A MONSTER by VIOLET

A MONSTER
by VIOLET

Laura Wake

urbanepublications.com

First published in Great Britain in 2017 by Urbane Publications Ltd
Suite 3, Brown Europe House, 33/34 Gleaming Wood Drive, Chatham,
Kent ME5 8RZ

A CIP catalogue record for this book is available from the
British Library.

ISBN 978-1-911129-27-1

MOBI 978-1-911129-29-5

EPUB 978-1-911129-28-8

Design and Typeset by The Invisible Man

Cover by The Invisible Man

Printed and bound by CPI Group (UK) Ltd, Croydon, CR0 4YY

urbanepublications.com

For Vanessa

Surely in no other craft as in that of the sea do the hearts of those already launched to sink or swim go out so much to the youth on the brink, looking with shining eyes upon that glitter of the vast surface which is only a reflection of his own glances full of fire.

From Lord Jim *by Joseph Conrad.*

1

Baby Maria had been crying for about thirty minutes. Lisa was still sleeping. Violet had been lying next to her for hours wondering how someone could consume that many amphetamines and still be able to sleep. Her eyes felt like sandy marbles grinding around in their sockets, and in her stomach was a sharp tugging sensation. She rolled onto her side and looked at Lisa. Her mouth was open, her cheek squashed against the pillow. A line of dark make-up ran from her eye to her nose. They had been awake for three days and Lisa was obviously going to sleep through all the hours they'd missed out on.

Violet picked her clothes up from off the floor and started pulling them on. Her jeans were stuck down between the wall and the mattress. As she pulled them free, coins fell out down the back of the bed.

"Fuck."

There was no way to get to them.

She walked down the mini-stairway to the lounge where Maria was crying from her playpen. The baby's little hands were clenched so hard into fists that her fingers showed white. Her gummy mouth was open as wide as it could go and her cheeks were dark red from screaming. She was shaking with the effort of crying.

Violet lifted her out and the smell of dirty nappy hit the back of her throat and she turned her head away. Maria's vest was wet round the neck, and soaked through at the bottom with cold greenish poo that seeped onto Violet's hand.

"Hey… hey calm down," she said.

Violet's brain felt swollen and about to explode out of her ears. She looked round the room for a fresh babygrow but the only one she could see had been used to soak up something spilt on the coffee table. She pushed some of the debris off the table with her foot. The glass surface would be cold so she picked up a magazine with one hand, shook it open and laid it on the table, holding her head away from the baby to avoid the smell. Violet laid Baby Maria on the magazine and tried to get the vest undone; Maria's screams seemed to shake the air. Violet tore the nappy off and pushed it to the far end of the table. There might be wipes in the bathroom but she didn't want the baby to fall onto the floor so she used the wet babygrow from the table to clean her. There was no point doing up the cold, wet vest again, so Violet eased it off over the baby's head and threw it towards the nappy. Maria was cleaner but her skin was mottled, clammy and cold. Violet picked her up again and held her against her chest. She was still crying but now her cries were less a yell and more a rhythmical kind of sob. Where Violet's hand lay across the baby's back she could feel the vibrations of each cry.

"Let's get you some food."

She lay Baby Maria on the sofa and went into the kitchen to look for the formula milk. There was a half-full baby bottle on the side. Violet picked it up then decided to start fresh. She threw the contents down the sink and cleaned the bottle out under the hot tap. There was a can of formula milk on the side. She tipped some powder into the bottle and mixed it with water. There was a bottle heater but it looked complicated so she turned the kettle on to put the bottle in a bowl of boiling water like she'd seen people do in restaurants. As the kettle boiled, she held her wrists under the cold tap, then cupped water in her hands and splashed her face.

Left alone, Maria cried louder.

"Okay, I'm coming, I'm coming…calm down."

She remembered something about testing bath water for babies with your elbow so the same probably applied to milk. She pulled up her sleeve and shook milk onto her elbow; it was lukewarm.

Violet's throat and nose stung and felt grazed inside. She sniffed hard and tasted blood. She returned to the sofa and sat down to feed Maria. The baby sucked hungrily, and seemed to relax into the crook of her elbow. Violet wanted to turn the telly on but couldn't see the remote.

On the coffee table lay the mirror they'd been using. Long fingerprints covered it where they'd licked up the last bits of powder before resorting to the big, tacky lump of base Lisa always bought as back-up. Violet scanned the mess on the table for a cigarette but could see only empty packets. One Camel Light had been torn open and half its contents used, but there was just enough left in it to smoke a few puffs.

The babygrow depressed her. It lay on the table soaked in whatever it was they'd spilt. It was dirty with ash and other scum. She couldn't remember Baby Maria being there at all last night, yet she thought babies needed feeding every four hours or something. She put her finger in one of the baby's hands and watched her grip it. "I'm sorry," she said.

When Maria had finished drinking, Violet removed the bottle and put it down.

"Hi there," she said, "you feeling better now?"

Maria reached for Violet's face and stretched out her legs. Violet tickled the bottom of her feet. After a while her eyes focussed on Violet's face and she flashed a brief, brilliant smile.

"What you grinning at?" Violet smiled back and settled Maria more comfortably into her arms. She held one of the baby's feet in her hand and touched the tiny toes; they were perfect, and cold like a doll's. Violet wriggled out of her cardigan and laid it over her.

Violet leaned her head back against the sofa and closed her eyes. All the muscles in her neck ached. She couldn't remember much of the last few days or even who had been here. Her body felt hollow as if it had been scraped empty from the inside. She opened her eyes and looked down on Maria who had fallen asleep.

At that moment she decided.

From the kitchen she took the half-empty can of formula milk, then wrapped Maria up in the cardigan, picked her up and walked to the door. She paused, turned back and grabbed the car seat, putting the bottle and the formula inside. Hanging on the door handle was a brown, fleecy babygrow with a hood and ears designed to look like a bear; Violet hooked it over her finger.

Outside she couldn't remember where she'd parked her car. Her arms ached with the effort of carrying Maria in one and the car seat in the other. She felt her pupils shrink painfully from the sunlight. Baby Maria seemed to be enjoying the daylight and was flexing her fingers towards the sky. Where was the car? The best thing would be to walk down all the roads she usually parked in until she found it.

People were waiting at the traffic lights, trapped in the one-way system. They were looking at her strangely. She hoped no one from work was around. As she stopped to push the button to cross she felt cold even knobbles under her feet, and realised she had forgotten her boots.

2

Adam does gymnastics. He climbs to the top of the octagon climbing frame where he swings and jumps from bar to bar. Most people stop half way up the octagon as it's so high. I think it is meant for teenagers or adults because the gaps in the bars are so far apart.

The octagon is made up of metal triangles. I'm the only girl who climbs on it. I play with the girls sometimes but most break times I just like to climb as high as I can and sit on a bar with one hand holding on above me. There is a sand pit underneath so if people fall they don't bleed.

Adam and I are in the same class. Last week we decided to be boyfriend and girlfriend. He gave me a *Milk is Great* ruler that is white and blue. It has a pencil sharpener attached to it and a rubber in a holder.

I am halfway up the octagon. Each triangle is a scary climb because I'm not tall enough to hold two edges at the same time. Whenever I make a move I have to let go completely for a couple of seconds.

Adam is right at the top. He swings by his arms and then reaches up with his legs so he can hang upside down. His school shirt and jumper have fallen down so his tummy shows. His hair is quite long for a boy and it hangs straight down below his head. It's the same colour as a conker and quite shiny. He waves at the children at the bottom of the octagon who are all watching him, then swings his body so he can grab on with his arms again. He pulls himself up and sits on the top like Spiderman does on a skyscraper.

I've climbed a bit higher every day this week. I want to go as high as Adam, climb over the top and down the other side, or maybe I'll get up there and swing like he does. I will do something spectacular that even he doesn't do. The bell for the end of break goes and I climb down. About four triangles from the bottom I decide to jump. It's quite high. When I land I fall on my bottom. The sand is cold and feels damp. I get up and run after the others.

In Bible Studies, we read a story from the Bible then have to copy it into our exercise books. If you finish you get to draw a picture. I'm quite fast at writing so I get to at least draw a camel before the bell goes for the end of school. I want to draw Isaac's red hairy son Esau but don't have time.

* * *

It is Thursday, and it is English, which is the last lesson before break. Today I am going to climb to the top of the octagon.

Sarah, puts her hand up, "Mrs Martin, I'm going to be sick," she says and starts to get up from her seat.

Mrs Martin looks cross. "Come here then," she says. "Rebecca, take Sarah to the care centre. Everyone else, carry on with your work."

Rebecca is a chubby girl whose parents are from Australia. She is a show off. She gets up from her seat and leads Sarah out. The care centre is horrible. Two hunchbacked ladies work there, and they never give you any medicine or plasters or anything. They make you lie down in a little room with pictures of Jesus dying everywhere. They don't make you feel better at all.

There are lots of hunchbacks that work in our school. The men do outside stuff. One of them has long dark hair and always pushes a wheelbarrow. I run past when I see them because they're creepy.

The wool of their jumpers looks stretched across the lumps on their backs.

I asked Mum why they don't give you medicine in the care centre when you are ill, and she said that those types of Christians don't believe in it. There is a girl in my class called Esther who is that kind of Christian. She has red hair and freckles with a pink mark on one cheek. She says God touched her there when she was a baby because she is special. I have a strawberry mark on the back of my neck that my Mum says is a birthmark. The thing on Esther's cheek looks the same but I don't tell her because she'll probably tell the teachers.

Esther is not one of my friends. Her friends are called Heather and Poppy. They are quite mean to other people, especially to Hannah who is very shy and often ill. I used to be friends with Esther and went to her house for tea once after school. She has a little brother who also has red hair and an older sister who is deaf and has light brown hair. I think her sister is a teenager, but she doesn't go to school. We all sat on the sofa and watched a film of Beauty and the Beast. Her sister's voice sounded strange and Esther kept elbowing and pinching her to be quiet. Even though she is the eldest, I think that Esther bosses her around.

The film was horrible. The beast was like a man but with a swollen lumpy face. His eyes were shaped like a cow's eyes and were close together, and his nose was like a lion's nose, but with pink and waxy looking skin. His skin looked like the earplugs I have to wear for swimming. I don't like wearing them because they always have fluff stuck on them but Mum says I have to because I get ear infections.

Every time the beast came on the screen I looked next to the telly so I could only see part of the picture. He kept coming close to the screen and looked like he was going to come out of the telly. I think he frightened Esther's sister too because when he was on she made little shrieking noises.

When Mum came to pick me up she was with Grandad. I told her I didn't want to go there again and she said I didn't have to. I don't think she likes Esther's family and she said something to

Grandad that I couldn't hear.

Grandad told me that people with red hair have fiery tempers and can withstand pain more than other people. He says they are descended from the Vikings. Esther would make a good Viking, although she is frightened to go up the climbing frame.

The bell goes for the end of the lesson and we go for morning milk. When we've drunk our milk we can go out to the playground. We each get a little bottle of milk with a blue straw. When you finish you take the empty bottle to the counter, rinse it in a bowl of water, and then put it in a crate with others. I drink mine fast because I want to be one of the first people on the climbing frame. I drink it almost in one go then hurry to the counter.

I am about the fifth person to the climbing frame; the boys always get there first. Adam and Matthew from my class are playing a game of 'it' on the climbing frame. They scramble away from each other fast like insects. Matthew keeps getting caught but Adam is even faster at climbing than some of the older boys.

I start to climb straight away because I know the octagon will get busier soon. I get to the point I got to yesterday and spread my arms and legs out wide ready to reach for the next triangle.

"Watch out Violet!" someone shouts and Matthew comes scrambling towards me away from a tall thin boy with white hair who is grabbing at his legs. I wobble and grab hold of the bar I've just left. They rush past me and I see the big boy tap Matthew's leg then climb away quickly downwards. My hair is blonde but the big boy's hair is much lighter than mine. He has bright blue eyes and light eyelashes. My eyes are grey which Grandad says means strength like a soldier.

"Oh, that's the fifth time I've been 'it'!" Matthew says.

The others are already at the other side of the climbing frame.

"Violet!" another voice shouts, "tell him to get a move on!"

Matthew and I look up. It's Adam. He has climbed right over the top and is crawling down towards us.

"Matthew," I whisper, "Pretend you haven't seen him."

"Okay," he says smiling, and stays where he is.

I can see Adam inching closer. The other boys are starting to come nearer too.

"What you doing Matt?" one of them shouts.

As Matthew looks round to answer them, Adam's hand shoots down and pats him on the head. Matthew grabs at him. His fingers just miss Adam's grey trouser leg and then he falls forward.

"Whoaaahh!" he cries as he loses his balance and his head and body turn upside down towards the sand pit. The last things to leave the climbing frame are his two shiny black shoes. A little "plunk" noise happens as his feet leave the bar and follow his body to the ground. His arms do doggy paddle as if he's trying to swim away from the sand that is coming up to meet him. The ground is too fast though and he lands on his face and hands. His feet and legs hit the sand last, and he crumples up.

Adam, me, and the big boys all look at each other across the climbing frame then back down to Matthew. It is quiet for a second then Matthew makes a gasping noise.

The boy with white hair gets to him first.

"Are you alright Matthew?" he says.

Another gasping noise comes from Matthew. He is moving slowly, pushing with one arm. The boy helps him to turn onto his back. The other boys have moved down from the climbing frame now and are standing in a circle round Matthew.

"Go and get a teacher, Adam," one of them says and Adam runs off fast. I stay where I am. Matthew's eyes are looking everywhere. There is sand in his eyebrows and he has a graze across his nose. He flaps one arm around at everyone. A sound like a backwards burp is coming from him and his body is jumping about like a goldfish that's been thrown out of its bowl.

"I... I can't ... breathe," he says. The words come in little gasps. The three big boys don't know what to do and they just stand staring at him.

"A teacher's coming," one of them says.

Matthew doesn't say anything he just keeps sucking burps back into his body and waving one arm around.

The teacher who comes is a tall thin man with a ginger beard. He teaches the older children. He kneels down to look at Matthew who is still making the burping noises.

"Just calm down, son," he says. "you've only winded yourself. In a minute your breath will come normally again."

"His arm looks funny, Sir," the boy with white hair says.

"We'll get him taken off to the care centre in a minute and they can have a look at it.... it's probably just a sprain. Did you land on it?"

Matthew's eyes have stopped looking at everyone and are trying to look at the damaged arm. I can see the arm from where I'm sitting. It looks wrong. The teacher pulls Matthew's shirt sleeve up.

Matthew screams.

Everyone jumps, even the teacher who takes his hand away quickly. I can see Matthew's arm where his sleeve is pulled up. Between his elbow and his wrist, there is an extra bend that sticks out. The teacher has seen it too. He lifts the arm between two fingers and lays it on Matthew's tummy. Matthew does a short squeaky scream, this time opening his mouth wide. He screws up his eyes and tears run down his cheeks.

"Be brave," the teacher says.

Matthew's eyes open again and turn away from the arm and look up at the sky. His face has gone all white, and he is crying. The teacher was right though, his breathing has gone almost back to normal.

"Go away everyone!" the teacher shouts.

The boys run off and the teacher helps Matthew to stand up. He doesn't know I'm still on the climbing frame.

They start to walk to the care centre together. Matthew's good arm holds on to the teacher, the other one just hangs down, not moving and still bent.

The bell hasn't gone yet and I have the octagon to myself. I stand up and start to climb making sure my arms are spread out wide ready to catch the bars as I move from triangle to triangle. Soon I am on one of the highest levels. I can see straight down to the sand pit. I don't need to stand up to move triangles anymore but can sit down and edge across the bars keeping my balance. The middle bit of each bar is the scariest because you can't hold on to anything apart from the bar you are sitting on.

I reach the very middle and sit with my feet hanging down, holding on with one hand. I lift the other hand above my head and wave although no one is around. I decide to practice a trick for when the others are here. I sit on the bar holding on with my hands then I let myself drop upside down. I let go with my hands so I am hanging by my knees like a bat. My hair hangs down below my head. I feel something move and my skirt falls over my face, but it's not that long so I can still see. I am glad no one is here now because they would be able to see my knickers. I start swinging myself a bit. My skirt knocks against my nose. If I swung really hard I could probably let go with my knees, leap through the air and catch hold of another bar with my hands.

Suddenly I hear the bell go.

I will wait for when people are watching to do my trick. I pull myself up so I am sitting on the top again. I think it is harder to get down than it is to get up. I feel wobbly and it takes me ages to get to the side. It seems like the bell went a long time ago. When I am almost halfway down I decide to jump. It is higher than I've ever jumped from before. As long as I land on my feet I won't get winded like Matthew.

I land on my feet but because I jumped from so high my knees come up and hit me in the mouth. I bounce and fall onto my front. There is blood in my mouth and a bit on my knee. I stand up and lick the inside of my lip where there is a lump. I wipe round my mouth in case there is blood there and then run to my lesson. My lip tingles as I run.

3

Violet pulled onto the drive, and stopped the car. She looked at Lisa's baby in her car seat on the passenger side. The seatbelt had come out of one of the slots, lifting the car seat up in a tilt, and the baby had wriggled out of Violet's cardigan and was naked, clenching and stretching her toes, and gazing at the roof of the car. Violet undid the seatbelt, then reached into the footwell for the bear suit.

Baby Maria wriggled as Violet tried to dress her. When Violet had got the bear suit over both legs and arms, she sat the baby on her lap and glanced at her house; the front door looked odd, shiny. A pain scraped in her stomach and she held her breath till it passed, then got out of the car.

"Mum?" Violet walked into the kitchen holding Maria, "Mum!" She went back into the hallway and climbed the stairs. The baby started to cry.

"You can't be hungry again."

Maria's mouth turned downwards, her eyes closed tight pushing tears out, and she let out a louder cry.

Violet rocked her from side to side, "Look, just wait a couple of minutes and I'll get you some food."

She headed to her parents' room. The door was shut; she touched the handle, held the cold metal for a moment, then pushed down. Violet expected darkness and the smell of sleep and trapped air, but as the door opened she saw the room was filled with sunlight, and the bed was made.

She walked to the window and looked out at the garden. The grass was striped dark and light with lawnmower tracks. The trees had turned bright red and orange, and seemed to blur and pulse as she looked at them. Violet shook her head. A movement at the bottom of the garden caught her eye. Their cat, Cokie, ran out from a flowerbed, flattened himself to the ground, and wiggled his hips about to pounce at something. Just beyond Cokie, behind the rhododendrons, Violet saw her mum. Her hair matched the auburn colour of the dying leaves. She was pruning something, and throwing the dead flower heads onto a pile behind her.

Violet put the baby down on the bed and looked in her dad's bedside drawer; there was a watch, a Mens Health magazine, a packet of Rennie, and some loose change. She put the coins in her pocket, then lifted some jeans off a chair, and found a twenty-pound note and some more coins in them. Baby Maria cried louder from the bed, and Violet checked to see if her mum was still at the bottom of the garden.

"Shh," she said, "just wait a minute."

She tried the drawer on her mum's side of the bed, but it was just stuffed full of broken necklaces, books, magazines and old bottles of suntan lotion. Violet picked Maria up, and left the room.

She stopped at her sister's bedroom and opened the door. On the windowsill there was a collection of stones and feathers, and a framed photo of Cokie. Maria grabbed hold of Violet's ear and pulled.

"Ow!" Violet said, and began jigging the baby up and down in an attempt to stop her crying. "Okay, we'll go and meet Mum and then I'll give you your lunch."

As she stepped off the back doorstep, something jabbed the sole of her foot and she remembered her bare feet. There was a pair of her sister's old flip-flops lying next to the outside tap; Violet rubbed a cobweb off them with her toe and put them on.

The breeze outside seemed to distract Maria and she cried

more quietly, sometimes stopping altogether to look around. Violet wondered if she could focus on things yet or if she was just seeing colourful blurs.

"Mum!" Violet called.

Her mum looked up and stared for a moment before coming towards them. She was smiling.

"I've been out here for hours, I've let it get in a right mess... Who's this?" She took Maria out of Violet's arms and began a similar jigging to the one Violet had tried indoors.

"It's Maria," said Violet. "I'm babysitting... Lisa had to go for some tests, and didn't want to take her."

Her mum looked at her for a second before turning to the baby, "Hello, Maria," she said.

Maria had stopped crying and was looking at Violet's mum with an expression of wonder. She smiled and said loudly, "Ba!"

"Ba!" returned Violet's mum.

"Why are you talking to her like that?"

"I talked to you like that when you were a baby too you know. Although you did always seem to prefer proper conversations. Still, it's best to do both I think... She likes it anyway."

"Right."

"She's communicating, it's important to let her know you're listening."

Her mum and Baby Maria were smiling at each other.

"I need to feed her," said Violet.

"Come on then," her mum cooed, "let's all go to the kitchen."

When they got inside, Violet noticed that the kitchen was tidy, the worktops clear and faintly shining.

Her mum stopped, and patted the baby's bottom.

"Violet, why isn't she wearing a nappy?"

Violet looked at her mum, "Oh, I think Lisa had run out. I'll get some later."

Her mum put her face close to Maria's, "You don't want to ruin your brilliant bear costume do you?" She smiled, shaking her head at the baby, then said, "She needs a nappy, Violet. I think there's a couple of cloth ones in with the dusters, and I've got an old nappy pin in my sewing basket."

"Thanks, Mum."

Her mum lay the baby down on the kitchen worktop. She was crying again, and thrashing her legs about. "Keep an eye on her."

"Yeah... I know."

Violet stared out the window and tried to think clearly. She had about £250 in her bank account.

Her mum came back in. "Here we go!" she said, putting a towel nappy and giant safety pin down next to Baby Maria.

Violet felt sick, and her hands were shaking slightly; she needed some air. "Can you do it Mum? I need to get her milk and stuff from the car."

* * *

After drinking her milk, Maria fell asleep in Violet's arms on the sofa. Violet laid her down in the car seat and sat at the kitchen table with her mum.

"Do you fancy lunch?"

"No thanks, I'm not hungry." The thought of food forcing its way into her speed-shrivelled stomach made her wince.

"Cup of tea then?"

"Yeah okay."

"Earl Grey?"

"Ooh lovely," Violet said in a posh voice making her mum laugh as she filled the kettle. She wondered when she would next see her mum.

"What time you picking Jodie up?"

Her mum handed her a mug, and Violet saw that she'd remembered not to put milk in, "She's getting the bus today."

"But she hates the bus."

"I know, I told her this morning that I'd get her, but she said she wanted to. Dad had a talk with her about being tougher, so maybe it's that."

Violet thought about meeting her sister at the bus stop but decided too much time in the area could cause problems.

"Tell her I said hi."

"You'll see her yourself soon won't you?" Her mum turned to face her "You work too much at that pub. You're starting to look like a vampire."

Violet lifted her mug to her lips and blew into it, "I'm going to stay at Lisa and Claude's for a while… it's easier when I'm on double shifts."

Her mum frowned. "Don't they mind you always being there? It must be exhausting enough with a baby, without always having you round."

Violet smiled, "I'll give Jodie a call, see if she wants to go to the cinema or something."

Her mum stood up and went to the cupboard with the faded monster picture on that Violet had drawn; one of his legs had a tear in it that had been there for about fifteen years. Big, blue letters at the bottom said 'A Monster by Violet'.

Violet looked over at the baby asleep in the car seat, she looked cosy in the bear suit. Suddenly she sighed, and stretched both arms out in her sleep, even extending her fingers. Violet watched as the tiny fingers splayed out then relaxed and her arms slowly dropped back down, still stretched out perfectly straight.

Her mum came up behind her "Chocolate?" she said holding out a dark square.

Violet looked up. Maybe her stomach could handle one square. "Thanks," she said and put it in her mouth.

"Eighty per cent cocoa," her mum said, "that'll give you a kick."

The chocolate was so bitter it made her taste buds twinge. Her throat felt scratched as she tried to swallow, and threatened to bring it back up again but she resisted the urge. When she'd swallowed it, the bitter taste was replaced by one of delicious cocoa.

"That's wicked, Mum," she said.

Her mum held out the bar to her. She had a speck of melted chocolate on her top lip, like a freckle.

"No, thanks," said Violet. As the chocolate taste faded the hint of chemicals returned.

"How old is she?" her mum asked, looking over at the sleeping baby.

Violet thought back to when the baby was born. Lisa had phoned and asked her to come to the hospital to celebrate with her and Claude. The baby was in intensive care as she'd been born a month premature; Violet remembered the papery looking babies in their rows of incubators. They went to a pub close to the hospital and drank double vodkas mixed with Smirnoff Ice. They'd sat outside so it must have been quite warm, April maybe.

"About five months I think," Violet replied, though her mum had stopped listening and was looking out of the window.

"Hey, Mum do you have any of Jodie's old baby clothes that I could take for Lisa, she'd be really pleased ... or has Dad got rid of them?"

"I rescued some, they're in the loft."

"Do you remember when he threw loads of my clothes away, and I got them back out of the bin? He was so annoyed."

"He hated your ripped jeans."

"They were my favourite."

But her mum was staring out the window again. "He's ruthless," she said.

* * *

At the top of the loft ladder, Violet felt for the light switch.

When the light flickered on she was surprised at the emptiness. When she was little the loft had been crammed full of stuff. Old toys, Christmas stuff, and photo albums had covered the floor, and hats and shoes hung from the beams, as well as the wooden sledge with metal runners that her dad waxed so they'd go faster than anyone else. Three massive dressing-up boxes were stuffed so full their lids were always open, and the clothes that didn't fit in the boxes used to hang all over the place so it felt like a jungle; there were wigs too.

Now the beams were bare and there was only one dressing-up box left. Where once you used to have to climb over bin-liners and boxes full of everything from stage make up to old slide machines, there was clear floor space covered in a thin, ridged fabric.

She stood up, and moved out of the way for her mum to get up.

"Where's the dressing-up stuff gone?"

"We had a clear out. I saved all the best stuff."

"What about my Minotaur costume?"

"It was going mouldy. I think the head's still in there though if you want it."

Violet opened the chest and dug through the clothes. As she pushed down feeling for horns, her hand scratched against something, and she pulled out some glittery silver leggings that she'd worn when she was The Star of Bethlehem in her nursery nativity. She remembered the prickliness of the leggings, and the big cardboard golden star that her mum had made. It was probably her earliest memory, the scratchy leggings, and feeling proud that she got to stand up through the whole thing while everyone else sat cross-legged.

"I'll get it next time," she said closing the lid, "where's the baby stuff?"

Violet followed her mum to the back of the loft where the light didn't reach as well. There were some dustbin bags of clothes labelled with marker pen on masking tape. Two read, 'Violet's baby stuff', another said, 'Jodie's baby stuff', and one at the back said, 'Jamie'.

Her mum tore open the 'Violet' bag and pulled out a tiny navy polo neck. It was made of velour. "You looked so trendy in this."

Violet took it and felt it between her fingers; it was still perfect.

"Don't give that one away," her mum said, "You ought to keep it for yourself."

"I think she's already bigger than that anyway," Violet said handing it back to her mum, who folded it and gently tucked it back in the bag as if it were a baby itself.

"You were so tiny, the best looking baby around. I know everyone thinks their babies are the most gorgeous, but you really were. I couldn't stop looking at you."

Violet smiled, "I know, I've seen the photos."

Her mum started making a small pile of baby clothes from the Violet and Jodie bags, "It's awful, there's hardly any of Jodie compared to you."

Violet picked up a small, grey leather suitcase and opened it for her mum to put the clothes in. She remembered running away with that suitcase when she was about nine. She had spent the day or what she remembered as the whole day going to the swings, and doing the bike jumps in the woods before coming home, and going under the tarpaulin of a car her dad was working on in the drive. She felt guilty at one point and looked through the kitchen window but her mum was just in there with Jodie like nothing had happened. She laid there until she saw the wheels of her dad's car come into the drive and heard him go in the house before she decided she was too hungry to hide any longer.

"It's Muffin the mule!" her mum said, taking the marionette puppet out of a box, and making him lift a front leg, "He's tangled."

Violet smiled and touched his woolly mane. Her mum had always called him Muffin even though that wasn't what Violet had named him. She'd called him Philip, and he was a foal, not a mule.

"I'm going down, Mum," she said.

"I'll be down in a minute," her mum said, "I want to untangle him."

Violet went into her bedroom, pulled a rucksack out from under the bed, and started stuffing things from her wardrobe into it, jeans, t-shirts, almost her entire underwear drawer, and some hats and scarves. It was only a small bag and filled up quickly. She wished again that she hadn't forgotten her boots; they were her favourite heeled, motorbike-style ones with white eagles on. Underneath some rollerblades she found a pair of sixteen-hole black leather boots she'd forgotten about; she couldn't recall ever wearing them. She pulled them on, not bothering to lace them up. There was some of her makeup on the side and she took a mascara and two eyeliners, and put them in the bag too.

Violet squeezed past the loft ladder and went into her parents' room. On the windowsill were her mum's radio, and a collection of CDs. Violet opened the CD tray; *Essential Reggae*. She couldn't see its case, so stuck it in with an Eddie Grant one, and put it in the bag with her clothes.

Downstairs, she went into the lounge. There was a glass on the table next to an empty bottle of Jamesons. She walked past and went into the walk-in cupboard with the alcohol and stereo inside. The stereo was massive and black, about fifteen years old now. She pushed the button, and the CD door slid open sideways, 80s cool, like those cars with the doors that opened upwards. Inside was her dad's *The Very Best of Al Green*. She stuck it in her cardigan pocket; he could get another one from any petrol station.

Violet put the suitcase of baby clothes, and her backpack in the car and went to get Baby Maria from the kitchen. The baby was awake, she watched Violet as she lifted the car seat. Violet stopped at the bottom of the stairs and called up, "See you later, Mum." From the loft, she heard her mum's faint "bye."

Violet buckled the baby seat in, then went round to her side of the car, and got in. She wondered if Lisa was awake yet.

"We're going on holiday," she said taking Maria's hand between her fingers.

The baby smiled at her showing her gums.

4

Dad picks me up from school because my new brother has been born. He drives really fast and goes over speed bumps so quickly that I'm thrown up into the air. I love my dad's driving.

At the hospital the nurse says Dad can't go in because his trousers are dirty. There is oil on them. She looks at the hole in the knee too, and then she smiles at me.

"You're alright," she says, "what a smart uniform!"

She is wearing thin tights, and navy blue shoes with holes in the ends that some of her toes are squashing through. They look like trapped pigs trying to escape through a little aeroplane window. "Thanks," I say.

Dad says, "Is there a place nearby I can buy trousers?"

The nurse looks at the small watch that is pinned to her shirt. "If you head back towards the town centre, you'll see a parade of shops. There's a sports shop there called Olympus. It's open till five."

We go back to the car and drive to the sports shop so Dad can buy tracksuit trousers. I ask if I can buy my little brother a present. I might get him a ball, but Dad says I'll have to wait a long time till he's old enough to play ball games, so should choose something soft and colourful.

"Anything you like," he says.

I want to buy a skateboard so I can teach him tricks but know that it will be ages until he can walk, let alone skateboard. Upstairs

I find a Woody Woodpecker toy. I like his spiky hair. I take it down to Dad and he says, "That's a golf club cover, Violet."

"He'll like it," I say.

We buy the Woody Woodpecker cover and Dad changes his trousers in the changing room. I put Woody Woodpecker on my hand and use him like a puppet, and practice his laugh, "Hu huh, huh HA huh, hu huh hu hah huh."

Dad comes out wearing the new tracksuit trousers. They are black with a luminous yellow puma on one side, by the pocket. It says PUMA underneath.

"Nice trousers," I make Woody say.

My Dad laughs and says, "Thanks Woody."

We drive back to the hospital really fast. I do the Woody laugh all the way until Dad says to be quiet because it's distracting him.

When we get to the car park entrance he says, "Ready?" and he winks at me.

"Yes."

Then he makes the car wheels screech all the way up the spiral ramp, and I shout, "Woooooooooooooh!"

Mum is in a room with lots of other mums and babies. Dad says it's a 'maternity ward'. Next to her in a plastic cot, my baby brother is sleeping. He is smaller than a teddy bear. My dad is resting his hand on my shoulder.

"Can I wake him up?"

Dad says, "No, let him rest, he'll wake up in a minute anyway when he's hungry."

I put my hand in the cot and stroke his hair. It's much softer than mine and it's black. He has really small hands with tiny fingernails. I wiggle my finger into his fist.

"Look Dad, he's holding my hand." But Dad is sitting on the bed, kissing Mum and he doesn't answer. "Do you think he likes Woody?" I ask.

They stop kissing and cuddling, and Mum says, "Do you like the name Jamie, Violet?"

"For him?" I point to my new brother. Mum and Dad are looking at us, they are both smiling in a funny way. He is still holding my finger. "Yes ... is that his name then?"

Mum says, "Yeah if you think it's a good one."

"I do... can I wake him up now?"

Dad says, "No."

"Mum," I say, "was I as small as him when I was a baby?"

"You were even smaller."

I still have Woody Woodpecker on my hand. I make him say, "Hello Jamie," and then I make him kiss him with his beak.

Because Woody is naughty, I make him peck my brother on the head.

"NO, Woody! Jamie is your master."

I make Woody peck him again.

"NO WOODY!" I shout.

Then Mum says, "Be gentle, Violet."

I make Woody say, "Sorry, Jamie... I'll be a good pet now," and give him another kiss on the head. Then I lay him next to my brother.

* * *

Mum and Jamie are staying at the hospital. Dad and I are at home on our own with my cat Cupid. Cupid is black with green eyes. Dad gets fish and chips and we watch a film about a car that can drive itself. Cupid usually sits on Mum's lap when we watch telly, but because she's not here, he sits with me.

In the morning, Dad and I go to visit Jamie and Mum again. It's boring in the hospital. Mum is tired, and Jamie sleeps all the time. Dad brought my sketch pad, so I draw pictures of Jamie and Woody. Then I draw the nurse with the squashed feet. I show Mum and she says it's brilliant, and she gives it Dad to look. They both laugh. The nurse comes in with Mum's lunch, and Dad turns the picture over so she can't see.

On Sunday, I go to Adam's to play. He always has loads of sweets at his house, and his mum lets us sit at our own table when we have lunch, and gives us french fancies. Adam has a tree house, where we play spies. There's a rope ladder that goes up to the tree house, and when we're in there, Adam pulls it up through the hole so intruders can't get in. Adam has loads of toys. On the garden wall we line up He-Man, Skeletor, Leech, Battle Cat, loads of little green plastic soldiers, two Star Wars storm troopers, and an Action Man, who won't stand up, so we make him sit. Adam aims all their weapons at the tree house.

He says, "Quick...to the base! The enemies are about to attack!" and we run to climb the rope ladder.

We take turns with Adam's slingshot to knock the baddies off the wall. I don't want to hit Battle Cat, so I shoot at the others first.

Adam says, "You get more points for the soldiers, cause they're hardest to hit."

The bag of stones and marbles is running out, so I shout, "We need more ammunition!"

Adam says, "You stay here, and keep firing...I'll make a run for it... Cover me!"

I hear the doorbell ring from inside Adam's house, and I know Dad is here to pick me up. With my last marble, I hit Leech. His crossbow pops out of his arm, and he falls off the wall. Adam climbs back in with his pockets full of ammunition.

"My Dad's here," I say.

"Let's hide," he says.

We lie down on our tummies in the tree house, until Adam's mum starts calling, "Violet! Adam! Violet, your dad's here!"

We stay hidden until she comes right under the tree house. Our faces are close to each other and it's hot because our breaths are mixing together.

Adam's mum says quietly, "I bet they're in here," and then she shouts, "Come on, Adam! Violet's got to go home."

Dad says, "Hurry up, Violet... Mum and Jamie are home."

Adam lets the ladder drop and we climb down.

* * *

Mum is sitting on a chair in the kitchen. She is breastfeeding Jamie, his eyes are closed, and he is dribbling a bit. There is a present on the kitchen table.

"What's that?"

"It's a present for you, from Jamie."

I tear it open, and inside is a book. On the front it says, *How to Draw Cartoons*.

I kiss my little brother on the head and say, "Thanks Jamie."

Mum says, "I'll put him in his Moses basket in a minute, and then let's look at the book together."

The book has got all different sections, animals, ghosts, monsters, people, and buildings. We look in the people bit first, and there's a bit about caricatures. I read it out loud to my mum, "The trick is to exaggerate the most prominent features of a person."

Mum says, "If someone has a normal mouth, but an interesting shape nose, then you would choose the nose to exaggerate, so if it was slightly crooked, you would draw it a bit more crooked."

"Can I try it on you?"

"Yeah, go and get your sketch book."

I make Mum sit still, and I draw her head, and eyes. I think about what is the most unusual thing about her face. She is pretty, and doesn't have a big nose or extra small mouth, or anything really unusual. She does have a little gap between her front teeth, so when I draw her teeth, I make the gap bigger. She also has really curly reddish brown hair, so I make it extra messy and curly. She is wearing a dressing gown, but I know she doesn't like it, so I draw her in her favourite turquoise raincoat. In the book it shows that when you want to make things look shiny, you draw about three small lines on them, so I put some on the raincoat.

When I'm finished I say, "You can move now."

"Let's have a look."

I show her the caricature and she looks at it for a long time. She moves her head from side to side and wrinkles her nose up, then she laughs.

"That is really funny," she says.

"Is it good though?"

"It's damn good!" Then she puts her hand over her mouth, and I laugh because she swore. "You need to sign it though, all artists sign their work." She points to the bottom corner.

I take it back and write BY VIOLET KALE.

5

Violet concentrated on the motorway. She repeated a routine of watching the car in front, then gradually extending her vision to the next car, then the next, then the next, scanning for any sudden stops. Her eyes were twitchy, and felt like they were moving quicker than they should. When she relaxed and drove automatically she couldn't be sure she that wasn't just daydreaming, so she forced her eyes to scan the traffic, and repeat the routine, trying not to let her gaze stop for too long on any one car.

She imagined a bird's eye view of them slowly orbiting London on the M25. No, not a bird's eye view, a flashing point on a computer map, they were marked as a moving dot, and around them were other flashing symbols indicating danger or significant locations. Her house would be a green, slowly-fading triangle, Lisa and Claude's an exclamation mark.

Violet watched the white centre line flick past. How long had she been daydreaming? She couldn't work out if it was a full few minutes, or just one, vivid second. She lifted a hand off the steering wheel and tapped her forehead and cheeks with her fingers. The tapping made little drumbeats behind her forehead.

She looked at the baby. The movement of the car had sent her to sleep again. Violet's stomach lurched and cold sweat prickled out on her face and down her arms. She gripped the wheel. Her eyes felt suddenly fuzzy, and she needed to sneeze, but she didn't want to close her eyes because they were going 80 miles an hour and how long would her eyes be closed for if she was sneezing, and for how many metres of tarmac? Violet resisted but her eyes tried to shut as the sneeze came. She held them open as best she could, trying not to imagine them popping out of her head, and bouncing off the windscreen. She sneezed three times. When she finished she was leaning forward, hunched over the steering wheel, squinting at the road.

"Fucking idiot," she said.

She turned the radio on. It was a man talking and laughing with another laughing person, she flicked stations. More talking.

"Just give me some fucking music!"

The only channel that always had music was Classic FM but classical music made her feel stressed. She wanted the CD out of her pocket but didn't trust her body not to make a sudden deliberate swerve while she reached down, so she kept hitting 'skip' until she heard music. Every bit of song she identified was something she hated. "Fuck it," she said, and left it on 'It's Raining Men'.

A blue motorway sign said 'M3 SOUTHAMPTON AND THE SOUTH WEST'; it was the next junction. Violet moved into the slow lane. They could get a ferry from Southampton. And there would probably be a cash point where she could take out all her money. Maybe it would be safer to draw the money out at a service station though, because if the police came after her they would check bank withdrawals, and the ferry port was too much of a giveaway. A motorway service station was good; she could be going anywhere.

On the radio Dolly Parton started to sing '9 to 5'. Another row of overhead signs came into view. There was a Welcome Break service station in 8 miles. Violet lowered the window a crack to keep her alert, and started to sing along.

* * *

Violet parked at the Welcome Break, and turned off the engine. Baby Maria was still asleep. The car clock said 14.27. She jumped as she noticed a lady walking straight towards them. The woman glanced at Violet and Maria, then squeezed past Violet's car to get into the car next to them. Violet got her wallet and the money she'd taken from the house out of her jean pockets. She put the money in her wallet, and got out of the car.

The lady in the car next to them was handing sandwiches and packets of crisps to some children in the back seat. The man in the driver seat looked up at Violet, a white bread sandwich hanging slightly open in his hand. Violet locked the car and headed for the entrance. She would have to be quick, it was probably against the law to leave a baby alone in a car.

The automatic doors opened to a blast of hot air and the smell of burgers and coffee. There was a food hall on her right and a brightly lit WHSmith on her left. Some people pushed past her and then split into two groups, one to Burger King, the other past Smiths to a tunnel under a toilet sign. Just past the tunnel she saw a cash machine.

Violet pulled her bankcard out, and noticed some crystals of powder on the edge of it. She looked around then ran her tongue down the side, before pushing it into the slot.

The screen said available funds £340.00; her wages from the pub must have gone in. Violet typed £340 in and a message came up saying maximum withdrawal £250.00.

"Fuck." To get the rest of the money she would have to use another cash point somewhere. She took the £250 out and put it in her wallet with her bankcard.

As Violet got close to her car she could hear Maria crying. She walked quickly to the door and got in.

"Shh," she said, and started the engine, "we'll be on a boat soon!"

The baby's cheeks were flushed, and wet with tears.

As Violet turned to reverse, she noticed the family in the other car, faces turned towards her, the purple glint of Cadbury's minirolls between their fingers.

6

The numbers of the hymns are on a wooden board at the front of the stage. I find them in my hymn book and keep my fingers there for when we sing. If you don't find them in time, the teachers see, and tell you off afterwards. Adam and Matthew are next to me. Matthew's arm is in a plaster cast, with a sling. At break time he's going to let everyone write things on it. I'm going to do a cartoon.

Mr Cobb has a huge lump on one side of his head. His hair is much longer on that side, covering the lump. It looks like an apple under a tablecloth. Adam and Matthew always joke about him slicing it off with a comb when he's doing his hair. Mr Cobb is talking about goals today. I think about football goals and the really tall rugby ones. There is a rugby field near my house. When I next go, I'm going to climb up one pole of it, and see how high it is. I wonder if Mr Cobb has ever scored a goal in football.

Adam taps me on the shoulder. He does a funny face like Mr Cobb and pretends to listen to music and comb his hair. He stops suddenly and goes, "HHHHkkkkkkk". Then he does a shocked face, and starts looking around the floor for the lump. I cover my mouth with my hymn book and laugh, but it makes me feel sick as well.

I feel sorry for Mr Cobb. I wonder if the lump hurts him, or if he really does catch it when he combs his hair. Maybe it has hair growing out of it, or it might be smooth and hard like a tusk. He is talking loudly with his arms out by the side of him. He is wearing a grey suit and a pink tie.

He says, "A life without a goal is like the captain of a ship without a map and a compass. His ship will just drift along with no direction for days or months, just hoping to maybe arrive somewhere."

Me and Mum have been reading about the first explorers who didn't have maps or compasses and used the stars to find their way. I put my hand up to tell Mr Cobb.

Mr Cobb says, "Does anyone have a goal?" and more people put their hands up. He points to a big girl and says, "Yes, Sarah."

Sarah says, "My goal for today is to play well in netball."

Mr Cobb says, "Good," then he points at Esther.

Esther says, "My goals today are to help somebody who needs it, and to do chores when I get home."

Mr Cobb smiles. His teeth are as yellow as sweetcorn, and I can see them even though I'm sitting far away. He says, "Those are excellent goals Esther, and one of them is the same as mine... a good goal that anyone can do, every day, is to help someone out... carry someone's shopping for them, or help your mum at home by tidying or doing the washing-up."

I put my hand down and try and think of a really good goal, like jumping from the very top of the octagon without hurting myself at all.

"The best thing about goals," says Mr Cobb, "is that they can be any size, from a little one like saying a prayer every day, or a more long-term one, like working hard to become whatever you want like a policeman, or to one day having a family... or to being a good Christian for your whole life." Mr Cobb stops talking and looks round the room. He smiles and the sweetcorn teeth show again.

Mr Cobb touches his hair where the lump is and says, "Now, I want every one of you to think of your own personal goal. It can be a goal for today, or one that you hope to achieve by the end of the week, or even the month. When you have thought of a goal, you must ask God to bless it, because it is for him that we carry out all our goals. Imagine the ship again. Your goal is your map, and God will be your compass, helping you to achieve it."

The piano lady starts playing the piano and I can't hear Mr Cobb anymore because everyone is looking through their hymn books to try and find the right numbers.

* * *

In the dinner queue Adam, Matthew and I stuff tissues in our pockets while the teachers aren't looking.

It is roast pork today. The meat is really thin and grey-coloured, and you can push the fat off of it easily. I eat the meat, some of the greens, and the carrots, but it is boiled potatoes, which I don't like because of the greyish bits in them that Mum says are called eyes. Pudding is jelly with little square bits of fruit stuck in it, which is nice.

There are three teachers doing lunch patrol, Mrs Martin, the teacher with the beard, and Mrs Cobb. If Mrs Cobb checks your plate, sometimes she eats what you've left, so you don't have to. The man teacher is talking to Mrs Cobb in the washing up area, so it is just Mrs Martin to look out for. When she is busy checking one of the other tables I put my boiled potatoes and the fat from the meat onto one of the napkins, then fold it into a parcel. I take another napkin from my pocket and wrap it round so the parcel doesn't leak, and then put it in my blazer pocket. Adam has eaten all his dinner, so only puts the bits of fat in his tissue, but Matthew is still trying to wrap his carrots up as Mrs Martin starts walking towards our table.

"Plates out in front of you," she says.

We push our plates forward so Mrs Martin can check them. Matthew has left his tissue on the table and has put the carrots straight in his pocket. Hannah is next to me, she has eaten hardly anything, not even the pudding. Mrs Martin goes up to her.

"What's the matter, Hannah?" she says

"I can't eat it," says Hannah.

Mrs Martin pushes Hannah's dinner plate back close to her, and says, "You must finish your food, otherwise it's ungrateful to God."

"I'm sorry, Mrs Martin," Hannah says, "I don't feel well."

"You've got five minutes," Mrs Martin says, "when I come back I want to see a clean plate."

Adam and some others stand up to go and wash their plates, but Mrs Martin shouts, "HALT! Nobody is to leave the table until Hannah has finished her food."

I think it's funny that she says 'Halt' like we are ponies.

Some of the older children at the end of the table start humming the school dinner song, and giggling. Hannah is shivering. She starts making mouthfuls of the food and eating it. Every time she takes a mouthful, she looks like she's trying not to spit it out. More people are singing the school dinner song quietly.

School Dinners, school dinners,
Mushy Peas, mushy peas,
Soggy Semolina, soggy Semolina,
I feel sick,
Fetch a bucket quick!

Hannah taps me on the arm and whispers, "Can I have a napkin, Violet?"

I look around for Mrs Martin. She is at the other end of the room.

"I haven't got any left," I say

Hannah says, "Please, Violet."

Adam and Matthew are singing the new bit of the song that I made up.

You're too late,
Done it on the Plate,
Teacher's coming QUICK!
Eat up your sick.

They burst out laughing, then put their hands over their mouths in case the teachers hear.

I run over to the napkins and grab a handful, then run back to Hannah. Just as I put them in front of her, Mrs Martin shouts,

"Violet KALE! Sit DOWN!"

Hannah starts putting her food into the tissue, but Adam says, "Mrs Martin's coming!"

Hannah puts the tissue in her pocket, but there's still food left on her plate. The older children have stopped singing because Mrs Martin is coming back.

Mrs Martin stands next to Hannah and looks at her plate, then she looks at Hannah. She smiles and I think she might let Hannah leave her dinner but then she says, "That's not a clean plate is it?"

"No Mrs Martin," Hannah says, and then she starts to cry.

Mrs Martin snatches Hannah's fork and a bit of potato falls on the floor.

"For Goodness sake!" she says, "If you're going to behave like an ungrateful, spoiled baby, I'll have to feed you like a baby." She makes a mouthful of food for Hannah on the fork, then passes it to her, and watches her put it in her mouth and eat it. Everyone is watching Hannah. I hope she eats it so we can go outside.

When Hannah swallows her mouthful, Mrs Martin gives her another one. Hannah keeps crying and eating, and Mrs Martin keeps making mouthfuls for her until there is no more food on the plate except for one of the long bits of fat off the meat.

Hannah says, "Please Mrs Martin, I've had enough...that's just fat."

Mrs Martin pinches Hannah's arm and says, "You're skin and bones... You need fat to keep you warm." She spears the fat with the fork and coils it round like spaghetti and then holds it up for Hannah to eat.

Mrs Martin looks really angry and I think Hannah is too scared to say no, so she eats it. I feel sorry for Hannah as it must have been like swallowing a worm.

"Good girl," Mrs Martin says.

But then Hannah does a huge burp. She starts rocking and then she is sick all over the table.

"EVERYBODY OUT!" Mrs Martin shouts.

Adam and I pick up our plates and Mrs Martin says, "Leave the plates, just go out to the playground."

We all run for the door to go outside. I turn back and see Mrs Martin pull Hannah up by the shoulder and drag her out the teachers' door.

When we get outside everybody starts laughing and talking.

Matthew puts his good arm up in the air and says, "Yes! No washing up."

Adam says, "I can't believe she was really sick on the plate, like the song!"

We start laughing and then I say, "I think Mrs Martin got sick on her." I smile and say, "Hannah's a hero!"

Adam says, "Yeah, three cheers for Hannah! Hip Hip Hooray!"

Everybody joins in except Esther and Heather.

Esther says, "Hannah's gross."

Me, Matthew and Adam run past her to the climbing frame doing Red Indian calls.

7

Violet stood on the deck of the Red Falcon ferry holding Maria. A group of grey looking people huddled behind a giant air vent, smoking cigarettes. Violet wanted one but couldn't face asking. She shifted Maria into an easier position on her shoulder, and headed towards the back end of the ferry. Some long, narrow puddles were starting to form on the deck. Violet couldn't tell if it was actually raining, or just the wind lifting the tops off the waves and hurling them across the boat. She pulled Maria's bear hood up and zipped it as far as it would go. The fleecy bear ears seemed ridiculous surrounded by sea. Violet closed her eyes and felt the spray settle on her face.

Maria started gurgling, and Violet touched the baby's cheeks, which had turned red from the wind. She held her closer and felt her cold fingers sink into the soft material.

"I like boats. Do you?" she said into the hood. She breathed in and smelt a faint dusty smell. Lisa would definitely be awake now.

Violet walked to the edge of the deck. At the railings she leaned over and looked at the sea which sped past as the Red Falcon ploughed its way through. The water next to the boat looked like heaving concrete; it was a long way down. The engines screamed but their sound was almost drowned out by the noise of wind and sea, to a small, vibrating hum. It was disorienting trying to distinguish the natural and mechanical noises. Violet licked her top lip, and tasted salt.

A hand touched her shoulder and she turned around to see a fat girl with a thick fringe. The girl looked at Violet's mouth as she spoke.

"Excuse me, have you got a lighter?"

Violet recognised her from somewhere, "Yeah hang on... you got a cigarette?"

Violet shifted Maria onto her hip and felt in her jeans for a lighter while the girl produced a pack of Sovereigns.

"Thanks," Violet said handing her the lighter.

Violet stuck a Sovereign in her mouth, and headed to a wet bench. It would be difficult to light the cigarette with the wind as well as Maria's head to watch out for. She hoped the bear suit wasn't flammable. A childhood flashback of a warning about shell suits, and being burnt alive inside them on Bonfire Night flashed through her head; she remembered a girl who used to shrink crisp packets in the oven.

As she sat down she felt wetness seep into her jeans. Maria grabbed for the cigarette. Violet lit-up, then gave her the lighter to hold to distract her.

The cigarette tasted dirty and strong but she inhaled deeply, sucking the rough smoke down into her lungs. She was leaning against a metal fan and it buzzed through her making her teeth chatter slightly.

The girl was still standing where she'd asked for the lighter, and the sea air and wind were causing strands of her fringe to stick to her face and cigarette. She turned towards Violet and Maria, shuffled her feet and then walked over, looking at the floor. She stopped in front of them, and without looking up from the floor said, "Mind if I sit here?"

"No," Violet replied, thinking that she might create some shelter from the wind.

When the girl sat down Violet was hit for a second by a smell of sweat and vanilla body spray.

Maria was enjoying the lighter and hit it over and over against Violet's arm saying "ba" almost in rhythm.

The girl was sitting leaning forward but not resting her hands on anything, as if she'd been paused just as she was about to stand up. She wore a powder blue fleece that clung to her sides, a black skirt with coloured tie-dye bits in it, and boots that were supposed to look like leather but shone too much. Her eyes were fixed on the floor in front of her, the cigarette smoking in her fingers. She looked distressed.

Violet definitely knew her from somewhere. Her voice had sounded northern so it wasn't school...the pub? No, it was a recent memory, something close. Violet took a drag on her cigarette, then let the smoke spill out of her mouth before exhaling.

She remembered; it was an age-gap episode of the Trisha show. The girl was only sixteen or something, and her boyfriend was like forty-five.

Violet looked at her again to make sure, and was about to speak when the girl stood up and threw her half smoked cigarette into a puddle. Still looking downwards she walked away, her top half bent over and her legs marching as straight as a soldier's.

Violet smoked the cigarette down to the butt. She took out her wallet and counted her cash. After paying for the boat she only had £220 in notes left and some change. The police could trace you through bank withdrawals so she would have to remember never to use her card; fuck, it was annoying that there was money still in there. She took the bankcard out and held it out to Baby Maria.

"Shall we throw it into the sea?" she said.

The baby's eyes focussed on the card, and she dropped the lighter on Violet's lap, and reached for it. Violet watched her take hold of the card. A hologram sparkled on it, unnaturally bright in the cloudy daylight.

Violet put her lighter in her pocket and tried to take the bankcard from Maria, but Maria's little fingers whitened as she held on.

"Okay, we can keep it," Violet said, "You look after it though."

Violet pulled out a couple of notes, shoved them in her jeans then tucked her wallet into the pouch on the front of Maria's suit.

The ferry was quite busy. People sat in rows, hands in laps, waiting to arrive; most of them looked bored, like commuters who had made this crossing hundreds of times. One lady was smiling and knitting, with a big bag of wool on her lap. Violet guessed that the holidaymakers were the noisier people in the bar. There were seats free next to Pets Corner but the strong smell of dog fur put her off. As she walked past, two Jack Russells strained at their leads, and a tired looking German Shepherd lifted its head.

"Hi, dog," she said, and a woman who had the look of an owner glanced up suspiciously.

There were fewer people at the other end of the boat but a group of fruit machines buzzed, rang and cheered in recorded sound loops. One of them was a 'Who Wants to Be a Millionaire?' machine, and every now and again Chris Tarrant's voice asked, "Would you like to use a lifeline?"

Violet's head resonated with each burst of noise. At least there was no one to stare at her. She sat down and closed her eyes, wishing she'd brought the car seat so she didn't have to keep hold of Maria.

As soon as her eyes closed, she started to plummet into the relentless sleep that follows a speed binge. Her arms and legs sank like beanbags onto the seat, and the metallic noises became suddenly distant.

Violet forced her eyes open and breathed in hard through her nose. She couldn't fall asleep yet; coffee; just till they got a room somewhere. As she stood up the smell of nappy hit her.

Violet went down onto the lower deck, following a sign that said 'shop'; she hoped it had baby stuff. There were no windows on this part of the boat and it was disorientating. She tripped and held Maria tighter, running the fingers of her left hand along the wall as she walked.

The shop was more like a booth, rather than an actual shop that you could walk around in. The walls were glass, but the door was locked so you had to ask a lady at a window counter for what you wanted.

Violet walked to the counter, "Can I have a pack of nappies?" she asked.

"Which age?"

"Sorry, I was miles away… what was that?" She stared into the shop, scanning the shelves for baby stuff.

"What size nappies?"

Violet squinted at the back wall. It was too far to make out the writing but she could see pictures of varying ages of babies on the front. The smallest was a sleeping baby, the size up from that was a baby with its eyes and mouth open. The end one had a picture of a child that looked too old to even be wearing nappies.

"The green ones," she said, pointing at the packet with the open-eyed baby. "Oh, can I have some wipes too, I've run out."

The woman slid off her stool and shuffled towards the nappies.

Violet waited until she'd climbed back onto the stool and was prodding the prices into the till, then said, "Can I have an Isle of Wight pencil too please?" The woman rolled her eyes, and let out a sigh.

Violet grinned at Maria, "Horrible lady," she cooed quietly.

She watched the woman reach towards the pencils and pick out an orange one with a map on it. "Can I have the fluorescent pink one!" Violet called.

The woman didn't respond, but thrust the orange pencil back into the pot, pulled out a pink one then made her way back to her stool.

"Thought she'd like a souvenir," said Violet motioning to Maria, "it's her first holiday."

"Four pound twenty," the woman said.

Violet hoisted Maria into a more comfortable position and pulled the money out of her pocket. With one hand she separated the notes and laid out £10 for the woman. "Can I have a bag?"

"We don't have big bags," the woman said and smiled for the first time as she handed Violet the change.

"Thanks," Violet replied, and turned away, "fuck you too."

She changed Maria on a flip-down changing surface in the toilets. Women came in and out and Violet wished she was better at the procedure. She should have brought the bottles and stuff in from the car. Maria would have to wait until they found somewhere to stay to have another bottle.

Doubt filtered into Violet's head as she realised what she had done. Her vision seemed to drop a couple of shades of colour and a feeling behind her nose prompted the urge to cry. It was just the comedown, the people looking, paranoia; and the internal sensation would be her shrivelled-up stomach begging for nourishment. Coffee; then once they were off the boat they would get sorted. She pushed her hair back off of her face, and headed back to the upper deck.

A red-faced man in a backwards facing cap took her order. He wasn't fat, but his skin looked squashy like an uncooked sausage.

"A black coffee please," she said.

"Cheer up sweetheart, it might never happen!"

Violet smiled and fought back the urge to tell him why what he'd just said was annoying, stupid, and wrong.

She watched him pull a cup out of a dispenser, and press a button on a coffee machine. Above the peak of his cap, "New York Bad Boi" was written in gold stitching.

"Someone's tired," he said returning to the counter and prodding Maria's hood with a mottled finger.

"Yeah, we both are," Violet replied, turning so his finger slipped off.

Maria's eyes were closed, her cheek crushed against Violet's shoulder.

"She's as lovely as her mother," he said.

Violet thought about Lisa who was probably awake and either drunk, thinking about smashing the features out of Violet's face, or both.

"Thanks," she replied.

As he handed the coffee to her, he gripped her hand and rubbed the top of it with two fingers, then let go as if nothing had happened.

Violet put her money on the counter and waited for him to get her change. When he turned back and held out her change for her, she waited for him to put it on the counter.

As she picked up her money, he leaned over and said, "You know smiling's the second best thing you can do with your mouth."

Violet put the change in her pocket, and walked back towards the game machines.

Sitting where Violet had planned to sit was the couple from the Trisha show. The age-gap boyfriend was there and Violet remembered that he was a lorry driver. The cardboard cup was burning her fingers, but she couldn't change hands because of Maria. She clenched her teeth against the pain.

Fuck it, she would have to sit with the Trisha couple. She crashed down on the seat and put the coffee down. She shook her burned hand, then moved Maria from her shoulder to her lap. The baby was fast asleep. Violet laid her down on the seat next to her, and picked up the coffee.

The older, lorry driver part of the age-gap couple was watching her, and the girl who'd given her the cigarette was leaning on him with her face turned downwards as if she was reading her own stomach.

Violet took the lid off her coffee. There were shiny patches on its surface which showed grease rainbows, hopefully it was strong. Behind her eyes she imagined tiny horses with foaming mouths, stamping their hooves, desperate to pull her eyelids shut. She put her lips against the cup and blew on the coffee.

The windows gave a view of the grey, foggy sky; it was almost as dark as the sea. In a film she'd have run off to Mexico or something, not the Isle of fucking Wight. She could feel the Trisha man still looking at her, so she carried on staring at the grey outside. Her Discman was in the car, with its CDs. She couldn't really remember buying the ferry ticket or parking the car on the boat. It was stupid to have left the milk and stuff in the car; Maria would need another bottle again soon, or would start screaming. They had to get to a hotel room, with a kettle.

She remembered her souvenir pencil and pulled it out of her jeans. It had a little map with a line drawing of the island, and all the big towns marked on it. Genius.

"You on holiday?" the Trisha man asked.

Violet looked up, and a nerve tugged in her right eye.

"Yeah," she said, "We're going to stay with my aunt... you?"

He sat up straighter and the girl's cheek slid down his shoulder a bit. "We live here," he said, "Where's your auntie live?"

Violet glanced down at the pencil and saw the town Ryde, "Ryde," she said.

His lips turned downwards and he took a breath through his nose. "You should've got the Portsmouth ferry, Cowes is the wrong side of the island. You could've got a ferry straight there."

His eyes looked like currants pushed in hard by a thumb into a dough face. Were they currants?

Violet blinked hard then said, "Were you two on the Trisha show?"

The girl glanced up and smiled quickly in Violet's direction, then looked

down at her lap again.

"Yeah, we were," she said.

"It was a good day out," the man continued, "You get put up in a hotel for the night, and get a £30 voucher to spend at the hotel restaurant, or a Hungry Hippo pub." He put an arm round his girlfriend, "I'm Paul, and this is Charlotte... What's your name?"

"I'm Esther," Violet said.

"You driving?"

"Yeah."

"It'll only take half hour to get to Ryde, everything's close on the island."

Violet sipped the bitter tasting coffee and wished she'd thought of a better plan. Scotland would have been a safer option; at least there would have been big cities to disappear into.

The Red Falcon started to vibrate, as big engines beneath began to kick into action.

"She's a big girl," Paul said, patting his seat.

There was a buzz and a high-pitched noise, and then a tinny voice came through the speakers.

"Would all passengers with vehicles please return to their cars. We are about to arrive in East Cowes."

Violet downed the last bit of her coffee and her throat stung from its heat. The baby was still sleeping and Violet picked her up gently.

"See you then," she said to Charlotte and Paul.

"You've got at least five minutes," Paul said, "they always make you go down early."

Charlotte was leaning on his shoulder chewing a piece of hair.

Violet motioned to Maria, "I've got to sort her car seat out."

Charlotte let the hair fall from her mouth, "Bye Esther," she said.

8

One morning I wake up and go to see Jamie but his cot is empty. I put my toe on the top stair to go down for breakfast but then I hear some horrible noises. I look down the landing to Mum and Dad's room. The door is shut but I can hear my dad's voice and my mum's which gets louder and louder. I run and open the door.

"What's wrong?" I say, but nobody answers.

Mum has got my baby brother on her lap and Dad's got one hand on my brother's tummy and the other is picking up the phone.

"He's not breathing, Sally," Dad says in a funny voice.

Mum says, "We can't wake him up Violet," and starts to scream.

She is shaking my brother but he doesn't move at all. He looks like a toy. I hold his hand and shout.

"Wake up! Wake up!"

Nobody tells me to stop shouting.

9

Maria had been crying hard for about two miles. Violet had put *Eddy Grant's Greatest Hits* on to try to calm her down, and it had worked at first, but now it seemed like she was too hungry to be distracted. Even with the noise of the crying, the need to sleep was overwhelming, and Violet opened all the windows to try and blast herself awake.

She turned off, following a Youth Hostel sign down a dirt road. The car settled into two tyre tracks cut in the ground and she hardly needed to steer. There was a line of grass between the muddy tracks and sometimes the bottom of the car scraped against clumps of weeds and earth. Violet's fingers lightly vibrated on the wheel. On the edge of her vision, little black spots flashed sporadically.

Finally she saw a wooden gate with a sign saying YHA hostel, and pulled in. There were a couple of cars parked outside. Violet parked next to a Clio with alloys and a sign that said 'Babe on Board'. On the grass a custard coloured VW camper was standing crooked on its wheel rims.

"I'll be back in a minute," she said to Maria whose crying was now at maximum volume.

She wound the windows up to a level that allowed a breeze, but prevented an arm from being able to reach inside and open the door. Funny, she thought, someone trying to steal a stolen baby. She locked the car and headed to the hostel entrance.

The hostel looked like an old mansion. It was about three floors tall, and painted in a yellowish creamy paint that was cracking off in places. In the tall windows were modern, vertical blinds. They had them at her grandad's hospice, and she remembered hating the way they moved, and the horrible little beads that joined the material slats together at the bottom. As she reached the front steps, she saw a face looking at her through the blinds in one of the windows. She smiled but it had already shrunk back out of view.

Violet went inside, and Maria's cries softened as the door swung shut behind her. She was relieved at the dimness inside. The room she'd entered was small and cold. She touched the wall and couldn't tell if it was damp or just freezing. On her left was a reception desk, and behind that a door.

There was a leaflet holder attached to the wall, which was stuffed with tourist attraction leaflets and maps, and straight ahead she could see a corridor with shut doors along each side. On the desk was a brass bell with a button on top, and next to it, a card which said 'PUSH FOR ATTENTION- IF NO-ONE ARRIVES DO NOT KEEP PRESSING'.

She was about to push the bell when a man appeared in the doorway behind the desk, and she recognised the face from the window. He was almost bald except for a cloud of fuzzy grey hair at the very back of his head, and his eyebrows which were thick, and jet black.

"Can I help you?" he said.

"Can I have a room for the night please?"

"No babies."

"What?"

He crossed his arms, "This is a youth hostel. Youths are aged between 15 and 24 years old, so you would be alright I suspect, but that," he motioned his head in the direction of the car park, where Maria's cries were still ringing out, "is a baby. No babies."

"Do you have any private rooms, just for the night?"

"Can't have that racket waking everyone up."

The eyebrows were clenched together, and Violet could see that he wasn't going to change his mind.

"Okay," she said, "but would I be able to quickly use a kettle...

47

so I can make up a bottle till we find somewhere else?"

He sighed and shook his head, "Follow me, I'll show you the kitchen. Baby stays in the car though."

Violet smiled, "I'll just run and get her bottle."

The man left her alone in the kitchen. While the kettle boiled, she scanned the cupboards. The first scratches of hunger were starting, but actual food was still out of the question. She needed an energy drink or something; another lump of base would've fixed the problem quickest. She had to stay awake and find a bed for the night, then she could think things through. In one cupboard was a well-used collection of jams. At the back she noticed the pointed hat of a honey bear. She took the plastic bear out, and looked through into his tummy. He was almost full, and there was no sign of crumbs or bits of margarine anywhere. She twisted his hat, tilted her head back and squirted honey into her mouth.

Violet mixed up a larger amount of formula milk this time. She screwed the top on Maria's bottle, stuck the honey bear honey up her sleeve, and returned to reception. The man was nowhere to be seen. She waited for a moment and looked at the tourist attraction leaflets, then stuck a walking map of the Isle of Wight in her back pocket, and left the hostel.

Back in the car, Maria was still crying hard. Violet shook some of the milk onto the back of her hand, it was boiling. She pulled the honey out of her sleeve to put in the glove compartment. Maria's cries hit a crescendo.

"Hey, calm down. You want to try some honey?" She squeezed a tiny bit onto her finger and wiped it on Maria's bottom lip. The baby paused for a moment, then squeezed her eyes shut and started up again. Violet put the honey away and turned the key in the ignition.

"Ten minutes and we'll park somewhere and you can have dinner."

As they turned back onto the road, *I Don't Want to Dance* came on and Violet put the volume up loud.

They stopped at a viewpoint where there were some dirty looking white cliffs. Violet leaned over and put the bottle to Maria's

open mouth. As soon as it touched her lips, Maria stopped crying
and started to suck; then closed her eyes. Her eyelashes were stuck
together from crying, and little tear tracks glistened on her cheeks.
The sky was an even darker grey now; it would be properly dark
soon. If Violet was home, evening shift would have started at the
pub.

Maria's gulps slowed down as she started to fall asleep. When
they stopped completely, Violet took the bottle away, and wiped
some dribbled milk off the baby's chin. She remembered there
was a town called Lake coming up in a few miles which would
hopefully have a B&B.

Violet slapped her cheeks to wake herself up, and restarted the
car. Eddy Grant blared out of the speakers and she stabbed at the
stereo to turn it off. The static air in the car made her eyes feel
even heavier, and she opened the window, hoping the freezing air
wouldn't wake up the baby. She wanted a cigarette, badly.

In Lake they passed a fudge shop, a pub and a Spar corner shop.
Violet carried on driving, looking out for houses with B&B signs
but soon she'd driven right out of the village. It was getting dark
and she didn't know how much longer before she fell asleep at the
wheel, so she turned round and headed back to the pub.

The pub was called The Bucket o' Mussels. The pub sign showed
a bird's eye view of bucket full of mussels, propped up in a rock
pool. The mussels were painted in detail, and their purple black
shells looked shiny and wet. Violet shivered, and lifted Maria in her
car seat, out of the car.

The bar was busy, and Violet waited at the quietest end, next
to a couple of women drinking white wine. There was one of those
internet juke boxes where the music video played, as well as the
song. Two men in football shirts were poking at it; someone had
chosen Shakira's 'Hips Don't Lie'. In the gap between the men,
Violet saw a tiny Shakira shaking her hips.

*I know I'm on tonight my hips don't lie, And I'm starting to
feel it's right.*

Where was Shakira from? Chile?

Violet remembered Juanito, the chef at work, doing the Shakira dance where she shakes all over. He always did it to Violet when she took him a blackcurrant cordial before the lunch rush. He was fat, and he wobbled and vibrated brilliantly in his white chef coat, and chequered trousers.

"Yes please," a voice said in front of her.

Violet looked up. The barmaid had arrived. A massive cleavage bulged out of a low cut vest that said BUCKET O' MUSSELS. She could've been any age between 17 and 30, the sort of girl who'd never get ID'd.

"I wanted a room for the night?"

The barmaid looked her up and down briefly, then turned and got out a ringbinder file.

Paranoia was setting in, and Violet tapped her fingertips gently on the cool wood of the bar. The words 'I wanted a room for the night' echoed around inside her head, in a stupid babyish voice, and the Shakira song seemed to get louder, then quieter as if someone was opening and shutting the door of a nightclub.

"It's £30 a night for bed and breakfast."

"Is that for both of us?" Violet asked.

Is that for both of us? Is that for both of us is that for both of us? Is that for both of us?

"Babies are free."

Violet pulled some crumpled notes out of her jeans and counted twenty pounds. She put the car seat and Maria down on the floor, then took her wallet out of the pouch on Maria's bear suit. She breathed slowly as she got the rest of the money out, then reached up for the bar. As she stood, she saw the barmaid roll her eyes at a man sitting at the bar. Violet was too tired to care, and put the money on the bar.

"Oi Martin!" the barmaid shouted to a teenage boy who was collecting glasses, "Show them their room."

She handed Violet a key, and said, "Follow him."

Violet followed the boy up two flights of stairs, till they reached room 5. He pointed at the door, "Do you want me to show you the room?"

"No thanks," Violet said, "I'll be fine." She smiled, and a blush spread over his face and neck.

"See you then," he said, and moved backwards towards the stairs.

Violet put the baby in her car seat on the floor, and went to get their stuff from the car.

Violet's legs felt hollow and unsteady as she carried her bag, and the suitcase of baby stuff up the stairs. When she reached the room she stopped for a moment with her forehead leaning against the wood, catching her breath.

Once inside, she dropped the bags on the floor, and leaned back against the door to shut it. The door closed with a bang, and the baby flinched in her sleep. She was kind of hunched in the car seat, and Violet wondered if she should put her on the floor. Babies bones were soft, wasn't there even a hole in their skulls that had to grow shut? She didn't want to warp her spine by leaving her in a sitting position all the time. Violet yawned, and pushed herself off the door. There might be an extra blanket that she could lay out.

She opened a thin cupboard next to the bathroom door. Inside, there was an iron, and a folded up blanket. She pulled the blanket out, and opened it. If she put Maria in the middle of the floor, she might forget about her and tread on her in the middle of the night. The grey suitcase was lying on the floor with the backpack. Violet unzipped it, and emptied the baby clothes onto the floor.

"Travel cot," she said.

She put the suitcase near the door, and in one side used the blanket to make a bed. Carefully, she unclipped Maria's seatbelt and lifted her out of the car seat, and laid her in the suitcase. Violet didn't want to risk waking her up, so left the bear suit on, it was probably warmer than a blanket anyway.

She pushed her boots off, and climbed onto the bed. There was a remote on the bedside table, and she turned the TV on, and laid back on the pillows; the News was on. As her eyes closed she thought she heard a tiny whinny of a horse. She felt a staggering feeling of weightlessness and relief, as her head sank into the pillow, and then the dreams started to rush through her brain, too fast and too vivid, like a horror film.

Jodie hugs a black snake dressed-up like a baby, Lisa laughing as she kisses Violet on a TV stage, drunk and pregnant, the audience hurl drinks at them, and boo, and hiss, sausage fingers stroking her eyes, probing her mouth. Jodie pushes the snake at her, says,

"Would you like to hold the baby?"

The snake opens its black mouth, black inside, tongue flicking, fangs clean like plastic, and cries like a real baby, lacy bonnet tied under its chin in a bow.

"Go on, have a hold."

Lisa's tongue flicks against hers, the audience boo; someone throws a can that leaves a dent in her forehead, as the snake's baby cries fill the studio. Yellow snake eyes spilling over with tears… opens its mouth wider and wider, dislocates its jaw, and strikes at Violet's face.

Violet opened her eyes with a jolt. Baby Maria was crying loud. Shit, how long had she been asleep? She looked at the TV; the News was still on.

She rolled over, pushed herself up, and went to fill the kettle.

Violet put the bottle on the windowsill to cool, and got Maria out of the suitcase; she needed changing again. Violet laid her down in the middle of the bed, and went back to the kettle. The crying wasn't as violent as usual, or maybe her ears had adapted to it. There was a tray with stuff to make tea or coffee, and some biscuits in plastic wrapping. She tore open four sachets of Nescafe, emptied them into a cup, and added water from the kettle. Honey would have been nice, but she'd left it in the car.

There was a mirror on the wall, and Violet stared at herself as she stirred. Her blonde hair looked dark and dirty, and was half pulled out of her ponytail. Somehow she still had traces of eye makeup on, and that combined with the shadows under her eyes gave her a kind of gothic look. Behind her she could see Maria's legs kicking as she cried. Violet took the spoon out of the coffee, clenched her jaw, and pressed it against her wrist. She squeezed her eyes shut as it burned her skin. She took it away, and looked at the mark. She would do Maria's nappy, and feed her before running it under cold water.

10

Mum stays in bed all the time. Sometimes I sit in bed with her and we both cry or lie down and watch telly. Dad goes back to work but he comes home earlier than he used to. He gets in bed with us and hugs and cuddles Mum, and he makes us beans or skippers on toast if we haven't had tea. Sometimes he goes up into the loft or stays in the garage for ages and when he comes out his eyes are red and I think he has been crying about Jamie too.

Sometimes Mum goes out and Michaela the neighbour comes and looks after me. She makes me peanut butter and banana sandwiches and reads me stories or plays snakes and ladders with me. Once she went into the toilet and came out with her eyes all puffed up and I know she had been crying as well, she did it once in the kitchen too. Whenever I think that I won't see Jamie again I get a bad pain in my tummy.

On Wednesdays Grandad comes to take me swimming. Because I'm not at school we can go in the daytime which is better because we get the whole pool to ourselves, and there are just a few mums and toddlers in the baby pool.

We are driving to swimming in Grandad's car and listening to some marching band music. It is cold so Grandad puts the heater on full blast. Yesterday I decided not to pray to God or to the angels anymore. I think that fairies and animals will help me to talk to Jamie instead.

This morning I drew a picture of two grizzly bear cubs and wrote 'To Jamie, love from Violet' on it. I took it to the end of the garden and put it on a branch so the blackbirds can take it to Jamie in heaven. At first I put it on the ground but then I thought it would be horrible if the blackbird was collecting the letter and Cupid caught him and ate him. So I climbed up the liquid amber tree and put the letter around a branch and then tied it on with two shoelaces.

I fly forward and my seatbelt stings my neck. The car screeches and then there is a bang.

Grandad says, "Shit."

I look up and there is a man getting out of the car in the front. He walks very quickly up to Grandad's door and opens it.

The marching band music is still on quite loud so the man has to shout,

"You bloody idiot! You've driven straight into the back of me," he yells, "I want your details."

Grandad presses the red triangle button in the car, turns the marching music down and undoes his seatbelt. The horrible man is huffing and puffing and staring at Grandad.

"You should be more bloody careful mate, specially with a kid in the car."

Grandad bends down and gets something out of the door pocket.

The man is standing there with his hands on his hips. He is nodding his head in an angry way and he reminds me of a goose about to hiss. Some other cars drive past, and I see the people in them looking at us.

Grandad gets out of the car, and then really fast he hits the man on the back of his head with a black stick. The man kneels down with his hands on the back of his head and Grandad gets back into the car and shuts the door.

Another door from the car in front opens, and a lady gets out, "Hey! HEY!" she shouts.

Grandad reverses quickly, then drives away.

He turns the music up again and I am a bit scared to say

anything so I look out the window.

After a while I hear him sniffing and I look over. His glasses have gone steamy, and he pulls a handkerchief out of his shirt pocket and wipes his eyes. I don't like seeing Grandad cry so I look out of the window again until we get to the swimming pool.

* * *

When we get home, Grandad makes me some toast in the kitchen and cuts it into triangles.

He puts his hand on my wet hair.

"Sorry about that man," he says, "I didn't mean to frighten you."

"I wasn't frightened," I say, "He deserved it… he was horrible."

He gives me a cuddle, "None of us are ourselves at the moment… Get that toast down you, an athlete needs fuel. I'm going to go and talk to your mum before I go."

When Grandad goes out of the kitchen I turn the telly on. It's Chucklevision which I don't like, but I leave it on anyway because there'll probably be cartoons on after.

11

Violet sipped her second coffee, which was weak and only made with one real coffee sachet, and two decafs. Maria was sleeping with her head tilted back. Her mouth was part open in a little pout. It was the deepest sleep Violet had seen her in yet. Usually, her lips were turned downwards, as if she wasn't quite comfortable. Maybe Maria found the suitcase cot more comfortable than the car seat, or Violet had made an especially good bottle of formula milk.

There were only four channels on the telly, Crimewatch came on after the News. A chill ran up Violet's neck, as she imagined a photo-fit of herself with dead eyes and grey lips appearing on the screen. No, it was too early. Lisa wouldn't want the police involved anyway, she was probably just drinking vodka and lemonade, expecting Violet to come back with Maria, and drugs. Did Lisa know where her house was? Violet couldn't remember.

She changed the channel to a film on ITV. It was an old James Bond film, a really stupid one with Sean Connery dressed-up and wearing eyeliner, with his hair tinted black to pass as Chinese. She watched as body double Sean Connery did a perfect pike roll off the side of a ship, and landed on a cargo pallet. Adam was a stunt man now. The last time she'd seen him was when she bumped into him in the chemist. He'd just got his first film job. He told her that he was supposed to be a Russian soldier and in his scene he had to run as fast as he could and then fall on the ground as if he'd been shot.

"It's much harder than what you'd think," he said, "It's the most unnatural thing in the world to be going full sprint, and then make yourself fall down."

"What stunt do you find easiest?" she'd asked.

She remembered him grinning, the same as he had when they were at school, "Getting set on fire," he said, "that's my speciality."

He asked her out for a drink, but she didn't turn up, getting high at work instead then going round to Lisa and Claude's.

Violet got off the bed, and sat on the floor next to Maria. She touched Maria's palm, and watched as the baby clenched hold of it, and held on. She wondered if Maria missed Lisa or not. She doubted she missed Claude, as he'd been gone a few weeks now. Violet felt the thoughts stir like worms suddenly exposed. She tried to concentrate on James Bond, the Trisha Show couple on the ferry, but the images pushed through and she felt the sick, heavy feeling roll into her guts and settle.

At least Claude left after that, after he'd 'punished' her. She remembered his anger when he couldn't make her cry and beg in front of the camera, and she'd clenched her jaws at the sex, punches and slaps to the face, focussing on keeping the high, and remembering a song the squirrel sang in Spongebob Squarepants. A smell like baby oil and rubber that made her stomach turn. Lisa was off her head on pills in the lounge, had she walked in a couple of times?

Violet just hoped her dad would never see any of it on the internet. She downed the rest of the coffee. Maria was better off without Claude, hopefully she hadn't inherited his mean streak. Lisa at least had a sense of humour, however fucked up.

Violet took her finger out of Maria's fist, and put the blanket over her properly. The bear suit was on the floor and she picked it up and pulled the rest of the money out. She took a £20 note, and stuck it in her jeans. The coffee had woken her up and she wanted a drink.

Violet looked at herself in the mirror, brushed her hair with her fingers and tied it up in a messy pony tail. She got an eyeliner out of the backpack, and put some on to detract from the dark shadows

Laura Wake

round her eyes. Her lips were split in one corner, probably from lack of vitamins. She opened her mouth wide and a tiny cut like an extra mouth appeared; she scratched off the dead skin around it.

Maria was still sleeping, and Violet leant down and listened to make sure she was breathing. She stuffed the rest of the money back in the bear suit pocket, and hung it on the back of the door. As she was about to leave, she changed her mind and switched the £20 note for a 10. They would have to be careful with their money as she didn't have a plan for making any more yet. She would buy one drink, and then find someone to pay for any others. If desperate, she was allowed to buy two, but she was coming back to the room with change.

The bar was almost empty, and the music had been turned down. Three men were sitting at a table in the far corner talking. Every now and again, one of them would slap his hand down hard on the table and laugh. An old, red-cheeked man in tweed was sitting at a round table staring at his drink. The bargirl with the big cleavage was still serving, and talking to the same guy as before. Violet stood next to him, and the barmaid said, "Room alright for you?"

"Yeah good, thanks." Violet jerked her head at the ceiling. "She's sleeping, thought I'd come down for a quick drink."

The barmaid leaned on her elbows in front of the man, who was rolling a cigarette. She turned back to Violet, and smiled hard.

"What can I get you then?"

"Vodka and ginger ale."

The man looked at Violet. He was thin with prominent cheekbones and weirdly bright eyes like an ill person, about 40. From the collar of his shirt a bad tribal tattoo crept and finished in a swirl behind each ear. "You can get a double for an extra pound," he said.

"Yeah, good idea," she replied, but the barmaid was already moving away from the optics toward the fridge.

"Joanne!" he called, "The girl wants a double."

The barmaid didn't turn round but went back to the vodka and added an extra shot.

58

Violet pulled up a bar stool next to the man. He licked the rizla and ran his thumb down the cigarette to seal it.

"Can I have a cigarette?" Violet asked.

He slid the tobacco and papers along the bar to her. She started rolling and Joanne put the drink in front of her, "That's three pound fifty," she said.

Violet pinched the half-made cigarette in her left hand, and reached into her jeans pocket to pull the £10 note out.

"Thanks."

Violet finished rolling her cigarette, tapped it on the bar, and put it in her mouth.

Joanne put the change in front of Violet, "How old's your baby?" she asked.

Violet took the cigarette out of her mouth, "Six months."

Joanne turned to the skinny man, "Ricky, why you goin' outside? You can smoke in here."

He touched the cigarette that was stuck behind his right ear, "Special one," he said, "You coming?"

She frowned and scanned the bar, "Can't till they've left, and Geoffrey's gonna need a taxi calling any minute."

Ricky looked at Violet, "Fancy it?" he said.

As Violet followed him outside, she heard Joanne loading the glass washer with a slam.

Outside there were round wooden tables with folded up parasols in the middle. The light from inside the bar dimly lit the patio area. On the stone walls hung lobster pots, buoys, rope with floats, and coloured glass fishermans' balls that shone faintly in the weak light.

Violet sat down at one of the wooden tables and rested her feet on a parasol base below. There were plastic Fosters, Carling and John Smiths ashtrays on the tables. Ricky and Violet had a black Carling one with a chip in the side, and a piece of ashy chewing gum stuck in the middle of it. The setting was quite authentic, Violet thought, like the sea with plastic rubbish floating in it.

Ricky passed her the joint.

They smoked in silence, passing the joint, pausing only to relight it. The wind had died down, and the smoke lifted steadily into the air. Violet hadn't smoked weed much since school, as it made her paranoid, and her head noisy. It would be alright if she got to bed quickly, and just benefited from its tranquilizing effects.

She took a last, long drag, and passed it back to Ricky, "Thanks."

"No worries... Hey, it's my birthday tomorrow, I'm having a house party, all day. Come if you like?"

Violet stood up to go, "I can't, I've got Maria..." she stopped suddenly, realising she'd said Maria's real name.

Ricky got the tobacco out of his pocket again, "She can come, there'll be loads of kids knocking about. It's across the road, number 29."

"Yeah thanks, might see you there then."

Ricky sparked his lighter and in the flame she saw him smile.

Violet pushed the door to the pub and it didn't open. She pushed it again harder, then realised it was a PULL door. The three men glanced up from their table, and she thought she saw one whisper something to another. The old man was gone, but Joanne was still at the bar, looking at her.

"Night," Violet said.

"Don't you want your drink?"

Violet turned back and picked up her glass. "I'll take it up. I'm knackered. Thanks."

Violet climbed onto the bed, and lay back against the pillows. She felt the uneasiness slip away, and a warm, weighty feeling fill her limbs. The ice had melted in her vodka & ginger. She held the remaining slivers on her tongue for a moment, feeling the cold come out, before crushing them.

Violet closed her eyes, and Maria started to cry.

12

I can never get to sleep anymore. When I tell Dad he gets annoyed with me, and says that I don't try. Mum says it's because he is a good sleeper and doesn't understand. She says I'm a night owl like her. It's boring when I go in their room though. Mum doesn't want to talk or anything, she lies there with her eyes closed, and we listen to Dad snoring. When I start talking she just says, "Shh, Dad's sleeping," so I don't go in there anymore.

I hate bedtime. The golden alarm clock that Mum got me for learning the time is on my bedside table, and sometimes I listen to it tick all night. I read loads of books. I have read all the Secret Seven, and Famous Five books about three times. I think they are a bit babyish now, and the only one I really like is when the boys in the Secret Seven go spying, and it tells you about how to follow someone without them noticing. There's also a Famous Five one that teaches you how to escape from a locked room. Now I always keep a folded up piece of paper and a bit of wire in my pocket. Mum bought me listening tapes about Lord Nelson and Napoleon, so sometimes I listen to those as well.

Dad comes in at half past eight every night and makes me turn my reading light off. I wait until he goes to bed, and then take my torch out from under the pillow. I have taken a book called 'A Chamber of Horrors' from the study. It's Mum's, and she says that it is full of 'horrific stuff', and not for children. Once she read me a chapter about a Greek god who ate all his babies. There are pictures of torture equipment in it like in the London Dungeon. My torch keeps running out of batteries but there is a drawer in the garage with lots of them so I sneak in and take them. I heard Dad swearing a few days ago, because he couldn't find any batteries. He and Mum had an argument about it, and he took the batteries out of the telly control. Behind the book of Black Beauty I have got six batteries hidden.

I am reading a story about a woman with a crippled arm. There are some words I don't understand, but I have a dictionary to look them up. I sit with my knees up and the quilt over me like a tent. I have the torch balanced on my shoulder, and the book propped up on my thighs because it is quite heavy to hold. I am just getting to a really exciting bit where the arm starts to do things that the woman can't control, when the torch goes dimmer and I know the batteries are wearing out.

I turn my bedside light on, holding the switch so that it doesn't click. My door is shut, and Dad probably won't see the light, but I have to be careful, because it's 3 o' clock and he will be really angry if he finds me still reading. I take two batteries from behind Black Beauty, and put the old ones down the side of my bed.

When I am putting the second battery in, something knocks inside my head. I stop what I'm doing and sit really still. It happens again. I feel something inside my forehead tapping, like it's knocking at a door. I don't know what to do, so I freeze, and only move my eyes. It knocks again, even louder, and makes me jump. Now I'm really frightened. I don't move, and I close and open my eyes to make sure I'm not dreaming, then a horrible little voice says,

"Oi."

I am going to cry, but don't dare make a noise. I sit there for ages, hoping it will go away if I don't say anything. I can feel whatever it is, waiting behind my forehead. Some tears roll down my face, and I have to hold my breath to stop the crying from coming out. I want to go into Mum and Dad's room, but I don't move in case it will make the voice come back. I sit totally still until the clock says twenty past three, and then I think it has gone.

I leave the bedside light on and get into the space under my bed. My nose almost touches the underneath of the bed which smells nice and dusty. I will sleep here tonight.

13

The car door wasn't shut properly, and there was condensation on the window. Violet climbed over the driver seat and got the honey bear out of the glove box. She twisted his hat, and squirted honey into her mouth. She was hungry. Her bag of CDs was stuffed behind the passenger seat, and she pulled it out to take back to the room.

Violet filled the kettle for Maria's bottle, then looked at the suitcase and saw that she was awake.

"No crying today then?" she said.

Maria was watching her. Violet leaned closer and the baby raised both arms above her head, and said, "Ba."

Violet lifted her out and carried her across the room, grabbing the CDs on the way. Violet emptied the bag out on the bed. She chose David Bowie's 'Hunky Dory', stuck it one-handed into the little Bucket 'o Mussels stereo, and pressed play. 'Changes' started.

"That's my mum's favourite. Too slow for today," Violet said, "Let's have 'Queen Bitch'." She forwarded to 11 and turned it up loud.

"Think you're gonna like this one."

"Ba. Ba!" Maria said and smiled.

"Yeah, bit of Bowie."

Violet danced around the room singing, and twirling Maria in the air above her head, then holding her and dancing from side to side.

"She's so swishy in her satin and TAT, in her frock coat and bipperty-bopperty HAT...."

Maria started chuckling.

When it got to the bit about the hotel room, Violet shouted the words out, "So I lay down a while, And I gaze at my hotel wall, Oh the cot is so cold, it don't feel like no bed at all!"

Violet gave the grey suitcase a hard kick that made the lid drop shut, and Maria let out a full, proper laugh, which made Violet laugh too.

When the track finished, Violet lay back on the bed with Maria on her chest. Halfway through the next track Maria started to cry. Violet wondered if it was the song with its creepy lines about brass teeth, or that she was hungry for breakfast.

She got up, mixed the formula, and put the 'Essential Reggae' CD in while they waited for the milk to cool down.

"Breakfast soon, don't worry," Violet said.

Maria paused in her crying and looked at her.

"Ohhh, oh, the Israelites," Violet sang.

Maria almost smiled, and then let out another forceful burst of crying.

Violet picked her up again, smelled nappy, and turned her head away, "How can milk turn to that?" she said. "Hey, you want a bath before breakfast?"

In the little bathroom there was a shower with a curtain, and a worktop with a sink, and a mirror on the wall. Violet wobbled off balance as Maria reached for the mirror and let out a shriek.

Apart from a greenish stain around the plug hole the sink was clean. With one hand she gave it a rinse round, then put the plug in and turned the taps on. Maria moved her head round as if she was trying to work out what the noise was.

"Bathtime!" Violet said.

There was a little basket next to the sink with a bottle of shampoo, one of shower gel, and a wrapped up bar of soap sealed with a rose-shaped sticker with 'Diana' written in the middle of it.

The sink filled quickly and Violet turned the taps off.

"Okay, let's ditch your nappy."

She lay Maria down on the bed and undid the nappy. Maria kicked her legs, and the sides opened. The poo had spread everywhere, it was even on her back.

Violet lifted Maria off the bed and put her down on the floor, then got the toilet roll and a towel out of the bathroom. Music still rang out from the stereo, *Pass the dutchie from the left hand side...*

Maria smiled and kicked her legs then slammed her hand down into the dirty nappy.

Give me the music make me jump and prance...

Violet turned her head to one side as she pulled the nappy out and lifted Maria's legs to slide the towel under so she could wipe the worst of it away with the toilet paper.

...give me the music make me rockin at the dance...

Violet left Maria on the towel as she went to check the sink. She stuck her elbow in, the water was warm not hot.

Violet opened the Diana soap and a strong smell of flowery perfume came out, she probably shouldn't use it on Maria, babies were supposed to have special soap or something; a couple of days later she might be covered in oozing sores. She took the lid off the shower gel and smelt it, it wasn't as strong as the soap. She poured a capful out, tipped it into the sink and stirred it with her hand.

When Violet went to get Maria she was gurgling and kicking her legs to the music, "I think you're a reggae fan," Violet said, lifting her up.

She got a firm grip on Maria and lowered her into the sink. As the water covered her legs she frowned and looked as though she was about to cry, then spread her arms and legs out like a spider and stared up at Violet.

Violet cupped her head and neck in her hand and let Maria sink lower into the water. Again, Maria splayed her limbs out.

"You making a starfish?" Violet said.

Maria frowned and moved her arms and legs up and down. Violet used her free hand to wash under her arms and down her back. "I'll get you a sponge for next time."

There was a plastic cup on the side, and she pulled it out of its wrapping. Carefully she scooped water, and poured it over Maria's head. Maria frowned again, moved her head from side to side, then smiled.

"Yeah... washing's fun," Violet said, and poured another cup over the back of her head. Maria shrieked and splashed her arms in the water.

After a while Violet's arm started to hurt from keeping hold of the slippery baby and supporting her head at the same time. She pushed Maria's hair into a lopsided Mohican and lifted her to show her the reflection in the mirror.

"Look at you," Violet said, "clean!"

Maria stared at the mirror, and kicked her legs. Violet felt suddenly embarrassed and half expected Maria to freak out when she saw that she was naked and being held up by a stranger. She lowered the baby back down and poured another cup of water over her head, flattening the Mohican.

Violet wrapped Maria in a towel, patted her dry then lay her on the floor while she picked out an outfit from the baby stuff her mum had given them. She chose a red babysuit, and denim dungarees that had a picture of two ducks on the front.

Maria's hair stood up in damp spikes, Violet picked her up, and smelled a faint, clean smell of shower gel.

"Looking good," she said.

Maria started to cry and Violet got the bottle.

Maria fell asleep before she'd even had half the bottle so Violet put her in the car seat and carried her down to breakfast.

Breakfast was in a room called Family Room, separate from the bar. There weren't many people there. An elderly couple looked up and said, "Morning."

"Morning," Violet replied.

There were two girls sitting together at the far end of the room, and a tall man with a book on his own. Violet chose a window seat that looked out on to the car park. She put Maria's car seat on a chair, and sat down next to her.

"Good morning," said a thin, dark-haired waiter with stubble. He had a foreign accent, somewhere Mediterranean.

"Hi," she said.

He handed her the menu, and asked "Coffee or tea?"

"Coffee," she said, "strong please."

He grinned, and a couple of gold teeth twinkled. "I understand. I get you proper one from the bar!" He motioned to the jug of filter coffee and lowered his voice, "I can't believe they can call this coffee. In Portugal, we will not tolerate."

Violet laughed, "Thanks."

The breakfast choice was either the 'continental', which was bread rolls with a jam selection, or combinations of fried breakfasts. Violet was craving kippers, and was disappointed to be by the sea and not eat fish.

She looked at Maria in the car seat, and felt a stab of panic. Lisa would definitely be looking for them now. She might've gone asking in the pub. They would give out her address, if she didn't already know where that was, Violet couldn't remember. She wished again that she'd chosen a big city to run to, not an island. She'd never been good at thinking ahead.

She thought of her tantrums at draughts, and Grandad giving her that look and slow shake of the head. Violet enjoyed draughts, before she realised it was about forward planning, not just jumping and beheading. Grandad would never let her win either. He beat her every time, managing to hop four or five of her pieces in one go. Once she threw the board at him so the pieces went all over the floor. He just laughed. Mum didn't think it was funny though. Violet remembered holding onto the rim of the washing machine as she smacked her with a flip-flop.

"You are ready?" The waiter put a tall black coffee in front of Violet with a flourish.

"Yeah, scrambled eggs on toast please."

"White or brown?"

"What?"

"What toast you like?"

"Brown please."

He left and Violet stirred a brown sugar lump into the coffee. There was a plate of fruit on the table and she peeled a banana.

Maria made a noise from the car seat. Her eyes were open and she was looking round the breakfast room.

"Hi," Violet said, "nice outfit!"

Maria's eyes settled on Violet.

Violet took a mouthful of banana. Her food-starved tongue seemed to shoot electric currents as her taste buds kicked into life. She'd forgotten how nice bananas were.

Maria reached out and grabbed at the banana.

"Are you serious?" Violet said, "You want to try some banana?"

She broke off a small piece and held it out to Maria who gripped it so it squashed in her fist.

"Idiot," she said, but then Maria raised her hand to her mouth, stuffed her fist in, and ate it.

Violet handed Maria a piece of scrambled egg to try, but she spat it out, and made a disgusted face.

Violet took the other banana off the table and put it in her jacket pocket. The scrambled eggs were good; she finished them quickly, and wished they'd been twice the size.

The waiter returned with the bill and she wrote the room number, then signed 'Esther Johnson', with a final flick that tore the paper.

"Sorry," she said.

But the waiter had lifted Maria out of the car seat and was holding her above his head and blowing raspberries. Maria's eyes were closed tightly and she was laughing more than Violet had ever seen.

"My God! She beautiful!" he said, "What is her name?"

Violet looked at him, he had hazel eyes with gold flecks in them, "Ma... Marley," she said. It was horrible, like some character from an American teen series, or something a self-righteous stoner might name their child. She needed to think faster.

The waiter lowered Maria to his chest and rocked her, singing something in Portuguese.

"I am Sergio," he said. "She is so gorgeous."

"Thanks."

Violet reached out to take her and he blew another raspberry at

Maria, making her laugh again. "Where are you from in Portugal?"

"Madeira," he said, "the most beautiful place on earth."

He turned from Maria, and looked at Violet. "How long you stay here? I don' work tomorrow, I can show for you the beach?" His gold teeth showed again as he smiled.

"I don't know yet, we're going to stay with my aunt. Thanks though." She held out her arms for Maria, and he passed her back.

"I think she's made a poo," he said.

"Oh. Sorry."

"She brilliant. Maybe I see you tomorrow?"

"Yeah... hey, do you know where the nearest supermarket is?"

"There is Sainsbury close to Shanklin. When you get to Shanklin you take the road for Sandown and after five minutes you can see him."

Violet held onto Maria, and Sergio hooked the car seat onto her other arm for her.

"Bye," Violet said and headed for the door.

When she looked back, he was still waving at Maria who was watching him from Violet's shoulder.

Violet changed Maria's nappy, then put her in the car seat. "My turn to wash now," she said.

Violet took the shampoo and shower gel and got in the tiny shower. The shampoo was harsh, and made her hair feel stripped-down and straw-like, but it was better than nothing.

When she came out, Maria was struggling and starting to cry. Violet got her out, pushed play on the stereo, and laid her down in the middle of the bed.

She sat in front of the mirror to put make-up on. Apart from the little scabby bit in the corner of her mouth, she looked surprisingly good. She ran her fingers through her hair. If people came after them, it would have to go dark, or come off completely.

Maria was making noises to herself and reaching up and grabbing hold of her feet. Violet went and sat next to her.

"What do you think?" she said, "Shall we stay another night... or go to the beach?"

Maria was dribbling, she looked at Violet and made a little

shriek.

"That's what I thought. Too risky."

She packed their bags, emptying her clothes out of the backpack and putting them in the suitcase with Maria's. In the empty backpack, she put a made-up bottle, two nappies, the wipes, the honey bear, and the bag of CDs. Violet felt energized after breakfast, but confused, like there were hundreds of things she needed to do, and couldn't think of any of them.

She pulled the fire assembly plan out of its plastic wallet on the door and looked for a pen. In the ashtray by the bed was a fluorescent pink pencil.

"Ah, I remember you," she said, and picked it up and held it between her fingers. She twisted it round, looking to see if Lake was on the tiny map, but there were only a few towns on it.

She started to write,

Nappies
Baby Wipes
Food for me
Food for Maria, formula milk & bananas
Shampoo
Oranges
Cigarettes
Coco Pops.

Violet didn't think Maria would be able to sit in the little plastic seat, so she left her inw the car seat, and put that in the trolley. As soon as she started pushing, Maria fell asleep. They were running low on cash; she'd counted it in the car park, £172.

She walked up and down each aisle, holding the pencil to eliminate items from her list, and adding the odd extra thing to the trolley, like Greek yoghurt; it would be nice with the squeezy bear honey. In the meat section, she stopped at a fillet steak for £8. If they were going to be successful in their getaway, Violet needed to keep her strength up. She lifted Maria's legs up, and slid the packet underneath the lining of the car seat.

Baby wipes and nappies weren't cheap either, and the cans of formula milk were even more expensive. Violet added a new baby bottle to the trolley. There were some baby books on offer, pop-up ones with farm animals and noises. She stuffed a few into Maria's car seat with the steak.

She chose a checkout with a punk girl cashier, who wore a chain linking her ear to her nose.

"Do you need help packing your bags?" she asked.

"No thanks."

"She's cool," the cashier said looking at Maria.

Maria must have woken up when the trolley stopped moving. She was frowning, and looked like she was about to cry.

"Thanks," Violet said.

"I like her dungarees."

The total was £32. She wished she'd stuck a few more items in the car seat.

Violet took the steak and books out from under Maria and put the shopping in the boot. As she was buckling Maria and her car seat in the passenger seat, she noticed a red warning sign: DANGER-NOT FOR USE IN FRONT SEAT- DEATH OR SERIOUS INJURY CAN OCCUR. Violet moved the car seat to the back, and strapped it in. Maria was crying and struggling, Violet realised she was probably hungry again. She got the ready-made bottle out of the backpack; there was nowhere to heat it up. Why did you have to heat up babies' milk anyway? She decided to put it between her legs while they were driving, that would warm it up a bit.

They drove away from the supermarket, through Shanklin and back to Lake. It was a bright, windy day, and red and brown leaves spun in mini cyclones on the pavements. Violet stuck 'Music for the Jilted Generation' in the CD player.

At the traffic lights, she remembered she'd forgotten cigarettes.

"Fuck."

Maybe she should check out that party, get a cigarette, or a quick free drink for the road. The clock in the car said 11:30, that guy had said it was an all-day party, and that there'd be children so it might have already started. She could park at the Bucket o' Mussels, give Maria her bottle there, and then walk across.

The bottle between the legs trick worked quite well, but Maria didn't fall asleep like she usually did when drinking. Violet lifted her up, and they walked across the road to find the party. She couldn't remember the house number but went to the one she could hear music coming from. Maria grabbed at Violet's earrings. She was dribbling again, and crying a bit.

"I don't know why you're moaning, I just fed you." She pushed the doorbell.

Someone opened the door and then disappeared up a stairway.

Violet followed the sound of thumping music. She pushed opened a door, and entered a thick cloud of weed smoke. The music was loud and bassy, some garage tune. The beat vibrated in her throat, and drowned out Maria, who had started to cry properly now. Violet bounced her up and down a bit, "I thought you liked loud music."

Two long, battered sofas lined the walls of the room. Each sofa held six or seven people. One sofa load was occupied with a bong, and the people on the other had a couple of joints on the go. It was murky, and difficult to see because of the smoke hanging in the air, and the windows which were blocked up with polystyrene painted silver.

The people were dressed like skaters, with beanies pulled down low, and baggy torn jeans. No one looked up, they were either smoking or banging their heads, eyes closed, to the music. Slightly masked by the pungent smoke, there was another danker smell, like stagnant water mixed with eggs. Violet had smelled it before, but couldn't place it.

She noticed crowded shelves above the peoples' heads. Apart from holding a huge pair of speakers, crooked piles of magazines, and tangles of electric cable, there were loads of big glass and plastic tanks. One of the tanks was huge, with a branch inside, and two iguanas with long, curly claws. Next to that was a stack of smaller plastic tanks. The first one was too misty to see inside, but in the second one up, two bent hairy legs were visible. Violet flinched, and held Maria tighter. She turned and saw that the shelves each side of the wall were full of creatures. Coiled snakes were pressed against the greasy looking glass, and although some of the tanks looked empty, she guessed the occupants were hiding. The smell was the smell of a reptile house.

Violet could see light through the smokiness, and made out a doorway with people dancing and moving about in another room. She headed quickly towards the light, then tripped on something and almost dropped Maria. Violet looked down and saw a foot in a beaten-up trainer.

"Nearly," a voice giggled next to her, and she turned to see a man with fuzzy blonde dreadlocks and a Rasta hat, looking at her through puffed up eyes.

She ignored him and carried on to the next room. One of the people in there was the barmaid from the Bucket o' Mussels. She was with three other girls, smoking cigarettes, dancing, and drinking the kind of fluorescent coloured alcopops that Violet hated.

The room was a kitchen with open sliding doors leading to a bare garden. There were children outside chasing each other around with plastic tennis rackets, and spades. The barmaid had obviously noticed Violet, but was ignoring her. There was a pack of cigarettes lying open on a worktop littered with plastic cups and cans, but Violet didn't risk it in case they belonged to one of the girls.

Maria was screaming, her tears dribbling down Violet's neck.

"Alright!" Violet said, "I'm just going to get a cigarette, and then we'll go."

Four men appeared from the reptile corridor, one of them was Ricky. He was wearing salmon pink shorts and a polo shirt, and looked more animated than he had the previous night. She saw him recognise her.

"Hey, you came. What's your name again?"

One of his friends nudged him, and they all laughed. Violet noticed they were talking too fast, their eyes darting round the room. One of them was chewing gum at about 100 miles an hour.

"It's Esther. Yeah I thought I'd stop by and say happy birthday, see what parties are like on the Isle of Wight."

Ricky's friends had joined Joanne and the other girls, and were jumping into each other, an elbow hit Joanne, and a spray of blue alcopop crossed the air. One of them ran back into the corridor shouting "Wankers!" as the music was changed to Happy Hardcore.

Ricky held out a bottle of Carling to Violet, and motioned her outside. They sat down at a picnic table. Maria's crying slowed down as she heard the noises of the children, and she started looking around.

Ricky started to roll a cigarette, the rizla trembling in his twitchy fingers.

"Do you want one?" he asked, and she reached for the tobacco.

Violet tried to position Maria on her lap, but she kept wriggling, till Violet spilled the tobacco. She started again, and put the cigarette in her mouth quickly before Maria could grab it, then leaned forward for Ricky to light it.

A small boy with chocolate round his face came running up.

"Uncle Ricky, Uncle Ricky!" he shouted, breathless. "Can we have a water fight?"

"Yeah, hose is over there."

The boy ran back to the others who were still running round in a circle, and shouted, "He said yes, he said yes, he said YES!!"

Ricky reached in his pocket and pulled out a small paper packet.

"Fancy a line?"

He opened it, and Violet noticed the powder's dirty tint. A burst of giggles made her look round, and she saw the barmaid and her friends piling out of the kitchen."

"No thanks, I prefer coke."

"Couldn't get that out down here, vultures'd get it." He nodded towards the sliding door, and Violet laughed.

Joanne the barmaid pushed between them and sat down on Ricky's knee, sliding an arm around his neck as he began chopping out thin lines on the table.

"Ooh, you shouldn't have!" Joanne said, and started rolling up a ten pound note.

Ricky stood up, and let the other girls take his place. Violet watched Joanne snort the fattest line, and saw her eyes fill with tears as it burned the inside of her nose; she almost felt jealous.

Ricky leaned close to Violet's ear, "We'll go upstairs in a minute, sort you out a line of the good stuff. Gotta treat the tourists nice."

Maria had stopped screaming and was sucking her fingers. Violet shifted her into the crook of her elbow, and flicked ash on the ground.

Joanne and her friends came up and started fussing over Maria. The speed was making them chatty.

"What's her name?" a big, blonde girl asked.

"Martine," Violet said.

"Ooh. Can I have a hold?" another one shrieked, "She's so cute!"

The girl was quite pretty, but her hair was scraped back tightly, and hardened with spray, giving her a mean look.

"This is Carol," Ricky said, "my little sister." He pinched her on the back of the arm, and she slapped at him, but missed as he dodged sideways.

"Fuck off, Ricky," Carol said, and turned back to Violet. She pointed to the boy with the dirty face, who was doing a wheelbarrow with a smaller girl. "Those are my two," she said.

Violet needed a rest, and wanted to smoke a cigarette without struggling with Maria, so she passed her over to Carol. The other girls gathered round, including Joanne who started elaborately playing boo behind her hands.

Ricky bent down, "You coming then?"

"Hey," she said to the group of girls, "are you alright with her for two minutes, I'm just going to the toilet."

Carol and the other girls were absorbed with Maria, but Joanne was staring after Ricky, who had disappeared through the sliding doors. As Violet followed him, Joanne gave her a hard look then turned away.

Violet followed Ricky upstairs into a bathroom. The bath was stained, and the front panels were crooked as if they'd been taken off recently. The mould-spotted shower curtain sagged where its hooks had been torn out. Ricky started chopping out lines next to the sink. The bathroom smelled damp, like the reptile corridor, and

Violet wondered if he gave the snakes baths in here.

Ricky had cut four lines. He passed her a rolled up note, and Violet did two of them. They were lumpier than she would have liked and would probably make her nose bleed a bit, but as she sniffed she felt her head clear with the first little uplifting flutters, and knew that her and Maria's first day on the Isle of Wight was going to be a good one. They would find somewhere to stay and could spend the rest of the day on the beach, maybe take Maria's new books.

Violet smiled, "Thanks," she said.

Ricky picked a little white rock out of his nose and licked it off. He moved towards Violet and pushed his fingers down the front of her jeans, pulling her towards him. Violet realised he was going to kiss her, and backed into the door. Because his hands were hooked into her jeans, he went with her, and she was pushed up against some hanging towels.

"Gross," she thought as his lips pressed against hers, and his tongue shoved its way into her mouth. He tasted of beer and chemicals. Violet kissed him back. She thought of the naff tattoos, and cringed as he pulled down her jeans.

He fucked her against the door, while she held on round his neck. Violet was surprised how long he was able to hold her, before moving to the floor. He had sex in a hard, jerky sort of way, with his head to one side, and Violet noticed wiry muscles straining in his arms as he pushed into her. She wondered what they would look like speeded up, and she thought of Woody Woodpecker *huh huh hu hah huh!* Her head felt light, bubbly almost; something about the sordid bathroom made her feel relieved. He must have been eating speed all day, and Violet realised that this might go on for a long time.

Someone banged on the door.

"Come back later!" he shouted.

Violet heard voices and laughter outside the door, then more banging. Ricky stopped, and shouted, "Fuck off!"

"Share the wealth," a voice said from behind the door, and Violet wondered if they meant her or the cocaine.

They started hammering the door.

Ricky got off her and pulled up his shorts, "Fuck's sake," he said.

Violet's jeans were around one ankle, and she still had a boot on. The other one was standing up by the bath. She dressed quickly, and Ricky opened the door and let in two of the guys Violet had seen in the kitchen. They grinned at her, and then headed for Ricky, who'd already got the wrap out, and was bent over the sink.

"One more here for you," Ricky said to Violet.

She paused by the door, then joined them at the sink, and did the small line he'd laid out for her.

The two men were watching Ricky, waiting.

"I'll see you later," she said.

Ricky sniffed, "Stick around," he said, "party's only just started."

She shut the door behind her, and heard laughter and a cheer erupting inside.

Violet went downstairs quickly. She didn't think she'd been more than ten minutes, but her awareness of time felt warped by her quickening heartbeats. She wanted to get out of here, and go to the beach with Maria.

When she reached the garden, Maria wasn't there. The music was still thumping. The fresh air hit her, and she felt high and awake. She couldn't see Carol or Joanne. There were two little girls left in the garden, sitting cross-legged in the mud. She listened for Maria's cries, but could only hear the banging of the music.

She ran into the reptile corridor. One sofa had emptied a bit, but the people with the bong were still passing it round, their heads lolling about, not keeping up with the beat.

Violet tried to shout over the music, "Hey, has anyone seen a baby?"

A hippy girl wearing flowery dungarees looked up and gave her a stoned smile. Violet climbed up onto the other sofa, reached over the spider tanks and pulled some wires out of the back of the speakers. The music stopped.

"Have any of you seen Ricky's sister, she's looking after my baby?"

A fat man in huge torn jeans, pushed passed her and began reassembling the speakers.

"Who are you?" someone said, and the people with the bong started giggling. Violet bit her lip, and tried to think how long she'd been gone. It couldn't have been more than fifteen minutes.

The girl in the dungarees tapped Violet's arm, "Carol, and her friends just left...didn't see a baby though."

Violet didn't know whether to run out the front door, ask Ricky, or check the house. She needed to calm down. She remembered there was another room off the kitchen, and went there. She pushed open the door. There were about six people standing with their backs to her. Music was playing, something folky, and the people were muttering and giggling.

Violet pushed through the crowd, and saw Maria sitting in the middle of the room. She was sitting up by herself. In a loose circle around her, a huge python was slowly circling. Violet felt her insides jolt, and froze. The snake was huge, at its fattest part, it was easily as wide as Violet. Two coils of snake circulated the baby. Maria wobbled, reaching for the moving patterns.

There was a man sitting cross-legged on the floor near the python.

"What the fuck are you doing?" Violet said.

He looked up and Violet recognised the fuzzy dreadlock guy.

"Hey," he said, "chill out. It's Ethel, man, she's friendly."

Violet heard a burst of slow giggles behind her.

"It's a fucking snake!" she shouted.

She lurched forwards, but someone grabbed her shoulders and held her back. Her shout startled Maria, who flinched, tipped over, then began a loud, racking cry.

The dreadlock man continued, "Wait, just watch, your baby was laying on her a minute ago, Ethel gave her a ride round. I'll put her back on"

"So fucking cool," someone said.

Violet felt a tightening in her brain. She looked for something to smash the snake's head in with.

In the far corner of the room she saw the couple from the

boat, Paul was laughing, his arm around Charlotte. Charlotte was watching Violet through her fringe. Violet thought she saw Charlotte mouth, "Don't."

Violet shuddered and pulled away from the person holding her shoulders. She stepped over the thick patterned skin, and grabbed Maria.

Someone started to boo.

Violet held Maria tight and kicked the dreadlock guy as hard as she could under the chin. She heard a rattle of beads, as his head snapped backwards dislodging his hat.

"You fucking freaks!" she said, and ran out through the corridor. She thought about pushing over the reptile tanks, but confused shouts were starting up behind her, so she opened the front door, and headed for the car park.

Violet felt in her pockets for her car keys and opened the door. She put Maria in her car seat, not stopping to buckle it up, then ran round to her door.

"Oi! Where do you think you're going?" It was a girl's voice.

Violet pulled open the door.

As she was getting in, her head was yanked backwards by her hair, and she saw a trainer kick the car door shut.

Joanne the barmaid was standing in front of her, she held a cigarette in her hand. Violet looked behind, it was Ricky's sister Carol who had her by the hair. Two other girls were making their way across the car park from a table in the Bucket o' Mussels beer garden.

Joanne took a drag on her cigarette, then said, "What were you doing with Ricky?"

Violet listened for people coming up the street. They needed to get out of here quickly.

"I said, what the FUCK were you doing with my boyfriend?"

"He gave me a line," Violet said.

Carol pulled Violet's ponytail, so she was facing the sky, "Grab her arms," she said to one of the other girls.

"He just gave me a line."

"Shut up!" Joanne said, and pushed up against her, so her

forehead was against Violet's.

Violet could feel the massive boobs pressing up against her, and started to smirk. She tried to stop the smile by biting her cheeks.

"You're a tourist," Joanne said, "you shouldn't take locals' drugs." Her face was so close to Violet's that their noses touched as she spoke. Violet smelled the stink of blue WKD misting over her face.

Joanne took a step backwards, and pulled on her cigarette. She flicked the ash off the end, and blew on it, then jammed it into Violet's cheek.

Violet let out a scream, and tears spilled down her face. She couldn't move as Carol had her arm round her neck and a firm grip on her ponytail. The pain seared through her face, and made something in her head lurch.

Joanne threw the fag on the ground. "Now fuck off, and don't come back here," she said.

"And sort your baby out," Carol said, "she's screaming the place down."

Violet felt Carol release her, and the girls walked back towards the pub, laughing.

Violet got in the car, spun it round and accelerated out of Lake. In the rear view mirror, she saw people piling out of number 29 into the street.

14

Violet craned upwards in her seat and looked at the damage to her face. The burn was in the middle of her left cheek. It was pale in the centre, and weeping, with a smudge of ash stuck in it. Around its centre point was a red circle the size of a penny. It would look worse when it scabbed and turned dark. She still felt high, and the pain wasn't unbearable, just a constant slow burning, like a ray of sun through glass.

Violet remembered that Maria wasn't strapped in, and pulled over. Maria's face was bright red, and she was crying so hard, she'd developed a hiccup between each scream. Violet touched her face.

"Yeah," she said, "I fucking hate me too."

Violet buckled her in and got back in the driver seat. She needed a kettle to make Maria's milk, but also to put some distance between them and Lake. Violet held her forehead in her hands, digging her fingernails into the skin hard.

"Fuck!" she shouted, dropping her hands and smashing her head back on the headrest.

She stared at the mirror again. Her big-pupilled eyes looked back at her, intense. On her forehead a line of moon shaped dents had appeared, a couple were starting to bleed.

"Fucking idiot," she said to herself, "Yeah, you!"

The mirror Violet stared back. Violet wished she would come out and take her place.

She turned back to Maria and said, "Let's go to the beach."

Maria kept crying.

"Yeah, I'll sort your dinner out first."

Within fifteen minutes they entered a town called Newport. It was the biggest town Violet had seen so far, but too close to Lake for it to be safe. There was a giant TESCO with a petrol station, so Violet went to fill up the car. The full tank cost £42. Violet tried to do the maths in her head, but as she was getting near to an answer, taking into account the shopping from earlier, the numbers dissolved and she gave up.

At the counter she bought a packet of Camel Lights. The lady serving kept looking at her blistered face.

"Anything else, love?" she asked.

"Yeah, can I get some hot water from the coffee machine?"

"You're supposed to pay for a token." The lady glanced at the security camera, "Silly really." She leaned forward and whispered, "Here," and handed Violet a plastic coin.

At the machine Violet filled a large takeaway cup with boiling water. The cup was so hot that whatever position she held it in, it burned her fingers. There wasn't a cup holder in the car, so she would have to risk burns to her thighs if they were going to carry on moving. As she crossed the forecourt, Violet looked back, and saw the lady at the counter watching her. When she caught Violet's glance, she nodded once and smiled.

Violet decided to risk the busy supermarket car park, and parked and started mixing a new bottle for Maria. She put the bottle on the roof to cool down, then got Maria out to try and cheer her up. She paced around the car and talked about the different shoppers, but Maria was too hungry to be entertained. It was cold too.

Violet breathed in the smell of Maria's hair, "Can't believe you sat up by yourself," she said.

15

I have missed school for three weeks since Jamie died. This morning I go back. Michaela has been helping mum, and she is taking me to school. She holds my hand to cross the main road.

"Do you like school, Violet?" she says.

"It's okay."

"Do you have to pray a lot?"

"In morning assembly and before lunch," I reply.

Michaela and my Mum think my school is weird, I hear them talking about it in the kitchen. They say 'Poor Violet having to put up with those nutters!' Dad says it's easy because it's just across the road. Mum doesn't like the other parents but Dad doesn't have to see them because he's at work.

When I am walking to our classroom, Esther comes up to me.

"You've got the wrong pinafore on. You'll be in trouble," she says.

Everyone else's pinafores are dark grey and mine is light. Mum got it from Woolworth's instead of the school shop.

"I don't care," I say, "I can wear what I like." I hope Mrs Martin doesn't notice.

We get into a line to go into the classroom. I have to stand next to Esther because her surname is next to mine in the alphabet.

She pinches me hard on the arm and I pull away.

"My Mum said to tell you something!" she says.

"What?" I whisper.

"She says she's praying for you and your family because God had to take your brother and you're probably all very sad. She told me to tell you that God will heal your pain."

I don't say anything. I hate Esther and I hate God. If God was nice then he wouldn't have taken my brother at all. I think God is actually evil. I wonder why if Esther's family are best friends with God, he doesn't heal her deaf sister who seems much nicer than Esther.

As we go in Mrs Martin says, "How are you Violet? I'd like to have a little chat with you later." She smiles and touches my arm.

"Okay," I reply.

She looks at my pinafore, and puts a finger on one of the buttons at the front.

"That's not quite right is it?" she says. She smiles and keeps the button between her fingers. "Don't worry, I'm sure your Mum's got a lot on her mind at the moment. We can probably get a spare one for you to wear for now. I'll keep a look out."

"Thank you, Mrs Martin," I say and move away so her fingers aren't on the button anymore. I go to my seat. I will wear my too small pinafore tomorrow. I know the Lost Property room is where she'll look for a spare one and it will be damp and stink.

Hannah had to borrow a tracksuit from there once when she forgot her P.E kit. The tracksuit smelt horrible. The Lost Property is in the basement of the old mansion that everyone knows is haunted. We said Hannah smelt of the dead. I said because it was a spirit smell it might stay in her skin forever. Everyone laughed and Hannah cried. I felt bad.

I won't wear a pinafore from that place.

I go to my desk and we get out our books. Mrs Martin starts reading then we all take turns. Afterwards we will be like reporters and draw eight small pictures showing what happened. I'm going to do mine like a cartoon. I've missed the first parts of the story because of being away. The story is about Joseph interpreting dreams.

I start drawing the pharaoh but I'm still angry with Esther.

I'm annoyed with everyone in the room especially Mrs Martin. If God is always right then why do we have to listen to her about pinafores? If God is good then why has he made me and my family so sad? My head fills up with words I'm not supposed to say, words Mum and Dad shout when they're fighting.

I stop drawing the pharaoh and turn the page. I don't mark out little boxes to do the reporting strip. I draw a big picture of a man with a beard. I draw food stuck in his beard and little red lines in his eyes so he looks tired and angry. I draw messy long hair with some flies above it, and put him in a dirty gown. His mouth is open and I give him yellow teeth. I put little movement lines around his arm that is in an angry fist. He is shaking his fist at the world and sitting on a tiny cloud. It looks like he will fall through the cloud because I've made him fat. I do a really bad thing and draw a cigarette in his mouth. Once at a christening I got a cigarette burn on my arm. My mum was especially angry as it was the vicar's cigarette that did it.

I finish my picture and write GOD above it in block capitals. He looks like a fat goblin gnome. I draw some little warts on his nose.

Mrs Martin comes round to look at our pictures. She will choose the two best sequences and get the people who drew them to stand in front of the class and show us all. She walks around the classroom. I hear her say that Daniel's is a bit messy and he should be careful not to smudge his work with his sleeves. Esther is smiling because Mrs Martin has said something good about hers. Adam looks round and smiles at me. I wave.

When Mrs Martin arrives at my desk she crouches down next to me. Her breath smells of coffee. She picks my book up and holds it in her hands. She looks straight at me and I know I'm in trouble. In the white bit of one of her eyes are two yellow splodges. I've noticed them before. They look like drops of paint and stick out a tiny bit from the white. I try to look away but she keeps her eyes on me till I look down at my desk.

"That's not right," she says. "You haven't done the exercise properly." Her voice is mean, it sounds like she's talking with her mouth shut. I keep looking at my desk. She's still crouching down and leans forward towards me so I can smell her breath again.

A ripping sound makes me jump as she tears the page out of my exercise book. She stands up and gives me back my book.

As she walks towards Sarah on the next desk I see her crush my picture of God in her fist.

Although I'm scared of Mrs Martin, I'm angry too. That was *my* picture of God. She's ruined my book too, there's a jagged edge where she tore the page out.

I look up and see Esther talking about me to the girl next to her.

"Fuck Off!" I mouth to her, and she sticks her hand up in the air fast.

Mrs Martin is on her way back to the front of the room. She turns round and sees Esther's hand then looks over at me. I think about all the trouble God has caused me. I stare at my desk and say, "Fucking bastard!"

It feels strange my tongue making those words.

I look up and see Mrs Martin moving fast towards my desk, her eyes fixed on me like a wolf's. It looks like her head is pulling her body. I stand up and my chair makes a screeching sound.

"GOD IS A BLOODY HEADED BASTARD!" I shout. There are tears in my eyes but I don't let them come out. I stand there staring at the floor squeezing my hands tight into fists.

Mrs Martin's cold hard hand wraps itself tight round my arm.

"I've had enough of you," she says. "You are a bad girl."

She drags me towards the back of the classroom. I dig in with my heels but I'm not heavy and she pulls me along. I knock into some tables on the way. Everyone is looking at me.

"Turn away," she says to them.

At the back of the room are all the art and crafts things and the big sinks where we wash up our painting trays. Mrs Martin pulls me towards one of the sinks. She gets behind me and shoves me so my chest is pushing against the edge of it. I feel wetness start to seep into my pinafore.

She leans away from me for a moment and turns to the class, keeping hold of my arm. "I want you all to turn to *Luke 2: 7.*

Esther, you read aloud and the rest of you follow along in your bibles."

There is a curtain where I think the room used to be a nursery and she pulls it across.

She turns back to me and my chest is pushed into the sink edge again.

"Where did you learn those foul words?" she asks.

"I don't know."

"Well, we're going to have to wash them away."

My hands are pinned in front of me between my thighs and the sink edge. Mrs Martin holds me there by pushing her body against me. I see her hands pick up the green bar of soap we wash our hands with. She washes her hands first then rubs the soap round under the tap till there are bubbles on it. I can see grey lines in the soap under the bubbles.

With her left hand she pinches me hard in the cheeks forcing my mouth open. Her fingers dig in. I try to say something but I can't and all that comes out is a babyish gurgle. The tap is left running and the water hits the bottom of the sink making spray.

"Open wide, Violet," she says, "we have to make you clean."

She pushes the soap into my mouth, and pinches tighter with her hand so my mouth opens wider. She rubs the soap hard over and over on my tongue. At first I feel the grey grooves but then the taste gets so strong spit comes into my mouth. My body tries to be sick but the more I cough the more the soapy bubbles seem to fill my mouth. Tears come each time I retch and spit. I start to choke and Mrs Martin lets go of my face and lets me spit in the sink.

I feel her hip bones pushing against my back and I watch as she cups her hands in front of my face. She fills her hands with water.

"That's it, drink the water Violet, and wash the soap out now."

I don't want to drink from her hands but the hip bones push harder into my back and I know I have to. I put my lips to the water in her hands, suck it into my mouth then spit it into the sink. I feel sick.

She takes hold of my face and shoves the soap in again. It rubs past my teeth as she pushes it in and I feel soap stick to them, then she starts cleaning my tongue again.

She washes my mouth out two more times. Each time she does it I have to suck water from her hands to rinse out my mouth. I am sick twice in the sink.

The bell for morning break rings and she goes and lets the rest of the class leave. She tells me to sit in a little chair. My pinafore is wet through.

When she comes back she has brought me a cup of orange squash.

"There you go Violet, what do you say?"

I take the cup from her, "Thank you Mrs Martin."

The soap taste in my mouth is disgusting and the orange squash helps to take it away.

Mrs Martin kneels down on the floor in front of me. "I know that wasn't nice," she says, "but those words have no place in the mouth of a nice little girl. They are the devil's words and I had to clean them away. Do you understand?"

"Yes," I say.

I think I see one of the yellow spots move a tiny bit, like a jelly, but I'm not sure.

16

Mrs Martin sits with me until the bell goes for the end of break. I look at her to see what I should do.

"Off you go to your desk now, Violet," she says and takes my plastic cup.

She lets the rest of the class back in and says, "Sit down everybody, Mr Sykes will be here in a moment."

Mr Sykes arrives for Maths and we all stand up and say "Good morning Mr Sykes", and Mrs Martin goes out.

Maths is a double lesson. We have different text books depending on how good we are at Maths. Mine is Level 4, it is mustard coloured with soldiers in busbies on the front. Adam is the same level as me. We are not that good, but not the worst. Daniel and Hannah are still on level 2 which is green with swans on the front. Esther is level 5. The new boy, Owen from Canada is on the highest book in the class. He is on Level 9 which some of the much older children in the school still use. It is black with a picture of the Egyptian pyramids on the front.

I don't talk to anyone as I get my books out of the drawer. My mouth still tastes disgusting and I don't want anyone to smell the soap. Some people look at me, but no one is allowed to talk so I just sit and start work. It is multiplication. I get to a bit I am stuck on, but instead of going up to Mr Sykes to have it explained I stay at my desk. People are working quietly and some are queuing up to ask questions. Whenever anyone looks at me I pretend I am reading the question or writing something down. All I can taste is soap, on my tongue, at the back of my nose, and in my throat. I stay at my desk like this until the bell for end of the first lesson goes. Everyone carries on with their work. I hear people in the corridors going to different lessons. I stay on the same page pretending to do my work for the whole of the second part of the lesson until the bell goes for lunch.

I go into lunch faster than the rest of my class and sit on a table with the class 2s. Pudding is treacle sponge with custard. Finally the soap taste starts to go away. The teacher checks my plates are clean, and then I rinse them and stack them for the dinner ladies. The only place I can still taste soap is at the back of my nose.

I stay away from the climbing frame today and play with Sarah, Rebecca, and Amy. They play 'French Elastic' which is quite fun when you have to jump really high. When the bell goes we all walk together to The Belvedere building for Home Economics.

I hate Home Economics. The only good Home Economics lesson was one Mrs Head took. Mrs Head's lessons are fun, but you have to be good because she shouts. She was teaching us about the Celts and brought in a rabbit, which she skinned and made into a Celtic stew. We put in loads of vegetables and old-fashioned herbs and plants, then we each got some stew in a little cup to try. Some people cried about the rabbit and wouldn't eat it. Heather told her parents and they complained to the school. Nothing happened though. Mrs Head is tough. If anyone told her off she wouldn't care anyway.

In Home Economics now we are making tapestries with Mrs Cobb. Only a few people can do it, even Esther's isn't that good.

Mine is just my initials in turquoise blue. The letters are made out of lots of tiny crosses which take ages. I sit next to Adam; his is worse than mine. In three weeks he has only made one stalk of the 'A' because Mrs Cobb keeps making him unpick his bad stitches.

Joanna in my class looks older than everyone else. She's tall and strong and wears her hair in a bun with hair grips like an old lady. She is excellent at Home Economics and is always knitting things and cooking in her free time. I made friends with her this year and she made me a badge with a tiny shrunken packet of Hula Hoops on it. I asked her how she did it and she said, "In the oven." She'd varnished it too so it was hard.

Joanna has done a brilliant tapestry, it's got a whole countryside scene on it. There is a pond with ducks, and a willow tree with a badger behind it. Along the bottom of the tapestry is a row of daffodils with bright green stems. I look at it each time we have this lesson. Joanna is the only person Mrs Cobb likes.

We're allowed to talk quietly in Home Economics, and I go and get my threads and tapestry from the drawer then walk over to Joanna. She is unpicking her tapestry.

"What are you doing?" I ask.

"I have to take out the daffodils," she says.

There is a daffodil shaped space in the front of her tapestry and she is unpicking the head of the second one.

"Why do you have to do that?"

She looks upset. It took her ages to do the daffodils. She didn't just use yellow and green but all different kinds of yellows and greens because she wanted them to be detailed.

"Mrs Cobb says that I have to put a message there so it can be framed and put on the school wall for parents' evening."

"Oh," I say, "what are you going to put?"

She shrugs her shoulders, "I don't know. I wanted to take it home really."

I feel sorry for Joanna. If Mrs Cobb says something you have to do it because her husband is the headmaster.

I go back to my seat. I start to wish we weren't allowed to talk as people keep coming up and asking what Mrs Martin did behind the curtain. I feel horrible, like I've done something bad. I don't tell them anything but feel my face go red.

Adam is showing me how to put pins under my skin. He has them stuck into the skin all around his nail. They stick out like porcupine spines.

"Go on," he says, "it doesn't hurt."

It looks disgusting. You can see the grey of the pins under his skin. He flicks one gently and his skin stretches.

"Ugh!" I say.

He smiles at me. I take a pin and start figuring out where I'm going to stick it in. Someone taps on my back and I turn round, and see Esther.

"Did you get punished?" she says. She looks back at her table where Heather and Poppy are grinning at her and whispering to each other. "Heather says you drew a disgusting picture... Did you draw someone naked?" She starts giggling, and looks back at Heather and Poppy and they burst out laughing.

"No," I say. I want to tell her to go away but feel tears coming into my eyes. I'm angry but embarrassed at the same time.

She looks at Adam and says, "Did she draw you naked?"

I frown and hold the tears back. I don't care what she says, I just don't want anyone to see me cry.

Adam says, "Violet, can you smell something?"

I don't speak but start slowly waving my hand in front of my nose. I know what he's doing. Esther doesn't, she stops laughing though.

He looks at Esther and then covers his nose, "Ugh Esther it's your breath!" he says, "it stinks!"

Esther looks round the room. Two other tables have heard and are giggling at her. She turns to Heather and Poppy. They're laughing at her too.

"You're gross, Adam," she says, but Adam suddenly opens his hands in her face. She sees the pins and screams. She steps backwards and knocks into a chair.

Mrs Cobb drops her knitting and heaves herself out of her chair.

Everyone goes quiet. Adam and I look at each other and put our hands over our mouths to stop laughing. Mrs Cobb is so fat that one day she will sit in a chair and get stuck. One of the boys made a joke once about having to saw her out and she heard and made him run round the playground for an hour with no shoes on.

"Esther?" she says, "What's going on?"

"Nothing Mrs Cobb, I just pricked my finger."

"I said you could all talk quietly but you've abused that right, so SILENCE from now on." She looks slowly round the room, "I suppose it's time I checked how you're all getting on anyway." Her eyes stop at Daniel and Owen's table and she starts to shuffle towards them.

I sit back down keeping my hands over my mouth. I look at Adam, he's doing the same. We both sit there shaking and laughing without making a noise.

The last lesson is silent reading and we have Mrs Cobb again. I am reading *The BFG*. We have to tell her what page number we start on and she writes it up on the board next to our names. Near the end of the lesson she asks us what page we've got up to then she writes that next to the first number. She works out how many pages we've read then scores us. I am the fastest reader in the class so usually get the highest score. It's always different teachers for this lesson. Mrs Head took us once and didn't believe how many pages I'd read. She made me stand at the front of the classroom and tell everyone what had happened in the book. Afterwards she said sorry, and that I was an excellent reader.

It rains all afternoon. At the end of school I walk past the climbing frame. There are puddles in the sand at the bottom and the metal bars look slippery.

As I go up the big gravely hill to the car park I see one of the hunchbacks with his wheelbarrow by the pine trees. I stop walking to watch him. The blue jumper is stretched tight over the hump and he is bent over so his head is almost next to his hands holding the handles. The wheelbarrow is full of chopped wood. I can smell the pine that seeps out of it. He has greasy black hair with a bald spot at the back. It shines because of the rain that's falling on it. Suddenly he stops and turns his face to me. He knows I've been staring at him. I run fast up the hill hoping he's not still looking at me.

I get to the top of the hill and see my mum. She's soaking wet and waving and smiling at me. I am surprised because usually she's one of the last parents to arrive. All the other parents have umbrellas. I run up to her.

"Hi Mum." I say giving her a hug and smearing the raindrops on her coat with my face, "You're really wet!"

"I can't be bothered with umbrellas," she says.

We both look at the other parents and smile to each other. She bends down and whispers to me, "They're for softies."

She looks happy for the first time in ages. Her curly hair is stuck to her face with rain. She takes my school bag from me and says, "Let's stamp in the puddles all the way home!"

I run and jump into the biggest deepest puddle I can see. The water goes up my skirt and all over my legs. My socks are soaked through. I jump again and again spraying myself and my uniform. Two of the other mums are watching and look cross.

Mum catches me up and does a big jump into the puddle with me. We run and splash all the way to the main road where we have to stop and hold hands.

17

It was unlikely they were going to get to a beach before dark. They were on the coast now, but high up, on cliffs. Violet turned off, and followed a lane with a sign that said VIEWPOINT. The wind shook the hedges, and she struggled to focus on the road, and not the twitching leaves and shadows. As she drove on, the hedges thinned out and the landscape became bare except for a few wiry bushes standing on the edges of empty fields. She opened the window and breathed in the sea air.

There was a muddy lay-by on the side of the road, and she parked, and got out. Violet went to the back of the car, and opened Maria's door. She was awake, and gurgling quietly to herself. Violet lifted her out, and locked the car.

"Shall we go and have a look at the view then?"

Maria seemed to search Violet's face, her eyes settling on the new splash of colour on her cheek.

Violet grinned, "Ugly isn't it."

Maria smiled.

They arrived at the edge of the cliff. There was a fence, and beyond that Violet could see the land tilting downwards, and ending. The sea crashed against rocks far below. A thick mist distorted the view, and it was only the far off, white flecks of waves that distinguished sea from sky. Violet closed her eyes and heard seagulls calling beneath them, coming in for the evening. She could sense the static of the huge expanse of the sea, and the drop beyond. She opened her eyes, and stared into the fog. Violet made out something big and white, slipping in and out of vision.

She walked up to the fence, and sat Maria on it, holding her under the arms. Together they listened to the noises of the birds, and waves. She put her lips against Maria's head. Her soft hair smelled nice, not just from the shower gel but something else too.

"I'll find us a beach tomorrow," she said.

Violet thought of the mouldy bathroom and wished she was underwater, bathed and disinfected by salt. She shivered and lifted Maria off the fence. The numbing effects of the coke had worn off and her cheek was hurting.

Holding Maria to her chest, she started walking back. When they got to the car, Violet realised she was too tired to drive on. Maria needed changing, and a bottle. It would have to be another cold one, made with evian, and it would be a night in the car.

Violet changed Maria on the back seat. The temperature was dropping; her little legs felt cold and clammy, and she cried and kicked as Violet put a new nappy and the babysuit back on. Maria still cried a bit as she drank the cold milk, frowning, and taking little bits at a time. They needed a base, with a kettle.

Maria didn't fall asleep. When she stopped drinking, Violet put the radio on. They got Radio 4, Classic and something called Smugglers with a squeaky DJ who chatted about a party he'd gone to, and didn't play any music. Violet changed to Radio 4, and they listened to a lady talking about being eco-friendly, and the different things you can compost. Maria was quiet through the programme. When it finished, Violet could hardly keep her eyes open, but Maria was wide awake.

Violet turned off the radio, "We'd better save the battery," she said, "Don't want to have to get rescued."

Her dad had given her a torch for the glove compartment ages ago, in case she broke down. She felt around, and found it, a little Maglite with a chequered flag design on it. She turned it on, and arranged it sticking through the headrest of the passenger seat. She didn't like the idea of them being lit up, and visible to wandering psychopathic farmers, but she liked the pitch dark even less.

Violet opened a can of Fanta. The hiss made Maria look up at her, and she stared at Violet, and said, "Ba."

Violet took a mouthful, and remembered the pop-up books. "Hey," she said, "I forgot to give you your presents."

The three books were Farm, Jungle, and Nursery Rhymes, "Which one do you want?" she asked, holding them out in a fan.

Maria looked at them all, and then reached towards Farm.

"Good choice," Violet said, "I was hoping for Farm or Jungle." She took a big slurp of Fanta and felt the sugar sting her tongue.

Maria seemed to enjoy Violet's noises more than the book ones, although the cockerel crow was good. Violet read the book about ten times. Each time, Maria reached out for the pictures more, until Violet realised she was hurrying her through the book to get to the page with the cow on. When Violet said, "The cow goes MOOOOOOOOOOOOO!" Maria giggled and kind of shrieked with laughter, like she'd done with the Portuguese waiter.

Eventually Maria's eyes started to close, and she fell asleep. Violet wanted to listen to a CD, but didn't want to risk the battery. Her body was exhausted, but she had the feeling that she'd missed the window of opportunity to fall asleep, and her brain had kick-started itself back into action. She reclined the chair and stared at the roof. The torch flickered. She tried to remember the Trisha episode with Charlotte and Paul. It was weird that they'd been at that party too, but it was a small island.

She pushed down the lock, and the central locking whirred into place. If someone wanted to come in, they could smash the windscreen. Violet imagined a hand slamming against the glass and then a face, and a big fucking hammer. She pulled the torch out, twisted it off, and put it in her jeans pocket. In the back of her head, a faint murmuring started up, like voices discussing her behind a closed door.

Violet finished her Fanta in the dark, and then felt around in the back for the bag with her toothbrush in. It was getting cold in the car, and she didn't want to open the door, so she brushed her teeth, washed her mouth out with evian, and spat it into the empty can. Maria was stirring in her sleep, and Violet realised she was probably feeling the cold too.

She risked the car light, and got Maria into the bear suit, then climbed into the back of the car and put down the seats. Violet opened the suitcase up, and used her clothes to line it, and make a little nest for Maria. She lifted Maria in, and put a hoodie first, and then her leather jacket over her. After insulating the baby, there were only baby clothes, t-shirts, and underwear left for Violet's covers, so she lay down next to the suitcase, and spread them over herself as well as she could.

For what felt like hours, Violet lay with her eyes shut while thoughts spun in her head: Lisa, Jodie, her mum, the police, her dad, how to get off this island, kicking someone in the face, that Trisha Show couple; she might be in the newspaper.

The cold woke Violet up. Her back was stiff and freezing, and her hair seemed wet. Even her teeth felt chilled, and brittle. The only warm part of her was her tummy, where she was curled around the suitcase. Violet could feel lumps where she lay on bits of clothing. Maria was still. Her cheeks were cold, but when Violet pushed her fingers under the bear hood, she felt warmth.

It wasn't light yet, but the blackness had been replaced by a chalky grey. She left Maria sleeping, and decided to jump around outside to warm up. She jogged on the spot, then touched her toes, reached up to the sky, and repeated the routine until she could feel heat trickling back into her fingertips. She bent down to touch her toes again, and stayed there, breathing slowly and letting her back stretch out. As the blood went to her head, she felt a sharp pain in her cheek and remembered the cigarette burn.

She got back in the driver seat. Maria would need another bottle. The constant search for boiling water was making them conspicuous. Petrol stations were a bad idea because of all the cameras. Maybe she could get hold of a camping stove, sort out somewhere to hide for a while.

Violet's stomach rumbled. She thought of the Shreddies advert with the hunger monster locked up behind cereal prison bars.

"Bum ba de bm bm!" she said, beating her hands on the dashboard, "...Hunger STRIKES".

Violet imagined her Hunger was more desperate than the cheeky Shreddies one. Hers would be an emaciated, hairless thing, almost translucent from lack of light, poisoned and jaundiced by alcohol and amphetamines. She closed her eyes and leaned her head back against the seat, then remembered the fillet steak.

Violet had seen Juanito throw steaks in the frying pan for only a couple of seconds on each side, so it was still cold in the middle when he ate it. He said one of the worst crimes of the English was the overcooking of meat.

She rummaged in the glove box and pulled out a Leatherman. Engraved on it in neat, slightly wobbly letters was *Violet Kale*. She ran her finger over the letters, remembering how enthusiastic her dad had been with his Dremel engraver, engraving everything she and Jodie ever took away with them.

She got the pack of steak out of the shopping bags, and opened the Leatherman. The blade was about four inches long, and partly serrated.

Violet cut open the packet, sliced off a thin piece of steak, and put it in her mouth. It was cold from being in the car all night, as though it had been in a fridge. When Violet bit into it, cold blood pooled into her mouth and she tasted iron. It would have been a lot nicer warmed up. She chewed it quickly and swallowed. The French ate steak 'blue', which probably meant it was served cold.

She cut off another chunk, and held it up saluting the vaguely rising sun. "Bon Appetit et Merci mon pere!" she said, and put it in her mouth.

After the steak breakfast, Violet felt queasy, and cold. She walked around outside the car, drinking a Fanta. The sky was lighter now, and she could see the ocean. The road sloped upwards and she walked towards its little summit.

Standing on top of the hump, she could see down to the viewpoint they'd walked to the night before. The white shapes she'd noticed were three huge rocks. They stuck out like giant molars, pulled out and laid down upended by some enormous dentist. Next to the last rock there was a red and white striped lighthouse. The line of toothy rocks had been almost invisible the night before, she could see why they'd put a lighthouse there. She hadn't noticed a light though; maybe it was broken, or only flashed occasionally. She heard Maria start crying from the car, and headed back.

Violet smoked as she drove. Maria's cries resounded round the car, and the rushing air from the window was almost a relief from the harsh noise. They passed a closed petrol station, and arrived at a village. Violet slowed down as they drove through, but the village was tiny, with only a post office, and a fish & chip shop with a Pukka Pies sign spinning slowly outside. Nothing was open yet. Violet pulled into a side road to turn round, and go back to the 24 hour TESCO. As she was reversing, she smelled a strong smell of baking bread. She stopped, and opened the window wider, sniffing to see where the smell was coming from.

Violet got out and locked the car. She crossed the road, and followed the smell to a thatched cottage with an open stable door. Inside, someone was singing. Violet knocked on the door, and the singing stopped, and a dog started to bark.

There was honeysuckle around the doorframe, and a doormat with paw print designs on it, and big letters saying, WIPE YOUR PAWS. A woman wearing a frilly apron appeared.

"Hello," she said, "Can I help you?"

"Hi," Violet said, "I wondered if I could use your kettle? My baby's hungry and all the shops and things are closed… I'm on my way to the ferry."

A yapping started behind the door, and the woman stooped down and came back up with a Yorkshire Terrier in her arms. The dog had its fur tied in a top knot with a blue hair bobble. It cocked its head to one side to stare at Violet; the woman did the same.

"Sorry," Violet said, "I know it's early. I smelled the bread and thought…"

The woman stroked the dog, "I'm an early riser too, always up with the birds."

Violet smiled.

"Go and get your little one. I'll put some water on."

Violet returned with Maria, and the backpack with the nappies. She knocked on the door again, and the woman reappeared with the dog, which started barking at Maria.

"Oh, don't mind him," the woman said, "he's just jealous. Doesn't like babies, 'cause he likes to be the baby in the house, don't you, Hector?"

The woman nuzzled the dog, who tilted his head back for his chin to be rubbed, keeping one eye on Violet.

"She'll stop crying soon," Violet said, "she's hungry."

The woman took Maria's bottle from Violet's hand. "I'll get that, give it a wash for you," she said, and started filling the sink. "There's nothing like the smell of baking bread...they say if you want to sell a house, you should put some bread in the oven, and it makes people feel instantly at home."

"Can we use your toilet?" Violet asked.

"End of the corridor, on your right."

Violet locked the door and laid Maria down on the carpet to change her. She heard the woman start singing again, something about a milkmaid. Maria was crying and struggling. Violet had forgotten new baby clothes. Maria kicked at Violet, as she tried to do up the nappy. Afterwards, she put Maria back in the bear suit, and laid her on the carpet while she went to the toilet. She flushed and saw Maria start at the sudden noise, and then carry on screaming.

There were small paintings of Yorkshire terriers in different poses on the wall, and a little shelf with a basket of potpourri, and a book called *Things to Read in the Loo*. Above the toilet there was a framed tapestry of Adam and Eve, with the tree and the snake, it would have been better drawn or painted rather than stitched. The stitching made it look like 80s computer game graphics.

Violet noticed her hands were bloodstained from the steak, and washed them under the hot tap. There was a cupboard over the sink, but no mirror.

"Shh," she said to Maria, "That lady's sorting your breakfast out, just wait."

Maria cried even louder so Violet picked her up and held her against her shoulder. There was some talcum powder in the cupboard and Violet put it in the backpack, as it was supposed to be good for babies' bottoms. Inside the cupboard door, there was a round mirror that you could pull out on a metal arm. Violet looked in it. Her face looked awful. The burn on her cheek was blistered and shiny with pus, and there was dried blood staining the lines of her lips. She smiled expecting to see dripping blood and raw meat hanging from her teeth, but they were alright. She cupped water in her hand, and cleaned off her face. There was a bottle of TCP in the cupboard, and she stuck it in her pocket to sort the blister out later.

A growling and scratching started outside the toilet door. Violet lifted Maria up high and pushed it open. The dog went wild, snapping at her ankles, and crouching down, baring its teeth at her. Violet was glad she was wearing the 16 hole boots. As she stepped forward, he grabbed hold of the laces. She didn't want to kick him, so she carried on walking to the kitchen dragging the dog with her.

"Hector! No!" the lady shouted.

The dog ignored her so she bent down and started pulling him off Violet's foot. Eventually she got him off and held him restrained under her arm, still snapping and snarling at Violet, trying to get to Maria.

The woman pushed hair out of her face, "We're not used to visitors, he's a rascal with the postman. Still, all dogs are entitled to a good snap at the postman aren't they?" She smiled, out of breath.

"Yeah," Violet said, "I'll do her bottle now if that's okay."

"I'll put him in the lounge," she said to Violet, then, "Hector, you're being very rude!"

She took the dog away, and Violet heard the barks quieten as a door was closed. Maria was crying with her mouth open, and Violet noticed a white ridge on her top gum.

"I think you're getting teeth," she said.

Violet held the bottle under the cold tap, and the lady came back, brushing dog hair off her apron.

"Sorry about that," she said, "he's very protective. Since we lost James, my husband, Hector's the man of the house."

It was a stupid way of describing death, Violet thought, 'losing someone', like they just got dropped out of a pocket, or left on a train, OOPS!

"You could be anyone really as far as he's concerned, a thief, or mugger, you hear such dreadful things in the news."

Violet's stomach turned. She might actually be on the news now. They'd been gone two nights, and Lisa must have realised they weren't coming back. She looked round the kitchen for a phone, ready to knock it out of the woman's hands if she went for it. She smiled, "Thanks for letting us in," said Violet, "We're not muggers, I promise."

"I had to," said the lady, "It's my Christian duty."

Violet tested the milk by drinking some herself; it seemed alright. She rearranged Maria in her arms, and gave her the bottle. Maria started drinking immediately, and closed her eyes. Tears shone on her eyelashes.

"I'm a Christian too," said Violet, "My name's Esther, by the way."

"I'm Anne," the lady said. She chuckled and shook her head. "God's got it all planned out! It seems that because my bread brought you here, you ought to stay for breakfast."

"Thanks," said Violet, "but I've already eaten, could I have a coffee though?"

"We don't have tea or coffee in the house. Stimulants," Anne said, "What about a glass of milk? It's local, the farmer delivers it."

Violet smiled, "Yeah... milk's great."

Somewhere in the back of her head she heard a snigger, and she shook her head. She wished she was getting coffee. Maria was heavy, and Violet sat down on a stool at the breakfast bar.

Anne turned round from the fridge, "You never told me your baby's name," she said.

"Jude," Violet replied.

"How old?"

"Six months."

Anne got two glasses out of a cupboard, "Bet you and your husband are over the moon with her aren't you?"

"Yeah we are," Violet said, "Geoffrey and I love her to bits." *Geoffrey?*

"You look so young to be married!"

"Well," Violet said, "we've been together since school, saving up, and you know... waiting to get married. We met at church." Violet stopped, wondering if she'd pushed it too far.

"Young love!" Anne said, bringing over two glasses of milk. "Hardly anyone waits to be married anymore before having a family. Some don't bother at all."

Violet smiled, and stroked Maria's hair. "We wanted to do everything properly."

There was a photo in a silver frame on the kitchen worktop. It showed Anne and a man both smiling, standing on the deck of a boat. Anne was wearing a scarf that was flying out to one side, and the man was holding a sailor's cap on his head. Both were squinting against the sunlight, and crouching, as if they'd put the camera on self-timer, and weren't sure it would work.

"That's James and I on our boat, how long ago now? I wasn't grey then, so maybe eight years ago."

"It's a cool boat," Violet said.

"'Revelations', she's only little. James wanted to call her Anne, but I said no."

"Do you go out on it much?"

"Hector and I go and keep her clean, sometimes just sit there in the marina, but she's too much work for just me."

"I guess lots of people have boats here," Violet said.

"Us Isle of Wighters love the sea. If you get the chance, you should go and watch the sailing boats down at Bembridge, there's some beautiful ones."

"Is that where Revelations is?"

"For the moment, but it's expensive."

Maria had stopped drinking, and Violet sat her up on her lap.

Anne cut a slice of bread and spread it thickly with butter and jam, "Is Geoffrey not holidaying with you?" she asked.

"No, he's working... He can't take the time off, because we're saving up for a house," Violet said.

"Property's so expensive these days too."

Violet nodded and took a tiny sip of milk.

"Oh," Anne said, "I've just had a brainwave!" There was a

dusting of flour on the fine hairs on her top lip. "I've got some things in the garage, for the church bazaar. If you'd like, you can have a look through before you go."

Violet looked at her wrist and realised she'd lost her watch. "That's really kind," she said, "we could always get the later ferry.... see Daddy after work?"

The garage was mainly full of things they didn't need like crockery and china ornaments. There were some bags of clothes, but Violet could see from the things poking out that they were mostly donated by elderly ladies. Although, a couple of bags were piled on top of a modern looking babies pram.

"Wow!" Violet said, "That pram looks brand new."

"Oh that! Silly really," Anne said, "I bought it for Hector. He started getting so lazy on our walks. Anyway, he hated it. Wouldn't go in it at all. I ended up having to carry him, as well as push that thing."

"That's funny," Violet said.

"I took him to the vet, and she said he was obese, so I cut down his treats, and now he's fine. We were ever so naughty, used to have snacks mid-morning and afternoon together." She passed Violet the clothes bags from the top of the pram. "I've slimmed down too, since we stopped snacking. Strange he got so fat cause we always did the snack times, although James used to take him for an evening walk too, and I'm not one for the dark."

"Me neither," said Violet.

"Anyway, the pram's been in here ever since. What with all the donations I get, I overlook it when I take stuff down for the bazaar. Would you like it?"

"No, you can't give us that! I bet it cost a fortune... though the one Geoffrey's mum gave us is really awkward."

"I think you're meant to have it," Anne said. "Look, I'll show you how it folds down. They demonstrated it over and over for me in the shop, so I wouldn't forget."

* * *

Anne stood in the kitchen doorway, Violet almost felt reluctant to leave. Maria was kicking her legs about in the new pram.

"Thanks for all this," said Violet, "You've been really kind."

Over Anne's shoulder, Violet could see a key rack. One set of keys had a large, buoyant looking cork ball attached to them.

"I don't suppose I could ask for one more favour?" she said, "Could I take a piece of your bread for lunch? It smelled delicious."

"I'll just get it for you."

As Anne headed for the kitchen, Violet grabbed the keys with the cork ball, and stuffed it up her sleeve.

Anne came back, and passed her some bread wrapped in kitchen towel.

"Well, thanks again," Violet said, smiling.

"It's nice to meet decent people," Anne said. "It seems there are less and less of us."

"Yeah, I know."

When the front door opened, Hector started barking.

"Bye then," Violet said.

She walked away from the house, pushing the pram. When she turned to look back, Anne was still standing in the door waving. Violet waved back. Through a window, she could see Hector barking manically, his spit marking the glass.

At the car, Violet put Maria back in the car seat and buckled her in, then collapsed the pram and put it in the boot. She did up her own seatbelt then took Anne's keys out of her sleeve, and shut them in the glove compartment.

In the back, Maria was looking out of the window.

"Bet you're pleased with your pram," Violet said, "we can go for some fast trips with that."

Maria looked at her, then put her fist in her mouth.

"Yeah I know. I feel bad too," Violet said, "Still, maybe she's right, and everything's planned out. She never uses it anyway."

18

I am allowed to stay up late when nature programmes are on. Tonight it is just me in the lounge as Dad is working in the garage and Mum is in bed. I watch a programme about vets and then it is a David Attenborough one who I like because he is brave enough to crawl into a termite nest. Tonight the programme is about the hazel dormouse who doesn't just hibernate in winter but sometimes just because there is not much food around. The programme says that the dormouse and the bat are the only animals in England who hibernate properly. The dormouse can live for months without moving at all. In the spring it comes out and starts running about in the trees and bushes eating acorns and berries. The branches are a bit like a high street with shops because it runs around on them like we walk on paths and chooses different foods as it goes along. If I was a dormouse I'd spend more time awake, walking about in the trees. In one part of the programme a dormouse is eaten in one bite by an owl. It is really sad but I know that it is nature.

At the end of the programme nobody comes to tell me to go to bed so I decide to stay up. I watch a programme where a woman has a husband and a boyfriend. The husband comes home from work early and the boyfriend has to hide and then climb out of the window. He is only wearing some pants and looks funny. I watch the whole thing. There is a bit of swearing and in one bit a man in a pub throws a drink all over a woman's fur coat. I think she deserves it as it's cruel to wear fur. The news is on after and it's boring and

I start to feel tired.

I wake up and on the television is just a picture of a girl, a blackboard and a clown; there is also a tiny screaming sound. I turn it off and the noise stops. The house is completely dark and quiet. I go upstairs to bed.

When I wake up I hear birds singing outside. Mum calls it 'The Dawn Chorus' but it is later than dawn and light outside. There are two blackbirds on the grass, one is pulling up a worm and the other is just hopping about. The one pulling up the worm is brown so I know it is the female. I go and brush my teeth then peek into Mum and Dad's room. Dad isn't there but Mum is still sleeping.

"I'm going to have breakfast," I say. She doesn't say anything, and I climb onto the bed. She is on her side and I lean over to ask her, "Do you want some?"

She doesn't open her eyes but says, "No thank you, Violet."

I get off the bed, and then she turns over fast and opens her eyes, "Not too many Coco Pops okay."

"I won't."

My mum is a bit like a dormouse at the moment, but it's springtime, and we always have food in the house. I open a bottle of milk and pour it over my Coco Pops. I eat my cereal and decide that today I am going to do a miracle.

When Benjamin from down the road comes round we usually play by the muddy swamp. The muddy swamp is at the very end of the garden behind the trees. When you are in there it is like being in a dark tunnel made of trees. The water is the colour of fire mixed with rust. If you look carefully you can see patches of rainbow coloured swirls like on petrol station floors. The muddy swamp stinks. Mum and Dad talked about filling it in. Mum says it looks 'nuclear'. In the end they decided to leave it because of drainage.

Benjamin is frightened.

"Go on," I say. "Jesus was just a normal person and he walked on water."

"What if it doesn't work?"

"Of course it works, you just have to believe…. I did it this morning."

Laura Wake

"Can't you show me first?"

Benjamin's nose is always runny and he never wipes it. In one nostril is a bubble of snot.

"I can't show you. A miracle is something you have to make yourself do without any help. Once you've done it once though we'll both be able to do it together."

"Really?"

"Yes. It'll be brilliant. We'll be able to run all the way down the muddy swamp to the sea."

"Okay."

As he climbs down closer to the edge he slips a little bit because his Wellington boots don't grip well.

"Go on!" I say, "You can do it."

He steps out onto the water and it works. I am sure he stands on top of the water, but then he goes through. I watch as he disappears completely. All that is left of him is a bubbling movement on top of the sludge.

I have to help him. I grab a stick and lie down on my tummy and poke at where he is. His head comes back up through the water. He looks like he is made of clay or chocolate; the orangey water has closed his eyes and nose. A hole opens where his mouth must be and he screams.

"I'll get help." I shout but don't know if he can hear me and he goes under again and all I can see is his orange brown arms waving. I run up the garden as fast as I can. I have never had to call for help before.

"HELP!" I shout, "HELP!"

It is the weekend but I can't see my Dad anywhere. I run into the house shouting as loud as I can. Mum comes down the stairs.

"What's wrong?"

"Benjamin's fallen in the ditch and can't get out."

She runs out of the house and into the garden. I can't keep up but run after her. She stops at the line of trees. She isn't wearing any shoes.

"Where? WHERE?"

I point to the place we enter the muddy swamp and she pushes

110

through the trees. I don't need to show her where Benjamin has fallen in because one of his hands is sticking up through the water. My mum doesn't lie down like I did but jumps straight in. It can't be as deep as I thought because she can touch the bottom. She pulls him out of the water. He looks like a little orange doll, he looks like Morph on Hartbeat.

Mum keeps patting Benjamin on the back then she lays him down on the bank and opens his mouth. She pulls mud out with her fingers then she puts her fingers into his nose and takes the mud out of there too. I think I see his legs start to move.

"Go to the telephone Violet and dial 999, then ask for an ambulance."

I don't move. I am scared to ring 999.

"Now Violet!" she shouts.

I run back to the house. I don't want to call 999, I almost start to cry.

The telephone is on the wall in the kitchen. I pick up the receiver and dial. I have always wanted to do this but now I don't. I know I will be in trouble.

A lady's voice on the other end says, "Emergency Services. Which service do you require?"

"An ambulance."

"Is there an adult we can talk to?"

"No. My mum is looking after my friend. He fell in a ditch and I think he's drowned."

"Okay Sweetheart," the lady says, "do you know your address?"

"Yes," I answer, and tell it.

The lady says, "Tell your mum an ambulance is on the way."

* * *

Mum has got our neighbours the Pearsons to come round. They are all in the drive with Benjamin and the ambulance. Mrs Pearson is German and has shouted at me before for trespassing in their garden. I told Mum and she said that Mrs Pearson is very protective of her plants and I should stay on our side of the garden. Mr Pearson's name is Peter.

The ambulance men put Benjamin on a little stretcher and lift him into the back. Everybody who has touched him has the orange mud from the muddy swamp on them. The ambulance men talk to my Mum and say that they're doing something to his throat so he can breathe easier. The word sounds like tractor and honey. I ask to go in the ambulance but Mum says, "No."

She says, "Mrs Pearson is going to stay with you until Dad comes home. I have to stay with Benjamin until his Mum gets to the hospital."

"Please can I come?"

"No, Violet."

The ambulance men hurry her into the ambulance and the doors are shut behind her.

Mrs Pearson puts a hand on my head and says, "Come on, Violet, let's go and read one of your books."

It's not fair. I don't want to stay with German Mrs Pearson. Benjamin is my friend and I want to look after him too. It's not fair that my mum is looking after him either, she should be with me. I hope his mum gets to the hospital quickly and she can come home.

Mrs Pearson and I take turns to read from *Nasty Tales for Nine Year Olds*. Even though I am only eight I have the whole set up to age 13. I choose a story about a boy who tries to steal an ogre's dinner. Mrs Pearson is brilliant at reading it especially the scary bits. She does a terrible booming voice for the ogre and yells, "VERRE IS MY DINNER BOY?" so loud that it scares me and then we both start laughing.

Dad comes home and tells me to wait in the kitchen while he talks to Mrs Pearson. They go outside to the drive. When he comes back he doesn't play with me or take me for a bike ride. He makes me sit down at the kitchen table and asks me lots of questions about Benjamin and the ditch. I don't want to tell him about the miracle.

"But why did he do it, Violet?"

"I don't know."

"He wouldn't have just jumped in."

"He didn't."

"Well what happened then? Did you tell him to jump in?"

"He didn't jump, Dad."

"Tell me the truth Violet." He looks me in the eye. He is holding one of my hands which I usually like but today it feels horrible and I wish he would let it go.

"I thought he would be able to walk on the water, Dad."

He takes his hand away and lifts both his arms up in the air and then puts them back on the table.

"So you told him to do it."

"Yes."

My dad leaps up from the chair and makes me jump, but then doesn't do anything. He turns and walks around in a little circle then goes to the sink and looks out of the window. We stay like this for a while. I wonder what the blackbirds are doing and if they have lunch like we do halfway through the day. I don't know if I am allowed to leave the table.

"Dad?"

He pours himself a glass of water and makes me a Ribena then comes and sits back at the table. He has forgotten to use my special cup but I don't say anything about it.

"Violet you did a very stupid and dangerous thing today."

I don't say anything, but it wasn't a stupid thing I did.

"You are a clever girl, and I don't understand why you would do something like that. You know how water can be dangerous and you know that people can't walk on water."

"Jesus can," I say.

My Dad screws his face up and says, "Jesus isn't a person, Violet... he's an angel. And anyway that doesn't matter. Benjamin is younger than you and you should be looking after him. He could have drowned today if your Mum hadn't got him out."

"He's okay now though isn't he?"

"No he's not. He's very ill and has to stay in hospital. You *know* how serious that is."

"Yes."

"Don't ever do something dangerous like that again." And then he says loudly, "Are you listening?"

"Yes."

"Promise me Violet."

I say, "I promise."

19

Essential Reggae filled the car as they drove. 'Girl I want to make you sweat' came on.

"I hate this song," Violet said, and skipped forward to 'Don't Rock the Boat'.

She looked into the back. Maria was watching bushes blur outside, as they sped past. The sun was breaking through the grey sky in thick stripes. Violet pulled the kitchen towel off the bread, and drove one-handed, gnawing.

"Please, don't you rock my bo-oat...Cause I don't want my boat to be rocking anyhow...."

Violet felt herself relax with the music. It was turning into a bright day. She opened the window, and cold air rushed in. She turned back to Maria, "Not quite Jamaica," she said, and shut the window again.

They entered a village called Shorwell. Where had Anne said the boat was? Berridge? Bembridge? In the foot well Violet could see the fluorescent pink pencil.

She pulled over as 'Mr Loverman' started, and picked up the pencil. Shorwell wasn't on there, but Cowes, Ryde, Newport, Shanklin and Sandown were. There were also some tiny illustrations. The three rocks were marked, and underneath, it said Needles. They didn't look like needles, but they had to be the tooth rocks. Violet could see the route she'd taken from the ferry, a kind of backwards

L across the island. There were some little sailing boats marked on the map. One seemed near to Cowes, but Violet thought Anne would have said Cowes if the marina was there. The other sailing boat was on the East side of the island, near Ryde. Violet decided to head there. There would be signposts, and she had a full tank.

"Shabba," she sang, and turned up the volume.

After about an hour of driving towards Ryde, she realised she had arrived in it. She hadn't noticed any signs for Bembridge the whole way. Two women were walking with shopping bags, so she pulled over to ask for directions.

Violet wound down the window and called, "Excuse me!"

Both ladies looked up,

"Do you know how I get to Bembridge?"

One of the ladies was quite old. When she saw Violet close up, she recoiled and muttered something, then put her head down and tugged on the other lady's arm, "Come on, Jennifer!" she said, and then glared at the pavement, "We're very busy!"

The younger lady half smiled, "Uh, yes," she said.

The old lady muttered and pulled away, then carried on walking up the street.

"You've overshot the turn," the younger one said, glancing up the pavement to see how far her companion had got. "Turn round and keep going through two, maybe three sets of lights and you'll be back on a country road."

Violet pointed up the road, "Back up there?"

The woman was starting to look nervous as her friend was getting farther away. Violet saw her notice Maria in the back.

"Yes," the lady said, "Go back on the country road for a couple of miles and you'll get a sign for St Helens. Once you're in St Helens, there'll be signs for Bembridge."

"Thanks," Violet said.

"Oh... okay. Head for St Helens."

Violet watched as she started to run up the street after her friend or mother. Fuck. That old woman knew. They must be in the papers now. No, she was probably just losing it a bit, Alzheimer's or something. She had looked terrified of her, as if she was some kind of goat-eyed devil. Violet glanced in the mirror to check her face, then changed the CD to Al Green. Next time she went to a supermarket she would check the newspapers. And maybe later, she'd cut her hair off.

The lady was right; once they reached St Helens, Bembridge signs appeared. The woods gave way to a horizon, and it felt like they were nearing the coast again.

Maria started crying in the back.

"Yeah, we'll get dinner soon," Violet said.

Bembridge wasn't as big as it sounded, and there were only two pubs that she could see: The King's Head, and The World's End. She parked at the side of the road and got Maria's new pram out.

As Violet started to push the pram, Maria's crying slowed down. Violet started to run. The pram bumped along, and Maria stopped crying and smiled.

Violet ran up and down the street three times until Maria was chuckling. She hadn't run for a while, and her legs felt heavy, her boots scuffing the ground with each stride. Her chest was tight, and she coughed something that tasted bad into her mouth, and spat it on the grass.

Violet stopped and wiped her mouth on her sleeve, there were tears in her eyes from the cold air and she was sweating and out of breath.

She looked at the two pubs again, choosing The World's End because of its decking and picnic benches where you could sit and watch the sea. As soon as she stopped moving, Maria started to cry.

"Calm down," Violet said, "we're getting your lunch now."

She opened the door to a rush of warm, smoky, beer-smelling air. A noisy chatter filled the bar, more like a Friday after-work crowd, than an early morning. She noticed that most people wore brightly coloured sailing coats with high collars, and brands that Violet hadn't seen before: Gull, Musto and Henri Lloyd. Henri Lloyd seemed to be the favourite.

Violet pushed Maria's pram through the crowd to get to the bar. Two men in rubber dungarees smiled and made a space for her to get through. On the back wall of the bar was a brass ships clock that said 10 o' clock.

The barman was tall with sandy coloured hair. He was suntanned with a white sunglasses mark, and wore a pink Henri Lloyd polo shirt.

"What can I getcha?" he said in a strong Australian accent.

"You serving alcohol yet?"

"Sure are!"

"Half a lager and a jug of boiling water, for her." She motioned to Maria, who was crying forcefully with clenched fists.

"Someone's hungry," he said.

He pulled Violet's half and passed it over, "One twenty," he said. Violet passed him a five pound note.

"Where you sitting? Someone'll bring the water over."

"Outside. You always this busy?"

"Regatta day," he replied, and handed her the change.

"Thanks."

"No worries," he said, and Violet smiled as she turned from the bar.

Nobody else was sitting outside, and Violet chose the picnic bench closest to the sea.

"Water for you," a voice called out behind her.

She turned and saw a lady in a chef's jacket walking towards her with a jug.

Violet took it from her, "Thank you," she said.

She gave Maria her bottle, and looked out to sea. There weren't many boats out yet, but there were two jetties which had smart looking yachts attached to them, covered in sponsor stickers. A few people were on board, making final tweaks before the race.

A far off, square ferry moved slowly across the horizon. Maybe it was the Red Falcon. Two men were driving around in a grey motor boat, putting down buoys with flags on. The engine buzzed quieter as they drove farther away, and the boat jumped and bounced over waves, skipping like a toy pulled too fast by string.

Maria fell asleep and Violet took the bottle out of her mouth and put it on the table. She took a mouthful of lager. The glass was uncomfortably cold, and she pulled her cuffs down with her teeth to cover her fingers for the next sip.

The whinny of a knackered fan belt made her turn around, and she saw a grey car pulling into the pub car park. Two figures sat in the front; the one in the passenger seat was rounder, and shorter than the driver. That couple again! She pulled her hood up and faced the sea.

She'd watched so much Trisha it was hard to pin down the episodes. The morning of the age-gap episode, she remembered being alone, probably in the loft room. Lisa must've still been in bed, Claude at work.

Violet would've woken to the smell of urine soaked sawdust and the watching eyes of Rabbit and Guinea Pig who never had enough water. Violet would fill it up, and get sticky food out of the sack in the corner until it ran out and she gave them toast that one time. They would still be up there. With only Lisa left they didn't stand much chance of survival, though sometimes she remembered and cuddled them, apologising and cleaning their hutch. Once she and Violet had picked dandelion leaves from behind the house, and sprinkled them round the lounge for them, like a treasure hunt.

Violet remembered the money Claude used to leave on the table, before he started getting pissed-off with them always being drunk or high before him. Then Lisa started asking Violet to buy alcohol, and Violet didn't want to, because Lisa was so pregnant. But then she did, because Lisa would've just done it anyway. She didn't like thinking of the baby inside getting hit after hit of vodka through its cord.

Violet didn't find the Trisha Show as funny on her own. She and Lisa would always laugh at the sad and scummy people. Violet watched the forty year old lorry driver and his fifteen year old girlfriend take their seats, smiled a bit when Trisha paled and asked "Did you know that was illegal?"

"She's sixteen now," he said, and Charlotte, yes it was definitely Charlotte, slumped, leaning into him like she'd been dropped from a height, and just landed there in front of that audience.

"We love each other, don't we babe." A squeeze of Charlotte's shoulder, and Violet remembered clearly Charlotte saying through her thick fringe, chin stuck to chest, "Yeah I love him to bits," because Violet hated that expression, like loving someone so much you squeezed and squeezed till their head popped off and went flying round the room like a deflating balloon, or their limbs detached, toes and fingers bouncing across the floor like party sausages.

Violet remembered going to buy vodka, but some cold feeling had got inside her from the Trisha Show, and stayed.

A burst of singing and laughter rang out from the car park, and Violet saw the teams of sailors spilling out of the pub. As they passed the steps to the right of the decking a guy with spiky hair looked at her, and called out, "You want Pink Fins to win! Number 22!"

Violet raised her glass, "Good luck," she said.

The guy was jostled by a stocky sailor with a dark ponytail, and stubble, "No, you want Number 16, Butterfly!" he called.

The people from team Butterfly all cheered, and someone cuffed the Pink Fins guy on the head.

She looked back at the pub. The car park was still busy with yachtsmen. The grey car was still there, but she couldn't see Charlotte and Paul. Violet shivered and gently lifted Maria into the pram, tucking her in with a hoodie.

20

Me and Mum are in the kitchen watching *Hartbeat*. It is the gallery part, and there are lots of different pictures. There is a really good one of a butterfly, and it says on the telly, EMILY AGE 8 ½.

"Mum, that girl's picture's as good as some of Tony Hart's."

"Yeah, it is good," Mum says, "Her parents probably helped her."

"That's cheating," I say.

"Yes, it is," says Mum. She sits down next to me and passes me a Ribena. "Violet," she says.

I want to carry on watching the telly, but she says it again, "Violet, listen for a minute."

I turn round. I can still hear the telly, and I'll know if a really good picture comes up.

"I'm pregnant again, Violet. You're going to have another brother or sister."

I hear Tony say, "That's a lot of marker work," and then the lady, Margot says, "That's a good bit of cartoon drawing."

Mum's hand is on her tummy, and I think about the baby growing in there.

"When will it be born?"

"Not for a while, about seven months time."

"How big is it now?" I ask.

She laughs, "I'm not sure, I think about the size of a grape."

I think about being as small as a grape. It must be horrible being inside someone's tummy with all the rumbling noises, and bits of eaten up food all over the place. I put my ear against Mum's tummy, but can't hear anything yet.

Tony Hart says, "See you next time," and the music starts. It makes me feel a bit sad, and I go and change the channel to ITV.

21

Violet got her leather jacket out of the car, and put another hoodie in with Maria. She jogged along the road that followed the waterfront, pushing the pram. Her boots thudded on the concrete and sent small shocks through the balls of her feet. Maria smiled at the bumpy ride.

They arrived at the gates to the marina and Violet saw a sentry box. She stopped. It was difficult to tell if there was anyone inside because the sun was reflecting off the windows. She walked past and glanced in. There was no one there. On the desk was a Kit Kat wrapper, a big diary, and a mug. She considered taking the diary to find out where Revelations was moored, but decided against it; they might spend some time here and it was better not to arouse suspicion.

A road ran through the middle of the marina, and there were lots of parked cars, but no people that she could see. A building in the middle had a sign saying 'Bembridge Marina Clubhouse'. She pushed past and carried on towards the end of the road and some big sheds. Beyond the sheds, there were three long jetties with boats moored. She would start at the farthest one and work her way back.

Revelations was the third boat along on the second jetty. It was a motorboat, with smart blue and white rubber ball things tied onto its silver rails. The boat seemed to shimmer in the sunlight. A thick rope linked the boat to the jetty where it was tied to a metal knob. Violet reached down and took hold of it. She pulled it, and Revelations moved gently towards them.

Maria gurgled in the pram.

"Hey," Violet said, standing up, "It's bigger than I thought... I bet there's bedrooms in there and everything."

Maria lifted her arms above her head, said, "Ba!" then threw them down on the hoodie again.

"Fuck," Violet said, "The keys are still in the glove box."

She looked around the marina. A car was driving out, pulling a trailer behind it. "We'll come back when it's dark," she said, "it's safer anyway."

Instead of going back the way they came, Violet headed towards the big sheds. One of them was open and inside there were stacks of small sailing boats without their sails, and a yacht, suspended, and shiny with new paint or some other stuff that made boats waterproof.

A door opened at the far end of the shed and Violet heard voices, laughing, and the sound of a radio. She walked away, and headed to the edge of the marina.

The ground was grassy with thin, muddy trailer tracks through it. Violet walked on the grass between the tracks.

"It's a high-performance racing pram," she said, "can't have mud getting in your wheels, and slowing us down."

All around them were small boats on trailers with covers stretched over them. If they needed to hide, they could get inside one and lie there for a couple of hours.

A fence surrounded the marina, and Violet walked along it, looking for a place to get through. Eventually they came to a metal gate, locked with a padlock and chain. Beyond the gate was a field of long grass.

Violet lifted Maria out of the pram. She held her against her shoulder and climbed the fence one-handed. The gate swayed as she went over the top. At the other side she laid Maria down on the grass.

"Hang on a minute," she said, and went back over for the pram.

She tried climbing with it, but it was awkward and heavy, and kept messing up her balance. Maria made a little noise from the other side.

"I'm coming," Violet called.

She climbed back down and tried collapsing it, pushing the red button which made half the pram fold down. It almost bent over perfectly, but the rear wheel end of the pram wouldn't bend.

"Fucking hell!"

Violet hoped there weren't bulls in the field, or a farm dog. There was another red button, but that only seemed to detach the bottom basket. She kicked the pram, but it just shook and stayed rigid.

She climbed up again, and sat on top of the fence, hooking her feet into the bars, and pulled the pram up.

Maria was wriggling in the grass, trying to turn herself over. Violet started to sing quietly, *Lions and tigers and bears OH MY! Lions and tigers and bears!*

She leaned backwards and swung the pram over her so it was dangling down the other side. She lowered it as much as she could, then let it drop down onto the grass. She stood up, held the fence for a moment, and jumped off, landing in a crouching position like a superhero. Her boots had made two perfect, flattened prints in the grass.

To her right she noticed a line of sheep watching her, chewing. She smiled, *Lions and tigers and bears...Oh MY.*

"You enjoy that?" she asked, but the front sheep turned away and hurried off, the others following behind. One of them let out a baa, and Maria made a noise in response. Violet saw that she was reaching out towards the sheep.

"Yeah," Violet said, "The sheep goes baaa!"

She picked Maria up, brushed some grass off her and laid her back down in the pram.

Violet pushed the pram through two fields and had to lay Maria down again to lift it over a stile. Eventually she reached a gate which opened out onto the road. They followed the road back to Bembridge and found the car.

Violet struggled to collapse the pram again, so laid it on its side in the boot. She got in the back next to Maria, and took out the pop-up books.

"Let's do *Jungle*," she said.

Maria put her hand out to the monkey on the cover.

* * *

Violet changed Maria on the back seat. She put the dirty nappy in a supermarket bag with the others. As she opened it, a waft of decomposing poo, filled her nose and mouth and she retched, tears filling her eyes.

"That needs incinerating," she said.

There weren't many clean outfits left to choose from, only dresses and one long-sleeved baby vest. She put Maria in the baby vest, and a navy corduroy dress. At the bottom of the bag were three pairs of tiny woollen tights and some socks. Maria's legs would be cold with only socks on so Violet pulled out some cream coloured tights.

"Who the fuck makes babies wear tights?" she said.

The tights were difficult to put on. She got both Maria's feet in, and then when she started rolling up the first leg, the other foot popped off. She tried doing both legs at the same time, first to ankle length, then knee, then thigh, but they were so restrictive at knee length that Maria started to cry. Violet lifted Maria up and held her with one arm, and then gradually pulled the tights up with her other hand, until they were halfway up the nappy.

Violet turned her round and held her up in front of her. "I hate tights," she said, "Sorry you've got to wear them. You actually make that outfit look good though, I can't believe it!"

Maria watched Violet as she spoke. She reached out a hand, grabbed Violet's nose and squeezed.

"Oh byy Godd," Violet said, shaking her face from side to side, "UUve got byy doze!"

Maria smiled and Violet carried on shaking, but then she felt a jolt and a shivery feeling as if there was someone behind her. She removed Maria's fingers from her nose, and turned around.

There was nobody in the street, but something seemed false. The sun was shining and everything was well-lit. There were some houses with drives and a couple of other cars like hers, parked on the curbs. Maybe it was because there were no people, and she couldn't hear any birds.

She looked out of the window and searched the sky. In the distance she saw the silhouettes of two birds flying around in a circle. She felt relieved for a moment, but then thought about zombie films where everything looked okay, horses, sheep and birds seemed normal, but something was wrong. Suddenly bloody hands and gaping mouths would thump against the car windows and she would have to fight for her and Maria's lives and drive away, running down zombies, bodies thudding under the car, and severed limbs shimmying across the bonnet as she mowed them down.

Maria let out a little shriek.

"Yeah," Violet said, "I need more sleep."

She looked through the shopping bags, found the Coco Pops, and tore open the packet. She shoved a handful in her mouth, crunched and felt the pops turn to powder. Maria could wait for a while before having her next bottle. They could try out that other pub, have a couple of drinks and by the time they finished, it would be dark.

Violet put the Coco Pops back and unpeeled a banana. She took a bite, and then sat Maria up next to her in the back. She was getting good at sitting. When she fell forward, Violet caught her and propped her back up. Violet broke off a piece of banana and handed it to her.

"Mmm, lovely nana," Violet said.

Maria put her fist and the banana in her mouth. Violet picked her up and put her on her lap while they both finished the banana.

Violet wiped banana off Maria's face and hands, put her in the car seat, and then curled up in a ball next to her on the back seat.

She pulled her hood up, and closed her eyes. The hood felt cosy against her skin. Next to her, Maria gurgled. Violet looked up and saw that she was watching the leaves outside. Her eyes felt heavy, and a warm sinking feeling filled her head.

She dreamed she was in a windowless corridor with hundreds of shut doors.

High-pitched baby cries echo off walls and she's knee-deep in honey. Eardrums rattling in her head like dropped saucepan lids... So hands over ears, and finds a knitting needle stuck through her head.

INTO THE RABBIT HOLE, ROUND THE TREE.

Trips through honey, leaves sticky handprints on the numbered doors, fluff sticking to fingers, lips, tongue. Follows the shrieking. Arrives at the door, pushes, falls, hands and knees. Three foetuses submerged in honey. They look like prawns. Tiny. Turns her head and the needle snags and hurts, fluid trickles from ear to cheek. Clumsy clot.

OUT OF THE RABBIT HOLE, RUN AWAY FREE.

Honey rises over their faces, fills their noses and covers their lidless eyes. She pulls one out as the others sink. The baby screams in her palm and in its mouth there are bees, huddling.

Violet woke with a jolt, and for a moment forgot where she was. She expected Maria to be crying, but she was awake, still looking out of the window. There was a sour, dry taste in Violet's mouth. She remembered a fly going into her mouth when she was little, on her BMX, and accidentally biting, the body surprisingly cold between her teeth. Fucking horrible dream. She ran a finger round her gums, checking for bees.

"I'm going to find us a better parking space," she said, "Then dinner. And then... our new boat!"

She brushed her teeth and spat outside, then put eye make-up on, using the rear-view mirror. Her burn was weeping again and she got the TCP out and put some on the cuff of her sweatshirt.

She dabbed it on the blister and wiped off some ashy scab. After a couple of seconds the TCP started to sting and she clenched her jaw and took a sharp breath through her teeth.

She had a quick look up the street and wriggled out of her jeans. Her clothes were all over the car from where she'd used them for covers, she couldn't see her socks or underwear. Eventually she found her thong with a chilli pepper in a Mexican hat on the front and the words 'Hot Stuff'.

She pulled on some grey jeans with frayed knees and torn-off back pockets. She was getting used to the sixteen-hole boots, and they looked good with all her tight jeans. She put a bag together with clothes for them both, the Coco Pops, bananas, talcum powder, TCP, honey, Greek yoghurt, and Maria's changing stuff and formula.

It was difficult to find an inconspicuous place to park. If she parked in the woods, someone might report the car thinking it was abandoned, and if she left it in a pub car park, it would probably be the only car there during the day. She needed a street like her parents', where loads of cars were parked, and no one knew or cared who they belonged to. Violet bet a car could stay in her mum and dad's road for months before anyone thought to report it. She settled on a street with about twenty houses on it, and a few other cars parked on the road. It was the other side of Bembridge from the marina and the pubs, probably a half hour walk. The road was called Ferney Crescent.

"Ferney Crescent, Ferney Crescent, Ferney Crescent, kind of like furry," Violet said, trying to fix an image of the road in her head. "Come on then," she said to Maria, "let's go."

Maria was asleep. Violet got the pram out, put their backpack on the tray underneath and started walking. There were more cars on the road now, and she guessed it was around three or four o' clock, school pick-up time.

The King's Head was less nautical themed than The World's End. It had low bumpy ceilings with thick black beams running through them. The traditional look was contradicted by a group of fruit machines, a virtual golf game, and a huge TV screen. A large banner saying *WATCH LIVE SPORTS HERE* hung above the bar.

A dark-haired man was playing a fruit machine with his back to Violet, and every now and again a whir of electronic noise burst out, followed by the quiet tapping of buttons, and a movement of spinning symbols. A half pint stood untouched on top of the machine as the man pushed pound coins into the slot, without looking up.

A narrow door opened next to the peanut and crisp rack, and a young barmaid appeared, chewing.

"Oh, sorry," she said, "I didn't hear you come in." She held a half-eaten sandwich in one hand, which she put down when she saw Violet looking.

"That's alright," Violet said, "we've only been here a minute."

The barmaid rested her hands on two beer pumps and smiled, "What would you like?" She had messy dyed blonde hair with red streaks running through it. When she said 'like', Violet noticed a tongue stud.

"A double bloody Mary for me, and can I have some boiling water?"

The barmaid saw Maria and leaned over the bar to look at her, "She's really pretty. Long eyelashes!"

Maria hadn't woken up yet, and her eyes were closed. "Yeah," Violet said, "thanks." She pulled out a ten pound note.

Violet watched the bargirl pour two measures of vodka over ice, and shake the tomato juice. She didn't put as much lemon in as Violet liked, but she did use celery salt, and put the drink in front of Violet along with bottles of Tabasco and Worcester sauce.

"Thought I'd let you do that, I never know how spicy to make it."

The barmaid looked her straight in the eye when she talked; it was unnerving, as if every word was a code for something else.

A flurry of mumbling vibrated in Violet's head, then a whisper: *Scab face, skank.*

"You alright?" the barmaid asked.

Violet rubbed her temples, "Yeah, just...exhausted. Do you sell cigarettes?"

The barmaid offered her a squashed packet of Marlboro Lights from her back pocket. "We have a machine, but it's a rip off. There's a newsagents down the road, I'd wait if I were you."

"Thanks," said Violet, taking a cigarette, "How much for the drink?"

"Two eighty." She put her hands on the pumps and smiled, looking her directly in the eye again, then went to the till. "I'll bring the water out to you."

"Thanks."

She didn't want to talk to the intense bargirl anymore, and wished she'd just waited for the hot water, and not got into the cigarette conversation. The girl would probably want to sit and smoke with her now too. At least she'd only charged her for a single.

The cold air woke Maria up, and she started to cry. Violet noticed the ridge in her gum again, and touched it. "Dinner soon," she said, and started pushing the pram back and forth with her foot.

She lit a cigarette, and inhaled hard, then held the smoke in her throat, blew three smoke rings into the air and watched them stretch and break. The twitchy paranoid feeling started to settle, as the nicotine hit her bloodstream. Rocking the pram wasn't working, and Maria's cries were escalating.

The door to the pub creaked and the bargirl appeared with a steaming metal jug.

"That alright for you?" she asked.

"Yeah, thanks."

Maria let out an especially loud cry and the bargirl winced, "She's woken up a bit hasn't she!"

"Yeah."

The bargirl headed back the way she came, and Violet watched the door swing shut.

"Nicely done, Maria," she said, "I couldn't face chatting either."

She held her cigarette in her mouth and rinsed out the bottle with some boiling water, then started to mix a new one. When she finished, she put it on the table to cool down, and lifted Maria onto her lap. She jigged her up and down, and smoked the cigarette down to the butt before grinding it out. It wasn't late, but the sky had a tinted orange quality that made her think of Halloween.

Violet wiped dribbled milk from Maria's chin as she sucked at the bottle. She was chewing the teat tonight, and making a snuffling noise like a piglet.

"We're gonna be alright," Violet said, "We've got a boat now. We can go anywhere we like."

Maria's drinking slowed until it was just one or two gulps a minute. When she was asleep, Violet removed the bottle from her lips. She held her against her shoulder, rubbing her back for a while, but didn't know if she could burp when she was sleeping.

Violet laid her back down in the pram and covered her with the hoodie. Her lips were defined and perfect, often in a pout like Lisa's. Other than that, Violet didn't think she looked much like her parents. She hoped she wouldn't develop Claude's hooded eyes.

She went back inside to get another bloody Mary.

"Thanks for the hot water," she said to the bargirl, "she's fast asleep now."

"Fuck!" shouted the man at the fruit machine, and slammed his fist down on the buttons.

Violet noticed two old men look up from a table across the room.

"Chill out, Serge," the bargirl said, "It'll pay out soon."

"I don't have more pounds," the man said. He turned towards the bar and Violet realised it was the waiter from the Bucket o' Mussels. He held a notepad in one hand, with numbers written on it. Violet saw him recognise her.

"Hi," she said.

He smiled quickly at her, "Hello," he said. His fingers were drumming the notepad. He glanced at Maria's pram, then turned back to the bargirl, "I go to get some more money. I will be back... Please can you do me big favour, and if somebody wants to go on this machine, just say he's broken."

The bargirl looked up at the ceiling.

"I'll try," she said, "But if Tim comes down, then I can't."

He put his hands together in a prayer position, "Thank you, Alex," he said. He smiled quickly in the direction of Violet and Maria, and then ran out of the pub.

"He's got a fucking problem," the bargirl said, "Comes in once or twice a week, and just plays that till it pays out. Nice guy though. He's from Portugal."

Violet added more Tabasco to her drink and stirred, "Yeah, I met him the other day."

"You and baby on holiday then?" Alex asked.

"We're visiting my aunt."

One of the old men came up to the bar and Alex went to serve him.

Violet pushed Maria back outside, and sat down with her drink. She'd never been into fruit machines, or gambling, but she didn't really like games. She wondered if there would be a shower on the boat, or electricity.

After a few minutes, the door creaked and Alex appeared, "Break time," she said, putting a cigarette between her lips. She offered the pack to Violet.

"Thanks," Violet said.

Alex sat down next to her and held the lighter out, cupping her hands round the flame. Violet leaned in and lit her cigarette.

"You're so slim to have had a baby," Alex said, "My sister had hers two years ago, and still hasn't lost the weight."

"Thanks," Violet said, "She was a small baby." Violet noticed that Alex had a slight double chin when she talked. Apart from her red and blonde hair, and piercings, there was nothing really distinguishing about her face or body.

"I get so bored working here," Alex said, "It's either yachties or old men. Where are you staying?"

The town names left Violet's head like liquid down a hole. She stammered, "Er, sorry... what?"

"Where you staying? There's not much going on round here, but if you haven't got to be back anywhere tonight, there's a free party in the woods."

"I can't," said Violet, "I don't have a babysitter."

"What about your aunt? Shame to come to the island and not go to at least one rave!"

"Thanks, but I think I just want a quiet one. Maybe another night though?"

An expression like pain crossed the girl's face, "That's cool," she said, "You just look like you'd enjoy it." She frowned, "How'd you hurt your face?"

"Last time I had a babysitter," Violet smiled, "Went out, got wasted and fell into someone's cigarette."

The girl laughed, "When was that? Must've been a good night!"

Violet dropped her cigarette butt on the ground, and squashed it under her boot. "Couple of weeks ago, I keep picking it though."

"I love picking scabs," the girl said, "Can never let anything heal."

She had moved closer to Violet, and it crossed Violet's mind that she might actually have a go at picking the scab on her face.

Violet finished her drink, and stood up. "I better go. Hey, thanks again for the cigarettes," she said, and manoeuvred the pram through the door.

"No problem, sexy," the girl said, as the door creaked closed.

Violet thought of the fairy tale with the troll under the bridge, bored, lonely, killing time all day till the goats came along. Maybe that was why Alex had come across a bit desperate. She was probably chubby because there was nothing to do in Bembridge if you didn't sail, apart from eat crisps and wait for something to happen.

Violet pushed Maria through the fields. The moon was out, but its light was smothered by a thick, milky fog. She stuck to the hedge line, and re-traced the journey back to the gate next to the marina. Her technique for stile and gate-climbing with the pram had improved, and she crossed them quickly despite the lack of visibility, and added slipperiness. Violet was crossing the last field when she heard a shuffling noise next to her. She felt the hairs on the back of her neck stand up, and she pushed Maria faster through the thick grass. A deep rumbling baa broke the silence making her jump, and she remembered the sheep. If there was anything really frightening in the field, the sheep wouldn't have stuck around. Violet wondered if there were wolves left in the Isle of Wight. She started to quietly sing 'Buffalo Soldier', until at last, the metal gate materialised out of the fog.

The mist wasn't as thick in the marina, and Violet made her way easily through the lines of small boats to the jetties. There was no noise, but she could see lights on in the clubhouse. A large searchlight meant that the jetties were lit up, especially the first one. Luckily the boats moored there were quite large and would obscure her a bit, but they would have to get onboard quickly. She reached into her jacket pocket and touched the cork key ring. Maria was starting to stir due to the lack of movement. Violet headed for the jetty.

Revelations bobbed gently as Violet took hold of the rope and pulled. When the boat touched the jetty she heaved Maria and the pram onto the front of it. Violet's fingertips were still on the handle as the boat started to move away. She tipped forward off balance for a second, then half-jumped, half-fell onto the boat. She landed on her knees and Maria's pram rolled forward with the jolt. Violet took hold of the pram and stood up. Her kneecaps stung from the impact on the deck, and she rubbed them to ease the pain.

The light was falling on them, so Violet pushed the pram to the side in darkness and kicked the brakes down.

"Please don't cry," she whispered to Maria, "not yet."

Violet felt the boat move beneath her as she shuffled the three keys on the key ring. The first one she tried fitted and turned smoothly. As soon as it was unlocked, the door swung open to reveal four steep steps down. She glanced back towards the clubhouse, and thought she saw a figure cross one of the windows, blocking the light for a moment. She listened to hear if there was anyone outside; nothing.

Violet lifted Maria out of the pram, and went through the door. As she started down the steps, she heard a distant cough. She shut the door behind them, and it closed with a smooth click.

22

Laurie is babysitting. He is my favourite babysitter. His mum is the teacher at the playschool I went to before my school. Laurie goes to a different school from me where you can do acting classes. He is fifteen, and wants to be a dancer. He is fat with curly brown hair and brown eyes.

"Don't you have to be thin to be a dancer?" I ask.

Laurie pats his tummy. "Yep!" he says, "I've got some serious training to do." He smiles and says, "Want to learn a dance routine?"

"Okay, I say."

"Cool," he says, "Where's the stereo?"

Laurie and I go into the lounge and I show him where the stereo is. My Dad loves the stereo. Sometimes he lies on the sofa for hours listening to music and drinking a drink that he calls 'Dragons' Blood'.

Laurie gets a cassette out of his bag and puts on a song called 'You got it' that he says is a 'top tune' and is by the New Kids on The Block. He teaches me how to do the dance and says that next time he comes round, we can perform it together for my mum and dad. We put the song on again and again and practice our 'routine'.

"Make a serious face, Violet," he says.

I frown and screw my lips up tight like Mrs Martin when she's about to shout.

Laurie says, "Ooh Violet, that's a bit severe!" then, "Right. Let's take it from the top! Five, six, seven, eight!"

We dance the whole song and I remember almost all the

moves. Laurie says, "You're a good dancer, Violet. It was a strong performance."

After dancing, we eat bourbons in the kitchen and Laurie makes me a Ribena, and then tells me it's bedtime.

"Do I have to?"

"Your mum and dad'll be home soon and they'll be upset if you're still up."

"Can I have a story?" I ask.

"Get into your pyjamas and do your teeth, then give me a shout and I'll come tell you one."

I run up the stairs using my hands and feet for double speed.

In the morning I wake up early and watch a *Storyteller* video in bed. After that I brush my teeth and start to get ready for school. Laurie told me that I should put my shirt and pinafore on the radiator before I went to bed. When I put them on they are lovely and warm, especially the shirt.

At seven o' clock I go downstairs and open the front door. There is a new bottle of silver top milk in the crate outside. I take it into the kitchen and open the fridge. There is still milk left in another bottle but I want the cream off the new one. I pretend I haven't seen the other milk and go to get the Coco Pops out of the tall cupboard. I drew a monster last year and Mum cut him out and stuck him on the door. His legs swing when I open it. I pour my cereal almost to the top of the bowl, then open the milk. I push down the foil top and carefully peel it off. When I pour the milk in there are two big spots of cream on the top. I will save that patch till last.

Mum comes down and starts eating a banana. "The teachers are impressed with you!" she says.

"Are they?" I say.

"Yeah, especially that Mrs. Martin, she says you're way ahead of the other children at spelling and reading."

"Mrs Martin's horrible," I say. I wish it was Mrs Head who was pleased with me.

"She wouldn't stop raving about you. You've got a fan there!" Mum says.

"I hate her."

My mum laughs, "Dad and I were a bit surprised. She's potty about you!"

It's funny thinking about Mrs Martin being my fan.

"In fact she said she'd spoken to the other teachers and agreed that you could be moved up a year."

I am about to put a spoon of Coco Pops into my mouth but stop halfway. "What, move to an older class?"

"Yeah, they all think you'd be great. The only thing you would be behind in

is Handwriting and Mrs Martin has agreed to give you special attention in that lesson."

We haven't been taught joined-up writing yet, but I have seen it on the board

when the older class has been in the classroom before us. I put the spoon of Coco Pops back in the bowl.

"What about my friends?"

"You'll love it in Class 4, and you'll still have all your old friends round to

play."

"Why isn't Esther moving up, she's the best in the class?"

"I don't know, Violet," she says. "She's probably not as clever as you think."

"She is."

"Well she can't be otherwise it would be her moving up and not you, Smartypants!" She tickles me under the arms, but I don't laugh, and move away from her.

I think I've hurt her feelings but I don't care, because she is stupid enough to be tricked by Mrs Martin.

"When do I change classes?"

She is looking out of the window and doesn't answer.

"Mum, when do I change classes?"

"Monday," she says.

"Oh."

I hate Mrs Martin. I'm not good enough at Maths to go into the class above. I think she has taken me away from my friends on purpose.

23

Nobody tells me what my first lesson is so I go to the school reception and ask.

The Lady there says, "Can I help you?"

"I've moved up classes and don't know where I'm supposed to go."

"What's your name?"

"Violet."

"Last name."

"Kale."

"Who was your form teacher?"

"Mrs Martin."

The lady looks through lots of papers. She has a plait twisted up into a ball on the top of her head and the longest fingernails I have ever seen. They curl over at the end and make a scratching noise on the papers.

"Hmmmmm," she says, "can't find anything here. Let's check the memos."

I hear the bell go.

"Ah ha, Violet. Your first lesson is Handwriting and you'll know your teacher, Mrs Martin. After that you have Maths with Mr Ford in The Mansion, but Mrs Martin will give you your new timetable, and that will tell you everything. You'll have to get used to finding your way around now you're in class 4."

"Thank you," I say. "Where is room 9?"

She points her curly finger out the window, "The long building behind the boarders' dormitories."

The long building is not old like the rest of our school. It looks like a caravan without wheels. There is a ramp that you walk up to get in. There is a thin corridor with pictures of people's work stuck on the walls, and three doors. The numbers on the doors say eight, nine and ten. I stand on tiptoes and peek through the window in the number nine door.

Mrs Martin is writing stuff on the blackboard. The children in the class look much older than me and my friends. The biggest girl has her hair tied up in a ponytail on the side of her head and pierced ears. I know one of the boys from the climbing frame, he's friends with Adam and he has brown hair and loads of freckles. The children start looking at the door and I see Mrs Martin is looking at the door too. I get off my tiptoes and Mrs Martin opens the door.

"You're late, Violet. And on your first day too!" She leads me to the blackboard and makes me stand in front of the class.

"This is Violet," she says, "she's moving up from class 3. Who's got a seat next to them?"

Nobody says anything, and then a really thin girl at the back puts her hand up.

"Thank you Ruth, you can look after Violet today and show her where all the lessons are."

Mrs Martin pokes her finger into my back. "Go on then, Violet, we haven't got all day."

I sit down and get out my pencil case. Two boys turn round and look at me. One of them frowns and sticks out his bottom teeth, I frown back even harder and they turn back round to their desks smiling.

"Books out everybody," Mrs Martin says, "I want you to copy the sentences on the board into your books in joined-up writing. Remember to draw lines with your rulers to help. If you don't finish, you will do it for homework."

The rest of the class get out their books and pencil cases and start writing.

I put my hand up because I don't have a book. Mrs Martin looks at me but doesn't come over. She goes to the desk at the front of the room, and sits down. I keep my arm pointing straight up at the ceiling. Mrs Martin just sits there writing something. My arm starts to get tired so I hold it up with my other arm. I keep looking at Mrs Martin and listening to all the other children doing their work. There are five sentences on the board. The first one says *Squirrels eat acorns, they collect them, hide them, and store them for winter.* Underneath this sentence is the same sentence but written in joined-up writing. The others we have to work out for ourselves. The last sentence on the board says, *Now make up ten of your own sentences and write them out in joined up writing.*

I look at Ruth who is supposed to show me around today. She has written about three sentences. She sees that my hand is up still and shrugs her shoulders, then smiles. Her eyes are a soft brown colour like a rabbit's.

"Concentrate on your own work Ruth," Mrs Martin says. Finally she has stopped writing and is coming over.

"Sorry Mrs Martin," says Ruth.

"How are you getting on, Violet?" she says.

"I need a book."

"Well why didn't you say something? Do you mean to say you've been sitting here being idle?"

"I tried to tell you, but you didn't see..."

But Mrs Martin is going back to her desk now. She comes back with a new exercise book.

I start to write my name on the front of it.

She snatches it from me, and makes me mess up my surname. "For goodness sake! You've wasted enough time, you can do that later. Now let me see you start the exercise." She opens the book and puts it in front of me.

I don't know what to do. Mrs Martin is leaning over me with one hand holding open the book. Her dress is touching my hair. I start writing the word *Squirrels* but I don't know how to join the letters together.

"That's not right," she says and takes my pencil. "Where's your rubber?" I take my rubber out of its holder on the *Milk is Great* ruler and she grabs it. I think about telling her that it is rude to snatch, but don't say anything. I wish she would stop leaning on my head, it is making me have to bend right down.

She rubs out my writing, then takes my ruler and draws two lines. "Right, Violet, keep your writing between these lines so it's neat, and copy the joined-up sentence from the blackboard. She hands me back my pencil and finally gets up so she's not leaning on my head anymore.

"You've got ten minutes, so hurry. I'll check at the end of the lesson to make sure you're doing it right. Otherwise, you can come to me at lunchtime and I'll explain it to you." She smiles, but still looks nasty.

It takes ages to copy the sentence off the board, and I know the bell will go soon. Ruth has stopped writing so I know she's finished. I don't want to spend my lunch with Mrs Martin. I write all the sentences on the board out in my own writing, then make up a couple. One says *Jesus likes bread wine and fish*, and the other says *My Mum is a fast runner*. The other children are starting to put their pencils away, so I know the bell is going any minute. Then I have a brainwave. I take my ruler and join the letters of each word up with a pencil line. I get to the last board sentence when the bell goes. Mrs Martin gets up and says, "Leave quietly everyone."

I put my pencil case and book in my bag and rush to get into the crowd of boys who are the fastest leaving the room. Because they are tall, I am hidden from Mrs Martin. I will wait for Ruth round the corner at the end of the corridor.

Just as I get out into the corridor I hear Mrs Martin calling my name. Fooled her! The only bad thing is that I never got my timetable, I will just have to stay with Ruth all day.

24

Violet waited in the dark, listening. Her pulse beat in her head. Maria let out a cry.

"Shhh," she whispered.

She paced up and down, rocking Maria, and running a hand along the smooth, narrow walls. She wondered if the boat had electricity, and if it would be charged-up or connected while it was docked.

The corridor area she was standing in was only a few metres long, and opened out into a larger space. She hoisted Maria onto her shoulder and felt in her jeans for a lighter.

She flicked the flame on, and held it out revealing a room with a sofa, and small shelves embedded in the walls. Maria cried louder.

"Please, shut up for a minute and let me think," Violet said. She laid her on the floor. Maria kicked her legs about and started to properly cry.

"Fucking hell," Violet said, "You're no good at being discreet."

Maria couldn't be hungry again; maybe it was her nappy. Violet remembered the pram and backpack were still on the deck.

"Keep quiet while I get the stuff," she said, "please."

Violet felt her way back up the stairs and grabbed the pram. With the door open, Maria's cries seemed to split the air, and echo across the marina. An image of herself stuffing Maria's mouth with socks played in her head.

The marina was lit up and figures still moved in the clubhouse windows. There was no chance of hearing the coughing person again, as Maria's cries were resounding out of the doorway, and spreading like sonar.

Violet pulled the pram through the door and fell backwards down the stairs. She felt carpeting burn her back above her jeans, and something hit her in the mouth and slid upwards tearing her gum. She lay for a moment, tasting metallic blood, then got out from under the pram, and scrambled up the stairs to pull the door shut.

Their stuff had fallen out of the pram, Violet felt around in the dark and found a banana. She clutched it in her hand and crawled towards Maria's cries, then sat her up against the sofa. Violet unpeeled the banana, and broke off a piece. She held one of Maria's hands, it was hot and damp; she felt the little fingers grip hers. She found Maria's other hand, and pushed the piece of banana into it.

"Okay, try and stay sitting up while I find us a light."

Violet used the lighter to go through some cupboards above, working her way along the seats on her knees.

The light fell on two glass mosquito candles. She lit them and put one on each side of the lounge area. The smell of citronella hit her nostrils, and she thought of her dad's barbeques, and hot holidays. Her thoughts rolled on to drunk sex, pavement, sweet shots, pills, and a taste of superglue in the morning. She couldn't remember the last time she had a suntan. The last year had been spent between work and Lisa's.

Violet changed Maria's nappy by the candlelight. It was cold in the boat, not much warmer than outside. The glass of the candles was red, and made the walls flicker pink, giving a false illusion of warmth.

When Maria was dressed again, Violet lifted her up and took a candle to explore the other rooms in the boat.

A small door at the end of the lounge area led to a kitchen. It reminded Violet of a caravan, with everything fitted to the shape of the walls. The cupboards had clips on them, and the plates inside had tight fitting compartments. The mugs were more precarious, hanging on hooks on the underside of shelves. Violet held the candle over the stove; it was gas. She turned it on and tried the flame, but nothing happened. There was a cupboard under the stove and she pulled it open to reveal a canister.

"Please don't be empty," she said.

Maria pulled on her ear. "Ba," she said.

Violet gripped Maria, and leaned in to find the valve. She twisted it round, and stood up to try the hob again.

This time when she turned the knob, gas hissed through. Violet tickled Maria and said, "Gas!"

Near where they'd entered the boat there were stairs that led to a locked room. Violet felt in her pocket for the keys, but they must've dropped out when she fell. She guessed it was the control room with the steering wheel and radios. Next to the door, in a holder attached to the wall, was a huge, black metal torch, security guard style.

"Nice," she said.

She'd gone out with a bouncer for a few weeks who had one just like it; he said it doubled as a weapon, and showed her how to hold it so you could hit someone. She pulled it out and held it in her palm; it was heavy, and cold against her skin. She put it back in its place.

Another small door next to the entrance opened to reveal two steps down to a double bedroom. It was shaped the same as the front of the boat and there was a wardrobe and thin dressing table set into the walls. The room felt colder than the rest of the boat. There was a horizontal, tinted window with a blind. The bed was made, and had two blue cushions embroidered with gold anchors arranged against the pillows. Violet was about to pull the covers off to take into the other room, but it was so neat, she would never be able to recreate it. At the top of one of the wardrobes were stacks of blankets, some pillows, and a single duvet. Violet took a pile of covers into the lounge area to make them a nest.

* * *

Maria was fed and sleeping in a doughnut of covers on the floor. Violet sat on the sofa eating Greek yoghurt with the squeezy bear honey. She wished there was power. A television with built-in DVD player stood useless in a neat alcove on one of the shelves.

It was hard to eat as a sick panicky feeling had taken hold of her body since she'd stopped moving.

She hoped Lisa wouldn't go to Jodie. Lisa had met Jodie the day they turned up pissed at the bus stop to intimidate the bullies. Fucking embarrassing. Lisa pregnant, getting pulled off some kid by the bus driver, and then kicking the driver and spitting in his face. Violet walking behind Jodie realising she'd made everything worse, looking back and seeing grinning faces pressed up against the bus windows, some snapping pictures with mobile phones.

Jodie had no self-preservation skills. Her prettiness should have saved her, but the other girls hated her for it, and Violet guessed the boys preferred more normal girls, because there was less risk involved. Violet hated everything about school and got out as soon as she could. It was a place where everybody tried to be standard issue. You couldn't be too pretty, funny, clever, ugly; you had to attain a kind of acceptable nothingness. It was like anti-depressants, you always felt okay, never really bad, but never really good either. Like the plainest black school shoe with a tiny required designer label.

Jodie was strange too, naïve; not naïve like a child, more like a tribal person who had no idea of Western society. When Violet was little she sometimes wondered if Jodie was really a child at all, and not a reincarnation of some ancient, enlightened buddha. She liked walking for hours in the woods, or lying on her bed with Cupid watching an old babies' nightlight make coloured animal shadows cross the walls.

"Aren't you bored?" Violet asked once.

"No," Jodie replied.

"What do you do in here all the time?"

Jodie looked as if she was abandoning a long journey to turn round for a forgotten toy. Her eyes focussed on Violet and she answered, "Daydream."

It wasn't Jodie's fault they didn't have much of a relationship. Jodie always wanted to be around her, but Violet always had a strong urge to be as far away from her sister as possible. She wished she was here now, even if she just lay on the sofa daydreaming like a freak. Violet felt a tightening in her throat and put the yoghurt down.

She wanted a drink. Maria's last bottle had used up the evian, but it wasn't late enough yet to venture out into the marina. A cabinet next to the television looked like a possible drinks cabinet. Inside there were a couple of board games, a pack of cards, and a cigarette in a glass tube. There were red letters printed on the tube; IN CASE OF EMERGENCY- BREAK GLASS. Violet was about to break it when she noticed a box of Hamlet cigars. If only there was alcohol, she could set herself up for a good night. She remembered Anne saying 'no stimulants' and felt the momentary flutter of hope fall down dead. She stuck a cigar in her mouth and took a candle to smoke by in the kitchen.

Violet lit the cigar off the hob and pushed open a thin window. Why hadn't she thought of alcohol at the supermarket? She kept forgetting not to inhale the cigar smoke; strange really, sucking smoke into your mouth then blowing it straight out again.

Maybe Anne cooked with wine. Violet clamped the cigar in her teeth and began opening cupboards. They were full of food.

"Revelations," she said through her teeth.

There were cans of soup, fish, dried pasta, stock cubes, baked beans and spaghetti hoops. A high cupboard had a packet of sugar inside, and a jar of Horlicks. Next to the Horlicks was an almost full bottle of Famous Grouse. Violet saw herself reflected in the bottle, cigar in teeth, and gave it a smile.

Violet sat drinking Famous Grouse in the lounge, with one candle on. Maria was asleep, gently illuminated. She remembered the Camel Lights from the petrol station. Where were they, and why hadn't she had them in the pub? The thick, mellow sensation that arrived with the whisky faded as the urge for a cigarette took over. She didn't want to break Anne or her husband's emergency cigarette thing. Something about smashing it would make her feel as if she'd taken part in a stupid joke. She took the whisky glass and candle to go and look in the backpack.

Violet righted the fallen pram. The boat keys were next to the stairs, and she hooked them on her finger. The bag was by the bottom step. She held it upside down and emptied its contents onto the floor; no Camel Lights. There was a small zip-up pocket in the front but she couldn't remember putting anything in there; she opened it anyway. Inside were the Leatherman, her car keys, and the Isle of Wight pencil. The cigarettes must still be in the car.

Violet took a big gulp of whisky. She swallowed, felt the unpleasant sting turn to fire in her chest, and headed up the stairs to the locked door. A small fire extinguisher was attached to the wall, and she remembered filling a school corridor with foam. Her and Gemma hiding under the school stage, gripping each other's hands, looking at each other in the dark, and digging their nails into each other's palms when footsteps crossed the hall.

The door opened to a room with radios, a switchboard, two small computer screens, and a steering wheel. Violet sat down on the wood and leather swivel chair, and put her feet on the desk. She leaned back and pushed with her feet expecting a slide, but the chair was bolted down.

From the captain's seat, she had a clear view of the marina. Violet remembered the candle and blew it out. The night was clear, she could see the Milky Way. A plane's lights blinked intermittently, and she thought of the people onboard in their headphones and aeroplane socks. A few windows glowed in clusters along the coastline towards Bembridge. There were still lights on in the marina clubhouse, but the night was silent. She pushed up a window to check, but there was no noise at all.

The boat's main window curved back quite far before joining solid roof, giving a view of the sky. Violet crossed her legs, spun the seat, and watched the stars shift. She opened a drawer and made out some papers, but it was too dark to see properly. She ran her fingers along the papers, and touched something cold; a Zippo lighter. Violet opened its lid and smelled paraffin. She lit the flame and held it over the drawer. It was full of maps and charts. A small, plastic-covered booklet on top said CROSSING THE SOLENT. She put another cigar between her teeth and lit it with the Zippo.

Violet needed another drink. As she got up, she noticed a frame fixed to the wall. It was the same photograph as in Anne's kitchen, Anne and James onboard Revelations. It didn't look like the Bembridge marina in the photo, and the sea was turquoise. She shut the lighter and felt her way back to the lounge.

Violet didn't bother lighting the candle again. There was a small window but apart from a small, black stretch of water between the pontoons, the view out to sea was blocked by moored boats. She'd lost the whisky glass somewhere, so she drank from the bottle. Maybe she could leave Maria for a few hours to find that party. The girl from the bar might be fun after all. If Lisa was here they'd be drunk together, laughing about the mess she'd got into, then phone up for drugs, call chat lines or fall into bed together with more vodka. What crap was she thinking? It was impossible to ever see Lisa again. And Lisa was bad; worse than her anyway.

Someone whistled in Violet's ear and made her jump. Chills ran down her arms, and she gasped cold air.

"What the fuck?" she said.

It was pitch dark. The whistle was so real she'd felt tiny hairs move on her cheek. She shivered, and went to sit next to Maria. Her limbs felt full of cement, and she stumbled, spilling whisky on her hand.

Violet crawled along the floor towards the backpack, feeling around in the dark for the Leatherman. Her movements were thick and uncoordinated. She didn't know where the candle was. The dark was safer than the light anyway, because you were hidden. The bottle clinked on the floor as she crawled around.

"Yo ho ho and a bottle of Grouse," she said, her voice sounding pathetic in the darkness. Her fingers found the Leatherman and she headed back to Maria. She opened the knife and waited in the dark, listening for another whistle, but there was nothing.

Violet took a swig from the bottle and rocked backwards off balance.

"Was that me or you?" she asked the boat.

She put the blade against her forearm, then pushed down, and pulled across fast. The sting cut through the whisky blur, and she felt the pressure in her head ease with the pain. She opened her mouth, "Ow," she said.

Violet lay down next to Maria, holding her sleeve tight round the cut. As she closed her eyes, cool tears ran down the side of her face to her ear.

* * *

Violet woke up because of the cold. Her limbs ached and her toes were numb inside her boots and socks. When she breathed, it made mist. Her mouth tasted disgusting, and her brain and eyes felt too big for her skull.

"Fucking Grouse," she said.

It was almost light outside, and she could see the room in more detail than the previous night. Maria was asleep, and looked pale. Violet touched her face and held her finger under her nose. She was breathing, but cold. Violet pushed her fingers under Maria's clothes to feel her chest; that was warm at least. She laid another cover over her. They needed water.

Violet was shivering hard, her teeth knocking together in her mouth. She grabbed the empty evian bottle, and her leather jacket. As she pulled the jacket on, something stung in her arm. She pulled up her sleeve, saw blood, and remembered the cut. It hadn't closed properly, and was wide in the middle, eye-shaped. She covered it back up and went out onto the deck.

It was so cold outside that her gums ached. The sun wasn't up yet and the sky was dark grey. She jumped off the boat onto the pontoon. The landing sent needle pains through her feet and ankles.

"Freezing," she said.

She started jogging but the scab on her face hurt too much, and her arm throbbed, so she slowed to a walk. She went into the boat shed, and walked to the back room, where she'd heard the radio playing. Just before she got to the room, she came to a sink.

Violet filled the bottle then entered the room. She turned on the lights. The room was a workshop with benches, vices, and racks of tools on the walls. Balanced on top of a tool rack there was a first aid kit, and she opened it to see if there were plasters to stick the cut in her arm together. Inside, there were only surgical gloves, big bandages, and a large piece of material for doing slings or something.

Violet scanned the workshop. There was a half-full bottle of Pepsi next to an empty Tracker bar box. She took the bottle and went to rinse and fill it at the tap. The large boat was still suspended, masked-up ready to be painted.

"Brainwave," she said, and picked a roll of masking tape, slipping it onto her arm like a bangle.

It was lighter outside now, and she hurried back towards the pontoon clutching the bottles. Engine noise rattled, and she looked round to see where it was coming from. It was so quiet, the sound could be from miles away, or out at sea. She hurried on to the pontoon, and jumped across onto Revelations.

Violet boiled water on the hob, and mixed up a bottle for Maria when she woke up. There was water left, and she poured it into a mug and squirted some honey in for herself. She got one of Maria's nappies from the backpack and tore it open, pulling out a chunk of cotton wool, then returned to the kitchen.

Violet dabbed the cotton wool in TCP and wiped around the cut on her arm. It made her queasy that it wasn't closing properly. Her other cuts scabbed quickly and turned to thin white scars in lines or crosses. When this healed it was going to look like a slug. When she'd cleaned it as well as possible, she covered it with cotton wool, then taped masking tape tightly over it and around her arm.

Violet sipped her drink and watched Maria. She was wheezing a bit, and it was unusual for her to sleep so long. Violet didn't know whether to wake her up. She remembered babies need lots of sleep, so she waited, listening for noises in the marina, and watching the light change outside.

Now they had gas, Violet could heat water to wash their clothes. She would go back to the car later, and fill a bag with their stuff. She could do with another supermarket trip to set themselves up on the boat for a while. Maybe she would get some baby books or a toy, and a sketch pad. Maria needed more formula milk; the cans went down so quickly. The sooner she started eating normal food the better.

It would be a good idea to move the car too. She could park it somewhere far away and spend the day trekking back. Then, if anyone was after them, the car wouldn't give away their location.

Finally, Maria started to stir, and Violet lifted her out of the covers. There was sleep around her eyes and Violet rubbed it off with her sleeve. Maria screwed up her face and began to cry.

"Alright, calm down. Your breakfast's here."

* * *

They stayed in the lounge area all day, with the blinds down. Violet hadn't remembered her Discman or Maria's books, so there was nothing to do. It was better when Maria was awake, but she only stayed awake for a couple of hours at the most, before falling asleep, or feeding, and then falling asleep. There was a little bit of Famous Grouse left, so Violet heated water, and made a hot toddy with no lemon. She tried to smoke a cigar, but it made her feel sick, and she put it out.

Violet went up to the driving room and entered on all fours in case people were outside. She crouched by the chair and peered over the desk. There were about twenty people scattered around the marina. A man was putting a mast into a small dinghy. Two children stood watching, a boy and a girl. They wore luminous orange life jackets and winter clothes, and looked bored, and cold. Other people were busy cleaning boats, and a group of guys in matching sailing outfits were scrambling over a large catamaran on the next pontoon.

Violet pulled a handful of books and charts out of the desk drawer. There was a large, plastic-covered Europe map, and another one the same style showed France and Spain, listing all the ports. She opened the Europe map and spread it out on the floor.

The English Channel was only little, and they were already on the Isle of Wight, which gave them a small head start. Navigating at sea was supposed to be complicated, but if they just headed south they would hit France. She wondered how much petrol they would need.

Back in the lounge, Violet looked through the cupboards again. There were a couple of Agatha Christie novels, but not much else. She chose *Sparkling Cyanide* and heated up some beans to eat while she was reading.

Maria woke up again for a while, and Violet played with her on the floor. From her front she could turn over perfectly by herself now, and she spent a lot of time with her chest pushed up off the floor looking around. She was dribbling. Violet wiped her mouth, and noticed that the dribble had soaked the top of her baby vest.

The Agatha Christie was quite gripping and Violet sat on the floor reading, occasionally doing farmyard animal noises for Maria.

"The sheep go Baaaaaaaaaaaaaaaa," she said.

"Ba," Maria said.

"Exactly."

"The cows go Mooo,"

Maria smiled and said, "Ba." She was lying on her back, kicking her legs. Violet watched as she turned herself onto her side. Violet supported her as she completed the turn to lie on her tummy. Maria pushed her chest up off the floor and looked at Violet.

"You're going to be crawling soon," Violet said.

After a while, Maria started crying again, and Violet put the book down and went to make her a bottle.

Maria fell asleep drinking her milk, and Violet lay her down in the covers again. It was cold in the boat, especially as they weren't moving around much. Violet picked up the Agatha Christie, and lay down next to Maria pulling another blanket over both of them. After a while her eyes started to tug, and she put down the book.

When Violet woke up it was just starting to get dark. She shivered, and went to get another cover out of the bedroom. Outside, the sky was dark blue, and the moon was just starting to glow. All the sailors had gone home, and the marina was quiet again. She glanced at the clubhouse, and saw the intermittent flashes of television light. She yawned, and went back into the lounge area.

Maria was still sleeping, and Violet touched her face to make sure she was still warm. They could wait until early morning to move the car. She lit a mosquito candle and picked up *Sparkling Cyanide*.

25

Ruth is nice, but not as fun as Adam. Her mum is a nurse, and she tells me that her mum knows my mum.

"It's really horrible what happened to your brother," she says, "My mum cried about it."

"Oh," I say.

"She says cot death is so bad because nobody understands it, and it isn't fair."

"No it's not."

"At least your brother's in heaven now with God."

"I don't believe in God," I say, and she puts her hand over her mouth. I look up at the sky then back to her. "If he was real and good like everyone says, then he wouldn't kill babies, just evil people."

"You shouldn't say things like that," Ruth says and we stop talking and go to History lesson.

Mrs Head has a stick that she points at stuff on the board with. It has a little metal hand on the end with a pointing finger. She uses it to point at us too. Today she is teaching us about the Aztecs. She says that they worshipped lots of different Gods, and also that they did human sacrifice, and cut out peoples' hearts while they were still alive.

The big girl whose name is Gemma says, "That's so evil."

Mrs Head says, "The Aztecs believed it was what their Gods wanted. They sacrificed people so the Gods would bless them with good weather for their crops so everybody would have enough to eat."

Mrs Head grins and some people laugh, some put their hands up to ask questions. Mrs Head moves her pointing stick from side to side to choose someone.

Gemma doesn't bother putting her hand up but says, "Ugh, pulling someone's heart out while they're alive, that's the cruellest thing I've ever heard."

Mrs Head looks cross and is about to tell Gemma off for not waiting her turn, but then I shout out, "In England, people used to burn people alive... and it was Christians that did it too!"

Everyone looks at me.

Mrs Head says, "Let's stick to the topic, Violet."

Gemma smiles at me. I think it's because I didn't wait to be asked to speak out either.

Mrs Head does a fierce look at me and then Gemma, "In my class we wait our turn to talk. One more shout-out, and you'll both get lunchtime detention!" Then she says to the whole class, "Who knows what kind of food was invented by the Aztecs? It's something most of you love."

"Pizza?" someone says.

"No, and, wait your turn, Mark."

I think Mark must be quite stupid because everyone knows pizza is Italian.

Mrs Head points at a boy with ginger hair who says, "Popcorn."

"No," she says, "But you're right Joshua, the Aztecs did farm corn, but I'm thinking of something delicious...made from cocoa..."

Lots of people put their hands up and I do too.

Mrs Head doesn't pick anyone with their hands up, she picks Ruth.

"What do you think, Ruth?" she asks.

Ruth goes red in the face. "Chocolate?" she says, and shrugs her shoulders.

"Exactly!" Mrs Head says, "Which is made from cocoa, and because it is an Aztec lesson, I've brought some in for us to all try."

* * *

I wait for ages in the car park. All of the other mums come and take everyone home. I sit on a wooden post and swing my feet, kicking them on the ground to get rid of the shininess. I hate shiny shoes. I wonder if I scrape them enough I can make a hole in them. It starts raining, and I watch the dusty mud mix with the rain and run down my shoes in lines.

Suddenly someone puts their hand on my shoulder. I look round and see the hunchback man. I get ready to run away. I look at his hand. It is suntanned and knobbly with mud under the nails and has a curved scratch on it. He sees me looking and takes his hand away and puts it in his pocket.

"Someone coming to collect you?" he asks and smiles at me. One side of his mouth lifts more than the other. I don't want to talk to him and wish he would go away. I don't know whether I should tell him anything. His bald head reminds me of a cartoon vulture. He walks forward and I see the huge hump on his back, pushing against his coat.

"My Mum's coming," I say, and look at the ground so I don't have to look at the hump.

"You can wait in my hut," he says, "save you getting wet."

"My Mum's here!" I shout, even though she's not.

He crunches his eyes up to look through the rain.

"Bye!" I say, and run across the car park as fast as I can. I run out of the car park and down the hill where me and Mum walk up. I don't dare stop running in case the hunchback has followed me. Usually Mum and I stroke the horses in the field, but today I ignore them and just keep going. I don't even check to see if they've got their coats on.

I don't look back until the road with the speed bumps is finished, and the main road is there. I stare back through the rain, but I can't see him coming down. I do see a car though, maybe one of the teachers' driving down the hill. There are some hedges next to the main road, and I crawl in and wait till the car is past. I think it is Mr Ford in the car. It is quite warm in the bush, and smells of mud. The rain is hitting the leaves and branches, but none is coming through. I wonder if there are other animals hiding in here too, but I probably scared them when I came in. I peek through the bush, and check the car is gone.

I have never crossed the main road by myself before. A lorry comes past with spray flying off its tyres. I wait for a gap, and just as I am about to step out, a horn goes and a motorbike goes past, and makes me jump. It sounds like an evil giant wasp. My school uniform is soaking. I can even feel rain between my toes inside my socks. I hope my school books aren't messed up.

This time I wait for a really big gap and then run across as fast as I can. I stand on the other side and look back at the road. I watch a few cars drive past, and the water spray from the road onto the pavement. I'm pleased I crossed it by myself.

There are some trees on my road, and I run from one to the other, sheltering as if I'm at war and the rain is bullets shooting at me. Eventually I get to my house, and make a last run for the front door and start ringing the doorbell.

Mum doesn't come to the door but I bet she's in, because she hardly goes out anymore, not even to Michaela's. I go round the back.

The back door is open so I go into the kitchen. I take my shoes off because Dad will be angry if I put footprints everywhere. I take my blazer off and leave it on the floor by my shoes. It smells weird now it's wet. The kitchen door is open and I can hear noise upstairs. I go into the hall, and listen. I can hear Mum crying really loudly. She's going, "Ahh huh ah huh ah huuuuuh…" and then doing squeaky screams.

I tiptoe back into the kitchen and close the door.

There's a little room joined to the kitchen that Dad calls the utility room. There's a washing machine and tumble drier, and a sideboard where Mum and I do painting and art stuff. My shirt has gone see through where it's wet. I get a towel out of the washing basket and dry my hair a bit, then I wrap it around myself and go back into the kitchen.

I put on the little telly in the kitchen and watch Childrens BBC, and then Newsround. I'm not supposed to have Coco Pops before dinner so I eat a pear from the fruit bowl and wait for Dad.

When I hear Dad's car coming in the drive I run outside to meet him. I still have the towel round me like a cape.

He picks me up and says, "You're shivering. Why didn't you get changed?"

"I forgot," I say, "Can we have Chinese takeaway tonight?" I hold on with my arms and legs wrapped around him like a baby orangutan.

"Hasn't Mum done something?"

"I don't know," I say, "she's in bed." I can feel his bristles on my cheek.

Dad puts me down and we go into the house. Dad goes straight upstairs. I wait in the hallway and hear him start shouting, and Mum crying again.

I go back in the kitchen and shut the door. I feel like I've got Mum in trouble. I fill up Cupid's bowl with biscuits, and give him new water. I wonder if he's hiding outside in a bush, or if he's sleeping on Mum's bed.

26

Violet packed the backpack with the changing stuff, some spaghetti hoops, a can of tuna, a made-up baby bottle, and the last banana. She boiled water, then filled the evian bottle with mixed formula milk. There was still some food in the car, and the rest of their clothes. She put the covers back in the bedroom, and hid the rest of their stuff in cubby holes around the boat. In a cupboard with some cleaning products, were lots of plastic bags folded into triangles. Violet stuck two in the backpack and unwrapped one. She filled it with their rubbish and put it on the pram's tray.

Maria was on the floor in press-up position watching Violet's preparations.

"Ready?" Violet said, and scooped her up.

Violet locked the door behind them and stood on the deck. The sun wasn't up and the sky was a cold, white colour. The first bird calls were coming from the direction of the fields.

Violet lay Maria down on her back by the door. "Stay still for a moment," she said. Maria blinked at the sky and stretched her arms out. Violet wheeled the pram to the edge of the boat, and pulled the rope. As the jetty came close she put one foot on it, and heaved the pram sideways. Its wheels hit the jetty, and Violet's thigh muscle pulled as the boat drifted away from the pontoon. Her boot slipped off the deck, and she wobbled on one leg, steadying herself with the pram. She rubbed her thigh, then pulled the rope again, and jumped back onto Revelations to get Maria.

Violet looked over to the fields, and yawned. Maria had kept waking up through the night, and her eyes ached; her arm was hurting too. She decided to go through the marina instead of the fields. It was quicker, and still early enough for there not to be anyone around. She tightened the straps on her backpack, and started to push Maria through the boatyard.

As she passed the boatsheds, she heard a door slam.

"Fuck," she said, and walked faster.

Just as the main gates were in sight, a loud voice called out behind her.

"Hello there!"

Violet kept moving.

"I said, Hi there!"

She wished she had her headphones on so she could feign deafness. There was no choice but to turn round.

A man strode up to her, puffing. He wore jeans, a bright yellow sailing coat that was tight over a big stomach, and a purple fleece hat that sat too high on his head.

"Morning," Violet said.

"Do you know this is a private yacht club?" His breath made steam explosions in the cold air.

"No... well, yes... my uncle sails here. He's a member."

"May I ask what you're doing here?"

Violet put a hand on her hip, and left the other on the pram. "My uncle was going out for an early sail. I bought him a hot drink."

The man waited.

"We're always up early, so I thought... but anyway, he wasn't here."

The man leaned his head to one side. His eyes were pale, watery blue and looked like they might spill out if he blinked. "Which is his boat?"

Violet pointed towards the covered dinghies, "One of those," she said.

He didn't look convinced, "Name?" he said.

"Esther," Violet replied.

"Your uncle's name."

Something about the interrogation and his hat seemed absurd, and she felt her mouth twist into a smile.

"Bert," Violet said, "Bert Clarke."

"I don't know any Bert."

An unwanted laugh started to wriggle up her throat. "People don't know him as Bert, here," she said, "His friends call him by some nickname, I can't remember... something to do with pirates."

The man took hold of her arm, and she flinched at the pressure on the cut. "You'd better come with me," he said, "See if he's in the book."

He led her towards the cabin keeping a tight grip on her.

Maria was awake, looking at the bright yellow coat. Violet didn't know what to do. The man was overweight, but she might not be able to outrun him with the pram.

They arrived at the cubicle and he reached in his pocket. He could execute them both and no one would know, or he might be an opportunistic rapist. He took out a set of keys, unlocked the door, and switched on a desk light. Violet watched him start leafing through the big diary; she should've taken it after all.

She watched him search the 'Cs' for Clarke, no Roberts or Berts apparently. He closed the book, and turned to face her, hands on hips. He parted his lips, about to speak, and she punched him as hard as she could in the balls.

The man doubled over and let out a dull groan. He reached out for her, and she stepped back and slammed the door, shutting him in, and hopefully catching his fingers. Violet took hold of the pram and ran for it.

The pram's wheels snagged and skipped in the mud. The jolts knocked the rubbish bag out, and Violet tripped over it, and fell forward onto the pram handle, sending the pram into a wheelie. Maria started to cry. Violet was out of breath already and they weren't even out the gates.

Beyond the marina gates was the main road. If they went up the road, the man would see them. She heard him shout after her. He would catch up with them soon.

There were bushes and what looked like the beginnings of a wood the other side of the road. Violet ran across, and pulled the pram through.

She lifted Maria out, "We're gonna have to leave your pram," she said.

Violet held Maria to her chest and pushed through the trees. Branches caught in her hair, and brambles pierced through her jeans, scratching her legs. Maria cried and struggled against her chest.

"Come out, you little bitch!" the man shouted.

Violet could hear branches snapping, but she had the size advantage over him, and could get through smaller gaps.

"I know you're in there!" he yelled, "I've got your pram!"

Violet carried on; she needed Maria to stop crying.

She ran when she could, but mostly had to push her way through tangles of bush and brambles. It was difficult to protect Maria's head and her own eyes at the same time, and her muscles burned from carrying her. The woods were wild and overgrown, and as she got deeper in, it was almost impossible to get through. She turned backwards, and used the backpack to break through the gaps.

Violet's chest was heaving, her breaths making a hollow rasping sound, and there was a taste of iron in her mouth. Sweat trickled down her back.

"Shhh," she said to Maria, "A bit further."

The man's cries became more distant, and she slowed down a bit. Violet could still hear movement, and snapping twigs. She jigged Maria up and down, uselessly, "Please! Shh."

Maria moved her head back, and cried loudly and forcefully.

Violet decided to risk a bottle. Her arms wouldn't hold out much longer anyway. There was a fallen tree with big curtains of ivy hanging down from it. Violet crawled through, sat against a broken bough, and wriggled out of the backpack. She pulled the still warm bottle out, and gave it to Maria. The baby took it straight away, sucking forcefully. Violet's breath still came in noisy gasps and she had to concentrate to keep quiet, and breathe slow.

The man wasn't shouting anymore. She heard some birds take flight somewhere off to her left, and she guessed he was giving up, or had gone in the wrong direction.

The woods were quiet, apart from Maria's sucking. She would hear if he came close again, and even if he snuck up on them, the bright yellow coat would give her a few seconds head start.

Maria moved in her arms, and Violet was aware of a bad pain in her forearm. She pulled up her sleeve. The running and banging into branches had opened the cut again. The masking tape was soaked with dark, fresh blood. Perhaps she should get another steak from somewhere to boost her iron count.

Violet leaned her head back against the damp bark. Her throat ached, and her eyes filled with tears. She wiped them away, and noticed her hand was covered in scratches and scuffs of mud and moss.

It was so stupid to have not taken the trusted route through the fields. The pram was lost now, and that man would be on the lookout for them. Fuck, he might tell people in the local pubs or anything. She looked down at Maria, her eyes were just partly open, and she was drinking slowly. Violet wiped some dribbled milk away with her cleanest finger.

"Don't worry," she said, "there's no way I'm giving up our boat."

Violet stayed sitting down until Maria was asleep. She decided to try to spread Maria's weight by zipping her into her leather jacket. She managed to zip the jacket halfway so it was supporting Maria's bottom half. A pattering started all around them; rain. Violet lifted her face to the sky for a moment, breathed in the damp earth smell, then started walking.

There wasn't much traffic noise to follow, but eventually Violet came out of the woods onto a road. It wasn't the road they normally followed, but a sign said 'Bembridge 1 ¼ miles'. When cars approached, she moved back into the bushes until they passed.

She wasn't sure how to avoid walking through the village centre, the only way she knew to the road they'd left the car in was straight through. It was probably good that they'd lost the pram. Maybe with Maria tucked in her jacket she could pass as a fat person from a distance. Violet's feet hurt. Her boots were damp from trudging through the woods and her toes rubbed against each other. She wasn't wearing socks, and blisters were starting on her heels.

The bushes and trees thinned out as they reached Bembridge and there was no choice but to walk on the side of the road. She guessed it was about 8 in the morning. An estate car slowed as it went by, and Violet saw two girls in school uniform staring out of the back window at her. She pulled her hood up.

They passed a newsagents with cars parked outside. The door swung open and an elderly couple exited, the man glancing in her direction. She kept her head down and walked on. They arrived at The King's Head next, and Violet wondered if Alex the bargirl was in there. Her neck and back hurt from carrying Maria; she imagined how nice it would feel to sit down and have a Bloody Mary, then she remembered it was too early anyway.

Bembridge was busy with schoolchildren and people heading to work in their cars, and Violet was glad for the rush. She made it out of the centre without being stopped and headed up the hill to find the road the car was parked in.

After a wrong turn down Ferney Rise, Violet found Ferney Crescent. At the far end, she could see the navy blue shape of her car.

When she reached the car, she noticed an A4 piece of paper in a transparent folder sellotaped to her windscreen. At the top of the page, in bold font was the underlined heading 'Polite Notice'. She tore it off, looked around, and got into the car with Maria.

Once inside she clambered into the back, put Maria in her car seat, and buckled her in.

Sitting back in the driver seat, she looked more closely at the notice.

"POLITE NOTICE: We have noticed your car parked here. Please be aware that this is a private road, and if the car is not removed we will assume it has been abandoned, and have it removed by the police. Mr and Mrs Hinds: residents."

Violet threw it in the back. Maria had woken up, and was wriggling in her seat, looking uncomfortable.

"I'm really starting to hate the Isle of Wight," Violet said.

She zeroed the mile counter, and decided to head back the way they'd driven when they first found Bembridge, as she remembered there being lots of trees. She would try not to go more than twenty miles. People walked at about 3 miles an hour, and a seven hour walk was manageable, and would put a good distance between them and the car. She got some CDs off the floor, and spotted the Camel Lights. She opened the packet and pulled the silver tab. Cigarette in mouth, she put The Pixies in the CD player, and waited for the car lighter to pop.

Maria squealed in the back.

"It's alright, we'll be moving soon...Yeah, don't worry, I'll open the window."

Violet lit her cigarette and inhaled. She wound down the window and left Ferney Crescent behind.

Maria stopped crying with the car's movement. Violet looked at her in the mirror, she was sucking her fist, and staring out of the window.

'Where is My Mind?' came on and Violet started to sing. The road was hilly with fast bends and she threw the car around, making Maria smile.

Violet turned down a small lane. The trees were thick and in places made an arch across the road, so it felt as though they were driving through a leaf tunnel. A muddy opening caught Violet's eye, and she pulled over to turn around. The muddy opening was an entrance to the perfect woodland car park.

The mile counter said 16. It was good that it wasn't more, as the walk would be difficult without the pram. She wasn't sure what to put in the backpack. There wasn't much supermarket food left; she packed Coco Pops, two cans of Fanta, the rest of the nappies, and a selection of their clothes. She also got the little Maglite torch out, and stuck it in the front pocket.

They had a bit of time to kill before starting their walk so Violet buckled Maria in and drove to get more formula milk.

They drove to St Helens, but it looked too little for supermarkets, and Violet didn't fancy stopping in another small town so close to Bembridge. She put The Pixies on again, and headed to Ryde. At a small roundabout she followed a sign saying Superstore, and arrived at a giant Sainsburys.

Maria sat in her car seat in the supermarket trolley the same as before, and Violet picked things off the shelf.

"One for you, Maria," she said, sliding a dark chocolate and almond bar down the side of the car seat.

She couldn't get too much, because it would have to be carried for miles on her back. The formula milk was unavoidable though, and more bananas.

Violet stopped at the meat counter and took a ticket. "What do you reckon, Maria?" she said, "steak tonight?"

Maria watched her, dribbling, Violet handed her the bunch of bananas to play with. The scab on her face felt tight, and itchy, she fought the urge to scratch, and pressed it instead feeling the itch turn to sting.

"Number 42!" the deli man called.

"Two fillet steaks please?"

He smiled at them, and wrinkles crossed his face. His uniform was bright white, and he wore a blue hygiene hat over his hair, and plastic gloves, "Certainly my dear. How thick would you like them?"

Violet held out her finger and thumb, "Two inches?"

"That's beautiful steak," he said, "Irish." His eyes were bright blue, and his eyebrows were long and white, and seemed to curl up when he smiled. Violet wondered what his hair looked like.

She watched him slice and weigh two thick pieces of steak.

He read off the display, "Eleven pounds and twenty pence, that alright for you?"

"Perfect," she said, and he printed off the barcode.

Maria chuckled in the pram.

"Yes, that was a wizard!" Violet said.

She walked away from the meat counter, and stuck the steaks behind Maria's back. Maria smiled and thumped the bananas on her lap.

* * *

Back in the car, Violet got out their money. Even with only paying for nappies, formula milk and bananas, she felt sick as she counted the notes. There were only four twenties left, and some change, leaving them with £81.27. She took a deep breath and tried to push the panic feeling to the back of her head, but it wouldn't go. There might be some cash in a pair of dirty jeans. In the back, Maria started to cry. Even with stealing half of what they needed, they couldn't go on much longer. She lit a cigarette and opened the window. A trolley attendant was heading towards them. She reversed out, and then drove out of the car park.

At some traffic lights, Violet flicked ash out of the window. A car pulled up next to them, and she looked over. The girl in the passenger seat put a hand up in a slow wave. Violet saw her reach to flick a heavy fringe out of her eyes. Violet looked away, quickly, a lump forming in her throat. They were following her. The cigarette slipped from her fingers and dropped down the side of the seat.

"Fuck," she said, trying to force her hand down the side to reach it. It wouldn't fit, and she felt sharp metal scratch her hand.

Car horns sounded behind her; the lights were green. A man in the car behind was shouting. She made out the words, 'Move' 'fuckin'…'STUPID COW' on his lips.

She glanced to the side. The car with Charlotte and Paul was gone. Violet moved forward and pulled over at the side of the road to try and get the cigarette. A plastic smell of singed carpet snaked into her nostrils.

The car with the angry man inside screeched past, as she got out and bent down to find the cigarette. Maria was screaming at full volume, as Violet finally grabbed the cigarette between her fingertips and pulled it out from under the seat. She stood up, and shut the door behind her. Maria's crying was softened and muted, behind the glass and metal. Violet leaned against the car and finished the cigarette. Her fingers shook; instead of blood running through her body, it felt like hundreds of glass marbles.

27

The good thing about being in class 4 is Art. Instead of doing Art in the Junior School rooms which are just normal classrooms with sinks at the back, we get to go in the art studio. There are huge wooden benches with marks on them like Dad's workbench in his garage. Some of the benches have little drawings on them, and scratches where people have been using knives. All along one side of the room are proper artists' easels. Not everyone in the class knows that they are called easels, but I do because Grandad has one. There are drawers with all different kinds of pencils and paints in: powder paints, poster paints, tubes of oil paints, some pastels, and lots of different kinds that I don't even know the name of. There are big cupboards at the back of the room with different sizes and sorts of paper like tracing paper, and bright coloured card. As well as that kind of art stuff, there is a long table down one side of the room where you can do pottery, and even a potter's wheel, and a huge, extra hot oven for clay called a kiln.

Our art teacher is short with spiky silver hair that stands up like a punk's. She looks older than Mum and Dad, but has really bright eyes like a pixie. She wears long skirts that touch the ground, and I imagine that she isn't walking, and doesn't have feet, but is hovering like a fairy. Her name is Miss Farr. Some people in the class call her Miss Fart, and say that we are going to Fart Class. It would be funny if instead of paints, all the bottles and jars of different things were actually collections of farts made by rare and extinct creatures.

There are a few people sitting at each of the wooden benches. In my group there is me, Ruth, and two girls called Mary and Harriet who look almost the same even though they're not sisters. They are nice, but hardly ever talk to anyone except each other. They've both got brown hair which they have in pigtails, and they wear glasses. Mary is a bit fatter than Harriet, and Harriet has two moles on her cheek. Gemma is sat on the bench behind us with John the boy with freckles from the climbing frame, a big boy with curly hair called George who is always sneaking food into his mouth from his pockets, and the twins, Alex and Aidan who I like because they are always making jokes. I think they invented the name Miss Fart, and they call fat Mrs Cobb 'Egg on Legs' which is funny because she even walks like an egg would if it had legs, with her legs moving out in a circle before going forward.

Miss Farr says, "Okay everybody, today you have some freedom!"

Everyone goes quiet.

"In a minute I'll give you all an A1 piece of cartridge paper, and then you can choose your tools... pencil, felt-tip pens, oil pastels, or poster paint. You can use any of those, but you can't mix them. Stick to one style."

Gemma puts her hand up, "Miss, can I use coloured pencil?"

"No," Miss Farr says, "I don't like coloured pencil, and if you're using pencil I'd be far more excited to see you do some shading, like we learnt last week."

Gemma shrugs, and makes a bored face, "Guess I'll use felt tips."

Gemma is the oldest person in our class. She is actually two years older than me because she had to go down a year because her family spent a year in South Africa and she didn't go to school there.

Miss Farr is handing out the paper. I lay mine out in front of me.

"What are you going to use, Violet?" Ruth asks.

"Fat felt-tip pens, like Rolf Harris on Cartoon Time."

"I think I'm going to paint," she says.

Miss Farr stops handing out paper and says, "I forgot to say, you can use a pencil to plan your work out. So everyone get yourselves a pencil if you like as well as the other stuff. If you prefer to just work straight on the paper, you can do that too... whatever you like."

The room gets noisy with everyone getting their pencils and paints.

"Another thing!" Miss Farr shouts, "This is a big project. We'll be working on it for the next four or five weeks, so take your time and make it something really special... a masterpiece!"

"Miss!" Gemma shouts, "What are we supposed to be drawing?"

"I don't know," Miss Farr says, "It's up to you. The only thing I want you to do is use the space you have. You have a big piece of paper, and I'd like you to fill it with anything you feel like. You could draw something to do with your family, or nature, or school, or something totally imaginary."

Miss Farr sits down at her desk and closes her eyes for a while, then opens them and stares out of one of the big windows.

"Are we allowed to talk?" Gemma asks.

Miss Farr keeps staring out the window. She smiles and says, "Yes, of course you can talk."

Ruth touches my hand, "What are you going to draw, Violet?"

"I don't know," I say, "Maybe a cartoon of the playground with everyone playing, but there are monsters hiding in the school and bushes. What are you going to do?"

Ruth is very quiet and sometimes it's hard to hear her speak. She is biting her nails, and I see that her nails are really short and the ends of her fingers are all pink.

"I think, an angel," she says.

Miss Farr sits at her desk drinking from a mug, and sometimes drawing something. She only walks around the room twice to see what we are doing. When she talks to people she is really quiet, almost whispering.

She gets to Ruth before me, and I hear her say, "The lines are lovely," and "Don't be afraid to make her bigger, she's beautiful."

I have sketched the octagon and Matthew falling in mid-air. Adam is on the top beating his hands on his chest like a gorilla. Underneath the two hunchbacked ladies from the care centre are holding out a trampoline to catch him. I have left spaces for the forest and the mansion. I don't know whether to put wolves in the mansion or monsters.

Miss Farr puts her hand on the bench next to my picture. She has short nails which are painted green, and a ring with an orange jewel in it on her little finger. She says very close to my ear, "Wow! You've got a lot going on there. Good details though, I can tell who everyone is. What are you going to colour it with? Paint?"

"Fat felt-tip pens."

"Mmm," she says, "Be careful not to do the pencil lines too dark, or they'll show through the pen."

She smells like lemons, much nicer than Mrs Martin and her sickly coffee smell. Then she says to me and Ruth, "You're a talented pair. If you like, you can come to my extra class on Thursdays after school. Ask your parents."

* * *

At the end of school I go and wait for Mum in the car park. I sit on a tree trunk kicking my shoes in the gravel. Someone's hands cover my eyes. I scream and kick because I think it's the hunchback. I jump up and trip on the tree trunk and my school bag falls in the mud. Someone starts laughing.

"Got you," Adam says.

I smile but feel strange inside like I'm full of cold water. "I thought you were the hunchback," I say.

"I crept up on you for ages, all the way from the gym."

I'm a bit angry that I didn't notice him. "Oh. Well done."

He is smiling a lot because he frightened me. "What's it like in the Middle School?" he asks.

"Okay. At least there's no Esther stinking out the classroom."

"You're lucky," he says, and stops smiling, "I brought my gameboy in today, and Esther told Mrs Martin, and she took it. My dad's gonna be really angry. I wasn't supposed to take it to school."

Adam's mum is really nice, and lets Adam do what he wants, but Adam's dad is a policeman and quite scary. He tells Adam and his brother off a lot.

"Say you lent it to me because I was sad about my brother," I say.

Adam holds out his hand, "Brainwave!" he says, "Gimme five."

"Adam!" someone calls, and we see Adam's mum calling from her car.

"Gotta go," Adam says, and runs to the car.

"Violet, come here!" his mum shouts, so I go up to the car. "Do you want to come swimming with us on Saturday? Ask your mum… tell her to call me."

"Okay, I will," I say.

When Mum arrives, we walk home together holding hands. She isn't speaking much, and only says 'yes' or 'mm hmm' when I tell her stuff. I keep talking anyway. Her hand feels cold and dry.

When we get home, she gives me lentil soup. We eat it together. I am eating much faster than her.

"Can we watch telly together tonight, Mum?"

She breaks off a piece of bread crust and says, "No, we have to go to the hospital tonight. Dad and I have got our special class, and you've got yours too."

Because my brother died, we have to meet up with other people who have had cot deaths.

"Do I have to go?" I say.

I hate the care group. Everyone just eats jam sandwiches and draws pictures, and the other children are babyish. There is a horrible fat girl who cries all the time. She had a little sister who died a whole year ago. I think she is just one of those people who can make themselves cry so everyone feels sorry for them.

Mum doesn't say anything. I tear my bread into pieces and drop them in the soup. I push them under with my spoon.

"Can't I come in your and Dad's class?"

The doorbell rings and Mum sighs, and goes to answer it. The pieces of bread have absorbed the soup, and now there are just lots of pieces of heavy bread in the bowl. I put one in my mouth. It's all squashy like baby food.

I hear my mum start talking loudly, so I go to see who is there.

There is a man at the door holding an encyclopaedia. He has a big shopping bag with lots of encyclopaedias in it. Mum is holding one and she is crying. The man is reaching out to take the encyclopaedia from her and looks like he wants to leave.

"Okay, Madam. Thanks for listening," he says.

Mum is holding the encyclopaedia really tight and shaking it like she wants to break it. "They're just fucking words!" she shouts.

"Please, if you'll just hand me the book," the man says. He sees me and sort of smiles.

I stay by the key cupboard. I don't think Mum has seen me yet. She sounds horrible when she swears, it's like it isn't actually my mum.

"Fucking books! Fucking KNOWLEDGE!" she screams, "It doesn't mean ANYTHING!" When she says 'anything', she kind of growls. She holds the book up over her head, and I think she might hit the man if he doesn't move. I go and hold Mum's sleeve. She moves her chin a little bit towards me, but doesn't look. She is shivering, and I can feel her arm shaking through her sleeve.

The man lifts his bag up and moves backwards. He trips as he steps off the doormat. He says, "I'll just come back later for the book." He looks frightened of Mum.

Mum doesn't care that she's scared him. She throws the encyclopaedia at him and he puts his arms over his head. The encyclopaedia hits the ground and skids on its cover. "Leave us alone!" she shouts, and slams the door so hard I think the glass almost breaks. Mum kneels down on the floor with her arms covering her face.

Everything is quiet in the house. It is as if the slam of the door

175

has blasted away all the other noises. I look up the stairs and see Cupid looking at us through one of the banisters. His eyes are big and scared and his ears are pointed back.

Then Mum makes a horrible groaning breathing noise, and starts rocking and crying. I put my arms around her and cuddle her, but I don't think she even knows I am there.

28

Trance Nation played as they drove up the winding road back to the car park. As they pulled in, Violet saw a silver car with two men and a woman standing beside it. They turned and stared at her.

"Fuck," Violet said.

She stopped near the entrance, and touched the radio, trying not to look across at them. Maybe they were dogging. Once Violet had found a clearing in the woods like a natural cubicle with loads of unopened condoms balanced in the branches ready for anyone who might need one. There were all kinds, in assorted coloured packets like sweets or decorations on some x-rated Christmas tree. She couldn't remember why she'd been there or who with, maybe it was a party that she'd walked off from, but the condom clearing was kind of amazing; it reminded her of Charlie and the Chocolate Factory.

Violet looked up, and saw one of the men walking over.

She tried to reverse, but accelerated too hard, and the tyres spun in the mud. She reversed again more gently and felt the wheels grip and bump over a root.

The man was tall with a skinhead that gleamed, and a wide, ham-coloured face.

"Hang on a minute, Darling!" he called.

He was walking fast, holding his hand up like a policeman.

Violet accelerated, and heard sandy gravel spray up and scatter behind as she left the car park. In the mirror she could see him standing, staring after them.

"Fuck!" she shouted, and punched the door.

A few miles up the road there was another car park, but it was too open, and visible from the road. She pulled in anyway, and got out.

Violet walked a little way into the woods and crouched down behind a tree. Dry leaves crunched under her boots. Her wee burned; she should drink more water.

Back in the car, she looked through the shopping; baby milk or Fanta. She took out a Fanta, and the Camel Lights, and went to sit on the bonnet. There were two other cars parked, both with dog gates in the back. It wasn't as cold today, and Violet smoked slowly, listening to a pigeon calling somewhere above.

Leaves rustled nearby and Violet heard low voices. A Dalmatian appeared, followed by a young couple. They glanced over, and she smiled. The man nodded, and they headed to one of the cars. Violet watched as they wiped the dog's feet with baby wipes, before opening the hatch back. "Good boy, Pongo," she heard the girl say, as the dog jumped in.

After a while, Maria woke up and started to cry.

Violet got back in the car. "Yeah, you definitely need changing," she said. She left the door open, and changed Maria's nappy on the back seat. Maria cried, and struggled.

"You'll enjoy your dinner more if you're clean," Violet said, "I'll do your bottle in a minute."

There was a plastic bag with another nappy already in it, and she put the dirty nappy, baby wipes, and some other rubbish in it, and tied it up. On the other side of the car park there was a red, dog poo bin, and she carried the plastic bag over and stuffed it as well as she could through the little opening. Maria's crying sounded strange in the woods, where the only other noises were birds.

Violet took out a ready-made bottle, and put it between her thighs to warm. She turned the radio on; 'My Achy Breaky Heart' sang out from the speakers, and Violet reached back and took one of Maria's hands, shaking it to the tune.

After Maria had her finished her bottle, Violet started driving back to their car park. Halfway there, she saw a man limping on the side of the road. He was dragging one leg badly, and his face looked bumped out of shape like a Buffy vampire. She recognised his hair from somewhere, and slowed down, winding down the window.

"Sergio?" she called.

He turned round. One eye was swollen shut.

"Hello there," he said, and moved his split lips into a half smile. Violet saw a flash of gold. "Do you want a lift?" she asked.

Sergio looked quickly up and down the road, then hobbled over and pulled open the passenger door.

Violet turned down *Trance Nation* to a tinny background beat. Sergio kept sniffing and wiping blood away as it dribbled out of his nose. He tilted his head back, and leaned against the headrest. Violet looked in the mirror; Maria was asleep, her mouth part-open.

"Do you want a cigarette?" Violet asked.

"Yes, thank you," Sergio replied and held out his hand for the packet.

They lit their cigarettes, and Violet wound down her window. She saw Sergio search for the switch, and then do the same.

Violet watched the muddy opening of her car park roll into view. She couldn't stop there now. Sergio had turned to stare at the car park too, and Violet accelerated past, a heavy feeling rolling into her guts as she abandoned her plan for a second time.

Violet threw her cigarette butt out of the window. "Where do you want to go?" she asked.

The cigarette in his fingers had a length of ash building up at the end. He turned to Violet. His eye was like something built for special effects, papier maché sculpted over a tennis ball to make a bulging Mr. Hyde eyeball.

"I'm sorry," he said, "I should not get in. I don' have somewhere to go."

Violet watched the road. She could feel him looking at her, waiting for some helpful suggestion.

His voice cracked as he spoke, "I have some trouble."

She saw blood gather in his right nostril, she thought he might start crying. His cigarette remained between his fingers, the ash on the end was about two inches long.

"You should flick that," Violet said, "it'll fall on your trousers."

Sergio held his cigarette into the wind, took a last drag, and then let it fly out of the car. He leaned his head back again, and sniffed.

They reached the main road, and Violet paused, then took the Ryde and St Helens direction. The sky was turning grey, and murky. Her head was too full, her thoughts muffled and suffocating as if there was stuff piled on top of them.

"We have some trouble too," she said.

Sergio coughed, and smiled, "Yes, I hear from Joanne."

Violet looked at him, and then touched the scab on her cheek. "Oh, yeah. No, not that," she paused. "We've got someone after us."

He sat forward, "Who?"

Too many answers came into her head, "Maria's Dad," she said.

Sergio frowned, glanced back at Maria, then back at Violet. She'd obviously given Maria a different name before. He was looking at her like a counsellor, waiting, prepared to be impassive to anything she had to say. She wished she hadn't picked him up.

"I was going to leave the car in that car park, and walk. So, I don't really know where to go now either."

They drove in silence, the trees rolling past becoming wiry hedges. A few spots of rain speckled the windscreen. Eventually Maria began to cry, breaking the quiet, and Sergio turned round to her.

"Hello, darrling," he said rolling his 'r'. He talked softly, and started to play 'this little piggy' with her toes. Violet wondered if Maria thought he was a friendly bumpy faced monster, or if she recognised him from the Bucket o' Mussels.

"This little piggy is going to marrrrrrkit, this little piggy is staying home, this piggy has rrrost beef, this little piggy has non...'

Maria had stopped crying. She chuckled when he said, "weeeeeeeeeeeeeeeeeeeeeee."

Without turning round, Sergio said, "If you like, I know somewhere you can leave the car?"

Violet yawned, "Yeah?" she said, "Is it far?"

He sat back in his seat; Maria seemed appeased, and was watching Violet.

"It's a place close to St Helen's," he said. "One of my friend's, Sam, he is away for winter, chartering the yachts."

"That sounds perfect," said Violet.

From St Helens Sergio directed them out onto a country road for a mile.

"Here," he said, and Violet stopped next to the start of a drive. There were thick hedges surrounding the entrance. Sergio got out to open a wooden gate. She saw him wince as he put weight on the injured leg, and then lean on the gate to wave them through. With the car slowed down, Maria began to cry.

"Keep cool," Violet said. "Hey, we're at a farm!" Maria frowned and cried louder.

Sergio got back in and Violet followed grassy tyre tracks past a dilapidated shed with a corrugated iron roof.

Either side of the track there were overgrown blackberry bushes and nettles.

They came to an open area with a stone cottage. All around were broken bits of boats, and bulky shapes under tarpaulins weighed down with bricks.

"This is great," Violet said.

"We can put your car under some plastic sheet," Sergio said, "or there is a garage, but maybe he's full."

"A plastic sheet is fine."

"Do you want to come into the house, and change the…. " he patted his bum.
Violet noticed the nappy smell that was filling the car. "Oh. Yeah, please." she said.

"I will come around to let you in," he said, and he got out and limped away behind the house.

* * *

Maria lay in a clean nappy, in front of the fire. Violet sat next to her, watching her kick her legs about, enjoying the heat.

"Fire," Violet said, "fire."

Maria looked at the flames and gurgled.

Sergio came into the lounge with a bag of frozen peas, a bottle of wine and two glasses.

"Chablis," he said, "very good one."

Violet watched him pour a small amount into a glass, and sniff it hard. He'd washed his face, but there was still a thin line of dried blood around his nostrils like an outline. He took a sip, and swilled the wine around in his mouth, blowing out his cheeks as if he was about to squirt it out of his mouth. He swallowed, "It's good," he said," and poured her a glass.

Violet took a gulp. It was good, and very cold. "We have to go soon," she said.

Sergio put his wine on a coffee table covered with a sarong, and lifted Maria up into the air above his head. He twirled her around and she smiled and opened her mouth.

"Do you go back to the mainland?" he asked.

"No," Violet said, "We're going to France."

"You can speak French?" He had Maria in his arms and seemed to be dancing to a rhythm.

Violet felt a warm fizzing sensation start in her temples from the alcohol, and she refilled her glass. "A bit," she said, "What are you doing in the Isle of Wight anyway, wouldn't you rather be in Madeira?"

Sergio stopped dancing. He laid Maria down on the carpet and put the frozen peas against his face, then knelt down next to her. His cheek and eye were still bumped out of proportion, and the firelight on his face highlighted all the unusual bumps, and made shadows where there wouldn't normally be any.

"I left because I didn't want to do the national service. I can not go back."

"Oh," she said, "So why the Isle of Wight?"

He turned to face her, "I have an uncle who has restaurant in

Newport. I came to work for him... but I left."

Sergio took the peas away from his face. "He was having affair with all the waitresses. One of them has only fifteen years old, and I tell him to stop, and he said to fuck off and mind my business and they are looking after me letting me stay, then I say if he doesn't stop I am going to tell my aunt. And he doesn't stop. One of these girls has pregnant and..." he stopped, slightly out of breath, and picked up his glass.

"Did you tell your aunt?" Violet asked.

"Yes. She tell him he have to sleep in another room until he stops."

"Right."

"Then my uncle says I must leave, and my aunt says it's better if I leave too, so I go and take a job at the Bucket of Mussel."

"How long have you been on the Isle of Wight?"

"Two year."

"Fuck," Violet said, "aren't you bored?"

"Summertime is very nice, more people are here, and I have friends around... go fishing, and sailing."

They watched Maria, as she turned herself over, and lay with her chest lifted off the floor, supported on her arms.

"Did your uncle do that to your face?" Violet asked

Sergio stared into the fire, "No, not my uncle... I owe some debt. I am making extra money with the horses to pay it back, and then I don' win for some time. So today they tell me that I am taking too long." He stopped talking and drank some wine.

Violet wondered what it was like to be addicted to something. Even though she drank everyday with Lisa, and took a lot of drugs, she knew she could stop if she wanted; maybe she didn't care about things enough to be addicted to them. "Is there anymore wine?" she asked.

Sergio smiled and the bump over his eye lifted a little. The eye wasn't completely shut anymore, and a dark slit gleamed in the middle of the distended lump. A black bruise ran from his eye to his cheek, the edges were bluish and unnaturally straight, probably from the edge of a boot.

"There is a crate," he said, "My friend won't mind."

Violet leaned back on the sofa. The room was scruffy, like the rest of the cottage, but full of stuff. There were crowded bookshelves, a couple of big canvas paintings of waves, and a standing wooden sculpture of a man in tribal dress holding a surfboard. It would be good chartering yachts, travelling the world and getting paid for it. She picked Maria up and put her on the sofa. Next to the fire was a rainmaker. She brought it over, turned it upside down and made it rattle for Maria. Maria reached out, and Violet let her take hold of it. Immediately she put her mouth on it, and started chewing.

The fire was hot. It reminded Violet of the Christmas she threw the Woody Woodpecker toy in the fire so it could go to heaven or something, some artificial material inside, stinking as it burned and filling the house so her Mum came in, and burnt the lounge carpet trying to pull him out.

Maria dropped the rainmaker, and it hit the floor with a noise of shifting beads. Her lips turned downwards, and she looked up at Violet. Violet picked it up, and watched her take it in both hands again and put it to her mouth.

* * *

Violet woke up alone in the lounge. She didn't know how long she'd been asleep. The fire was still glowing but not giving out much heat. The cottage was completely silent.

"Sergio!" Violet called out. Her shout was swallowed up in the thick silence so quickly she wasn't even sure if she'd made a noise.

"Sergio!" she shouted again, "Where's Maria?" *Where's Maria where's Maria…Oh Seeeeeerrrrrrgio, Surgeeeeeeoh.* Her own voice filled her ears, and she rushed out of the lounge to get away from it. The room she ran into was a small kitchen. An empty wine bottle and a half-full one stood on the side, next to a glass still with wine in it. "Sergio!" she shouted.

She pulled open the back door and went outside. It was getting dark; her car was still there at least.

"Maria!" she shouted, her voice sounding shrill and dramatic.

From the other side of the cottage, Sergio called out, "Esther? We're coming!"

Violet headed towards the voice and saw Sergio walking towards her, carrying Maria.

She reached out and took Maria.

"Esther?" he said, "Are you okay?"

"My name's not fucking Esther!" Her heart began to slow from frantic to normal, and she put her chin against Maria's hair.

"I am sorry," he said, "You are sleeping, and she's starting crying so I bring her to find the plastic sheet."

"Don't take her like that again. I don't know you."

"I don' know you either," he said, and walked away.

Violet went round to the rear of the cottage where there was a muddy field. It didn't look as though anything was growing in it. About halfway down a scarecrow with gleaming eyes made out of CDs was leaning over on his pole, a long jacket swaying in the breeze.

Violet shivered.

"Creepy scarecrow," she said.

Maria looked in the direction Violet was pointing then turned round and pulled Violet's hair.

Violet extracted her hair from Maria's fist, repositioned her on her shoulder and started to walk back towards the house.

When they went into the lounge, Sergio was putting more coals on the fire.

Violet said, "I'm going to make her a bottle. Can you watch her for a minute?"

"Sure." He threw a last block of coal in, then stood up and took Maria from her.

"Thanks," she said

"So, what is your name?" His mouth lifted at one side in a half smile, and she saw the gold tooth.

Violet pushed her hair back and looked at him, "Violet."

29

Mum's tummy is really big now. She says that soon the baby will be born.

"Is it a boy or girl?" I ask.

"I don't know."

"Can't you tell a bit?"

"No, not really…. Violet, the baby's kicking, feel it quick!"

Mum lifts up her sweatshirt and I put my hand on her tummy. Her tummy button has stretched and is really big. I wonder if because Mrs Cobb is so fat, her belly button is as big as a plate. Suddenly the baby kicks hard. I see Mum's tummy bump up just next to my hand. I put my hand where it kicked and it does it again.

"Ooh," she says, "I felt that one!"

"It's really strong!" I say, "Maybe it's going to grow up to be a karate expert."

Mum goes upstairs and I finish my breakfast. When I lift the cereal bowl up to drink the milk, I spill some on my blazer. Cupid is on the windowsill, and I hold my blazer out to him. He looks at me, wondering what I want, but then he sniffs the milk and licks it off. I wish me and Cupid could swap bodies for a day, and he could go to school, pretending to be me, and I could run up tree trunks, and explore all the neighbours' gardens without getting told off. Even if one of them did shout, or try and spray me with a hose, I would be too fast for them to catch me anyway. Cupid jumps down, and goes out of his cat flap.

I get my school bag, and then climb onto the windowsill to see if I can spot him. Mum comes back into the kitchen. "Come on then," she says, "let's go."

Cupid is crouching down in a flowerbed going to the toilet. I bang on the window, and he turns round quick, and then runs off.

Behind me, Mum says, "That wasn't very nice."

"He doesn't care," I say.

"Yes he does," she says, "You wouldn't like it if he came in and scared you when you were on the toilet."

I climb down, and pick up my school bag.

"Come on, Violet," Mum says.

As we are crossing the main road, I get this funny feeling in my head, and all down my back, like someone has just jumped out and frightened me. I think I feel something move in my head, and my arms and legs go all tingly. I let go of Mum's hand so she doesn't feel it. It is like there is something sitting in my head, and it knows that I know it's in there so it's staying really still.

When we are halfway up the hill Mum says, "Oh, I forgot the carrots for the horses."

I don't want to feed the horses anyway, I want to go home and back to bed. I won't be able to though. If I pretend I'm ill, I'll end up in the Care Centre. The thing in my head feels like it might jump out.

"I'm going to run the rest of the way, Mum."

Mum looks a bit funny, and she says, "I can run with you."

"The baby will get bumped around."

"Don't be silly," she says.

Then this grown-up voice in my head says, "Bog off!"

I don't think Mum hears it, but I feel scared. I want to cuddle her, but I don't want her to hear the horrible things.

"Bye," I say, and start to run.

"Good Riddance to bad rubbish," the voice says, and then snorts and starts rustling about in my ears. I run really fast, and hope that the thing falls out or gets knocked about and dies.

Behind me I hear Mum say something about carrots after

school.

I think if I don't see anybody the voice might get bored and go away. I go through the car park, and see Adam getting out of his mum's car. I run off down the hill. Instead of going to registration I go into the trees near where the hunchback caretaker's hut is. I push my way through the bushes. I am a bit out of breath and I can hear panting in my head. I'm not sure if it's me doing it, or if the voice is out of breath too. I make sure I'm in the bushes really deep, and then climb up a tree. The bark has got moss on it, and it's slippery. I sit on a branch and wait. I put my arms round the trunk, cuddling it like a koala. The bark is cold and knobbly on my cheek, and I close my eyes. I can hear some people shouting in the distance, and some laughing. After a while I can't hear anyone anymore because they are probably all in registration. There is a far away ringing noise, which is the bell.

I sit in the tree for ages, and the thing in my head doesn't say anything. I get a bit bored so I climb another tree. It doesn't have any low branches so I have to run and jump to grab the lowest branch with my hands, and then pull myself up. I hang upside down like a bat. Mum says you go dizzy when you hang upside down because all the blood runs up to your head. I stay upside down for ages. My head hurts, and I can hear a noise like a heartbeat banging in my ears. I squeeze my eyes shut tight, and imagine I'm someone who can't feel pain like a fire walker, and maybe the horrible voice is drowning in all my blood that is rushing down into my head.

I pull myself back onto the branch, and everything turns grey and white. I wobble and almost fall off. The dizzy feeling is nice, and all the trees look strange with no proper colour. The colour starts to come back, and the dizzy feeling goes away. I can't remember what first lesson is, so I get my timetable out of my bag, it's Maths. I will wait till I hear the bell for the end of first lesson and then go straight to second lesson, which is Art.

Everybody else is sitting down already when I get there. Miss Farr is explaining what we're doing today. She doesn't stop talking, but hands me a piece of paper.

I normally sit with Gemma and the boys in Art, but all they do is talk, and today I just feel like being quiet and drawing. I go and sit in my old place next to Ruth.

She smiles at me as I sit down.

"Okay, everybody!" Miss Farr says, "In pairs you can go up to the table and choose two or three of the objects there for your still lifes."

I look at the things on the table. There is a sheep's skull that I quite want to draw, but Alex and Aidan get it because their table is called up before mine and Ruth's.

"Violet and Ruth. You two come up and pick your objects," Miss Farr calls.

I follow Ruth and look at the stuff on the table. Ruth chooses a small, bluey green eggshell and a bunch of dried purple flowers. I don't really want anything apart from the skull so I just pick an apple and a banana. Underneath the banana is a small ornament of a donkey with a blanket over him, and a rope around his neck. One of his ears has got chipped off. I take him too.

We all start arranging our still lifes and I lean the banana against the apple, then stand the donkey there like he's sheltering in a cave. There is a chipped bit on his blanket. I think he's the donkey from the nativity scene but Mary has got broken off, and the chipped bits are where her legs would be. Ruth touches my hand.

I look at her and feel funny like I'm sleepy, or awake in the middle of the night.

"What?" I say.

She points to her dried up flowers, and says, "They're violets... like your name."

"Oh."

"They're lucky."

"I hate my name," I say, "It's soppy."

"I think it's nice," she says, and starts to sketch out her flowers.

* * *

At break, instead of going to find Adam, or hanging around with Gemma, I go and sit on the wall by the boarders' dormitory. I look up into the clouds. I think about spinning round really fast and lying down to watch everything spin, but I can't be bothered so just stare up at the sky which is bright blue today with a few clouds. The clouds look like the ones in cartoons, and are perfect cloud shape. I get off the wall and lay on my back so I don't have to look up to stare at the sky.

A shadow goes across me, and I stop daydreaming and see Mrs Martin. The wind blows a bit, and I see her petticoat and horrible beige coloured tights, and bony legs like a really old man's. She is staring at me in a strange way, and smiling.

"Well, get up then!" she says.

I am still lying on the ground and will probably get a detention for not standing up straight away and saying 'Good Morning Mrs Martin'. I stand up.

"How's your mother doing?" she says.

"She's okay."

"It was nice meeting her at Parents' Evening. It seems like ages ago. Your father's very good-looking isn't he!" Then she giggles like Heather or Poppy would do, and puts her hand over her mouth.

I start to walk away, but she grabs my shoulder, and turns me round to carry on talking.

UGLY BEAST UGLY BEAST UGLY BEAST UGLY BEAST UGLY BEAST UGLY BEAST UGLY BEAST UGLY BEAST UGLY BEAST UGLY BEAST UGLY BEAST UGLY UGLY UGLY UGLY UG

Mrs Martin crouches down next to me. "You're very quiet today, Violet; that's not like you! You know, it's very rude to not say thank you when someone pays you a compliment."

The voice starts singing GO AWAY DOG'S BREATH, GO AWAY DOG'S BREATH! It sounds the same as the school dinner song.

If I don't say anything, Mrs Martin will probably give me detention, and she'll find out about the voice anyway.

I say quickly, "Sorry, Mrs Martin... I've got a sore throat."

I shut my mouth quickly, and move away so her hand slips off my shoulder.

DOG'S BREATH, the voice says.

Mrs Martin stands up and puts her hands on her hips. "Perhaps you should stay inside if you're not feeling well. We could sit inside..."

"I'm doing an errand," I say.

Before she can tell me off, I sprint towards the mansion. I don't think the voice likes it when I'm running, because the school dinner song gets quieter and quieter and my head fills up with the noise of my footsteps hitting the ground. Maybe the voice isn't evil, it might just be naughty, though it said those horrible things to Mum.

I slow down, and listen to the place in my head where the voice sits. I think it is gone. I am panting from running so fast, so I slow down and sit down against the wall of the mansion.

There is a little barred window next to me on the ground and I peer down into it. I think it's where the basement is. It is too dark to see anything, and there is a quiet noise coming from down there like the sound when you put your ear against a sea shell, and it doesn't sound like the sea, but something else. I stand up and walk to the bushes behind the mansion.

There's a place in the bushes where you can crawl through, and it is like a room inside. Some children call it The Glen, but Adam, Matthew and I call it The Green Chamber. We sometimes go there to play, or if we want to do anything secret. Adam and Matthew are probably on the climbing frame. I like them better than the boys in my class, and I miss seeing what Joanna is making in Home Economics.

As I'm crawling in I hear people talking. I stand up, and go through the next layer of bushes, and see Esther, Heather, and Poppy. Poppy sees me and taps Esther on the shoulder. They all turn round.

Behind them, Hannah is tied up to a tree trunk with French Elastic. Her arms are sticking out and tied to another branch so she looks like Jesus. Heather is holding a pair of nail scissors, and a piece of Hannah's hair, which she hides in her fist when she sees me.

There are tears on Hannah's cheeks, and she is crying, but trying to hold it in so she is gulping, and sniffing.

It is all quiet in my head now, but I'm tired and wish they weren't all here where I was coming to hide. I feel sorry for Hannah, but annoyed with her as well for always crying, and letting people like Esther boss her around.

"What are you doing to her?" I ask.

Esther puts her hands on her hips, "Mind your own business!" she says.

Poppy smiles in a sneaky way like a cartoon cat, "We're punishing her," she says.

Esther turns round and puts her finger on her lips, "Shh!" she says, and Poppy stops smiling, and looks at Heather who has put the scissors behind her back.

"What are they doing, Hannah?" I say.

Hannah looks at me, and just gulps and sniffs again. Esther is glaring at everyone.

"Go away," Esther says, "Or we'll get you!"

I look at Poppy, who is twisting one of her long plaits around, "What are you doing, Poppy?"

Poppy looks at Esther, and then says, "We're cutting her hai…"

"Shut up, Poppy!" Esther shouts, "Or we'll do yours too."

Poppy stops smiling, and holds on to her plait. We're not supposed to have really long hair, but when Poppy's is down she can sit on it. She got a note written so she didn't have to cut it.

Hannah's hair is flat and brown, and only as long as her chin.

Esther says, "Hannah's vain and we need to teach her a lesson."

Heather and Poppy start giggling, and Esther says, "Behold this wicked girl! Heather, raise the scissors!"

They burst out laughing and it sounds horrible, like pigs squealing.

Hannah is just standing there. She's only tied up with French Elastic so she could probably just pull her arms out of it anyway.

"Move Hannah!" I say, but Hannah just closes her eyes, and stays still, waiting for Heather to cut her hair.

"For God's sake, Hannah!" I shout, and Esther, Heather and

Poppy all look at each other, not knowing whether to grab me or not.

"You're dead!" Esther says, but I push her out the way and go up to Hannah and start untying her.

There is a crash behind us, and we all turn around and see Mrs Martin bent over, pushing through the bushes. "Freeze!" she shouts, and we all stop moving.

We all look at each other, and then me and Esther start speaking at the same time.

"Silence!" Mrs Martin says. She is still crouched down because it is too low for her.

"Poppy, untie Hannah please."

Poppy looks like she might cry, and she walks up to Hannah and starts unwinding the elastic.

"Come over here, Violet!" Mrs Martin shouts, so I walk up to her. "I knew you were up to no good."

"I was stopping them!" I shout, and she grabs hold of me, and covers my mouth with her hand.

Poppy has untied Hannah and now Esther, Heather, Poppy and Hannah are staring at Mrs Martin and me.

"What was Violet doing, girls?" Mrs Martin asks.

Heather looks at Esther. I wish Hannah would say something, but her and Poppy are both looking at the ground.

Nobody knows what to say, and we all stand there looking around. I try to move, but Mrs Martin holds me tighter and a bit of her hand touches my teeth, so I stay still and watch Esther and Heather.

Then Esther says, "Violet was cutting Hannah's hair."

"Liar!" I shout, but Mrs Martin holds my mouth even tighter and grips me against her. The scissors are still in Heather's hand.

Grandad says there's not much you can do if someone's got you in a headlock, but it's always worth trying a kick to the shins. I pull my foot back and kick Mrs Martin as hard as I can where I think her shin is.

"Ah!" she screams and bends down to rub her leg. I run so I'm standing next to Heather.

"I'm sorry Mrs Martin," I say, "But it wasn't me, I was trying to stop them. Heather was cutting her hair, look at the scissors!"

Mrs Martin has tears in her eyes, and looks angrier than I've ever seen. She rushes towards me, and I think she is going to hit me, but she stops.

"Liar!" she shouts.

My face is getting hotter and hotter. "It wasn't me!" I say, "Ask Hannah."

Nobody else has said anything for ages. Esther's face has gone white, and Poppy has started to cry. Heather's mouth is open.

Mrs Martin stands up straight and her head goes into the leaves, so she has to lean it to one side. She looks at Hannah, and smiles her mean smile.

"Alright then, Hannah. Who cut your hair?"

Now we all look at Hannah. Her legs are shaking and she is just staring at the ground.

"Well, spit it out!"

Hannah looks at Mrs Martin, then down at the ground again. "Violet," she says, then she lets all the cries out that she's been holding in and cries really loud like a baby.

"You three take Hannah to the Care Centre," Mrs Martin says to Esther, Poppy, and Heather. She puts her hand around the back of my neck and pushes me in front of her.

"You're coming with me."

The others start to walk. Esther turns round to look at us. I think she might smile, but she's still all white. I decide that I hate Hannah more than any of them.

30

I walk with Mrs Martin behind me. Two of her fingers are poking into my back. When I slow down she jabs me with them.

I can't believe what Hannah did. Why is she more scared of Esther than Mrs Martin?

I bet Esther's never seen a teacher that angry because she's clever and if something goes wrong with one of her plans it's always somebody else who gets in trouble. When we stop walking I'll be able to tell Mrs Martin what happened. I should not have kicked her in the shins. When Mum and Dad are angry and fighting, they always shout that they're not listening to each other. Mrs Martin was probably just too angry to listen to me.

I can't believe what Hannah did. I hate her. I am never helping her again. Her face looked so stupid and horrible when she lied, and then started crying. I wish they had cut her hair off, so she was completely bald. Grandad says a coward is the worst kind of person. I wish Hannah would die.

We have to walk through the playground, and people start looking at us.

Aidan shouts, "What's Violet done, Mrs Martin?"

Mrs Martin's fingers stay still, poking into my back like a fork. "Mind your own business," she says.

Gemma and Alex have come to stand next to Aidan.

"Where's she going?" Gemma asks.

The fingers push in, and I start walking again.

Mrs Martin says, "Shut up, Gemma!"

We go past the boarders' dormitory, and into the building where my old classroom was. Mrs Martin takes her hand off my back and puts it on my hair.

We go into Mrs Martin's classroom.

"Sit there," Mrs Martin says, and points to a desk at the front of the room. She sits down at her desk, and opens the drawer.

"Mrs Martin," I say.

"Shh!" she hisses, and puts her finger on her lips. She looks through the drawer and then gets a little blue book out and starts writing.

I look around my old classroom. The frieze that we all made for Easter is still on the wall. I can see the chicken and nest full of eggs that I drew, with one chick breaking out of its shell and a piece of shell on its head like a hat. Next to my chicken is the rabbit that Joanna did really well, and Adam's frog that looks a bit like a green man.

On the other walls are paintings and things done by my old class and by other classes. Joanna's tapestry is there too. It still looks good, even though instead of daffodils, now the ducks and badger have to look at these big dark green stitch letters that say, 'THE LORD GOD MADE THEM ALL'. Joanna must have rushed the letters because they're not as good as the stuff she usually makes, and are just made with thin straight bits of thread. I bet if the badger and ducks could come to life at night, the ducks would come out of the tapestry and find Mrs Cobb and fly at her and peck her for making Joanna take away the daffodils. And the badger would use his claws to tear the letters out, or break them up into lots of green bits, so it was at least more like grass.

I sit there for ages. I realise that I forgot to go to lunch.

Mrs Martin puts a chair next to me and sits down. She is still holding the blue exercise book, and she puts it down on the table in front of me. She puts her finger underneath the writing on the front that says 'Violet Kale', in her handwriting. It is written in the blue fountain pen ink that she marks homework in.

"I want to look after you, Violet," she says.

She opens the book. Each page has the date, and lots of her neat, blue ink, joined-up writing.

"I've been keeping a record of all the good and wicked things you do," she says, and puts her hand on top of mine.

I pull my hand out and say, "I don't do wicked things."

"They're all in here," she says, and takes my hand again, lifts it off the table, and holds it in both of hers.

"Mrs Martin," I say. Her face looks different from usual, and I can't tell if she's angry or pleased. "It wasn't me today. Hannah and Esther lied."

Mrs Martin takes a deep breath and waits for me to carry on talking.

"I was trying to stop them."

Mrs Martin smiles and shakes her head. She is still holding my hand. "Don't lie, Violet," she says.

I pull my hand out of hers.

"I'm not lying," I say, "Heather cut Hannah's hair."

She stands up, and snatches the book away.

"That's not what I'm cross about," she says, and goes back to her desk and sits down.

"Do you know that it wasn't me?"

"I know that you are being wicked today."

I can feel my cheeks getting hot as I get angrier. "I'm not wicked!" I shout, "I was trying to help stupid Hannah! I was doing something GOOD!"

"Don't shout at me, wicked girl," she says, and her mean smile is back.

My face is really hot, and my head feels like it's full of fizzing bubbles.

"You kicked me, Violet," Mrs Martin says in a little voice like she's sad, "that was a wicked thing to do."

"I'm not wicked, you IDIOT!" I shout, and get out of my chair.

I know I'm in even more trouble now.

Mrs Martin doesn't do anything though. She smiles, shakes her head and opens up the blue book to start writing.

I think maybe I should run out of the classroom and go home and tell Mum, and she can tell the teachers what really happened, and that I shouldn't even be the one in trouble.

"Sit down, Violet," Mrs Martin says, and I think she must know what I was thinking, so I sit down.

She writes for a bit longer. I'm angry that she's writing stuff that isn't true in her horrible book. Maybe I'll sneak in one lunchtime and steal the book, and take it home, and push it to the bottom of the muddy swamp. Or when Dad falls asleep in the lounge I could put it in the fire.

The end of lunch bell goes, and it makes me jump. I think my next lesson is History with Mrs Head. If Mrs Martin doesn't listen to me, I will tell Mrs Head all about what happened and she can explain it to Mrs Martin.

"Mrs Martin," I say.

She doesn't look up, but says, "Stay where you are, Violet."

"I have to go to my lesson."

"You will stay here for as long as I want you to."

"What about your class?" I ask.

She stops writing and looks up, "They've got P.E. Plenty of time for you to think about your crime."

"I'll get in trouble with Mrs Head."

"You're already in trouble," she says. She is not smiling or frowning. She is just looking at me.

"I'm sorry for kicking you, Mrs Martin," I say.

Now she smiles and comes back, and sits down next to me again.

"Thank you Violet. That's a good start." She looks at me again like she's waiting for me to say something, but I can't think of anything else, so I look at my hands on the desk.

Mrs Martin takes my arm and rolls up my sleeve. I look up at her, but she's doing that face again that isn't angry or happy, and suddenly I feel a sharp pain in my arm.

She has got a bit of my skin between her nails and is pinching it. She pinches it really hard, and I feel her nail go through my skin and it stings. I bite my teeth together so I don't cry. The pain gets worse and worse as she pinches, and then when I think she might pull the bit of skin completely off she lets go.

"Ow," I say and rub the pinch mark with my other hand.

Mrs Martin hugs me and pulls me over so I'm almost sitting on her lap. I can't move my head, and my face is pushed against her chest that smells of talcum powder. She squeezes me tight, so I can't move. I feel her hand on my arm, touching the bit where she pinched.

"There, there," she says, "Good girl."

She rubs my arm. I want to escape, and go and show Mum the mark. I try to wriggle but Mrs Martin hugs me tighter and my face is pushed more into her chest, and I can feel the buttons of her blouse on my eye and lip, and it makes me feel sick, and horrible like I'm a baby and she's trying to breastfeed me.

I try and pull out of her grip and slide down in my chair, but she holds me tighter, and now I'm sitting on her lap. She rubs all up and down my arm, and then on my side, and up and down my legs, like mum when she used to dry me after a bath.

"Be my good girl, Violet," she says.

I wish Mum was here.

"Be my good girl," Mrs Martin whispers, and I feel her lips moving in my hair, "Good girl, Violet."

If I bite her, it might make everything worse, so I stay still, and make my muscles go hard, so I can't feel her stroking as much and close my eyes tight and try not to think about her horrible mouth on my hair. I hold my breath so I don't have to breathe in.

Eventually, her arms get looser around me and I can move my head away from her chest. She lets go, and I stand up.

I look at my arm, and the curved pinch mark is still there, with a bit of white skin hanging off it.

Mrs Martin reaches out, and I jump. She smiles and pulls my sleeve down over the mark.

"You hurt me, Violet," she says, "Do unto others..." She starts walking back to her desk.

I rub my arm.

I don't know whether I'm allowed to go or not.

"Well go on, then!" Mrs Martin shouts, and she sounds normal again, "Off to your next lesson!"

I run out of the room.

31

I cross the playground and run towards the caravan building. When I get to the boarders' dormitories, I stop and look to see if Mrs Martin is following me. From here I can see across the playground to the junior building. One of the hunchbacked ladies is outside the Care Centre talking to the hunchback gardener. I think he might be nice after all. Hannah looks like a normal girl, but actually she is evil. Maybe the caretaker is enchanted and at night when he goes back into his hut his body changes into a prince or something nice like a hedgehog or a deer. I think about the Storyteller episode with a man in it who is half-man and half-hedgehog, and everyone hates him except for his mum, but he is nice and gentle and is friends with all the wild animals in the woods and his best friend is a rooster. Then a stupid princess finds out he is actually enchanted and at night he becomes a naked man and his spines and everything come off and they are soft and she sleeps on them every night. One night she throws his spines into the fire because she thinks it will break the spell, but she hears noises outside and looks out of the window. She sees him outside and he has his spines and his snout back and he is on fire and burning and screaming in pain, and then he hates her and runs away.

The hunchbacks turn and look over to the junior building. Mrs Martin is standing there. I see her face moving slowly around looking across the playground. I go behind the dormitories and into the caravan building where my lesson is.

I stand on tiptoes and see everyone writing in their books, and Mrs Head checking peoples' work at the back of the classroom.

I go out of the caravan building, and back to the edge of the dormitories. I can't see anyone anymore. I am a bit worried about where Mrs Martin has gone, but decide to go home.

I run up the gravel path to the hill that goes up to the car park. The stones crunch and scatter everywhere as I run and I wish they weren't as noisy. When I get to the hill, I go into the woods where the caretaker's hut is and walk up the hill that way.

There is one big coach in the car park with its engine on and doors open. I can hear talking on the radio then a buzzer noise, then laughing. The coach driver is sitting in his seat. The stuff on the radio is making him smile. As quick as I can, I run around the edge of the car park and onto the hill that leads to the main road.

When I get home I go round the back. Mum's music is coming out of the kitchen window. I open the door and she smiles at me. She is cooking.

"I'm making pancake batter," she says. She passes me an egg, "You can help if you want."

"It's not Pancake Day."

"You don't have to wait for Pancake Day to have pancakes." She puts a chair against the cupboard for me to stand on.

Mum's music is on really loud. The cassette case is next to the kitchen stereo, it is Bob Marley which I like. There's a picture of him on the front with his long thick plaits called dreadlocks and his hat with the colours of Jamaica on.

I look at the chair and I suddenly feel all slow like Tick Tock in Return to Oz must feel like when his clockwork runs out. Mum turns the music down and fast forwards to the next song which is my favourite one where he sings 'Every little thing's gonna be alright'.

I go to Mum and put my arms around her. I still feel like Tick Tock, like in a minute my arms and legs will completely freeze and only my brain will be left working. I cuddle her, and she turns the music off and kneels down and moves my hair off of my face.

"Violet?"

I hug her and push my cheek into the big bump of her jumper where my baby brother or sister is growing. I listen to her tummy but don't hear anything.

I bet it is a bit like hell inside someone's tummy, hot and blood coloured, but safe too, like a joey kangaroo in its mum's pouch.

Mum puts her hands on my shoulders and pushes me away from her tummy, "Violet, what's happened?"

Probably because of the miracle nobody will believe me about Mrs Martin without proof anyway. If I tell Mum she will go straight to the school and probably punch Mrs Martin and then everything will get worse. And Mum could end up going to prison because I bet Mrs Martin is clever enough to fool the police too.

Mum shakes me. "Violet!" She looks worried. There is some flour on her cheek, "Why are you home so early, I was coming to collect you?"

I smile at her, "I had enough of school today."

She frowns and puts a hand in her hair, then she shakes her head. "Bloody hell," she says, "We're a right pair!"

I crack the egg on the side of the glass bowl while Mum goes to get my apron out of the cupboard with the bin in. I pull up my sleeve and look at my arm. There is a thin fingernail shaped cut where Mrs Martin pinched me. The skin around it is a bit red. If I pull the scab off every time it comes then it will scar and I will have my first bit of proof against Mrs Martin. When the cupboard door slams I pull my sleeve down again.

"You don't do this again though, Violet," Mum says, and hands me my apron with zoo animals on. "I don't want you crossing that main road on your own again."

"Yeah I know," I say.

I think about the times she forgets to pick me up when I always walk home on my own, and wonder if when that happens I am supposed to stay at school all night. I don't say anything about it though, because I know Mum's not really cross, and soon Dad will be home and he will be happy that we've made pancakes.

32

"Do you want to stay here tonight?" Sergio asked.

Violet looked over at Maria, sleeping on the sofa. "We can't," she said.

"Do you still leave the car? If you want I take you where you need and then bring him back for you?"

"No thanks, I'll just leave it here."

She started to gather up their things, and went out to the car to make sure there wasn't anything else to take on the boat. She pulled out her bag of CDs from behind the passenger seat and some loose discs out of the door pockets, stuffing them into the bag. The backpack was already heavy, and she would have to carry the car seat too. She felt the bump of the Camel Lights in her jeans pocket.

"Violet."

The voice made her start. She turned round and saw Sergio holding a tarpaulin.

"I bring the plastic sheet for you."

They covered the car, and weighed down the tarpaulin with bricks. Violet reached under and put a hand on the tyre. "Bye car," she whispered. She hated the car when she first got it, never picturing herself in a £500 ugly blue estate, but it was the only solid thing she owned apart from clothes. "Fuck," she said, "this is harder than saying goodbye to my Mum."

She took her hand out and stood up to check the car was

properly covered, and the tarpaulin wouldn't fly off in the wind.

"Do you sail off the island?" Sergio asked.

Violet took out a cigarette.

"I think you are not going with ferry, so... do you have a boat?"

She searched her pockets for a lighter, "I shouldn't really talk about it," she said, "Maria's Dad could come here and it's better if you don't know anything.

Sergio limped around the car so he was next to her and held out a lighter, "I don't talk to anyone about you." He looked down at the ground, his fingers shook, probably disconcerted not hitting buttons or feeding coins into a slot.

Violet passed him a cigarette.

It was getting dark, and the temperature had dropped again. She hoped the cottage wasn't much farther than the car park would've been from the marina; she might not even remember the way. The clouds had filled the sky and it looked thick and blank. She couldn't work out where the moon was.

Sergio still held the lighter and cigarette, "Maybe I can come and help you?"

"It's better if you stay away from us."

"When I am young, we have a boat in Madeira. I know about the sea, and I can fish very well."

His good eye was fixed on Violet. Her Grandad used to say people with hazel eyes are descendants of the sun or something, and really powerful. She remembered wishing she'd got hazel eyes because they were the best. If Violet went mad at sea, what would Maria do? No, you'd have to be at sea for months to go mad at sea, and they were just crossing the channel.

"Thanks. But I think it's better if just the two of us go."

His iris seemed to flicker at her hesitation. He lifted his arms, "I speak French, and also very fluent Spanish. It is difficult on a boat alone. Even parking you need two people."

It was stupid to involve someone else. But the police would be looking for a girl and a baby, not a family. Sergio might find out that she'd stolen Maria and throw her overboard. He was right though; it would be easier with two of them.

Violet took a hard drag on her cigarette, and inhaled. She blew the smoke out and watched it rise and disappear, "I told you I'm in some trouble," she said, "You have these people you owe money to, so we both have our secrets…"

Sergio watched her.

"I love fish," Violet said.

Sergio put his hands together in prayer position, the cigarette and lighter sticking out awkwardly, "Thank you, Violet," he said, "When do we go?"

* * *

They walked along the road, Violet carrying Maria in her jacket, and the car seat over her arm. Sergio took the backpack. He walked slowly and, Violet could see he was in pain from his leg.

Occasionally a car approached, and they moved into the bushes until it passed. It was good that Sergio was in trouble too, it made her caution and secrecy seem normal. She thought he even ducked into the shadows faster than her.

The baby seat was awkward, and Violet had to keep changing arms. The cut was throbbing too, and she could feel that the blisters on her feet were now just exposed skin that burnt with each touch of leather.

After a while she asked, "Do you know what time it is?"

Sergio got out a mobile phone and turned it on. Violet stroked Maria's head. She was sleeping, her breath dampening Violet's neck.

"It is ten thirty," he said, "I guess we have been walking for maybe two hours." A text beeped on his phone, and he read it, the light illuminating his chin and mouth.

Violet watched as he turned the phone off again and put it back in his pocket.

"My mother," he said.

Violet passed him a cigarette, "I think we're halfway there," she said, and they moved off again.

They walked in silence, like passengers on their legs. Violet felt sick, and unsteady by the time they got to a sign saying 'Bembridge 1 mile'. She put the babyseat on the ground. "Can you pass me the bag?"

Sergio stopped next to her.

"You want a break?" she asked.

There was a bank next to the road, and she climbed up, her boots slipping on the damp grass. She turned and slumped down halfway up. Sergio's shoes were worse, and he took a few slippery steps, then fell, landing on all fours. Violet heard him take a sharp breath with the impact, and he crawled the rest of the way. He passed her the bag, and lay on his back. Steam came off him.

"Do you want a Fanta?" she asked.

"Yes, thank you," he said, and reached out for the cold can. He put it against his eye and let out a quiet sigh.

The sugar rush made the last part of the walk pass more quickly. When they reached Bembridge Violet guessed it was about one in the morning. The clouds had started to clear and the moon gave out a faint, silvery light. No house lights were on, but a few street lamps gave out an orange glow. There was no breeze; it was good they weren't going by sailing boat.

Violet saw something move out from behind the newsagents. A tall fox, lit-up in the streetlight stopped, and stared at her. It held her and Maria in its gaze. Violet stayed still, watching. Sergio stumbled up behind them, his shoes scraping the ground, and the fox galloped off.

They walked on and a smaller fox ran out, and turned to them, its eyes gleaming white in the streetlight, then ran away after the other one.

"Foxes are brave here," Sergio said, "They are not like this where I come from."

"I like them," Violet said, "My mum used to feed them cat food."

When they arrived at the marina, Violet carried on walking. She leaned down and touched Maria's hair with her lips, then glanced towards the woods; she wanted their pram back. The man wouldn't have just left it though. It was evidence, and bait.

Sergio's voice rang out behind her, "The marina is here, no?"

Violet turned round, "Yeah," she said, "but we go this way. The gates are locked anyway."

Sergio followed her through the fields. She held the gates steady for him to climb. He was slowing down, and the moonlight showed sweat shining on his pale face. Violet hoped rest would fix his leg, and it didn't seize up altogether; it might need amputating at sea. She laughed out loud, then cleared her throat to cover it up. They'd be proper pirates if he had a wooden leg. Maybe her arm would turn septic, and she would end up with one empty sleeve like Nelson.

When they got to the marina, Violet said, "We have to be quiet, there might be security guards."

Sergio's pupils were huge and black, "It is not your boat?"

"It's a friend's."

She hurried through the lines of dinghies towards the jetties. Maria was starting to squirm, and whimper. "Shh," Violet said, "not long now."

Maria let out a squeal and Violet started to run, holding Maria against her. She heard Sergio's bad leg scraping faster behind them.

Violet stopped next to the boat shed and listened. The marina was quiet.

"Ready?" she said.

Sergio nodded, and they ran across to the jetty.

Violet pulled the rope and tugged Revelations towards them. She motioned for Sergio to jump aboard. He stumbled on landing and grabbed hold of the railings.

"Is your leg okay?" Violet asked.

His face was white with pain. He smiled, "Yes, I need only some rest."

Violet passed Maria to him, and then jumped across. She unlocked the door, and they went down the stairs.

Violet lit the candles and heated water for Maria's bottle. Her head felt full again, there were too many details. She wanted the pram back from the fat man. They needed to leave soon, within the hour if possible.

Sergio came into the kitchen area, "Do you need some help?" he said, "I can make a coffee?"

"There's no coffee, just Horlicks.'

Sergio frowned, "Horlicks?"

"It's like the opposite of coffee, it'll send you to sleep." She took the boat keys out of her jeans and handed them to him. "The driving room is up the stairs," she said. "Do you want to have a look and figure out the boat?"

"I can't believe there is no coffee," he said, "I should have bring some from the cottage." He started to climb the stairs.

"Wait!" she called, "Don't turn the light on, there's a torch you can use, but..."

Sergio stopped. She couldn't see his face in the dark; the candlelight only showed the bottom of his jeans, and his shiny, office-style shoes, "Don' worry," he said, "I will be careful."

Violet fed Maria, and laid her down in the car seat to sleep, "I'll make you a better bed when I get back," she whispered.

She dried Maria's neck with her sleeve where milk had dribbled down, and leant down and kissed her on the head.

Violet climbed the stairs. Sergio was sitting on the floor studying a map with the torch. He looked up when she came in.

"So, is this the kind of boat you're used to?"

"No," he said, "But it is okay."

"Okay," she said, "I'm going to get some water and stuff from the marina. What petrol is it?"

He didn't look up, "Unleaded petrol, not the diesel."

"Maria's asleep down there, I'll only be twenty minutes. She shouldn't wake up."

She sounded like a parent talking to a babysitter, *If she cries just read her Farm or Jungle and she'll settle again in no time! A bit of Bob Marley always does the trick too.*

Violet realised Sergio was watching her, words hanging in the air that she hadn't heard, "What?"

"Where will you take petrol? Do you need help?"

"No, I'm fine."

She left the cabin door open so he would hear Maria if she cried, then went back down to the lounge. She emptied out the backpack on the floor, making sure the leatherman was in the front pocket.

Outside the boatsheds there was a hose attached to a tap. She pulled a length loose and cut it off with the leatherman, then rolled it up and headed into the sheds. She needed some big containers. There was a stack of buckets, but that wouldn't work. If the petrol didn't spill, it would evaporate. Maybe there would be petrol cans on other boats.

Violet couldn't see any petrol caps on the boats. All the surfaces were smooth, and shiny, the petrol caps discreetly placed where she would never find them. Maybe boats didn't have normal petrol caps. Fuck. She was wasting time.

One of the boats might have a spare can of petrol that she could take, then they could figure out where to put petrol in Revelations when they were safely at sea. It was a shame; she had been looking forward to siphoning out petrol with the hose. She stuffed it into the backpack, they might need it for something. Maybe she could make a toy with it, or one of those swinging baby chairs that hang from doorways.

Violet headed to the jetty with the biggest, most expensive motorboats moored to it. The first boat was locked. She had a quick look round the deck, but there were no petrol cans. There was an unlocked chest, and she pulled it open, and saw a pile of lifejackets. There were a couple of normal ones, and a tiny toddler size life vest in fluorescent pink and turquoise, which she put in the backpack.

Violet jumped across to the next boat. She tried four more boats before she found one that was unlocked. She wished she had the torch. It was bad enough not knowing where to look, and almost impossible without light.

The boat was much bigger than Revelations, with more rooms. The kitchen was twice the size. Violet opened the cupboards. There was a wine rack with four bottles of wine, and she put two in the backpack. As she was leaving the kitchen, she remembered coffee, and added a large, unopened jar of Nescafe to the bag.

On the back of one boat there was a grey dinghy hanging on a kind of pulley system. Action Man had dinghies like that; they were called ribs, she thought. She stepped onboard, and headed for the dinghy. She stood on her tiptoes and looked inside. There was a large, orange metal can of petrol.

On her tiptoes, she took hold of the handle; it was so heavy she could hardly lift it. Violet took a deep breath, and with all her strength, pulled it up onto the side of the dinghy. She balanced it there for a second as the heavy liquid swilled around inside, then dragged it towards her. With the change of angle, the petrol shifted, unbalancing the can. Violet couldn't hold the sudden rush of weight, and the can crashed onto the deck. A noise like someone playing a washboard rang out across the boatyard. Violet crouched down underneath the dinghy. She stayed there listening for new noises, but there was nothing except the quietening ringing of the petrol against the walls of the can.

She dragged the petrol can back to Revelations, and put it down next to where the boat was tied to the pontoon.

"I want our pram back," she said.

The sky was beginning to take on a chalky glow; she would have to be fast.

A floodlight attached to the gates was directed straight onto the cabin, and it glowed like a vending machine left on at night. Violet waited in the dark, watching the cabin. There was no one inside, unless the man was lying down on the floor, in wait. The pram probably wasn't even in there.

She ran to the cubicle door. It was awful in the floodlight, lit-up where everything else was dark, and disorientated by the concentrated unnatural light. Violet pressed her face to the window and looked in. The pram was standing against the wall inside. She tried the door handle, expecting it to be locked, but it opened. She went in and grabbed the pram, but the wheels stuck.

Panic ripped through her and she almost ran, but then saw that the brakes had been put on. She kicked the brakes off, and swung the pram round. As she turned she noticed something flicker, and saw at the very top of the cabin, the red LED light of a camera recording. Nothing she could do now. She smiled at the camera, and ran out of the cabin into the safety of the dark.

Violet pushed the pram quickly through the boatyard, the wheels whirring in a way they hadn't done before. She lifted the pram across onto the boat, pushed it through the door and down the steps, then went back outside.

Violet crouched on the front of Revelations, and pulled the rope so the boat moved towards the pontoon, then reached out and took hold of the petrol can. Quietly, she counted to three, then stood up and heaved the can up onto the side of the boat, then tugged as hard as she could to get it over the little rails. As she pulled she felt the cut on her arm tear, and wetness on her skin. Finally the petrol can hit the deck and Violet slumped down with the can between her legs, gasping in the cold, fresh air. In the distance she heard the sound of an engine, and she got to her feet, dragged the can away from the edge of the boat, and went back inside.

Maria was still sleeping, and Violet covered her and put the car seat buckles on in case the waves were rough. As she passed the pram, she pushed its brakes down, then went up to the driving room.

Sergio looked round, "We are ready?"

"Yes," Violet said, "Let's go. Quick."

He turned a small key, and some dials lit up. He seemed to be counting them. Violet expected the engines to start, but Sergio swivelled round in the chair. Violet waited for him to say he'd changed his mind, or couldn't really drive a boat.

"You need to untie us," he said.

"Right, yes," Violet replied, and ran down the stairs and back out onto the deck.

She jumped onto the pontoon, and untied Revelations. In the top window she could just make out Sergio's face. She didn't want to shout, so made him a thumbs up sign.

She saw the white of his hand against the window make the same signal.

From the marina gates she heard the sound of a car.

"Fuck," she said, but her voice was lost as the boat's engines roared into action. Violet heard the chug of the propellers quieten as they sunk into the water, and the boat began to reverse gently away from the pontoon. Violet jumped across the widening stretch of water, and landed heavily on the deck.

She went upstairs, and stuck her head out of the window next to Sergio. The lights along the coast twisted as the boat turned.

"Okay," Sergio said, "We are moving." He pushed a gear stick forward, and Violet felt the front of the boat lift up as they accelerated out of the marina. She turned back around, and saw two headlights moving through the boatyard.

"Goodbye, Isle of Shite," she said and got them both a cigar out of the drawer.

33

The cold air rushed over them from the window, lifting and snatching the cigar smoke, as it puffed off the ends. Violet watched the scatter of lights on the Isle of Wight diminish, and disappear, the island changing from a coastline, to a shrinking block of land. Her eyes watered from the breeze. The moon was behind a cloud, and the sea looked black and bumpy as they cut through it. It was 3.48 in the morning.

"Violet," Sergio said, "If you drive, I can go to cook some food?"

Violet brought her head back inside the boat, and looked at the dashboard. "Yeah, okay… What are we heading for?"

He pointed at a dial with a moving compass inside. "You are not having to look too much," he said, "Keep this pointer like this. If he moves, just steer little bit."

"So I don't even need to look out the window?"

Sergio frowned, "Watch for the very big ships and ferries, any other can move out of the way."

Violet took the backpack off and got out a bottle of red wine, and the coffee. "I got wine to go with dinner," she said.

After a while she slowed the boat down, and went downstairs to get Maria.

Violet touched Maria's cheeks, and leaned down to listen to her breathing. Maria was wheezing a bit, maybe she'd got a cold from their damp run through the woods. Violet picked up the car seat, and carried her up to the steering room. There were controls for heating, and she switched them to full and shut the window.

The compass had swung to the left, so she turned the steering wheel until it was back in the position Sergio had showed her, and pushed the gear stick forward to a faster speed. All Violet could see through the window was the black and blue of the sea and sky. The heating started to kick in, and she leaned back in the chair and closed her eyes. The smell of onions and garlic frying started to creep into the room. Violet's stomach felt strange and twisted inside, like knotted rope. She opened her eyes to check the compass again, and then bent down and eased her boots off, trying not to tear the skin off her blisters. She pulled her feet up onto the seat, and sat cross-legged letting her eyes fall shut.

Violet woke up as Sergio bumped into the captain's chair. She watched him turn the wheel, and check some of the dials. On the desk was a tray of food.

"Are we okay?" Violet asked, hoisting herself up in the seat. "Still on course?"

"Yes it's okay," Sergio said, "I come up twenty minutes ago, and you are both sleeping, so I am checking."

Violet nodded. She felt annoyed for some reason.

She waited until she heard Sergio going down the stairs, and then swivelled round in the chair. There were two saucers with a small piece of fish on each. Next to the fish, there was a neat mound of mushy peas, and two triangles of brown toast, standing propped up against each other.

Violet heard Sergio coming back up the stairs, and went to check on Maria. The door swung open, and Sergio came in holding two big plates of spaghetti on one arm, along with wine glasses, and a corkscrew. In his other hand, he held the bottle of wine and some salt and pepper shakers in the shape of lighthouses.

"How many plates can you hold?" Violet asked.

"Six," he said, "But I have done seven a couple of times."

"The food looks nice. Where'd you get the fish?"

"I find inside the freezer with this bread. I cook him inside the oven, then take off this batter, and fry very fast with some dry garlic and salt. There are not so many herbs, but it's okay."

"What's the pasta?"

"Spaghetti Arrabiata with tuna."

Sergio poured a little bit of wine into his glass, and stuck his nose in and sniffed it hard. Then he took a gulp and did his wine tasting routine. Violet speared some fish on her fork.

"It's good wine," Sergio said, and filled both their glasses.

The fish was delicious. It didn't taste like a frozen ready fillet at all. The only part Violet didn't like much was the mushy peas, because the consistency reminded her of school dinner mashed potatoes.

The wine affected Violet quickly, and a warm electric feeling started to run under her skin. The spaghetti was the nicest spaghetti she'd ever tasted. The mixture of garlic, chilli and tomato turned the dull metallic flavour of tinned tuna into the most delicious thing she'd eaten in ages. That wasn't hard though, she thought, compared to cereal, and bananas.

"Thanks," she said through a mouthful, "it's really nice."

Sergio smiled and filled up her wineglass. "There is not much ingredient in this kitchen...when we get to France I cook something very good."

He looked at her, and Violet felt aware of the scab on her cheek, and the fact that she hadn't washed since the Bucket o' Mussels. In the morning she would go for a swim.

"Who taught you to cook?" she asked.

"My mother," he said, "and then I work in many kitchens."

"I used to work in a kitchen doing washing up. I did the salads sometimes too, when it was busy." She twisted spaghetti onto her fork, "But then the boss decided he wanted me on the bar. It was more fun I guess, and you could drink... But I liked the rush of the kitchen, and you all had this really nice dinner together before you started work." She took a mouthful, "And you got to finish earlier."

"Where is this?" Sergio asked.

"What?"

"Where did you work?"

Violet took the wine bottle and emptied it into their glasses, "London."

Sergio picked up his wineglass. "I have never been in London. When I come to England I think for sure I will go. And then when I leave my uncle's restaurant, I'm almost going."

"Why didn't you?" Violet asked, "There's loads more restaurants than the Isle of Wight."

"I don't know. It was risk maybe I don't find a job quickly... and then I take this job at the Bucket Mussel. Also, in Isle of Wight there is maybe the chance to find a cook job on a yacht."

Maria groaned from her chair and Violet saw she was awake. Her nose was running, and there was crusty yellow stuff around one eye.

"She wants her dinner too," Violet said, lifting her up.

"I can do her bottle if you want finish the spaghetti."

"No, thanks," Violet said, "I'm full. I'll have the rest for breakfast ... Hey, there's another wine in that bag."

Downstairs Violet boiled water, and mixed up a bottle. It was good having a kitchen, so much easier than having to beg hot water off people. Maybe they could park the boat somewhere and live on it. Though they would need petrol, and the gas would run out eventually. She put Maria's bottle in the fridge to cool, then looked in the tiny freezer compartment and saw the frozen peas, a half-full tray of ice cubes, and some curly fries. Violet thought of her car, left under the tarpaulin on the Isle of Wight, and felt a cold, creeping sensation in her neck.

She poured some of the boiled water into a bowl, ground salt in then left it on the side. Maria was crying, and Violet laid her on her back to change her nappy. She stopped crying and watched Violet.

Violet smiled, "You're putting me off," she said, using baby wipes to clean her. She noticed that Maria's bottom and the back of her thighs were red and dappled with a rash. There was talcum powder somewhere, but she couldn't remember where it was.

"You can go nappy-less for a while," she said.

She put the cleanest looking babygrow on Maria, and a knitted blue cardigan with a hood. Maria wriggled and began to cry again.

"I'll do our washing tomorrow," Violet said.

Maria's nose was running, and the ugly yellow stuff was still stuck in her eyelashes. Violet made a tear in a new nappy, and pulled out some cotton wool. "Wait a minute," she said, and went back to the kitchen.

There was a roll of kitchen towel with little anchors and lifebuoys on, and Violet tore off a sheet, then she dunked some cotton wool in the salt water and went back to Maria.

Maria was red in the face and screaming now, kicking her legs about. Mucus pulsed in and out of her nostrils. Violet took the kitchen towel, and folded it into a thin rectangle, then she gently pinched Maria's nose, and looked to one side, as she squeezed away the snot. She felt the kitchen towel dampen, and she retched.

"Sorry, Maria," she said, "I fucking hate snot."

Maria's crying was now like a racking howl, her were eyes squeezed shut, and her cheeks purple.

"Hey, it's not that bad." Violet picked her up, and started to rock her from side to side, then cleaned her eyes with the cotton wool and warm water.

"I know, it's disgusting having a cold," she said.

Maria struggled in Violet's arms.

Violet walked about in the lounge. The floor vibrated beneath them, and she felt a tremor of excitement as she thought of the moving water underneath. Above the little drinks cabinet was a door that opened upwards. She pulled it open and saw a stereo.

"Maria, look!" Violet said, "We've got music." She craned her neck to one side to distance herself from the screams, and pressed POWER. A green light came on next to the button, and Violet smiled, and stroked Maria's hair, "Things are looking up for us."

Maria let out another desperate burst of crying, and her hot face bashed against Violet's, wetting it with tears, and dribble.

"Okay, okay," Violet said, "Your milk's probably ready now."

Violet took Maria upstairs, and handed Sergio the bottle. He held out his arms for Maria.

"Hello Darrling," he said, "Don' cry. Are you hungry?" Violet noticed purple wine stains in the cracks of his lips.

She watched as he settled Maria into his elbow, and she stopped crying, and started to drink. "I'll do the washing up," she said, and picked up her wine glass and went downstairs.

Violet pushed up her sleeve, and pulled the last bits of sodden masking tape out of the cut. It stuck to the bits that had scabbed, and she winced, as it re-tore new skin. She used the cotton wool and salt water to clean it out, and saw that it had got smaller, although the middle of it was still open and bleeding. It didn't look so much like a gaping mouth now, but partly closed lips, about to whistle or blow a kiss. Her arm throbbed, and she guessed it was slightly infected. She poured the rest of the salt water over it, then dabbed it dry with kitchen towel. Her forearm looked swollen, and she rolled up her other sleeve, and held both arms out to compare. It was a bit bigger than the other one, but nothing too alarming. She would feel properly ill if she had something like blood poisoning anyway.

There were lots of scars on her left arm. Most of them were thin and white now, in series of two or three parallel lines. A few were raised, and others were an uglier, deep red colour, like muscle. There was a half-finished star that looked more like a broken holly leaf, some faint circular cigarette burns, and a faded 'smiley' from a clipper lighter. Her right arm was almost perfect in comparison, with just two thin scars like teardrops on her middle finger, and one on her knuckle that she did when she was about eight and her Mum had broken a window trying to kill a wasp. Violet had climbed onto the windowsill to help clear it up or something and got cut. She couldn't exactly remember.

A hand touched Violet's shoulder, and she gasped and turned round.

Violet saw Sergio take in the bloodied tissue and cotton wool around, and her two bare arms stretched out in front of her.

"What have you done?" he said.

Violet pulled her sleeves down, "Nothing," she said. She could see the thoughts ticking behind his eyes; disgust, fear, embarrassment, panic, disgust.

Violet tipped the salt water down the sink, and picked up their dinner plates. Sergio stood behind her. Violet felt the static energy between their two bodies, thick like a force field.

Sergio reached forward slowly, not looking at her face, and took her wrist. "You bleed," he said.

Violet stared at plates. "I had an accident the other night.... I knocked it, and it reopened... It's fine."

Sergio pulled up her sleeve, and looked at the cut. Little bubbles of blood were forming at the edges. "I think he needs to make a stitch."

Violet tightened her hold on the plates, "Okay."

"Do you have something to make stitch?"

It was obvious she'd done it herself; the cut surrounded by others all a similar length and angle. "Um, I don't know," she said.

"I go to look."

Violet threw away the bloody tissues and cotton wool, and downed the rest of her wine. She went upstairs to the steering room, and poured another glass. The compass had moved again, and she steered the boat back on course. Maria was sleeping in her car seat. Her cheeks were flushed, and her breathing was wheezy with cold.

Violet took a gulp of wine, and sat back in the captain's chair. She could hear cupboards opening and closing below. The sky was much paler now and there was a set of slowly moving lights in the distance, and the small dark shape of a boat: nothing close though. It shouldn't take long to reach France. She'd been on the ferry from Calais once, but couldn't remember exactly how long it had taken, only a few hours though.

Footsteps clattered on the stairs and Sergio appeared in the doorway with a bowl of water, kitchen towel, and a plastic travel sewing kit.

He held out the sewing kit. "I find this."

"Great," Violet said, and emptied the second wine bottle into their glasses.

"You wash your arm, and I clean the, 'how you call this'?" Sergio asked.

"Needle."

"Neeedawll," Sergio said, and they both laughed.

"Fucking hell," Violet said.

She picked some fluff out of the cut, and wiped it clean again with the warm water, then watched as Sergio threaded the needle with turquoise blue cotton.

"Why blue?"

Sergio looked up serious, "I think black stitches will be ugly."

"Okay... thanks," Violet said, and pushed her sleeve up to her elbow.

"Maybe we need a drink before," Sergio said.

"Don't get pissed and put buttons on it or something."

Sergio smiled, not quite understanding. His face still looked mashed up, the black eye bulging out, and his smile pulling tight the scabbed split in his lip.

Violet downed her glass, feeling slightly sick, as the rich wine gushed down her throat.

Sergio drained his glass too, then opened the drawer and flicked open the Zippo lighter. "My father had one the same," he said.

"You can keep it if you want."

"Thank you... but I don' really like to think of my father. He is a bit of a bastard."

Violet laughed. "Sorry," she said, "it's just funny."

He held the needle in the flame, and she watched it blacken then glow bright orange.

"Are you ready?"

Violet nodded, and looked away as Sergio pinched the cut together. She put her right thumb between her teeth, and bit down, as the needle pierced the damaged flesh. The pain seared through her arm, and she held her breath.

The needle scratched as it found its way through the cut and stuck into the little wall of skin the other side of the wound.

Violet looked and saw her skin lift and then the needle poke through like a burrowing creature. Sergio took hold and started to pull. Violet winced as the thickest part of the needle tugged through followed by the thread. The thread travelling through the skin felt almost nice, scratching and tingly, but when the needle stabbed back into the other side of the cut, Violet looked away and bit down on her thumb again.

After a while she felt a tug then a stinging, tightening sensation, as Sergio pulled on the cotton.

"Almost finish."

Violet watched as he tied a knot in the end, and used a miniature pair of scissors to cut off the extra thread. He gently wiped some blood away with kitchen towel and salt water.

Sergio stood up. His face was white. "I am going to the toilet," he said, and walked quickly out of the room.

Violet looked at her arm. The cut was closed with two neat stitches, the skin slightly puckered where the thread held it tight together. Over the hum of the engine she heard Sergio coughing and throwing up in the toilet.

He came back into the steering room with a bottle of the white wine from the cottage. He sat on the edge of the desk; he was sniffing, and his eyes were watery from being sick.

"Are you okay?" Violet said.

"Yes."

"Thanks for doing the stitches."

Sergio didn't look up. He opened the bottle, poured two wines, then raised his glass to his mouth and drank.

"Aren't you going to taste it first?" she asked, smiling.

He took another gulp and looked out of the window.

Violet pulled her sleeves down, "Where did you learn that anyway?"

There was a strange, cold look on his face. "I was not sick," he said, and stood up fast, knocking the chair and sending it into a spin. Wine spilled from Violet's glass and ran down her wrist.

"Fucking hell," she said, starting to laugh.

"Stop talking about it!"

"Okay. I was just trying to say thank you."

"It's disgusting what you have done with your arm!"

Violet walked to the window, and lit a cigarette. "It was an accident," she said.

She stared into the cold breeze and didn't let herself blink. After a while her eyeballs started to prick and burn. Eventually they welled up and she closed her eyes and felt the tears roll over and wet them. The cigarette smoke felt warm as it travelled down to her lungs. She held it there before letting it rise back up to her throat and parting her lips so it spilled out.

Violet heard Sergio's shoes tapping on the floor, and then the chair creaked and she guessed he'd sat down. She heard the motor speed up, and felt the boat rise higher in the water. The sky was glowing, and an orange tint showed on the horizon above the dark water. Apart from the noise of the engine, and the odd wave slapping the sides of the boat, there was nothing.

She remembered being shown a picture of what people thought the edge of the world was like when they thought it was flat; a boat full of screaming people about to drop over an immense, god-sized waterfall.

Violet heard the engine noise change again, and the boat slowed down. Sergio walked up and stood behind her. She could smell sweat and aftershave.

He put his hand on her shoulder, "Do you like some wine?"

Violet turned around, and took the glass.

"Let's get drunk," she said, "to celebrate our first night at sea."

* * *

Essential Reggae played on the stereo downstairs. Sergio was sitting on the floor leaned up against the wall. His head nodded to 'The Israelites'. They were down to the last wine. The empty bottles rolled in slow semi circles when the boat went over a wave. Maria was asleep in her car seat by Sergio's feet. It was light outside. Violet turned the key in the ignition, and the engines stopped.

Sergio looked up, "What are you doing?" he said.

She stood up quickly the room twisting a little. "I'm going for a swim, you want to come?"

"I don't like much to swim."

223

"Come on!" she said, watching him.

"No." He shifted himself on the floor and frowned, "Maybe you are drinking too much for swim."

"I think you're just scared of the cold."

Sergio put a cigarette in his mouth, and moved to the captain's chair, "I will watch in case you need the life saver ring."

"Whatever," she said.

* * *

Violet unwrapped a bar of Imperial leather soap and put it down next to a 3-rung ladder attached to the boat. Revelations bobbed in the water as she stepped up onto the side. She could faintly hear 'Red Red Wine' coming from the open door, and from above where Sergio smoked out of the window.

Violet pulled her top off, careful not to snag the stitches. She undressed until she was standing in her thong and bra. Her teeth started to chatter. Violet looked at her toes gripping the edge of the boat, and then the water. The surface was still and glass-like, dark blue showing the wobbly bright-white reflection of the boat. If they were floating in the Caribbean instead of the Channel it would be paradise; she could be going for a morning swim, ready for a day of fresh fish, freezing bottles of beer, and sunbathing. It would be winter soon; they couldn't stay on the boat through that, unless they made it as far as Greece or Africa.

Violet glanced back at the window and saw Sergio bend down, pretending he wasn't watching. She unclipped her bra and threw it towards her pile of clothes on the deck. She lost her balance for a moment, then stood up on tiptoes, stretched her arms above her head and dived.

As Violet broke through the surface, cold shocked through her body, obliterating the warm wine-blur. An ice-cream headache gripped and tightened across her forehead and temples. It was as if icy fists grabbed hold of her lungs and squeezed, and she turned and kicked, reaching for the surface. She broke through, gasping.

"Fuck," she said, "fucking freezing!"

Her toes and fingers ached with numbness, and the cut on her arm stung like acid. She began to do front crawl around the boat.

After a while the cold started to subside from her shoulders and feet, till only her fingers were left numb. As her body plunged through the water Violet began to feel revived. Her skin tingled all over. She trod water and called up to Sergio, "Come in!"

Sergio leaned out of the window, "No, thank you. I prefer in here."

Violet lay on her back, the water pooling in her ears, her hair floating around her face. Her body looked pale, mermaid green through the water.

She reached up for the soap, and started to wash. Although the salt water would feel greasy on her skin when it dried, Violet felt the dirt of the last few days of sleeping in her clothes coming away. She moved her thong aside and touched herself with her middle finger. For the first time in months she wanted to have sex. Her nipples were hard from the cold water, and sensitive. She imagined the scrape of someone's teeth on them.

The last time she'd really wanted sex was that first time with Lisa. Claude had gone to pick-up. They did the remaining couple of lines, watching Cartoon Network. Then suddenly Lisa was on top of her, kissing her hard and pulling off both their clothes. The bump of Lisa's pregnant stomach pressed into Violet's as she pushed her fingers inside her. Ed, Edd and Eddy shuffled across the TV screen while Lisa got down on her knees and started to use her tongue, fucking her with her fingers at the same time. Violet felt a twinge in the base of her stomach. She swam for the boat and took hold of the ladder.

She climbed the stairs, her wet feet skidding a bit on the smooth surface. Sergio's face went red, and he smiled as Violet walked in still wearing her wet thong.

He got up off the floor and sat in the captain's chair. Both wine glasses were empty. Violet reached for the bottle, drank the last gulp and stepped out of her underwear. She put her knee inbetween Sergio's legs, and he leaned forward, and held her waist. Violet let him kiss her, as she undid his belt and zip. He kissed gently, his tongue running lightly over hers. The gold teeth were misleading she thought. She could taste the salt from her lips, on his tongue.

Sergio stopped to pull his trousers and boxers off, and Violet sat astride him and put her hands in his hair. Some of his curls were crunchy from hair gel. She pushed his head down so his mouth was on her left nipple, and looked out at the sea.

"Bite them," she said, and reached down for his cock.

Violet moved so he was just inside her, then pushed herself down onto him. He moaned, and finally, his teeth closed hard around her nipple.

The chair kept swinging into the desk, as Violet fucked him, lifting herself up, and then pushing down so he went deep into her, making her ache. Sergio reached out to take hold of the desk, and knocked the wine bottle onto the floor. Violet laughed.

"Shall we go to the floor?" Sergio said.

Violet climbed off, and waited for him to sit on the floor. He was still wearing his white shirt, and socks. His legs were thin, and hairy; one of his knees was swollen and bruised with a dark cut across the kneecap. Sergio watched her, slightly out of breath, his eyes moving slower than normal from the wine. He lay back on the floor, and Violet sat on top of him. She saw his pupils enlarge, as she climbed onto him, rested a hand on his chest, and pushed him inside her again.

The sun streamed in through the window and lay in hot stripes on Violet's back, as she moved. Her thigh and bum muscles were beginning to ache. She felt her skin dampen with sweat; she didn't think she was going to come. After a while Sergio started to get soft too, and she stopped.

"I think I am drinking too much," he said, frowning.

"Yeah, me too."

Sergio sat up. His eyes seemed to look into Violet's and right through the back of her head.

"I can give you though," he said, "with my mouth."

He looked so serious, like he wasn't there anymore and had gone into a sort of autopilot. Something about him made her think of the Terminator.

Violet smiled, "Yeah... okay."

She sat in the captain's chair and Sergio kneeled down between her legs. He started to lick, gently, the same as he'd kissed. Violet closed her eyes and leaned her head back. Gradually he started to lick harder, moving his tongue from side to side, pushing on her clit. His stubble prickled against her skin. Violet felt the throb of an orgasm beginning, and opened her legs wider, resting a foot on the desk to stop the movement of the chair. She concentrated on the sensation, growing more intense as he licked and sucked on her. Violet bit down on her lip as she came, wave after wave kicking out of her, her leg muscles spasming under her skin.

She opened her eyes. Sergio was masturbating. Violet put her hand on his head and gently pushed his mouth away from her. He looked up and stopped, his face flushed. Violet could see he was hard again.

"Do you want me try again?" she said.

His eyes were dark and intense, concentrated. He frowned, and stared down at the floor, "Maybe I can do it in your butt?"

Violet started to smile, and bit her lip to contain it. She stood up and turned around to face the desk, then bent down and rested her arms on it. Her legs were still shaky from the orgasm. "Okay," she said.

Violet felt Sergio pushing himself into her bum, and she heard him spit into his hands. Then he began to push more forcefully, and she felt the coldness of the saliva. There was a tight, splitting sensation that took her breath away as he pushed himself fully inside her, and then started to thrust into her hard. The sensation was somewhere between unbearable, and kind of nice. She'd had anal sex before but it was always as a novel extra to sex or something, not like this. This was someone having full on sex with her bum. Sergio fucked her harder and harder, and she put a hand against his thigh to try and slow him down, but he carried on banging into her.

The cut on her arm stung and pulsed, the stitches straining with the effort of holding herself up until she couldn't bear it anymore and let her chest fall, and she lay across the desk. Sergio gripped her waist, his fingers digging in round her hip bones. Violet's skin stuck and rubbed against the wood as she was pushed across it.

With one last thrust, Sergio exhaled hard, and shuddered into her. Violet felt warm liquid like glue spread inside her.

He pulled out of her, and sat back down on the floor. Violet stood up and felt wetness trickle onto the back of her thigh. She picked up Sergio's trousers, and wiped it off.

When Violet looked round, Sergio was watching her. He didn't look like the Terminator anymore, he looked sad. He reached up, and pulled her down so she was lying on top of him, and then held her in his arms.

Violet felt him kiss her head. She wished she hadn't gone for the swim, as she felt sober and awake. She looked at Maria, hoping that she would start to cry and she could go and make a bottle, but she was still asleep wheezing gently. Their bodies were sticking together, and Violet could feel his pubic hair damp and itchy against her skin.

"Do you want a cigarette?" she asked, pulling herself out of his grip.

Sergio sat up, and brushed his hair back. He smiled, and Violet felt jealous that he was still drunk.

"Yes, thank you," he said.

"They're downstairs, I'll get them."

Violet walked out onto the deck, the sun was warm on her naked skin. Her eyes ached. She climbed onto the side of the boat again, and dived into the sea.

34

I have a new baby sister called Jodie. Even though she was born three weeks ago she has only just come home from hospital because she had blood transfusions because of antibodies. Dad and me visited her there but Mum was allowed to stay at the hospital.

Jodie had all tubes going in and out of her and she had to stay in an incubator. There were other babies in incubators too. One was even smaller than my sister and was only about the size of a guinea pig. Jodie looked a bit like a baby Frankenstein or a robot being built because she was like a machine that needs to be connected to electricity to live. Now she sleeps in a normal Moses basket in Mum and Dad's bedroom, but she is still very small and doesn't look as strong as Jamie did.

35

Violet climbed on board, and walked to her pile of clothes. She looked at the cut in her arm with its two neat stitches, it felt numbed from the cold water and wasn't as pink as before.

She dried herself with her t-shirt, and then pulled on her jeans, bra and jumper. As she dressed and started to warm up, little stings of pain began to prick at her arm again. Her hair was tangled and sticky from seawater. She tied it back into a ponytail, and went back inside.

From the bottom of the stairs Violet could hear Maria just starting to cry, so she went to the kitchen to make a bottle.

A slow trickle of water came out of the tap. She filled her palm and tasted it. It smelt faintly of dirty fridges. She wondered if Sergio had been using it for Maria's bottles. Her and Sergio would have to drink the tap water from now on, and Maria could have the remaining Isle of Wight water, which was in a Pepsi bottle somewhere. They couldn't be far from France now anyway.

There was a bit of water left in the saucepan, and Violet turned the gas on to boil it again. Upstairs Maria started to cry more forcefully. In a cupboard Violet found a lid, and covered the pan. Pirates must have had to carry barrels of water. She tried to think if Jim Hawkins had said anything about it in *Treasure Island*, but Violet could only remember the barrel of apples.

When the bottle was ready, Violet put it in a bowl of tap water to cool, and went upstairs. Sergio must have gone to bed because

Maria was alone in the steering room. She was crying and kicking, squinting against the bright sun. Her nose was running again. Violet lifted her out, and saw that the legs of the babygrow were saturated.

"Shit," Violet said, "I never put your nappy back on."

She changed Maria outside. The fresh air seemed to cheer Maria up, and her crying became less desperate.

Violet held the soaking babygrow up. "Shall we throw it overboard?" she asked Maria.

Maria stopped crying and watched Violet as she threw it into the sea. Violet held Maria up high on her shoulder. The sun reflected off the waves, and the sea sparkled so bright that she had to shield her eyes to look at it. The babygrow was floating half underwater, its arms outstretched on the surface as if it was waving for help. The sea held it there suspended, the underwater currents making the dirty legs kick gently.

Back in the steering room, Violet fed Maria her bottle. Maria wheezed as she drank.

"Please don't get ill now," Violet said.

Maria had survived loads of alcohol and drugs when she was inside Lisa and come out undamaged and healthy. Violet had pissed in a bottle only a couple of weeks ago so Lisa would pass some test and Maria wouldn't get taken away. Funny that Violet took her away in the end.

Violet stroked Maria's hair. She wondered if Maria would ask about Lisa one day. If Violet never mentioned mums she'd never know what one was, but then you couldn't get away from mums. Even if Maria didn't go to school she'd see animals with babies. She thought about what she'd say.

I took you from your Mum because your mum was evil.
She didn't want you to get taken off her.
I think I loved your mum.
She was letting you die.
I had sex with your mum when you were inside her.
I took you because I didn't want you to die.

Violet thought about the morning she took Maria; it was only a few days ago but it felt weeks, and the memory was vague and dream-like. The previous days all seemed like that, like mornings when you're still off your head from the night before, and when you get to the evening, you can't remember anything you did in the day, or how you got to where you're standing. Violet pictured herself lying on the bare mattress, damp with fuck knows what, listening to Maria crying. A morning like so many others that she didn't know if it was a real memory, or just an image of another morning the same.

She scratched at the stitches on her arm, and felt a little sting, as a bit of scab came away taking a hair with it. The compass was in the right position, and Violet pushed the gear stick forward to speed the boat up. The sea was clear in front of them.

"Keep your eyes peeled for land," she said to Maria, but Maria's eyes were already closed, her gulps slowing as she fell asleep.

Violet turned the engine off and took Maria down to the lounge where it was cooler, then made her a bed on the floor by the sofa. She took the cushions off the sofa to build a wall around her so she wouldn't roll out.

When Maria was tucked in the bed, Violet went into the kitchen. Their dinner plates were still on the side. She stood at the sink, and ate some cold spaghetti. The boat was silent, everyone asleep except her. On her way to the stairs she stood and listened at the door of the double bedroom, but couldn't hear anything. She tried the door handle, but Sergio had locked himself in.

Back in the steering room, Violet turned the engine on and pushed the gear stick forward to full speed. The nose of the boat lifted, and they ploughed on towards France. Fuck saving petrol. Maria needed milk, Violet needed water and cigarettes; the sooner they got there the better.

After an hour or so, Violet slowed the boat down and went to check on Maria. She was still sleeping, but breathing heavily. Violet listened at Sergio's door but it was quiet, and she headed back upstairs. Maybe he was embarrassed about the sex, or was sleeping off all the wine. She was a bit embarrassed for him. She felt a kind of mixture of excitement and disgust when she thought about the sex. Her stomach twisted as she thought about it, and then a dark, heavy feeling filled her head as she thought of Lisa again. She wondered how many times they'd gone to bed together while Maria was crying for milk. Violet gripped her head in her hands and pushed her nails in. She pictured the people laughing as Maria was carried around by that snake, and a smell of rotten eggs seemed suddenly present.

Violet stood up, shook her head hard and leaned out of the window. "I won't let you die," she said.

She stared at the water rolling past like a fat, blue motorway.

* * *

Violet sat at the desk with a coffee, her hand buzzing where it rested on the gear stick. Her head nodded. She wished there was a coastline to aim at, or something to let her know how far they'd gone, or how much longer it would be before they could at least see France. The empty sea gave away nothing.

In the desk drawer was a leather-bound book with gold lettering that said *Captain's Log*. There was a thick strap and a buckle to keep the book shut. Violet opened it. The paper was thick, cartridge paper. The first few pages were full with ink writing, and entries that ran from '16ᵗʰ June 1995' to '4ᵗʰ August 1995'. Next to each date were coordinates, and a couple of sentences describing the events of the day. Anne, James and Hector had gone to Mallorca and back on the boat. She read about their trip. Mostly, it was harbour fees and petrol stops that were listed. The most interesting entries were about wildlife they'd seen. James had written about a huge flock of white birds they saw at a harbour. The birds flew from Africa each year and always stopped on the same cliff.

He wrote, 'the sky looks like a normal cloudy sky, and then you realise that it is darker, creamier in colour, and it's 'foaming' with birds. The air vibrates with their beating wings.'

They'd also seen a floating dead whale, some flying fish, and near somewhere called Barbate a school of dolphins swam beside the boat for an hour.

Violet suddenly felt tired. "Captain needs caffeine," she said, and slowed the boat down while she went downstairs for more coffee.

There was a small amount of boiled water left in the saucepan, and she lifted it to her mouth and drank it, then refilled the saucepan to boil water for her coffee.

Violet found the Pepsi bottle of Isle of Wight water in the lounge area. Next to it was a plastic supermarket bag of something bloody and cool. She lifted it up, and held it in her palm. "Fillet steak," she said, "Bought from a wizard."

Violet stood the bottle of water next to Maria's can of formula milk. She didn't want Sergio to wake up and drink it, so she used the masking tape, and taped the can of formula, and the water together. Next she took the steaks out and laid them on a plate. She rubbed them in salt and pepper like she'd watched Juanito do at work, then poured olive oil on, covered them up and put the plate in the fridge. Later, she could collect some sea water to boil and wash their clothes in.

Violet made a coffee with two tablespoons of Nescafe, and squirted some of the squeezy bear honey in.

"Hello my friend," she said, and rubbed his tummy with her finger.

The bear returned her smile with his, and she twisted his hat shut, and put him in her pocket.

"Bored on a boat," she said, "All we do is float."

36

Lunch was shepherds' pie, and had lots of chewy bits of gristle in it. Mine is already wrapped in napkins in my pocket like a warm parcel. I am eating the pudding which is jelly and ice cream. Mrs Martin is on lunch duty today, which means that I can try the desk drawer.

Almost every lunchtime I go to Mrs Martin's room to check if she has left the desk drawer unlocked. When I have her book I can take it to Mum and Dad or straight to Mr Cobb and hopefully he will give Mrs Martin the sack. Or at least Mum and Dad might make me change schools.

Gemma is talking about strippers, she says, "If you give a stripper money she'll take all her clothes off and do a dance for you."

Alex and Aidan laugh.

"Do they have to?" I ask

"Yeah it's their job."

"All their clothes?"

"Yep."

"Can men be strippers too?"

Gemma rolls her eyes to the ceiling and says "Duh!... They're called Chippendales."

I think of some chipmunks doing a sexy dance.

Gemma nudges me and says, "Alex and Aidan should be Chippendales."

Alex says, "Shut up!" but Aidan stands up, puts his hands on his hips and wiggles about like a bellydancer.

We all start laughing and then Mrs Martin shouts, "Aidan Harris sit DOWN or you'll get detention!"

Aidan sits down but he is still smiling.

I put my plates on my dinner tray and get up, "See you at the wall," I say.

* * *

My school bag is heavy because I've got one of Dad's claw hammers in it. I can feel the handle digging into my back as I walk. At the junior building I look behind me to check no one is around. The building is very quiet at lunchtime because we're not supposed to be inside. I walk down the corridor to Mrs Martin's room.

Just before I go in I close my eyes and listen for any footsteps or voices nearby. Then I open the door. There are only two small high windows in the room so it is quite dark which is good. I pull the desk drawer but it is locked as usual, so I open my bag for the hammer.

There is a small gap above the drawer where you can just see the little lock going up. I try poking the claw bit of the hammer in and twisting to see if I can push the lock down but it doesn't do anything. I watched Dad pulling the doorframe off when he was decorating the kitchen. He used the claw hammer to pull off the thin bits of wood. I push the hammer into the gap as far as I can, then pull on its handle hard. The gap above the drawer gets bigger and the wood makes a creaking, cracking noise. The wood is strong though and when I stop pulling the gap closes again.

I put the hammer in again, and pull. The wood creaks and makes a snapping sound. I can see more of the little lock this time.

I pull the handle of the hammer so there is a gap above the drawer, then hold the handle in my elbow so the hammer doesn't slip. It is hard work, and I can feel sweat coming out on my back.

I keep my elbow as strong as I can and push my fingers through the gap. The gap is too small, and as hard as I push I can't get my wrist through.

I shut my eyes and touch the pens and papers with my fingertips, trying to be like a blind person and seeing with my hands, but it is no good and I can't reach anything anyway.

My elbow is shaking where it is holding the hammer so I move it a bit. The hammer falls onto the floor and makes a loud bang, and the gap above the drawer snaps shut on my fingers. My fingers hurt as if they've been trapped in a door but the pain gets worse and worse like the drawer is going to squash them completely flat. I think some of my skin is caught on the lock because it feels like a cut. I feel a bit sick because it hurts so much, but I don't want to pull anymore because the lock might pull all the skin off my finger.

With my other hand I reach down and pick up the hammer. My fingers are hurting so badly it is making me want to cry. Mum took me to the Operating Theatre Museum which had all saws and things that people used to use to cut infected legs and arms off with in the olden days. There were no injections to make you sleep or take away the pain so people used to bite hard on cloths or bits of wood, but I don't have anything like that so I bite down on my lip and push the hammer claw into the gap again. It is extra difficult because it is my left hand.

Finally, I manage to push the hammer in the gap again and I use my shoulder to make sure the claw is in properly. My fingers are hurting so badly that the pain is starting to go into the rest of my body. I concentrate to keep the hammer in the right place, and then I pull the handle as hard as I can with my left hand and the gap opens with a bad, snapping noise, and a loud pop, and the drawer falls down on one side.

I take my hand out. My fingers are whitish and a bit blue as if I've been cutting off the blood with an elastic band. There are two blood blisters on the finger that was trapped by the lock, and already a black line under the nail. I hope the nail doesn't die and fall off because that happened to Dad once and it was disgusting.

I shake my hurt fingers and then suck them, then I listen for noises but it is still quiet in the building.

I have broken something underneath one side of the drawer, and there is a big gap now, and I can see inside. I move some envelopes away, the register, and Mrs Martin's bible. I put my arm completely in up to my shoulder and feel along the back of the drawer. There is something slippery like a pack of Christmas cards and more envelopes, but then I feel the little book. I pull it to the front of the drawer and see my name written on the front. I take it out and put it in my bag with the hammer then do it up.

I don't have time to try and fix the broken drawer, because Mrs Martin will probably come in soon, so I leave the room and head to the playground.

* * *

I sit with Gemma, Alex and Aidan on the wall. From here we can see the octagon. I can see Adam on it right at the top, he is playing 'it' as usual. I hold my school bag on my lap tightly and think about the book inside. I don't know whether to take it straight to Dad and then he can tell Mr Cobb, or whether to just throw it in the fire and burn it. I feel like burning it because of all the lies Mrs Martin has been writing about me, and what if nobody believes me even with the book? But that's stupid because the book is proof. I think I will read it first and then decide what to do.

The bell goes for end of lunch and Aidan says, "Ugh what's next Al?"

Alex says, "Double maths."

Gemma says, "My brother's having a party at the weekend and I can have someone to stay over... you want to come, Violet?"

"Yeah okay."

* * *

Mr Ford is our form teacher so we have Maths in our own classroom. He is usually okay but last week he lost his temper with George and it was horrible.

We were having a desk inspection and George keeps crisps and sweets in his desk which you are not allowed to do. Mr Ford looked in George's desk and slammed it shut really hard, and made everyone jump. He shouted and went bright red in the face and everyone was scared because normally he's quiet and serious. He said George's desk was disgusting and then lifted it up by the legs and turned it upside down so the lid flew open and all his books fell out, and loads of sweet wrappers. The lid hit George on the legs and he looked like he wanted to cry but he held it in. Mr Ford shook the desk and then threw it on the floor. George started to pick it up but Mr Ford told him to stop and made him stand with his nose against the wall for the whole lesson and come back at lunchtime to clean his desk.

Me and Gemma kept looking at the desk fallen over on the floor with all the sweets and books and smiling at each other.

I look at the clock and it's 3 o' clock which means only half an hour until home time. The next time I look it is seven minutes past. I carry on with my fractions.

The door opens and Mrs Martin comes in.

Mr Ford stands up and she talks quietly to him. I slide down in my chair and stand my maths book up. I feel my face go red. I push my ankles against my school bag. Everyone is still writing. I hold on to the Maths book and wish for Mrs Martin to go away.

"Violet," Mr Ford says, "Mrs Martin needs a word with you outside."

I stay hunched down.

It goes quiet because everyone stops working and looks round at me.

"Violet," he says again.

I sit up.

Mrs Martin and Mr Ford are staring at me, and so is everyone in my class.

"I don't want to," I say.

Mrs Martin says, "Stop messing around now Violet. I need to ask you something."

"No!"

I look around the class, everyone looks surprised. Gemma is watching me, and so are Alex and Aidan.

Mr Ford comes up to me and takes my school bag. I stand up quick, but he is already handing it to Mrs Martin. She looks round the room and then kneels down and then opens my bag. She pulls the hammer out.

"Violet has committed vandalism," she says.

People start whispering.

Mr Ford frowns and shakes his head like he's working out a maths problem. I think Mr Ford liked me but now he talks to me in a horrible way, "Put your books in your desk young lady, and go with Mrs Martin."

"But Mr Ford... Mrs Martin's been..."

"Now Violet!" he says and I don't want him to go mad like he did with George so I put my books away. I feel tired. Mrs Martin is doing her sad face, and holding onto my school bag. Nobody says anything and I bet they all think that I'm a vandal. I walk to the front of the room and Mrs Martin opens the door for me to go out.

"Thank you Mr Ford," she says, "sorry to disturb."

When we are outside Mrs Martin puts her hand on my shoulder and marches me like she did after Heather cut Hannah's hair. We go to the girls' changing rooms and she says, "Sit down."

I sit on one of the benches, and she opens my school bag and starts taking things out. She is shaking her head as she does it and breathing in a funny way as if she's been running. Maybe because the book is small she won't see it, but she does. She puts it into the pocket of her dress and then turns and puts a hand on the wall, and rests her forehead next to it. "Why are you so cruel to me?" she says in her little sad voice.

I don't say anything. I'm really tired and it is almost hometime so she will have to let me go.

She shakes her head fast and then stands up and sniffs.

"You've got a month of lunchtime detentions," she says, "I won't tell Mr Cobb that you've stolen, because *that* on top of the vandalism could lead to expulsion."

I try to look through her to the wall and she goes blurry.

"I believe in you Violet. I believe you can change and be a good girl."

I keep staring through her and imagining the coat hooks on the wall.

The bell goes.

"Put your things away," she says, "I'll talk to Mr Cobb tonight, and try to convince him to let me deal with this, rather than informing your parents and upsetting them when they're already busy with your new sister."

She keeps hold of the hammer, "I'll see you in my room tomorrow lunchtime. No later than 12.30."

I don't say anything, and suddenly she crouches down in front of me and grabs my head and makes me look at her properly.

"Yes Mrs Mar…"

"Don't think you can deceive me. You and I are going to be spending a lot of time together and I will teach you to be good."

Her eyes are sparkly as though she has cried a bit. She lets go of my face and I kneel on the floor and start putting my things back in my school bag.

37

CAPTAIN KALE'S LOG:

DAY ONE: OCTOBER 2000 MAYBE THE 6TH OR 7TH?

No calendars onboard. Even if there was, don't know the day so would be pointless anyway. Need a television.

TIME: 14.00?

Successfully departed from Isle of Wight. Sailing time approximately 10 hours.

No sight of land.

Some signs of sickness in crew.

Ate spaghetti. Still nice.

Running low on water.

Boring. Nothing to report

Water from taps possibly foul. Been boiling it, and making very strong coffees to hide the taste.

DAY ONE/ ENTRY 2-

TIME: EARLY EVENING. 1800 HOURS?

Put ice cubes into saucepan to melt.

Still heading South

Cabin boy still sleeping

No sight of land.

Youngest member of crew has a cold. Signs of discontent observed in youngest member of crew. Gave one ration of milk.

Drew a portrait of youngest member of crew while she was sleeping. Out of practice. Not great.

Had coffee.

Drew another portrait. Better. Maria is good subject. Looks like Lisa, not like Claude at all.

DAY ONE/ ENTRY 3-

TIME: 2100 HOURS?

Need to put petrol in vessel.

Found cigarettes. Coffee and cigarette on deck. No noise. Clear night, loads of stars. Heard talking inside the boat. Thought Sergio had turned the radio on, or maybe he was on the phone. When I went inside everything was silent. Hate the silence. Cities are better, although if I suddenly heard the noise of a double decker bus drive past right now on the boat, I'd probably be terrified.

I hope sex with Sergio won't mess up us being friends. At least we sort of had a couple of arguments already. I don't think people are really friends until they've had at least one fight. What the fuck is he doing locked up in that room all the time? Maybe he's having some kind of masturbation marathon, doing his terminator face and fantasizing about 'butts'. Funny.

There are definitely noises on the boat, like feet shuffling, and boots on the stairs. Maybe the boat is haunted by Anne's dead husband. No, I bet he's with Anne. Maybe he's going to haunt me for stealing the boat. Ghosts don't exist. Even if they did, people are far more fucking scary. I wish ghosts did exist. Maybe I can send Anne a postcard when we get to France and tell her thanks and sorry or something and let her know where the boat is. Maybe I can write to Jodie. No more stupid ideas dickhead. Can't even email in case police are looking into emails. Even if I make up a new email address it's not going to work because how would she respond without them knowing? She's better off without me anyway. I haven't ever looked after her, why do I suddenly want to when it is not an option? Things are always more desirable when you're not allowed. I have been a bad sister.

ENTRY 4-

TIME: 2200 HOURS.

Put petrol in vessel. Difficult due to darkness. Accident. Dropped can overboard. Shame as it was buoyant, and probably valuable in the event of sinking.

Crew restless. Gave her one ration of milk.

Ate cold beans out of can.

Captain feeling signs of fatigue/exhaustion. Ringing ears, shivers, unease. Need to keep sailing on. Want to land in France. Croissant, and maybe one of those giant hot chocolates that they drink out of bowls.

Had two rations of coffee.

ENTRY 5-

Still no sign of cabin boy. Maybe suffering seasickness or scurvy.

Captain feeling more symptoms of tiredness. Drank many cups of coffee.

Captain vomits coffee in sink. Black.

Found treasure in bag. Fanta.

ENTRY 6-

0200 OR 0300 HOURS DAY TWO?

Too tired to keep driving. Seeing black flashing spots, and weird dark shapes like panthers walking across the surface of the sea.

Engines off.

Feel like my body is slightly above my body. About a head too high, so I can almost see the top of my head, and transparent feet that are mine, seem to be poking out of my shins. Wiggle my toes to figure out which ones are the dreamy ones, but all twenty wiggle.

Fed Maria. Her tooth has fully come through the gum now. Will have to buy special baby toothpaste in France. I remember the word for toothpaste from school. Dentrifice? Is that right. Dentrifice por bambino? Dunno. How the fuck am I going to get Euros? Maybe Sergio has a bank account he can use.

Sleep. Sleep. Sleep. Sleep. Sleep. Sleep IS THE ANSWER.

Tried to wake Cabin boy for nightwatch. Heard noises of crying behind door. Homesick? Seasick? Mothersick? Weird.

Let anchor down to sleep.

Hopefully nothing will crash into us and sink us during the night.

ENTRY 7-

No sign of land. Just more fucking water.

Thirsty, but tap water tastes bad, even when boiled. Tiny bit of Isle of Wight water left in Pepsi bottle. Even with lid on saucepan there will not be enough for more than one of Maria's bottles. Water water everywhere and not a drop to drink? What is that from? Why do I know that?

Lips are cracked, and tight and scabby in corners of mouth. Ha ha! Scurvy! Laughed and split mouth again, hurting. Opened can of tinned pineapple and drank juice. Good for me vitamin C. When water runs out for making Maria's milk, perhaps she will be able to eat tinned fruit. I won't eat anymore, and save it for her.

Discovered terrible treasure in cupboard. Pickled wiener sausages! They're not even made from pork, they're made from chicken? Drained them in the sink, and took them onto the deck. Threw them over the side of the boat, lit a cigarette, and watched the wieners float like small logs. Ahh!!!!!!!!!!! Imagine being a tiny person in a river and logs rushing down to crush you, and then when they hit, they were actually disgusting smooth sausages made of chicken dyed pink.

Nasty.

The wieners split up in the water and went their separate ways, although there was a group of three that seemed to stick together touching ends in a little frankfurter triangle. Kept the wiener jar, because I might choose the best sketch of Maria, roll it up and release it into the sea. That's the best way of contacting Jodie! I can write her a letter and put it in the jar too. I can even write the full address on it, because no one can trace a jar that's been in the sea for days, or months or years.

DAY 2

(maybe Day 3 if I slept for a whole day, but unlikely as had that messed up sleep where you feel like you're awake the whole time, but somehow thank fuck, time passes. Maria wouldn't have slept through the night so pretty certain it is still Day 2).

DAYLIGHT.

Pulled up anchor. Boat in distance. Waved then remembered there may be people looking for me like the police. Maybe should not include that information in this book. I'm keeping the book anyway. It is a good sketchbook. Could get good at drawing again, maybe sell portraits to make cash. There's a place in Paris I think, a square that's full of artists doing portraits.

Engines on. Driving. Still no sign of land. Still following compass South. Driving time about an hour and a half.

Took a break. Drew biro picture of Maria on the carpet kicking her legs. Best picture yet. Rolled it up, and was about to put in the sausage jar for Jodie, but Maria might want it when she's older. Emptied Horlicks into the sea, it looked like ash from when someone's cremated as it blew all over the place in a big, disintegrating twist. Used Horlicks jar for stuff for Maria. Put the

leg-kicking picture in, and another one of her sleeping.

Heard footsteps again on the boat. Keep thinking it's Sergio but when I go to the room it is quiet. Getting bored of his spiritual retreat or whatever it is.

Maria woke up, had breakfast then when straight back to sleep. Sounds better today, not as much wheezing.

AFTERNOON-

Sergio still locked in his room. Started to think he might be dead from internal bleeding from where he was beaten up.

Banged on door. Shouted for ages.

Eventually he answered. Said he had a migraine and couldn't take the light.

I think he's crying though, he might be married or have a family or something. Or he might be gay. I wish he would unlock the door. What's the point in having someone else on the boat if you can't even talk to them?

EVENING-

There are other people in the boat. I can hear them talking. Maria's down there too. Where did they come from anyway? There's nowhere for them to hide, although I never checked the toilet. Fucking great, stowaways. Going to retrieve Maria and investigate noise.

38

Gemma is coming round tonight. She's stolen a scary film called *The Lost Boys* from her brother's room and we're going to watch it.

Laurie was supposed to babysit because it is Dad's Christmas party, but Mum didn't want to go, so Laurie's not coming. Gemma never has babysitters anyway. Mum is in bed already, so me and Gemma can do what we like.

I go into Mum and Dad's bedroom. There is a hump in the covers where Mum is. The television is on really loud, it's making shaky blue light on the walls. It is football on and it's making a horrible noise. I climb onto the bed and look for the remote to turn the volume down. Mum is mumbling in her sleep. I lean on her and feel under the covers and pillows until I find the remote.

Jodie is sleeping in her Moses basket next to the bed. She has kicked her blanket off. I look and check the baby alarm. The bright green light is shining so it is on, then I make sure the plastic tube that goes from the alarm down to Jodie's tummy is plugged in properly and it is. I put my fingers on the blue tube and run them down to Jodie's tummy. I lift up her little t-shirt and look at where the tube is stuck to her. Mum showed me how to put it on, so sometimes I do it now. At the end of the blue tube there is a circle-shaped bit of material like the soft bit in the middle of a plaster. You put in on her tummy, and then get the special soft sticky tape and cut off a piece to stick it on with. If Jodie stops breathing for more than ten seconds the alarm goes off. When it goes off we rush upstairs to check her, but usually she must have just been holding her breath in her sleep or something. You can set the alarm to 15 and even 25 seconds but we keep it on ten. Jodie's hair is much darker than my hair, and her eyes are a more dark silvery grey than mine, which are a kind of grey like a pigeon.

Next to Jodie is Geronimo her toy giraffe. I pull the blanket up over her tummy and put it over Geronimo's legs too.

At 8 o' clock when Gemma is supposed to arrive, the doorbell rings.

I open the door. It is Sharon the secretary from Dad's work.

"Hi, Violet," she says.

Behind her I see my dad kneeling by the wall.

"What's wrong with my dad?" I ask.

Sharon smiles and shivers a bit, "Oh he's alright... he's just had too much to drink. Is your Mum in?"

My Dad starts being sick on the wall.

"She's asleep," I say.

"Oh."

Sharon goes over to the wall and starts talking to Dad. She helps him to stand up, and he tries to walk but he goes too fast and drags Sharon so she almost falls over.

"Violet!" she calls, "can you help me?"

I put my school shoes on, and go outside. I look at Dad. His eyes look at me but then they look sideways. He smiles but because of his eyes it looks horrible like a monster.

Dad leans on Sharon and she puts his arm around her neck. I push against his hip so he doesn't fall on me, and he trips and puts his hand on my head. He walks and wobbles all the way to the front door. His hand on my head is making my neck hurt.

We all start to go up the stairs but Dad says, "Ss' okay, I'm okaaaay," and crawls up by himself.

Sharon and I follow him up the stairs. He holds onto the banister and stands up. He looks at me and it is like he didn't know

I was there before and he smiles and puts his hand on my face and says, "Alright daaarling!"

There is a bit of sick on his tie.

"Come on, Jack," Sharon says, "you should go to bed."

"No," I say. "He'll wake mum up."

Sharon looks like she doesn't know what to do and we are all just standing in the hall, then Dad mumbles and grumbles then says, "Bath. Bathroom... brush mm' teeth."

In the bathroom Dad falls over and hits his head on the radiator.

"Shit!" Sharon says.

There is a cut on Dad's forehead that is starting to bleed. He rolls over and then sits leaning against the radiator and the towels. He touches the cut on his head and smears blood in his eyebrow. He looks really confused like a cartoon character that has just been hit on the head.

Sharon says, "Violet why don't you go and get some ice for his head?"

I run downstairs and get some frozen peas from the freezer.

When I come back Dad has fallen asleep and started snoring.

Sharon says, "Listen Violet, I'm sorry... I have to go. Will you be alright?"

"Yes."

"Just put those on his head for five minutes and then if I were you I'd just leave him there to sleep it off. Anyway I better go. Your dad'll be fine in the morning. Er, see you soon."

She goes down the stairs and I listen as the front door closes. I hear the car start up in the drive, and then I climb on the sink and watch her drive off.

I go downstairs and put the peas back in the freezer. I make myself a bowl of Coco Pops and put the telly on. It is Only Fools and Horses Christmas special. Del and Rodney are dressed up as Batman and Robin. A lady gets her bag stolen by muggers. Del and Rodney's car has broken down so they are running to their Christmas party. When the muggers see Batman and Robin running towards them they drop the handbag and run off.

"It's Batman!" the lady says and opens her mouth wide in shock. It makes me laugh.

I wonder why Gemma isn't here yet.

I go upstairs and check on Jodie again. The light on the monitor is still on. One of Jodie's hands is lying on Geronimo's back, and she is smiling a bit in her sleep. I put my face close to her nose and listen to her breathing.

A crashing noise comes from the bathroom.

I go quietly past Mum's bed and close the bedroom door, then go in to the bathroom.

The doorbell rings.

My dad is being sick in the bath and has knocked all the shampoos and conditioners in too.

I take the key from the inside of the door, shut the door and lock him in.

39

Violet woke up on the floor of the lounge. She was curled around Maria who was asleep, breathing gently. She laid her ear on Maria's chest and listened to her heartbeat. For a few moments everything seemed quiet and normal, then she heard lowered voices in the kitchen.

She cuddled Maria, and spoke into the pillow, "Please, let me be insane and there not really be people in the kitchen."

Violet stood up slowly, walked to Sergio's door and tried the handle; still locked. She didn't dare bang on it in case the people came out of the kitchen. Her body was rigid. The voices got louder as if they were walking closer to the kitchen entrance. One was a deep, male voice; the voice that responded was softer and less frequent. Violet strained to hear, but it was difficult over a buzzing that rattled in her ears. They were discussing something, the louder voice speaking, the quieter one murmuring responses.

A shiver ripped up her spine as she realised who they were. It was the Trisha Show couple.

Maybe they were serial killers, fixated on Violet and Maria since the moment they'd met on the ferry. What was that statistic, 99% of people know or have met their killers at least once? Or maybe it was because she'd recognised them from the telly. What were they doing here? How had they hidden all this time without her noticing?

Paul's voice sounded again, and this time Violet understood the words, "MY baby… fuckin kill her… dumb bitch."

He must have turned away because the talking went muffled, and then Violet couldn't hear either of them. She stayed rooted to the spot, her tired eyes scanning the room as she tried to think.

It was light outside, sunny. She couldn't remember falling asleep. The Captain's Log book, and the Horlicks jar were tucked in next to Maria like another couple of babies.

Violet lifted Maria up, and tiptoed past the kitchen to the stairs. Halfway up she heard a loud bang, and the shout, "Blood's BLOOD!" and she ran the last few steps to the steering room. The rattling in her ears had sped up, and become a high-frequency squealing.

Violet slid a tiny bolt across, laid Maria on the floor, and sank down with her back against the door, waiting for the inevitable footsteps.

She pressed her ear against the wood and listened.

They were still just talking.

With a sudden, doom sensation, Violet realised that the anchor must still be down and they wouldn't be able to move.

She would wait until the couple fell asleep, then get Sergio, and see if they could somehow trap or throw them overboard. It was unlikely though, as both Paul and Charlotte were bigger and heavier than either of them. Violet could probably frighten Charlotte with a knife. She could sneak up on her, and use her as a hostage. Maybe take them out on deck, throw Charlotte in the sea, then while Paul was scrabbling for Charlotte, Violet could run back inside, Sergio could lock the door, and they could carry on to France. Fucking genius.

The anchor would still be down though. She would have to go out the window, climb down to the deck and pull up the anchor before doing anything else.

Maria woke up and started to cry.

A scurry of footsteps sounded on the stairs.

Maybe the best thing was to go down and appeal to their

humanity. Charlotte seemed alright, if a bit weird and sad. And Paul was probably just a harmless pervert. If they were serial killers they wouldn't have gone on the Trisha show... unless they were that sure of themselves, and it was like a 'Fuck you!' to the police for not catching up with them, and finding the bits of bodies that they buried all over the country. That was why they were getting day trips to places like the Trisha Show! Cover for when they disposed of corpses they had no further use for.

Perhaps they really did 'love each other to bits', and just wanted a friend like Violet to love to bits too. Violet put her hand on the bolt, but at that moment footsteps banged on the stairs and something thudded against the door. She recoiled, and walked backwards slowly to the captain's chair, hugging Maria close to her, her eyes fixed on the door handle.

Maria's cries rung out like a siren, overpowering any noise the heavy presence might be making the other side of the door.

Violet whispered into the back of Maria's head, "I'm sorry, Baby. We've just got to wait. Too dangerous."

They stayed there, Violet watching the door with Maria struggling in her arms, screaming.

* * *

It was possible that she'd slept, but Violet wasn't sure, as the whole time she'd been conscious of Maria's crying, and of making sure she didn't relax too much and let Maria fall onto the floor.

The sun was quite low in the sky, it must have been late afternoon. Maria's crying was slower, and had a painful tone to it.

"Just go to sleep," Violet said, "When you wake up, I'll have sorted everything out, and your bottle will be ready."

A low voice came through the crack under the door, "Violet...it is Violet isn't it? ... Violet... It's okay...come here."

She put Maria down on the floor, and crawled over. A shadow was visible at the base of the door, and she lowered her face to it.

"It's okay, Violet... I can help."

Violet put her cheek against the wood floor, and spoke to the gap under the door, "Maria wants a bottle," she said.

"I believe you," the voice said.

Violet felt the warm breath dampen on her lips. She leaned in and said, "Maria needs milk, her bottle's in the kitchen."

"It was a wicked thing to do."

"What?"

"You know."

Violet tried again, "Maria needs milk... Can I come down?"

The shadow disappeared and a plain, uninterrupted line of light replaced it. Violet pushed her fists against her eyes. Maria got louder.

She waited until the sun went red and sank into the horizon. The car seat was downstairs, and there was nothing to pad Maria with, or stop her from rolling over onto her face and suffocating. The room was filling up with the smell of dirty nappy.

Violet couldn't really hear Maria's crying anymore; it felt more like pulsing waves of energy than an actual noise. "Maria," she said, "I'm going out the window. Don't move. Ha ha, if I die like a dog, I'll die doing my dooty."

Violet opened the window as wide as it would go and squeezed out. There was no handy ledge to stand on, just a very thin, rounded ridge, that her feet kept slipping off. She gripped the window with her fingertips, while her toes struggled to grip the ridge. It was only a few metres down to the deck, but it would make a noise if she jumped.

Her fingers and toes were already aching with the strain and wouldn't hold out much longer. A wave of sadness hit her, and she wished she'd done something useful like become a climber, and could support her whole bodyweight with her fingertips.

"Think fast," she said, imagining her fingers and toes snapping off, then crashing digitless to the deck.

She would grip, and slide.

Violet spread her arms and legs out like a rainforest frog,

imagined suckers on her hands and feet, and let herself drop.

Her jeans button scraped down the side of the boat making a sound like an electric saw. Her right ankle twisted, bent over, and crunched as her weight came down on it.

She lay curled up on the deck rocking and gripping her ankle, her mouth open silently releasing the scream she couldn't let out.

"Elevate," she whispered, and rested her ankle on the hand rail, then leaned back against the boat.

It was quite dark, and raining softly. The cold sea breeze felt soothing, and she closed her eyes, waiting for the pain to ease. Maria's crying still rang out above her.

"Ay that stung," she said, and closed her eyes, letting her head roll to one side.

A few minutes later she was woken by pins and needles in her leg. She lifted it off the rail, and tried to stretch her foot. Her ankle was already swollen and becoming shapeless, as if it was being slowly injected with liquid.

She stood up, putting her weight on her left leg, and then gingerly rotated her right ankle.

"Not broken," she said, "but useless for now."

She used the hand rail and the side of the boat, to swing herself around the deck keeping her bad foot off the ground, until she reached Sergio's bedroom.

The window was open about five centimetres. Violet was about to knock when she heard talking. She shrank back out of sight, and listened. He was talking too quietly for her to hear the words.

A chill ran down her neck. He was in on it; the three of them, Paul, Charlotte and Sergio.

Feet beating out of time… three together, hand in hand.

Violet gripped the rail, stood on her bad ankle and started kicking the window. Her bare foot thudded against the glass ineffectively, so she got down on her knees and started to pull at it.

"You fuck!" she shouted, "What have you done, you idiot?"

Sergio appeared the other side of the window, his eyes puffy and blinking. He put his hand against the glass, and she saw his lips making words.

He frowned and started to unlatch the window. Violet waited till he reached out to push the window open, and threw her body against it trapping his hand outside, and bit his wrist.

She heard him swear, and then he put his other hand outside the boat, and she felt his fingers go into her mouth prising her jaws apart.

She spat on the window. "We trusted you!"

"I do not understant," he said.

"You told them!" Violet said, realising that she was crying.

Sergio opened the window and helped her in. She winced as she stepped down onto her bad foot.

He glanced quickly at the bed where his mobile phone was laying, "I'm sorry," he said, "I don' understan."

Violet hit him in the face, and saw the Terminator eyes flash for a moment.

"You fucking crazy!"

"I heard you." Violet said.

On the bed, a little voice came out of the phone, "Sergio?"

They both dived for it at the same time.

Violet gripped the phone, before Sergio's hands closed round hers.

"Why did you bring them here?" she shouted.

Sergio's face looked grey, his forehead becoming shiny. He put a finger to his lips.

"Please, Violet," he whispered, "it is my mother."

Violet shook her head, "How do you even know them?"

Sergio's hand still held hers tight, the phone trapped in the middle.

"I don' understan," he repeated. "Please give me the mobil... my mother she doesn't know where I am."

"I don't care about your mother!" Violet yelled, "Why are those people in the fucking kitchen? How have you got signal anyway? We're at sea!"

"There are some more people on the boat?"

"Fuck you!" she shouted, her voice breaking with a screech.

Sergio put his hands either side of his head as if she'd just said. 'stick 'em up'. He watched her hand that contained the phone.

Violet took her chance and climbed out of the window, clutching the phone tight. She felt Sergio take hold of her ankles, and opened her palm. The little phone voice said again, "Hallo hallo? ... Sergio?"

Sergio pulled, and Violet began to slide back in through the window. With one last effort, she threw the phone across the deck and watched it skid under the hand rail and drop over the side.

Then she was pulled into the room and Sergio scrambled out screaming, "No, no, no, no, no, NO!"

She watched his feet kicking, as he beat his fists on the deck. Maybe it really had been his mum.

Violet climbed out, and stood over where he lay. His arms were dangling down over the side towards the water.

"I do not tell her where I am," he said, "I was try to tell her about France."

Violet's head felt swollen with pressure, as though it was full of helium, and trying to lift off her shoulders.

Sergio sat up.

"Just call her when we get there," Violet said.

He turned to face her. His eyes were red. He didn't know about the Trisha couple.

"Until two weeks I don't talk with my mother for six year... my aunt she's giving me the new telephone number." He stared at the water, "I have the number only on this."

They were wasting time. "I'll phone your aunt when we get to France... get the number again."

Sergio stared at his knees, "My mother when I try to call she cancel the call... for five years. And then she start to speak with me again. She is banishing me when..."

"Sorry," Violet said, "I thought you were talking about us... and that you knew *Them*." She motioned to the inside of the boat.

Sergio carried on staring into the water. Violet imagined the phone travelling slowly downwards, bubbles coming out of the speaker as his mum called 'Hallo! Hallo! Hallo!' And then it would land on the bottom with the sea lice, and blind fish with oversized jaws.

"Sergio," she said, "there are people on the boat."

He didn't move.

She poked his side with her foot.

He got to his knees, "Where is Maria?"

Violet couldn't remember. Maria seemed like a dream that you try to recall when you're awake, features disappearing and shifting as you try to picture them.

"She needs her dinner," Violet said.

Sergio stood up, and walked to the back of the boat to the door.

"Don't!" Violet called. She started to run, but forgot about her ankle, stumbled to the deck, and crawled after Sergio.

Violet reached the door to see Sergio disappearing up the stairs. She was about to shout about the door being locked when two big shapes rushed after him like heavy speeded-up shadows.

Violet lay in the doorway with her hands hanging down on the steps, and closed her eyes. She listened as a loud banging started and then the sound of splintering wood. Violet opened her eyes again and everything turned red, then brown, then black.

40

I am in detention. Mrs Martin has given me a piece of paper where she has written *Things I Can Do To Be A Better Girl.* I am allowed to write a list or just think about it and we can discuss it when she comes back.

I stare at the badger in Joanna's tapestry.

Mrs Martin gives me these kinds of things to do quite a lot and it is better if I write something because she takes a long time reading them and sometimes copying them into her little book and by the time she's done that it's almost the end of lunch.

Today I can't think properly though and every time I have an idea of something, when I start to write it down I can't remember it anymore. I think of the bright pink scar on Benjamin's neck, and I get a weird ache in my tummy. Then I think of the voice. It usually comes at night time when I can't sleep. Sometimes I can stop it by reading really fast out loud and filling my head up with words. The best books for this are the Famous Five ones which I don't like much but they are easy and very quick to read.

I will never tell anyone about the voice, except maybe Jamie if he comes back as a ghost because spirits can keep secrets.

I pick up my fountain pen and write *I will look after people who are younger than me.* It takes me a long time to write it because I have to do it joined-up and I get stuck for ages on the word 'people' because I can't remember how to join the p to the e.

I hear Mrs Martin coming back and I pick up my pen again.

The door creaks as she opens then closes it. I listen to her footsteps as she walks up to me. The room is really quiet, only her footsteps and the clock ticking on the wall, her footsteps are loudest.

I look at the page with only one sentence on it. My hand looks funny holding the pen.

Mrs Martin stops behind me and puts a hand on my shoulder. I can see her bony fingers out of the corner of my eye. The floor squeaks and I hear her breathe as she bends down behind me. She moves my hair to one side and I can feel the cold air of the room on the bit of my neck that she's uncovered. I stare at the paper and make my muscles tight as she puts her mouth on the back of my neck and gives me a kiss.

41

Violet was lying with her arms above her head; they were cold like her face, but the rest of her body was warm. There was a dull pain in her ankle, and a cramped feeling in the toes of that foot.

The door was open, and she could hear Sergio talking in an exaggerated voice in the kitchen, and Maria gurgling back at him. Violet lifted the bedcovers, and saw that Sergio had put her bad foot up on a pillow. She looked out of the window, but the boat was surrounded by fog. She put her arms under the blankets, and shuffled down till she was covered up to her nose. The coldness of the room and the stillness reminded her of a room at her old school where you went when you were ill. She rolled onto her side, curled up tightly and went back to sleep.

Someone was pushing her head into the pillow. Hot hands that smelled of copper covered her face and shoved it downwards. Then a heavy body climbed on top her. She felt the heat of him, his big face millimetres from hers, currant eyes, shining and dilating uselessly in the darkness.

"Paul?" she said, and a cold tongue licked her face from chin to cheek. It flicked across her earlobe, then it was probing the concave of her eye socket, running across her eyebrow and forehead, before stopping at her hairline; its tip resting, vibrating a little on her skin.

"Paul," she repeated, but she felt the weight release her, the pillow rising with her face as the hand was removed, the smell of metal and saliva dispersing as sleep started to drag again, and she retreated into the blanket heat.

It was hot, and black under the covers. Her whole body was heavy, a warm, appealing heavy that it would be pointless to resist; as if she was full of gradually setting honey instead of blood. Sometimes she heard Maria cry, or footsteps stopping next to her bed. But then sleep came again, and she sank through the sheets and mattress into a somnolent underworld where she lay in something like black treacle up to her nostrils.

At some point Violet felt a breeze. She tried to ignore it, but it persisted, focussed on a point above her eyebrow. Violet felt the covers moving off her face, and the cold area spreading. When she opened her eyes she saw the pinkish blur of a face. It leaned down, and a thick, brown fringe swung forward. The fringe settled on Violet's forehead, and as Charlotte bent down it spread like a dropping curtain, covering her eyes, before slipping off sideways as Charlotte whispered in her ear, "He's scared."

Violet tried to sit up, but Charlotte put a hand on her boob. Violet saw the hand recognise what it was resting on, and it was quickly removed and put back down on Violet's neck.

The visible part of Charlotte's face was turning red.

"Why are you following us?" Violet asked.

She felt the hand on her neck turn clammy, as Charlotte whispered, "I don't mean to be rude... but you need to sleep more if you're going to be the mum."

Violet tried to shake off the sleep feeling and hold onto Charlotte who was disappearing behind some fog.

"No, don't go," she said, "I'm sorry I laughed." She grabbed Charlotte's wrist, but her fingers were removed gently, and tucked back into the covers. A faint smell of sweat and vanilla body spray mixed with vinegary ketchup filled the air for a moment. Violet sniffed hard, but the smell became imperceptible as it mixed with the mist in the room.

* * *

A hand tapped Violet's shoulder and she heard a little shriek. She opened her eyes, and saw Maria smiling, reaching forward to take hold of her nose. Violet prised Maria's fingers off, and let her take hold of her finger instead.

Sergio was standing beside the bed. "Sorry for wake you," he said, "We have some problem of the boat."

Violet sat up, "How long have I been sleeping?"

"I think maybe ten hours."

She sat up, and re-did her ponytail.

Sergio watched her, "How do you feel?"

"Okay."

She sat Maria between her legs and put her lips against her hair for a moment before replying, "What problem?"

Sergio put his hand against the window, and looked out at the fog, then back at her. "When I go for start the boat, I see ignition key is on already, and the boat is in drive position."

Violet waited.

"I think you are sleeping maybe, and the boat he still goes."

"What do you mean?" Violet said, kicking the covers off her legs.

"The boat goes until the gas is finish."

"So we're just floating?"

"Yes. Floating."

"Where are we?"

He clasped his hands together and stared at them, "I'm no sure. If you keep the pointer where I say you, then we are arrive already to France."

Violet lay Maria down next to her, then curled up in a ball and covered her face. She squeezed her eyes shut tight until she saw red. They were going to die or at best get caught by someone and arrested. She could hear Maria, and the sound of the floor creaking as Sergio shifted his weight.

"Violet?"

She felt the bed sink as he sat down and put a hand on her back.

"Violet," he repeated, "I am sorry for leaving you to drive all the time."

She kept her face covered and spoke into her hands, "There's no more water."

He left his hand resting on her back, and she heard him take a couple of slow breaths. "I find some ice in the freezer and we can use today. Listen, when you are driving the boat what numbers is the compass point to?"

Violet took her hands away from her face and stared at the wall, as she tried to remember driving.

"Violet?"

She got up off the bed. "I didn't use the numbers," she said, and walked out of the room, to the lounge.

The captain's log was tucked under some blankets next to the Horlicks jar. She picked it up, and looked through the pages. Her handwriting had always been bad, a mixture of non joined-up letters, and messy joined-up sections that looked like broken springs. She ran her fingers along the words as she tried to read.

Violet walked back into the bedroom, holding the book to her chest, "I went south the whole time," she said, "but I don't know what happened when I fell asleep."

Sergio lifted Maria off the bed, "Come on," he said, "Let's go for look to the map and see if we can find where we are."

Violet and Sergio knelt on the floor with the maps spread out in front of them. The Europe map showed the small space between France and the Isle of Wight. Sergio was right, if they'd gone in the right direction, they would have arrived days ago. It was clear that somehow, she had missed France. But she had been driving south for most of the journey. If she'd gone east, then they would have hit Belgium or Netherlands, but her clearest memory of driving the boat was heading south.

The most likely thing was that she'd somehow gone west or south west for a while and just missed the sticking out parts of France. If she'd gone south for as long as she thought, and as she'd written in the Captain's Log, then they were probably in the sea called Bay of Biscay, and had cruised down the side of France and were headed to Spain. She just hoped they hadn't gone west for long.

Violet remembered a programme about the Bay of Biscay; it was supposed to be one of the roughest seas or something, and loads of people scuba dived there because of all the shipwrecks. Francis Drake came into her head too, but she didn't know why. The reason the Bay of Biscay so rough was something to do with it being shallow she thought, but she couldn't remember exactly. Even if she did, it was probably better not to mention it. She hoped they were close to France or Spain, and weren't stranded right in the middle of it.

Sergio was looking out of the window, but fog still surrounded the boat. It was like being inside a cloud. Violet thought of a trip to Tenerife just after Jodie was born. Her dad drove them all up a mountain. You couldn't see the top because it was in the clouds. Violet watched the clouds as they got closer. She was excited to touch one of them. They looked solid and white and bumpy. She remembered her dad announcing, "We're entering the clouds now, Violet!" and then a horrible feeling of being tricked when the clouds were just mist, and your hands went straight through when you tried to touch them.

Fuck, she hoped they were near the coast. Without the engine, there was nothing they could do if huge waves started to hit them. In films, sailors always seemed to aim straight at the massive waves, and ride over them. If they got hit sideways on, the boat would probably just tip over.

She stood up, "I'm going to see if there's an inflatable boat or something."

Sergio turned to her. The swelling in his face was gone. Now there were dark purple and green shadowy bruises that looked like makeup around his eye and down his cheek. He smiled, "I go to make a bottle for Maria."

"Thanks," Violet said, and left the room.

The fog was thick outside, she couldn't see more than a couple of metres in front of her. The gentle rocking of the boat seemed ominous and disorientating now that the sea was invisible. She held her hand out in front of her and took a couple of steps forward until the hand rail came into view. She took hold of it and looked down at the water. A bird screeched high above, and she looked up but could only see more of the bright white mist.

Violet put her hand on the boat's cabin, and began to walk slowly around. Her ankle twinged and she felt a little crunch with each step as if there was a screwed up crisp packet inside the joint.

There was a u-shaped seat that looked like it might open up to a storage compartment; she felt under the rim and found a catch. Inside there were more of the rubber floats that hung on the boat's rails, and an empty petrol canister.

The other parts of the seat unclipped and lifted up. In one compartment there was an old-fashioned orange lifejacket, it looked like a giant's travel pillow. When Violet picked it up she smelled mould, and some wet dusty stuff came off on her fingers. She hooked it over her arm and made her way round to the other side of the boat.

A smell of cooking came out of the kitchen window, and she could hear Sergio singing. The window was tinted dark so she stood on tiptoes and cupped her hands round her eyes to peer through.

He held Maria in one arm, a spatula in his other hand, and he was dancing as he cooked, something in a frying pan. Violet's stomach rumbled and she ducked down.

She recognised the song, and stood back up on her tiptoes to listen,

"Give a little bit... I give a little bit of my life for you, da-dah da-dah... Give a little bit, give a little bit of your time for me."

Whatever the song was, it was pretty bad, and annoyingly catchy; she was already starting to hum it in her head.

A bit further along from the window there was a box-shaped panel attached to the wall of the boat. It was about 2 metres long and stuck out 30 centimetres. It looked like part of the boat, but there were some hinges at the bottom. Violet felt above the box and undid a catch. The panel opened downwards and strapped inside it was a pile of folded-up yellow and black rubber. On the inside of the panel were some instructions printed on the plastic, 'INFLATING THE LIFE RAFT'. She opened the straps and let the contents fall out onto the deck.

There was a valve that you twisted and the boat would blow up automatically. The instructions said there was another pump that you could use if the boat wasn't sufficiently inflated by the automatic one.

Violet could still hear Sergio singing but the song was different now, that one about having a lovely day.

"When I look at you... and I know it's going to be... a lovely DAYYYYYYYYYY.... When I look at you."

The life raft made a hissing sound as it filled with air. The bits that she hadn't unfolded properly creaked as they inflated and opened out. It was too big to stay where she'd laid it, so she lifted it onto its side as it carried on expanding. When it was fully inflated, it was about five metres long, and two metres wide. It had rounded rubber walls with rope handles, and two rubber hoops that she guessed were for the paddles. The bottom was also inflatable but with longer, thin tube panels. Underneath it was reinforced with some harder material, which was a relief because she'd seen a film where turtles had bashed into the fabric bottom of a raft and torn through.

She dragged the life raft to the back of the boat, and tied it to the guard rail. Attached to the inside with elastic straps was some kind of rubber sheet with a pole and ropes folded into it, and two miniature paddles. She pulled one out. It was light, hollow, metal with a black, plastic paddle on the end. She ran her fingers down it, and felt a thin line in the metal. Violet gripped either side of the join and twisted hard. It worked the same as the extendable mops at work. She felt the handle twist in opposite directions, and loosen till she was able to pull it open and extend it. When it was extended to full size, Violet tightened it again.

The door opened, and Sergio stuck his head out, "Violet I..."

She turned quickly, Sergio looked at her but then his eyes fixed on the life raft.

"I blew it up," Violet said, "in case we need it."

He walked up to the boat and touched its side. "You blow him up by yourself?"

She felt suddenly embarrassed of the boat, "There was an automatic pump thing."

Sergio watched the dinghy as if he expected it to do something unpredictable. He frowned, shook his head, and then smiled.

"I cook steak," he said, "Would you like?"

* * *

Violet sat at the table in the lounge area to feed Maria. Maria drank fast, her eyes concentrated on the bottle. She'd started putting her hands on it while she drank. This time, she had one hand resting on the bottle and the other she held against her ear.

The fog outside was making everything glow. Violet looked at the furniture in the room, the strange light made everything seem to have an outline. She realised she was still humming the tune from earlier. She tapped her foot and started to sing Bob Marley instead. Maria's eyes flicked up from the bottle to watch her.

"Three little birds... upon my doorstep... singin' sweet song of melodies pure and true.." Violet could tell from Maria's eyes that she was smiling behind the bottle.

"Singin' don't worry... about a thing..."

She stopped as Sergio came in and put their plates down.

"You don't have to wait for me," Violet said.

Maria's eyes were closed and she'd virtually stopped drinking. About every minute, she did a little sucking motion, but it didn't look as if she was actually drinking any more. Violet took the bottle out, and lifted Maria into her car seat.

Sergio had cooked the fillet steaks and some curly fries and peas. Violet cut off a piece and put it in her mouth. It was delicious, almost crispy on the outside, and juicy in the middle.

"What did you cook it in? It's amazing."

Sergio smiled, "Is honey and mustard. I am doing pepper sauce but then I find the honey."

Violet felt a stab of panic.

"Did you finish him?" she asked, standing up.

Sergio looked confused, "No I don' finish."

She went into the kitchen. The honey bear was on his side, his tummy dented in where he'd been squeezed. She twisted his hat so air could get in and pushed his elbows till he re-inflated to his normal shape.

Violet wiped a bit of honey off his face and put the bear back in her pocket.

Sergio looked up as she came back to the table.

"I was just checking something," she said, and sat back down.

They ate in silence. Violet was so hungry she had to concentrate on chewing and not just swallowing everything whole.

Sergio finished his dinner first, and lined up his knife and fork in the middle of the plate. "It is very good meat," he said, "Where did you buy?"

"Sainsburys. It's Irish."

He nodded, "Very nice."

Violet pushed some peas onto her fork, ate them and then speared another bit of steak.

Sergio tapped his fingers on the table, "You know for to have signal on my mobil, we must be close to the land."

At the mention of the mobile, Violet kept her eyes fixed on her plate. She put the steak in her mouth.

"I mean it is normal when you are on a boat that you don' have signal, like you say me before."

Violet pushed some peas inside the 'u' of a curly fry.

"I am talking with my mother three maybe four time since we are on this boat... the signal he is here and then sometime he goes, but usually there is."

Violet counted twelve chews before letting herself swallow. If they still had the phone they could probably tell which country they were in by the phone network. She wondered how long it would take for it to decompose underwater.

"I'm sorry about your phone," she said.

"It does not matter."

"You think we're close to the coast then?"

Sergio looked up, "Yes, I think," he said.

When they finished, Sergio took their plates into the kitchen, and Violet heard them clunk down in the sink.

* * *

They sat at the table, sometimes watching Maria, and sometimes staring out of the window at the fog cloud.

"Have you got any cigarettes?" Violet asked.

"No I finish."

"Yeah, me too."

She got up and opened the stereo. Some of her CDs were piled on top of it. "What music do you want?"

"I don' mind."

She lifted her Dad's Al Green CD up, and pictured him listening to it, glass in hand, sometimes tears in his eyes. He used to call alcohol dragons' blood. She put Al Green in with her Mum's *Essential Reggae*, and put on *Black Sunday*.

"Do you like Cypress Hill?" she asked.

"I don' know this, but it's quite nice."

Violet sat back at the table, "What was that song you were singing earlier?"

"Which song I sing?"

"I dunno," she said, then sang, "Give a little bit."

He smiled and joined in loud, "Give a little bit of you time for me!"

Violet laughed.

"Supertramp," Sergio said, "I love this... I go to the concert in Lisbon."

"What kind of music is it?"

"Is rock music."

"Oh. What else do you like?"

"I like Queen and U2."

"I like a few Queen songs," Violet said.

Sergio drummed his fingers on the table, and looked out the window.

Violet put her finger into Maria's fist.

She imagined what the boat must look like from underwater, a tiny solid thing surrounded on all sides by miles of ocean. The sea was strangely calm, the boat hardly moving, static within the fog which seemed to be getting thicker. At least the life raft was inflated. She started to work out what they'd need to take with them in an emergency, formula milk, leatherman, nappies, some clothes, a couple of cans of beans. The toddler lifejacket for Maria was important, and she and Sergio could take turns with the antique one. If they ended up in the water, though, Maria might die from the cold.

"Do you want something to drink?" Sergio asked.

Violet smiled at him, "Yeah, but we haven't got anything that doesn't need water."

"I will go to check," Sergio said.

Violet looked in the cabinet. She could read Sergio and Maria the Agatha Christie novel. It might kill a whole day reading a book aloud.

Violet glanced at Maria and then turned the stereo off. She had got them all stranded. Her stomach twisted and for a second she thought she might throw up her steak. She rolled the glass cigarette tube under her finger, then let it drop to the floor.

Looking down at her feet, she realised Sergio must have put socks on her while she was asleep; they were men's sports socks. She shifted her weight onto her bad ankle, put her other heel over the glass tube and pressed down till it crunched.

Violet picked up the cigarette, dusted off the splinters of glass and laid it on the table for Sergio. She lifted her foot up and examined her heel. Two little spots of blood had come through, but it wasn't hurting.

The kitchen door opened. Sergio was holding two bright red drinks with cocktail umbrellas in.

"What are they?" Violet asked.

"Virgin Mary," Sergio said, "We have tomato juice, Worcester sauce, and Tabasco... but no lemon, no vodka."

She held out her hand and took one, "There's a cigarette on the table if you want."

Sergio picked the cigarette up, "Come on," he said, "We can share outside and drink these drinks in the clouds."

* * *

There was a small amount of melted water left in a bowl and Violet mixed it with formula for Maria, and put it in the backpack with the other stuff: One can of formula milk, Leatherman, two cans of beans, a can of peaches, nappies, sewing kit, a pair of jeans for her, two cleanish babysuits for Maria, a lighter, the rest of the money, and the Horlicks jar with Maria's pictures in.

Next she unfolded two dustbin bags, and tied them around the backpack like people did in films when they needed to swim with their bags. As she was sealing the knots with masking tape, she noticed the boat had started to rock.

When Maria woke up, Violet decided to save the last bottle of milk and gave her some tinned peaches instead. When Maria took them in her hands they slipped out like goldfish and skidded across the table. Violet broke off a little piece and put it in Maria's mouth, then panicked because Maria couldn't chew. She stuck her finger in and flicked it out onto the table.

Maria licked her lips, and then put her fist in her mouth and sucked the juice off her fingers.

"I'll mash them for you," Violet said.

Maria seemed to enjoy the mashed peaches and ate almost half the bowl.

Violet finished it off. "You're right," she said, "they're better like this."

* * *

Violet lay curled around Maria on the lounge floor. It was dark outside now, and the sea had got rougher. The boat tipped and every now and again a big wave slapped against its side and water ran down the windows. Something on the deck creaked when the biggest waves hit.

Sergio sat staring out of the window. Every time the boat tipped he put both hands down quickly on the seat either side of him.

"Are you okay?" Violet asked

"Yes. Little seasick I think."

"It's just waves," Violet said, "if it was a proper storm there would be rain and wind."

Sergio had lit the mosquito candles and the reflection of the flames flickered in his eyes as he looked around the room.

"Do you want to sleep in here with us tonight? It's cold in that cabin."

"I think I will not sleep," Sergio said, but he moved down from the seat and sat on the covers next to her and Maria.

Violet breathed in the smell from Maria's hair, it wasn't shower gel anymore but something like hay, and a hint of Sergio's aftershave. She closed her eyes, and said, "I hope the fog's gone tomorrow."

"Also me."

"I found a lifejacket," she said, "and there's some kind of tent thing in the boat."

* * *

Violet woke up cold with a cramp in one side of her neck. She sat up. A greyish light filled the room. Sergio was asleep next to Maria. Violet touched Maria's cheek, and pulled the covers up higher. As she stood up, a wave rocked the boat and she lost her balance for a moment and grabbed the side of the table. She looked out of the window, and saw that the fog was thinning out.

Violet's throat was sore and she was thirsty. The peach can was on the side in the kitchen and she drank the last bit of juice out of it. Her body didn't want sugar though, and the sweetness seemed to burn her tongue. She kept one hand on the walls to keep her balance and went out onto the deck. Her ankle was stiff and achy, but the pain wasn't as sharp as the day before. The fog was almost gone and the sky was the colour of milk after Coco Pops have been in it. The sun wasn't quite up yet, but there was a light patch in the sky where it was starting to rise. The sea looked black and the water was heaving slowly.

Violet watched a set of three large waves approaching. They seemed to span the ocean. As the first wave hit, Revelations tipped over to one side, and then lifted as the highest part of the wave passed. As they slipped down the back of the wave, the boat tipped back the other way. It was quite a nice sensation. Violet held the hand rail and waited for the next one. The third wave was the biggest and she heard a creak come from where she'd tied the dinghy up.

Violet went to check the dinghy. The creaking noise came from where the rubber wall of the dinghy was pushed up against the railings. Violet moved it a bit to take the pressure off then went back to the rear of the boat to carry on watching the waves. The waves seemed to come regularly every five minutes or so, three or four at a time. If they were from a boat, then they would either get bigger or smaller depending how close it was, but these looked more like waves you would see on a beach. She stared in the direction the waves were travelling.

It was just more water. The more she stared, the less she trusted her vision. All the blue was confusing, and the moving water made it hard to judge distance. She might be looking fifty metres away or five miles.

Something flickered far away and Violet strained her eyes to make it out. It happened again, a brief flash of white against the dark black blue. Stupid; it was probably just a bird diving for a fish. Another big wave rocked the boat and she reached to steady herself. After a couple of minutes Violet saw another white flash, and she gripped the hand rail tight.

She waited for the sun to burn through the clouds. It was cold so she started to windmill her arms one at a time, facing the point where she thought she'd last seen white. It would be nice to put some music on, but she didn't want to wake Maria up yet. She would be hungry and Violet would have to decide if she could have the last bottle or not.

As the clouds began to clear, Violet could see the white splashes more clearly, and a distant patch of something other than dark blue. It had to be a land. She scanned the sea for more boats but there were none. She shook her head and stared again, more flicks of white, and when they stopped there was a tiny speck of something green.

She ran inside the boat, "Land!" she shouted, "Fucking Land Ahoy!"

42

Sergio held Maria as Violet lowered the dinghy into the sea. She checked that it was still tied tightly to the back of Revelations, and then climbed in. The rubber walls were blown up hard, but when the waves came the floor wobbled, and her feet sank into it as she moved around.

"Throw your shoes down... I think we should go barefoot in case we tear it."

Sergio kneeled down and handed her his shoes one at a time.

"Can you pass the bag as well?"

He pushed the bin-bag wrapped backpack to the edge of Revelations and Violet lifted it into the dinghy and tucked it under one of the elastic straps. She pointed to the rubber sheet and poles bundled in the bottom, "Hey, this is that tent... we can put it up if it rains."

Sergio frowned, "I don't think we will be inside the boat for this long."

"Yeah," Violet said, "But if it rains..."

She climbed back onboard Revelations, and threw the paddles down into the dinghy.

Most of the clouds were gone, and it was a bright, cold morning. The waves were still coming regularly every few minutes. The bursts of white also seemed more obvious.

Sergio held a hand up to his eyes, "I wish we are having some..."

"Binoculars," Violet said.

"If we had these, we can see that this is not just waves hitting some buoy."

"It's not always in the same place. It's got to be the coast."

"It could be some platform for oil boats. Maybe it is better if we stay?"

Violet shook her head, "What if no boats come for days? And... if we get rescued then Maria might be taken away."

"By her father?"

"Look," Violet said, "let's just try." She held out the ancient lifejacket for him, "You can wear this."

"No, you take."

"I've got the lifesaver ring."

Sergio passed Maria to her and started putting on the lifejacket.

Violet lay Maria down on the deck. She'd dressed her in a velvety babygrow and put the bear suit over it. She lifted her up gently and put the toddlers life vest on. Maria watched her; the fluorescent material cast a pink shadow on her cheeks. Violet was surprised she wasn't crying as she must have been hungry.

Even with the straps pulled as tight as they would go, the lifejacket was too big and the neck of it framed Maria's head, and made her look as if she was staring out of a cave.

Violet looked at Sergio, "You get in first, and I'll pass her down to you."

Sergio was pale, his knuckles white where they gripped the rail of the boat. He watched the water as he spoke, "Actually. I don' really swim."

"What?" Violet said, "I thought you grew up by the sea?"

"Yes. But I don't learn for swim."

"What about the boat you had?"

He watched a large set of waves approaching. "It is my father's... but usually he's going with my brother and I am staying with my mother."

"We won't be in the sea, we'll be in the boat." Violet said. She smiled, "Anyway with the lifejacket on, if we need to swim you can just kick your legs."

Sergio looked at her and Maria, closed his eyes for a moment, and then nodded his head. "Okay." He waited until the set of waves had passed then moved his hands along the rail, and began to climb down.

Sergio wobbled as he stood in the dinghy. He took hold of one of the float things to steady himself, and then reached up for Maria.

Violet checked that the anchor was down then went to lock the boat. As she put the key in the lock, she tried to think of anything she might have forgotten. She rested her forehead against the door for a few seconds, then turned the lock and stuffed the key with its cork key ring into her jeans pocket.

Sitting on the floor of the dinghy in their bulky lifejackets Sergio and Maria reminded her of dressed-up toys. They looked out of place, like someone had picked them up, put them in sea outfits, and decided they were going to play sailors.

She started to untie the rope, "Ready?" she asked.

Sergio looked up, he held Maria's hands, "Yes, we are ready," he said.

Violet stepped onto the side of the dinghy and used her foot to push them away from Revelations.

Sergio held Maria out to her, "I can row first," he said, "You tell me for which way."

He sat with his back to them and started to row, slow, hard pulls that pushed the dinghy forward. Violet guessed he was keeping an eye on the waves. She sat with Maria in the front point of the boat, keeping her eyes fixed on the area where she'd seen the splashes of white.

The oars creaked against the rubber hoops. When the paddles lifted up, water ran off them back into the sea, and as Sergio dug them back in for each new stroke, Violet could hear a small, underwater plunk noise below the surface. The dinghy felt different from the motor boat; it shook and wobbled over the waves. When Violet put her hand on the side she could feel vibrations, like when you put your ear on a bouncy castle and can hear everyone's bounces echoing inside.

A cold breeze started to flick her hair across her eyes. In the distance a flash of white exploded, followed by another puff of spray. It was definitely waves.

Sergio turned round, "When I'm younger I prefer motorcycle to beach. In Portugal we also have these prickly bastards, I don' think you have in England."

"What?"

He stopped rowing and turned and held out his palm as if he was holding a tennis ball, "How you call them? We have many in Portugal. Black...with needles."

"Sea urchins?"

He carried on rowing, "Yes! Sea urchin. Sometimes my brother he's swimming for collect them and selling the dead ones which look like little basketballs to tourist shops."

"Yeah, I know what you mean," Violet said, "I trod on an urchin once on holiday, a lifeguard had to get the spines out."

"I never trod," Sergio said.

"It hurts. I kept a piece of spine, they have hooks on the end."

"I always hate these urchins," Sergio said.

"I feel sorry for them," Violet said, "sitting underwater waiting to get stepped on. I guess at least because of the spines people usually take their feet off quick and don't completely crush them to death. Or they get snatched out of the sea and their dead bodies sit in someone's house getting dusty, probably miles away from the sea in some shit, cold country. They can't even move out of the way." She touched Maria's face, then held one of her feet in her hand. "It's got to be one of the worst things to be."

Sergio started rowing again and the dinghy bounced over the waves. Violet could see the impressions of his vertebrae through the back of his shirt as he leaned forward for each stroke. She looked at Revelations, and saw the distance between them gradually increasing with each pull of the oars. She realised that she'd forgotten the lifesaver ring.

Sergio turned his head and looked over the thick collar of the lifejacket, "How old are you when you trod?" he asked.

"I don't remember," she said, "ten maybe?"

After a while they swapped positions, and Sergio sat with Maria. He couldn't sit as far forward as Violet had because it made the boat nose heavy and water kept splashing in when the waves came, so he and Maria sat behind Violet.

"Is she asleep?" Violet asked.

"Yes, she's sleeping for already twenty minutes."

"Can you see anything?"

"I think it is beach," Sergio said.

Violet stopped rowing and turned around. The white splashes were definitely waves, and a thin dark line on the horizon was a coastline.

"The coast?"

Sergio smiled at her, "I think it is France, or maybe Spain."

"How far?"

He squinted at the horizon, "I don' know, but it is still morning. I think we arrive in the afternoon."

The sky grew cloudier in the late morning, turning the water dark, and the wind got stronger. Sitting in one position all the time was making Violet's ankle throb. Blisters had formed on her hands where the oars had rubbed. She let go of the paddles and looked at her palms. "Didn't this hurt your hands?"

"A little. I will row again if you like."

"Thanks."

She stood up, keeping her legs wide apart for balance, and stretched her back, "I preferred our other boat," she said.

"Also me."

She took Maria, and sat in the front of the boat again. The dinghy rose and fell on the waves, sometimes slapping the water with an echoey sound.

Violet stared at the coast. Either side of the beach there were large areas of dark green forest. On the left the forest spanned unbroken as far as she could see, but to the right it wasn't as dense, and there were gaps between the trees that looked like other beaches.

There were lots of white splashes now, but only occasionally a really big one like she'd been able to see from far away. When the wind blew, Violet felt spray dampen her skin.

She scanned the beach and saw two tiny dark figures on the sand. They moved towards the sea, but as they met the water she lost sight of them. She searched for splashes of colour like towels or maybe a beach shop, but there was nothing.

Some gulls circled in the sky, and higher up a single, dark-coloured bird was hovering. Its wings trembled as it balanced on the wind, and sometimes it dropped for a second and made a couple of little flaps to maintain its position. Something ached in Violet's throat and she felt suddenly scared, properly scared like a child, and she realised she was holding her breath. Then quickly, the bird dipped its head downwards and dropped out of the sky like a stone. She watched as it hit the water and disappeared, leaving circular ripples that spread outwards towards their dinghy.

"Sergio," she said.

He turned round to look where she was pointing and the bird surfaced silently with a fish in its beak and sat like a duck. Shrieks rang out from above as the seagulls saw the fish, and swooped. The black bird lifted up from the water and flew off, water dripping from the silvery head and tail of the fish still twitching in its beak.

"Whoah," said Sergio as a wave lifted the boat and he lost his balance, gripping the side.

One of the oars slipped out and Violet reached forward and grabbed it.

"Sorry," Sergio said.

The jolt made Maria open her eyes, and she frowned and wriggled, getting ready to cry.

They were close enough to the shore now to hear the waves breaking, Violet squinted at the beach. "I can see some cars parked."

Sergio glanced round quickly, "The waves are big."

Violet looked behind them. A row of waves approached like moving hills. She turned again to the coast. Waves were breaking along the whole coastline. If they paddled on they might not find a calmer spot, and even if they did it could be deserted. The beach was sandy, not rock, and the cars meant there would be people. If they ended up somewhere empty Maria might have to wait another whole day for food.

A wave crashed about twenty metres in front of them and spray hissed up into the air. It prickled as it landed on them, and Violet started to shiver.

"Keep going," she said, "we're really close."

The dinghy lifted sharply on the next wave and wobbled before sliding down the back of it. Another passed in the same way, but the boat stuck a little longer on its crest before sliding down.

The third wave was the biggest. She knew Sergio would be watching each one rising up behind them. Again the dinghy teetered on the highest point of the wave and then surged forward for a second as if it was going to surf down it. Maria made a little cry and moved her head from side to side. Violet checked again that the lifejacket straps were as tight as they could go.

The wave made a noise like thunder cracking as it broke ahead of them, and the water boiled and foamed behind it as it reformed and rushed towards the shore. As the spray hissed down on them Maria started to cry properly.

The dinghy dipped downwards and Violet gripped one of the ropes at the side, and held onto Maria. She turned round and saw that they were on a huge wave that was still rising. The boat dipped more sharply downwards, and she scrabbled back towards the seat. "You okay?" she shouted to Sergio.

"Yes Okay!" he called, but she heard his voice crack.

"I'm going to move right to the back," she called, "to stop us nosediving."

The dinghy stopped for a few, long seconds on the peak of the wave, and Violet climbed onto the back of it and hung over the edge to stop it travelling forward with the wave. Sergio made two hard paddles backward and finally the wave released them and rushed forward exploding ahead of them.

"Violet," Sergio said, "I don' think this is good idea."

"Stop paddling till they pass," she said. Maria struggled in her arms as another wave rose up behind them then tipped the dinghy forwards. This time the boat was seized harder by the wave, and even with Sergio paddling, it started to take them with it.

"Lean!" Violet shouted, and Sergio moved as far back as he could without dropping the oars.

Violet saw panic flash in his eyes and his hands loosen on the paddles just before the wave let them go, and keeled over. The spray from it flew back and rained down hard, stinging as it hit, and bouncing off the rubber of the dinghy.

The boat bobbed on the water. Another set of waves was just visible on the horizon. Sergio looked at her.

"Now!" Violet said. "Paddle as fast as you can, try and make it to the beach before the waves hit again."

Sergio's eyes flicked from the approaching waves to Violet and Maria then back again as he started to row hard.

Maria cried with her mouth open as wide as it would go, and her eyes squeezed tightly shut. Her cheeks were red from tears and sea spray. Violet stroked her hair, "We're almost there," she said, "We're close now."

Sergio panted with the effort of rowing, his gaze fixed on the dark lines moving steadily towards them.

As they inched closer to the beach, the water seemed suddenly calm. Level with them, a flash of red caught Violet's eye; it was about the distance of two swimming pools away. Then, Sergio shouted.

"Violet!"

A wave started to rise behind them.

Violet looked at the shore, "Keep going!"

The wave was lifting fast, becoming concave and dark.

As it arrived, it lifted them vertical. Sergio fell backwards, dropping the paddles, and slid down to the nose of the boat his hands scrabbling for something to grip.

Violet clutched Maria and moved as far back as she could, grabbing onto a strap at the back of the dinghy, as her feet started to slide.

"You okay?" she called, but Sergio was frozen, staring at the wave as it started to curve over.

"Remember!" Violet shouted, "Just kick your legs!"

The wave heaved forward and they started to turn upside down. Violet held Maria tight, and pushed her arm through the back of the lifejacket. The wave seemed to breathe in, and everything went quiet for a second. Violet let go of the strap, and hugged Maria to her chest as they began to fall.

The dinghy dropped above them and Violet saw the tent thing still in its elastic strap, and Sergio's shoes and the backpack falling out then travelling downwards next to her towards the water. She covered Maria's head with her elbow, and then noise roared in her ears as the wave came down on top of them, and they were slammed underwater.

The water spun Violet round and round. It pulled and sucked at her, and she had to use all her strength not to let Maria get torn from her arms as she was thrown into a backflip. At one point she hit the bottom and felt gritty sand rush across her face, and she curled into a ball around Maria.

Then the thundering cyclone of water released her and she kicked not knowing which way the surface was. Her chest burned with the lack of breath, and she could feel her lungs beating as if there was a giant bird inside her ribs trying to break out.

Just as she felt her chest was about to burst open, Violet surfaced. She trod water and gulped air, lifting Maria's face away from her chest to check that she was okay. Maria opened her eyes, and looked at Violet in accusation, before opening her mouth and letting out a loud cry.

The light dimmed and Violet looked round and saw another huge wave lift up and arc over them. She took a breath, covered Maria's nose and mouth and swam as deep underwater as she could. The wave broke on top of them and they were forced down to the sand again, bubbles exploding everywhere. The rolling water started to suck her into it, and she kicked hard, fighting not to get pulled into the cycle, but the wave was too powerful, and dragged her and Maria backwards and spun them around for fifteen seconds before releasing them again.

This time Violet kicked off from the sand and broke the surface quicker. As they hit fresh air, Maria opened her mouth and cried loudly, she shook all over from the shock of it.

Another wave reared up, and Violet covered Maria's mouth again, and tried to swim underwater away from it. She didn't swim as fast this time, and the full weight of the wave hit the arch of her back, knocking the breath out of her, and making her hand slip from Maria's mouth. She struggled underwater, fighting the force of water that was pulling them backwards ready to be dunked by yet another wave.

Violet didn't know how many more times she could do this. She closed her eyes, and held Maria as they were dragged upside down, and held under for another half a minute that felt like ten. They whirled round and round, the thrashing water wrenching at her arms. Her chest thumped and burned, desperate to inhale.

This time when the wave released them, Violet felt too weak to kick to the top. She half swam, half floated to the surface, then lay back gulping in the delicious, cold air.

Part of her wanted to stay like that, and forget about the other wave that was going to break on them, just keep breathing as long as possible. Maria's screams didn't seem as loud somehow, but maybe it was just because there was water in her ears.

Violet opened her eyes just as another wave peaked and leaned over. There was sand in Maria's nostrils and she weakly scooped it out then covered Maria's mouth and nose. Just before the wave broke, she heard a shout. Then the wave pounded them underwater again. Violet held onto Maria with the last bit of strength she had.

She opened her eyes underwater; the white bubbles rushing around them reminded her of the inside of a snow shaker, or a hundred broken snow shakers in a washing machine. Her chest didn't hurt anymore, but her lungs seemed to tug harder and harder until she opened her mouth and took in a long breath of cold water. The almost calm sensation was gone as she started to choke. Her vision went red, and her temples felt too full of pressure.

As she popped up this time, she realised that she could touch the bottom with her toes, but she was too tired. Seawater blocked her throat and she felt her chest flapping ineffectively trying to cough it out and breathe at the same time. Maria screamed and Violet loosened her hold on her, letting her bob in the water in her lifejacket, and breathe.

A wave rose behind them, Violet watched it grow, darken, then gleam as it curved over them. It wasn't as big as the others, but she was exhausted. She loosely held Maria to her, covering her mouth and nose for the last time to stop water coming in. As the wave hit, she heard another shout close by.

"Van Sont! Van Sont! E.C!"

The cold water wasn't so shocking now. Sand rubbed her back as she was dragged along the seabed. They were so close to the beach. She remembered that people can die in five millimetres of water. The sea rumbled in her ears, and then the shout made sense to her, it was the name 'Vincent' in a French accent.

With one last effort Violet pushed Maria upwards to the surface, and held her as high as she could under her arms. She felt cool air on her wrists, and was happy that they weren't so deep now.

Something still flapped and fluttered in her lungs, but instead of a bird it was small, like a bluebottle knocking against double-glazing.

A hand roughly grabbed Violet's collar, and pulled her out of the water into the cold air. She felt something painfully scraping her toes, and heard someone shouting in French. A hand thumped hard on her back and she imagined the bluebottle hitting the walls of a glass jar.

Violet opened her eyes and realised she was coughing. Her eyes and throat stung from the salt, and she felt grazed from her mouth to her lungs like she'd been breathing building sand and nails. She retched, coughing up salty liquid. Her stomach felt cold inside as if it was full of sea. A boy in a wetsuit had her arm hooked around his neck, and was helping her walk up the beach.

"My baby?" she said, panicking, "Bambino." She tried to turn back to the sea but stumbled and fell on her knees.

The surfer knelt down next to her and pointed up the beach, "Bebé okay," he said. Violet saw the bright pink of Maria's lifejacket and distant cries seemed suddenly loud, and alive. She let him help her to her feet.

Violet leaned her face against the wetsuit and smelled rubber.

"Okay?" he asked, "Anglaise? Inglish?"

She coughed again, and her throat scratched as she spoke, "English."

He smiled and banged her hard on the back.

They were almost at Maria when the boy stopped. He pointed down the beach. She saw two surfboards, stuck nose down in the sand like colourful gravestones. Just beyond them was a tanned, curly-haired man in a red wetsuit holding what looked like a full dustbin bag. He was waist deep in the water, facing out to sea. Then Violet saw another figure in the water wearing an orange lifejacket, and white shirt. Sergio was wading out of the water towards the man.

"I go now? Okay?" the boy asked.

Violet nodded, "Yes, I'm fine... Oui. Bon."

He ran down the beach to Sergio and the other surfer.

Violet took Maria's lifejacket off, and rocked her in her arms. Maria's skin was cold, and she was shaking. Violet put a hand inside the bear suit and was relieved to find that her chest was still warm.

"We're going to be okay," she said, "we'll be in a warm car soon and get you some dinner."

Maria cried painfully, but Violet was pleased that she still had energy, and wasn't still and quiet. Violet was shivering too. She shuffled back into a little hollow in the sand dunes and cuddled Maria tight, as Sergio and the two surfers hurried towards them.

As they got nearer, Violet could hear that Sergio was speaking to them in French. His white shirt had gone see-through in the water, and the old fashioned life-vest was twisted the wrong way round. As he got close, he started to run.

"You are both okay?" he called.

Violet smiled, "Cold," she said.

He knelt down in the sand and touched Maria's face. "These guys saying we can sit inside their van to dry."

The surfers stood behind him. The one that had helped Violet was staring at her, he had short, black hair, and bright blue eyes. The tanned one's curly hair was brown, gone orangey blonde at the ends from the sun. He looked about Violet's age, the other one a couple of years younger, maybe seventeen or eighteen. The one with curly hair smiled at Violet, and put a hand on his chest, "Vincent," he said.

"Je m'appelle Esther," she said.

She looked at Sergio, but he looked calm. He must have told them the same.

"You swim good," Vincent said, "I see you take some very bad hold downs. Gabriel he saw you first, and we come to catch you."

The dark-haired boy smiled, then looked back towards the surfboards.

Violet took his hand. It was cold and sticky from salt, "Merci," she said, "You saved us."

He smiled and nodded at her.

Vincent turned to Violet and said, "Come on. Follow me." He put his hand on the small of her back, and walked her towards the car. Maria struggled and cried in her arms. Sergio followed behind with Gabriel, talking in French.

There was a small car and a white camper van parked in the car park. Vincent stopped at the camper van.

Gabriel said something to Sergio, and laughed patting him on the back. Vincent said to Violet, "He say you fucking crazy trying to row to the shore in a dinghy in this swell."

Violet and Sergio both smiled.

Vincent unpeeled the top half of his wetsuit, and pulled a car key out of a little pouch on the inside. Gabriel handed Sergio the bin bag with their backpack wrapped in it, it was torn, and shreds of black plastic hung from it dripping.

Vincent unlocked the van, and pulled opened a sliding door. It was messy inside and there was a smell of damp mixed with cooking. A sponge mattress folded in two took up most of the standing room. Piled on top of it was a bundle of sheets and blankets, and another surfboard. The two front seats swivelled like captains' chairs and were both angled for viewing the surf. A faint smell of coffee lingered.

Vincent turned the engine on and started the heater, "Your husband said you have called already the coastguard for your boat."

Violet looked at Sergio and he smiled, and nodded his head.

Vincent continued, "If you would like we will drive you to Hossegor or Capbreton where you can call them again, or take a hotel."

Sergio started to speak at the same time as Violet, "That would be great," Violet said, "We'll give you some money for petrol."

"It is no probleme. Hossegor is only twenty minutes driving."

Gabriel tapped Violet on the arm, and handed her a towel, and a thick hoodie.

"Thanks," she said.

The heater was starting to take effect, and she wasn't shivering as hard.

"You can undress now if you want," Vincent said, "while we get our boards."

As they disappeared behind the sand dunes, Violet swivelled the driver's seat so it faced forward.

She put her hand on the gear stick and looked at Sergio, "I'm going to take it," she said, "are you coming?"

He glanced towards the beach, then back at her. Maria still cried and thrashed about as he held her.

Violet looked at the sea and saw a surfer ride up a wave, and spray fly off in a perfect arc as he turned on top of it. He rode along the wave gathering speed, and then up to the top again where he jumped off the back of it and disappeared. Vincent and Gabriel came into view jogging towards their boards, and she turned back to Sergio. He rocked Maria, holding her tight to his chest.

He slid the door shut. "Yes," he said, "I stay with you both."

Violet turned the heater up to full blast, and accelerated out of the car park.

Epilogue

"Que quieras Guapa?" Gino says.

I climb onto the bar seat, "One cocktail especial with lots of grenadine."

"Sî Senorina Maria."

He gets a cocktail mixer and puts ice in, then he pours some zumo orange and some pineapple from up high like a fountain.

I get my homework out and put it on the bar while he gets the cans for the next bit.

He winks at me then starts to juggle cans of Fanta lemon and Fanta orange. The cans go faster and faster until I don't see their shapes anymore.

Gino opens his eyes real wide and shouts "Which one you want? Which one you want? Tell me now, tell me now. Now! AHORA!!!!"

I laugh and point my finger to one, and he smacks the others down on the bar bang, bang, bang, bang, and catches the one I said on the top of his foot just before it lands on the ground. He stands on one leg, balancing the Fanta, and waits with his arms out wide. He kicks the can up into the air then real fast he flicks it open and pours it into the mixer.

"Ahora, grenadine." He smiles and his teeth are bright white like his eyes. I like Gino the best of all Mama's friends and he is a very funny, cool guy.

He spins the sirop di grenadine very fast in one hand like a cowboy spins a gun, then points his arms and bows down low like a matador while behind him he lifts up the grenadine and pours, and it drops perfect into the mixer that is in his other hand.

I start clapping but he stays serious and then stands up and starts to go super fast, chopping some lime, squeezing it, spinning a cocktail glass in sugar, and then shaking the mixer all over so it sounds like music. I hear the zippy noise of a straw opening and then he turns and puts my cocktail in front of me.

"Gracias," I say.

"Una cosa mas," he says, and spears some cherries on a cocktail stick and lays it across the glass like olives on a martini drink, "Now try that on for size," he says in a funny American accent.

There is a curly straw and a straight straw. I slurp a big slurp through the curly one. Gino is waiting for me to tell him if I like it. He crosses his arms and leans on the bar.

"Very delicious," I say.

He nods his head and smiles a big smile, then goes to the other side of the bar to some other people and gives them cervezas. There are two little kids with them that are playing with the table tennis outside but they are too small to know how to do it right.

I get my exercise book out for my homework. It's English which I am best in the class at anyway. Some music starts and I look up and MTV is on. It is the song *Warriors Dance* and the video is really good with all these cigarette packets that make themselves into small people with faces a bit like ants and they break into a bar and put the music on and start dancing. Mama likes the song too, and after we first heard it we made some figures out of cigarette packets that look exactly the same as the ones in the video.

I took one to school and everybody wanted to know how to do it, so I told them if they bring empty cigarette packets I would show them. That is actually how I got my two new friends Ana-Lucia, and Catarina. This school is okay. Most schools are okay when you get used to them, but I like this one because it is not very far to the beach and I also like this town which is up high on a hill and has very big and ancient walls around it.

I wonder if Mama has done lots of portraits today. I think she likes this town too because she got another job apart from the portraits that is in a very cool big building that used to be a bread factory. She got the job when we were both on the beach, and we were sitting at her art stand. This guy started to look at all these pictures that Mama puts up on her extra easel. It makes me feel a little shy because a lot of them have me in, but doing things like driving a tank or jumping out of an aeroplane. And because she does portraits for tourists, there are also lots of portraits of me now and when I was a baby.

The guy said he had a studio and did graffiti art and they wanted a new artist because they have a lot of work at the moment because of the very big music festival that is coming this summer. So now Mama has another job that gives us more money and we stay in an apartment real close to the beach and there is a swimming pool that we share with the people in the other apartments.

Actually I would quite like to stay here for the school holidays but we always go away for two months, sometimes to see uncle Sergio at the restaurant in Sevilla, and sometimes a holiday where it's just us. Once we drove all the way to South Italy and then took a boat to this Greek island but I can't remember the name. It was really good and we went snorkelling every day and had our own little boat when we were there, and Mama told me lots of Greek stories and legends.

But tonight I think I will ask Mama if we can stay here for the summer and we can just relax a bit by the pool and in the sea, and Sergio could take a holiday here, and maybe we can even go to the music festival.

I slurp my cocktail through the curly straw. First comes the Fanta and zumo mix, and then just a little bit after comes the thick grenadine which I suck slowly through my teeth so the sweet taste stays for longer. I take the cocktail stick, pull a cherry off with my teeth, and wait for Mama.

Acknowledgements

Thanks to my family, The Wakes, John, Katy, Maisie and Lyndon, for your support, and individual specialist knowledge.

I am grateful to all my tutors, colleagues and friends at Sheffield Hallam University, especially Linda Lee Welch, Jane Rogers, Mike Harris, and Rachel Genn, thank you for the wisdom.

Thank you also to my friends who inspire me to write, and share my love of fiction, Robin Nelson, Tricia Durdey, Susan Clegg, Suzanne McCardle, and Noel Williams.

Laura Wake

About the author

A Monster by Violet is Laura's debut novel, and she is currently working on a second. She teaches Creative Writing for the Workers' Educational Association and is an Associate Lecturer at Sheffield Hallam University.

Urbane Publications is dedicated to
developing new author voices, and publishing
fiction and non-fiction that challenges, thrills and
fascinates. From page-turning novels to innovative
reference books, our goal is to publish what
YOU want to read.

Find out more at

urbanepublications.com